THE
POWER

of Fate

A SOULS REUNITED NOVEL

ALISON E. STEUART

Preface

"Ian! Come over here, I have to show you this!" Charlotte says, excitedly pulling Ian across the hall that leads to the resort's restaurant. "This is the display I told you about last night."

"I only remember one thing about last night," Ian says before stopping her in the middle of the hallway and pulling her into his arms. "How did I survive all those months without you?" he asks before devouring her mouth again with the same pent-up emotion that nearly drove him mad for the months they were apart.

Minutes pass before she can reply. "I'm sorry, Ian. I'm so sorry for what I put you through." Her voice is thick with sadness and regret.

"Don't, Charlotte," he says, tucking her hair behind her ear. "I don't want you to focus on regret. We are together now, and we will never—ever—part again." The command swirls inside Charlotte's stomach, sending chills across her skin. Her breath hitches when his thumb glides across her lips, then presses harder, forcing them to part so he can take her mouth in another deep and sensuous kiss. "Fate has insured us of that."

"Yes, it has," she agrees. "You have to see this. Come look." She pulls him along to follow her to the display case she found the day before. "When I found this, the strangest feeling came over me. Like nostalgia, I don't know...it was...just familiar somehow. This man, Alasdair Stewart, wrote these letters and poems to his wife, Ella. Look how sweet these are." She points at the fancy script on yellowed paper.

Charlotte can't help but notice Ian's intense expression and focused intent on Lord Galloway's letters and poetry. But when she sees his reaction to Lady Ella's portrait, it raises the hairs on her neck.

"What is it?" she asks.

He doesn't answer right away and continues to stare at the beautifully painted portrait of Alasdair Stewart's beloved wife. A minute later, he finally replies, "Charlotte...I...I feel like the wind has been knocked out of me. Jesus. I could swear I know that woman and..."

"And that you cared for her?" Charlotte finishes.

"Yes," he whispers, still staring down at the display.

"That's exactly what happened to me when I saw Alasdair's portrait. But Ian, he's the same man from the vision I had. The one I told you about when we were in the Abacos." She moves down to the next display, and once again, her entire body is covered in chills. "It's him." She laughs nervously. "I almost fainted when I first saw it."

"I'm feeling a bit strange myself."

"Then look here, at this letter he wrote to her. He says..."

Lady Ella ~ My dearest faerie maiden,
  I thank God every day that our souls found each other

again. Let us grow old joyously, knowing they will do so from now through eternity.

> *Your humble servant and loving husband,*
> *Alasdair Stewart*

Charlotte pauses, her hand resting on her chest, then turns to Ian, a glorious smile lighting up her face. "Their souls found each other and will again through eternity. Ian, it is not a coincidence that I came here and that you followed me. Fate brought us here on purpose. We were meant to be here." She stops as the idea of being guided by a higher power, to find the history of their souls that loved in another life, overwhelms her. "It's just...I mean...it's so beautiful, Ian. Don't you agree?" she asks as her happiness wells up the tears in her eyes.

Ian pulls her to him again, and they take a moment to gaze upon one another. "I do. It's rather extraordinary, to say the least." he agrees, letting the poignancy of the moment wrap around them.

Smiling up at him, she says, "It's funny, but of all the wonderful things about this display, you know what's my favorite?"

Ian raises a brow and tips his head in curiosity.

"I love that he called her faerie maiden."

ONE

Ella

MARCH, 1798 LONDON, ENGLAND

I f she pulls them any tighter, I'm going to faint.

"Beatrice. Please, not so tight. I told you I have a terrible headache." Turning to give her a stern look, I let out a huff. "I don't even know why I have to go. It seems like nothing more than an event for military superiors and their wives. It's sure to be dreadfully boring and will only exacerbate this terrible ache." I take a deep breath and rub my temples as Beatrice loosens the ties of my stays.

"Yes, dearie. I'm sorry you are suffering, and I cannot say it is likely this evening will bring you any relief. But it is important for you to make appearances. You are at that age where you have to show society what a lovely lady you have become." She turns me toward her so the rest of my ridiculous ensemble can be added to the layers already covering my body and shaping me into something that pleases everyone *but* me.

With my hands on my hips, I wait for Beatrice to finish her lecture. This is routine, so I know she is not done yet.

"You never know when or where the perfect, handsome gentleman will be waiting to sweep you off your feet. It's a very exciting time for someone so young and beautiful." She's starting to excite herself, like she always does when she dresses me up for a fancy evening. Her face lights up with a smile that warms my heart, and she's doing her little dance where she sways back and forth, going up and down on her toes, head tipping from side to side, while humming a sweet melody as she completes my final touches.

Beatrice has been with me for as long as I can remember. She was my nanny, my governess, now my lady's maid and everything in between. She is the one constant I cannot do without, and her love and loyalty anchor me. I laugh as she spins me around and giggles like a girl my age, rather than one of sixty-one years.

"Maybe you would like to go in my place, hmm?" I ask, tapping my chin in mock contemplation. "I know of a hundred other things I could do instead."

The statement stops Beatrice mid-sway. "I'm certain you do! Like riding that horse of yours faster than what is proper for young ladies, and searching through the forest for God knows what." Her eyes pinch with disapproval, and I can't help but throw my head back and laugh.

"Oh, Beatrice! I do love you so. Your disapproval is so entertaining." I pause and turn around, finding her exquisite work reflecting in the mirror. As always, the gown is magnificent, flowing with elegant cream layers and delicate leaves stitched with golden thread along the edges to match the gold sash around my waist. The dress is maidenly and innocent, if not angelic, which will make my mother happy, but it's a bit too monochromatic with my light skin and blonde hair. "Could you do me a favor? Would you please fetch my mother's aquamarine choker?"

"Yes, of course. The one with the pearls?" Beatrice asks as she walks toward the door.

"No, not that one. The one with the gold chain and the smaller gems dangling from the focal stone."

"Now, Ella dear, that will only draw attention to your..."

I cut off her nervous rant before she can more. "To my ample bosom? Well, it's going to be a little hard *not* to draw attention to it, so I might as well make the best of it."

The fullness of my breasts has been an issue since they started budding a little earlier than normal. Beatrice thinks they draw inappropriate attention from the opposite sex and consternation from the same sex, both of which I generally ignore. Beatrice, on the other hand, is occasionally more prudish than my mother, and she knows the pendant of my chosen necklace will fall perfectly down my cleavage. But I will sit back and laugh, converse with everyone as I am forced to witness their gazes fall upon the only color in my ensemble. They will then blush at my "unfortunate fullness," as my mother would say. At least I'll have some kind of entertainment for what is sure to be an otherwise boring evening.

Beatrice re-enters the room with my conversation piece in hand. "I still think it's a bit much, dearie." She comes up behind me as I stand facing the mirror. As she loops it around my neck and rests it against the bare skin of my throat, my smile beams back at me.

"It's perfect!" I say, turning to face her, then perform a mock curtsy. "You don't have to agree, but I can see in your eyes that you *know* it is the perfect finishing touch to an otherwise colorless presentation."

"Hmph. If you were married, I'd say it was perfect. But you're not, so I don't think it's proper." Under her breath, she mutters, "Little good my opinion will do."

"I love your opinion, Beatrice, you know that. But I also know when you disapprove, I'm on the right path." With a mischievous laugh, I come up from behind my dearest companion and give her a tight hug. "And I love you. Thank you for helping me prepare for this evening."

"Go on, dear. Have fun and behave yourself. I'll see you in the morning, and you can share all the details." Smiling and shaking her head, she turns to tidy up my room.

The hallway is dim, only the occasional candle lit to highlight some of the framed artwork my mother loves to collect. Before I reach the staircase, I realize my headache has drastically diminished. I know it's because Beatrice managed to distract me from my frustration. She knows me better than anyone, and although she is strict when it comes to etiquette and every rule and nuance that is to be followed by a proper lady, I can always count on her to be my true confidant. Beatrice, not my mother, has always given me the freedom to speak my mind without fear of judgment or punishment. Whether it goes against her prudish grain or not, I can be open and honest, and she will always help guide my way.

At the top of the staircase, I pause, staring down at its grand structure curving gracefully around ending on the shiny marble floor of the foyer. I see my parents patiently waiting for me by the front doors as the footmen stand by to be of service. Mother catches a glimpse of me and her face lights up with pride. "Ella, darling! You look absolutely stunning." She leaves my father's side and comes to me as I make my way down the stairs. Her gloved hands fall gently to my shoulders as she pauses to take in my glamour. Apparently, my ensemble meets her approval—I think I see a shimmer in her eyes. "Oh, my sweet little girl isn't a little girl anymore. You're so grown up all of a sudden."

I tip my head to the side, giving her a questioning look. "Mother, my coming-out was over two years ago. I'm almost nineteen. That doesn't quite seem so sudden."

"Yes, well, I suppose that's true." She stops to contemplate the truth in my words. "But something is definitely different this evening. You seem more..." She stops and takes a step back to get a better look at what is baffling her.

That's when my father comes up next to her and says, "Libby, it's the necklace. How can you not see that? Clearly our daughter is rebelling against your insistence on making her look like she will walk into the room and start passing out blessings and answering prayers. By God, look at her! An archangel of the eighth order is a bit intimidating to most men. She's just making herself more approachable, aren't you, love?" He gives me a mischievous wink.

My father is always coming to my rescue when it comes to Mother. Likely because he knows I take after him in every way but our looks, and the rules of society—my mother's bible— tend to make us both want to rebel. Although for him, as a man, it is much easier to get away with.

Acknowledging his wink with a raised brow, I answer, "Excellent observation, Father. More approachable—that's what I had in mind." Holding in the mirth that will undoubtedly send my mother into a fit about how a proper lady conducts herself, I turn to her and say, "Mother, you must agree the pop of color is fantastic! Look, it matches my eyes." I bat my eyelashes at her.

She appears skeptical as her eyes fall to where the blue-green stone rests. When they shift down to follow the trail of smaller matching stones that disappear into my cleavage, her eyebrows come together, and her mouth turns down into a disapproving frown. "Ella, I don't think you should draw attention..."

Before I must hear it again, I try to whisper while gritting my teeth, "Mother, there is nothing I can do about them. It's not like I asked God to give them to me..."

"Ella! You do not need to speak so openly!" She turns her

head toward the footmen and huffs with exasperation before looking back and whispering, "There are men present, young lady."

"Well, this man thinks you're being ridiculous and wasting valuable time." Father jumps in again to dampen my mother's fire. "Ella, you look lovely. Try not to break too many hearts this evening. Libby, you need to quit trying to make molehills out of mountains." He tries hard to keep a straight face. I, on the other hand, cannot, and we both end up in fits of laughter as we watch my poor mother try to decipher my father's words.

"I'm glad you two think this is so amusing. I'm just trying to look out for your reputation, dear. Any mark against you could drastically reduce your chances of finding a suitable husband!" With a loud swoosh of her skirts, she spins around, nose in the air and all the hauteur she can muster and heads toward the door.

While observing her dramatic exit, I think, perhaps, Father and I shouldn't tease her so. She means well, she truly does, and she doesn't know differently. As the second daughter of the Duke of Brunswick, Mother's upbringing was a life of privilege that mimicked a prison sentence—or at the very least, a strict military term. Her marriage to my father was arranged from the time they were children. When the happy day finally arrived, it turned out to be her first taste of freedom, and she devoured it. From then on, their relationship grew into a happy, respectful, loving marriage. Thankfully, my parents decided early on that I should have some say in choosing my own husband, increasing the chance for a companionable match and perhaps even love.

At this point in time, I can honestly say my mother is regretting that decision. Charles Percy, the heir presumptive to a dukedom, an earldom, two viscountcies, and who knows what other titles, has shown a great deal of interest in me, and Mother thinks this is the most wonderful thing that could ever happen. She can't understand why I don't share her opinion, but Lord Percy does nothing for me other than grate on my nerves with his nasally voice and make my skin crawl with his clammy hands. Thankfully, Father seems to understand completely and doesn't push the issue.

When I peer over at him, we smile at each other and he shrugs his shoulders. "I do apologize, dear. That was very forward of me, but it was going to drag on forever if I didn't stop it." Placing his hand on my shoulder, he gives me a tender look. "Don't let her constant fussing upset you. She worries about you and only wants what's best. You know that, right?"

Our arms link together as we walk toward the open doors and our awaiting carriage. "Of course, I do, Father. I make the best of it though. She and Beatrice have become a source of entertainment for me." I glance over at him with a sly smile. "It is great fun to see who will get into the biggest tizzy about anything from riding my horse to picking out jewelry to wear to a ball."

His deep laugh echoes through the porte-cochere. "That's my girl," he boasts as he waits for me to enter the carriage, "a true Seymour, through and through."

Mother is still pouting as I take a seat next to her. It won't last long; Father won't let it. He has a genuine charm about him that puts people at ease without them even knowing he has diffused their ire. I feel a great sense of pride come over me as I think about the good man that is my father. Edward Henry Seymour, Duke of Somerset, is an admiral in the Royal Navy and is currently serving as the First Lord of the Admiralty. He was initially reluctant to take a political position as the government's senior advisor of naval affairs, director of the Admiralty, and general administrator of the Royal Navy and the Royal Marines. However, he quickly embraced the role that seems to have been made for him. The King, himself, has complimented my father on several occasions for his excellent performance and leadership.

The door closes as he takes a seat across from us, looking very distinguished in his formal uniform—the magnificent dark-blue wool jacket with wide gold embroidery on the high collar, chest, and cuffs, the fancy gold fringed epaulets on the shoulders, and various badges and medals that speak of his military accomplishments. I may be somewhat biased, but of all the military uniforms, the navy's formal dress is the most spectacular. There is no denying the commanding presence and appeal of a properly dressed, high-ranking navy admiral.

Reaching forward with his sword-cane, a beautifully crafted accessory that was a gift from the Prime Minister, he taps my mother's knee through the layers of her brilliant red skirt. "Libby, my love, did I happen to mention that your beauty is so dazzling this evening that I am likely to have difficulty paying attention to anyone else in the room other than you?" I can see the sparkle in his eyes, and it makes my heart swell with love for him. He adores my mother, possibly even more than she adores him.

Mother shifts her attention to him, but only briefly before looking back out the window. "Yes, Edward, I believe you've mentioned it several times. Although your previous compliments were not glazed with as much honey." I cannot see her face as it is turned away, but from the endearing look on my father's, I suspect he must find a smile.

His foot moves to slip underneath the hem of her dress, silently claiming her attention. Once their eyes meet, he offers her a charming wink and a half smile that tells her everything she needs to know. With that simple gesture, all is right in the world again. I sit quietly and observe their exchange, finding comfort in the love and trust they share, wondering if someday

I will find the same in the man with whom I choose to share my life. I pray to be so fortunate.

~

Entering the ballroom, my first thought is that someone needs to open the French doors. It is stifling, the air stagnant from a crowd that is far larger than I anticipated and overheated by the number of candles used to illuminate this vast space. Beyond the lack of fresh, cool air, this ballroom is a stunning feature in an already palatial estate. The high ceilings are elaborately embellished with moldings so ornate, they are works of art themselves. In between the gilded frames that span the entirety of its length are lovely painted scenes of cherubs floating playfully in the clouds. I pause for a moment to enjoy the artistry and wonder at the subject's mischievous intentions. In spectacular contrast, the walls are covered in a rich burgundy wallpaper with small geometric designs of metallic gold. There are layers upon layers of gold swagged drapery that accent the floor-to-ceiling windows from top to bottom and pool onto the floor in an intentional excess that shows off our host's ability to afford it.

My favorite touches, however, are the massive potted palm trees that fan out proudly at every column and stand guard at each entrance, making the grand room more inviting and less intimidating. The bright green fronds contrast perfectly with the warm burgundy of the walls as they cast curious shadows around them.

Opening my fan, I try to cool myself before a sheen of perspiration has a chance to form across my face. If this room becomes any more crowded, it will be unbearable. I begin my search for a servant, seeking a refreshment to quench my sudden thirst, when my cousin, Mary, sneaks up from behind and grabs my shoulders, squealing as she spins me around. "Ella! You're here! Thank the Lord for small miracles. I thought I would have to endure this all by myself." I can tell by the beaming smile on her face that she is truly happy to see me.

"Mary! What are you doing here? I didn't think you were coming tonight. Oh, this is a wonderful change of plans!" These events just aren't the same without her.

"Mother changed her mind, as usual, and decided we should delay our visit to the country for another week or so." She rolls her eyes and releases a huff. "I can honestly say that I cannot wait to be married, living my own life, and no longer forced to follow my mother around with the hope that she will stick with a plan from one day to the next."

"Well, perhaps tonight is your lucky night. Surely there is a handsome young officer here that is lined up to be the next duke or marquess or some important title," I say encouragingly as we hook arms and continue to search for a refreshment.

"Listen to you with that fanciful notion. Look around, Ella. I think I am more likely to find myself matched to a stodgy old curmudgeon with a round belly and ear lobes that hang to his shoulders."

I cover my face with my fan as a giggle escapes. "Oh Mary, you are too cynical. You'll find your match, and it won't be to the frightening character you just described."

"So you say. I fear my mother is growing impatient and in discussions with my father to sell me off to the highest bidder. And I assure you, her standards are far different than mine."

"That's interesting considering the size of your dowry. How does the bidding work in that scenario? Your future husband is the one who receives the gain."

"Yes, well, don't confuse things, Ella. It's all about title with my parents, especially Mother. If he has status and a name, they are more than happy to fill his coffers." She squeezes my arm tighter. "It's really a terrible thing. Do you have any idea what has come to call recently?" she asks with a mock shiver up her spine.

"You act as if monkeys and mules have come to ask for your hand in marriage."

It's her turn to laugh as she throws her head back, unabashed. "I shall start matching my callers to creatures just for fun, and perhaps to keep them all separated. Lord Pennington is most assuredly the monkey." She pauses, tapping her chin as she thinks of the next comparison. "The mule is either the Earl of Falsworth and Lord Paget, the Marquess of something-or-other. Oh, Ella, it's truly terrifying. I cannot imagine being married to any of the men that have showed interest. I wish I did not have a dowry at all. We both know that is all they are interested in. Well, that and providing them with a son." Bringing her hand up to her chest, the angst escapes in something between a groan and a cry. "I simply will not be able to do *that* with a monkey or a mule."

Before I have a chance to distract her with something more positive, her head pops up, her face lit with mischief. "A stallion! That's what I need, a thoroughbred stallion. Tall, shiny, muscular, and handsome. I'll be the mare, and he'll be the stud."

Taking my fan, I snap it closed so I can hit her on the shoulder. "Mary!" I try not to draw any more attention than she already has. "You cannot talk so freely here. Someone may have heard you," I whisper sternly. "If your mother heard you, she'd send you straight to the convent."

"I can't become a duchess or marchioness if I'm a nun. Trust me when I tell you, her mission is clear. You've never seen such determination. That lunatic Napoleon doesn't hold a candle to my mother when it comes to the will to succeed!"

I can't help the burst of laughter that has me turning my

back to the crowd to hide my face. Mary's laughter starts to mingle with mine as she continues, "Oh dear, I've just had a vision of my mother, stern-faced and determined. Wearing that ridiculous hat—" She can barely talk now, and I've got tears coming out of my eyes. "that Napoleon wears."

Leaning into each other for support, we try to hide behind a column so no one can see that we have completely lost all decorum and are laughing riotously in the middle of a formal ball. Mary and I have been poking fun of Napoleon's hat since the first time we saw an image of the French leader. We decided it is a cross between bull horns and a burnt pastry that is three times too big for his head. Now, picturing Napoleon's signature accessory atop her mother's head is so absurd, neither of us can maintain control.

Unfortunately, we appear to have drawn the attention of the subject in our comedy, and she is not happy. "Mary! What on earth has come over you? And Ella, you as well? The two of you know better than to draw this kind of attention to yourselves."

Mary cannot bring herself to look at her mother, clearly imagining her standing there wearing Napoleon's oversized burnt pastry. I, on the other hand, force myself to do so and attempt to quickly defuse her ire. "I'm so sorry, Aunt. You are right, Mary and I got carried away with our silliness. I think we are just excited about this evening's gathering." I step aside so I can make a quick escape and finish with a polite curtsy. "Please forgive me. It will not happen again." I turn around and scurry along the back wall until I make it to a doorway that leads me away from the crowd, the stifling heat, my mischievous cousin, and her furious mother.

My steps are quick as I continue down the hall. I notice the air growing cooler the further I get from the ballroom, and I decide to keep going in hopes of finding a place to sit down and regain my composure. I see light coming from an open door just a short way down the hall. Approaching somewhat cautiously, I find a room with massive windows that seem to glow with the full moon's light. The room is filled with gardening equipment and plants of all kinds. It must lead to the conservatory that has a reputation of being one of the most extensive and impressive in all of London.

I find what I'm looking for on the other side of the room, and when I walk through the door, I am not disappointed. My eyes widen as I enter the indoor garden of my dreams. It is enormous, and I am in awe as I make my way down the path that leads me to the center where a magnificent tiered fountain stands at least fifteen feet high. I approach the encompassing pond and sit upon its wide edge. The water is trickling at a steady rate, its sound almost hypnotic, each droplet and stream highlighted by the moon's light glowing through the glass ceiling.

I stay there for a moment, letting my body relax and absorb the natural essence of this magical place. I may never make it back to the ballroom, it pales in comparison to this spectacular display. Something in the pond catches my eye, and I see there are orange and white fish swimming gracefully through the rippling water. Several appear to be very large, and I wonder if the darkness deceives my eyes. But, as a white one reaches the surface, almost glowing in the moonlight, I see they have not and that these fish are quite large indeed.

I stand up and leisurely spin around in a full circle, taking in all that the dim light allows my eyes to see. I must have a place equivalent to this one day when I have a home of my own. A smile lifts the corners of my mouth as I think about spending my time here instead of practicing the piano or stitching designs so intricate, my eyesight goes blurry and my fingers ache.

There is so much to this garden that I cannot see in the darkness of night. So, I decide to explore, and soon I am happily lost in the maze of paths lined with a variety of plants and trees I could only dream of visiting every day. This is the place I love to be, enjoying the smell of green plants and moist soil—the place where silence has a sound. Further down the path, massive leaves drape toward me, and I stretch my arms out wide, allowing my fingertips to sweep along each one.

It is completely peaceful here, with only the fountain's trickle sounding in the distance, and the gentle swoosh of my layered skirts as I walk along the manicured trail.

The moment is tarnished by the feeling of guilt that washes over me as I wonder about Mary's fate and her mother's wrath. I hope my aunt wasn't too hard on her. Interrupting my thoughts, an abrupt sound steals what's left of the tranquility in my paradise.

I follow the noise out of curiosity and annoyance, finding my pace quicken as I search for the distinct male voice, and perhaps another person as well. Instinct tells me I will likely find a gardener working hard to maintain this botanical masterpiece. However, when I make my way to the furthest edge and step off the path, I pull down the colossal leaf of a philodendron, unknowing of the moment my life will change forever.

My heart pounds painfully in my chest, blood swooshing within my ears as I try not to gasp at my discovery. Presented before me, shielded in darkness, yet highlighted by the moon's pale blue glow stands a man more masculine than I ever knew possible—naked, sinuous, spectacular in a way that makes my stomach ache. He seems herculean, tall, broad, and beautiful. His muscular form is like that of an ancient Greek statue, each muscle flawlessly carved, an extravagance meant for show.

My eyes will not look away. I am fascinated by the harsh shadows cast across his spectacular form. The way his wide chest expands proudly across his upper body then twists and wraps around his powerful shoulders that lead into arms so defined they cannot be real. My stare drifts lower and my stomach tightens as a wave of unfamiliar heat flashes through my body. His torso is sculpted into perfect squares on either side of a center line. Involuntarily, the fingers of my right hand come up to my mouth. I bite down on my lip to stop the terrible desire to touch his chiseled core. The tips of my breasts become painfully hard as I follow the line down to the dark patch of hair framed by more carved muscle, directing me to the one thing I know I should not see.

By all that is holy. How is that possible? His manhood is thick and long, protruding from his body like the sturdy branch of tree. Its form is like nothing I have ever seen, its details on obvious display as the light reflects off its shiny surface. *Is that even real?* I wonder to myself, perplexed and fascinated all at once. My body ignites from within as he reaches down and takes the massive appendage in his hand to slowly stroke it from base to tip. I swallow the gasp threatening to escape, then squeeze my legs together as another wave of sensation travels directly to my most private place where heat, wetness, and a strange pleasure are forming.

His deep voice startles me out of my trance. "Ye look lovely tonight, lass." My breath lodges in my chest at hearing the richness of his voice. *Surely, he wasn't talking to me.* When I pull the leaf all the way down, I see a woman bent over the half wall of a planter. She is completely unclothed, her smooth pale skin ghostly white compared to his. She responds to his compliment, but her head is turned away from me so I cannot hear what she said. However, her body translates the meaning as her legs spread further apart and her hips rise upward,

15

causing her backside to move toward him in silent invitation, one that he accepts without pause.

I should leave. It is not my place to spy upon them, and it is so improper I fear I may have to pray for a month straight to release me from this sin. Not only the sin of watching them, or the sin of finding pleasure in simply staring at him—watching his sculpted body move, each muscle flexing and relaxing, bunching then stretching—but for the sin of jealousy. I don't want him to touch her. I don't want her to enjoy his touch. But why? I don't know him. I don't want to know him. Yet my body is alive with a need so intense; I could mistake it for something that is achingly familiar—as if my body is haunted by the feel of his touch.

I watch him reach forward and touch her most intimate place, her own sound of pleasure echoing around them. My teeth grind together and my jaw clenches. I want him to touch *me* just like that. A heavy surge of envy lands in my chest where it mingles with a confounding mixture of fear, curiosity, and shame. The voice in the back of my mind tells me to leave now, but I see her starting to move. It's as if she wants more contact than he is already giving her, causing more desire to expand through my core. Her moans intensify as his touch becomes more aggressive. My heart races faster and I start to sweat as a strange pressure starts building between my legs.

I need to run away, but I can't. Not yet.

Without warning, he pulls his hand out from between her legs, his fingers shiny and wet, then rests it against her backside. He rubs her gently before drawing back his hand, fingers spread wide, smacking it against her just as he brings his stiff manhood to her entrance, driving it in with a brutal force. She screams out in erotic pleasure, and my knees become weak as an unbearable sensation takes over where the wetness is secreting from my body. I pant as I watch him thrust in and out, hard and fast, grunting and straining. The muscles of his legs and backside are taught from exertion, his body glistening with sweat.

Please...please! the voice inside my head screams. To stop? For more?

A cry escapes his partner as her head is thrown back in what is either intense pleasure or terrible pain. My hand involuntarily reaches down to put pressure between my own legs. I am desperate for some kind of relief, ready to beg him to help me find it or else I will go mad.

As if he read my mind, a fierce growl escapes him as he pulls himself out of her body, taking his hardness in hand and milks himself, allowing his essence to spew out across her naked back.

I am unable to hold in the sound that escapes me as the pressure that was building between my legs releases into a throbbing pleasure so intense, my body curls forward, my head bows, and my breath gets caught in my chest.

I can't breathe. I can't breathe.

My God! What have I done?

As the sensation dissipates, the pulsing continues, and I'm overtly aware of what has happened. Shame engulfs me as I rest my hands on my knees for support, trying to steady my breaths as my body returns to normal. Tears build behind my eyes, I must leave. Now.

With caution, I straighten my posture, trying not to make a sound. I raise my head and almost choke on the cry that has been clogging my throat. Between the long stems of the philodendron that I thought kept me hidden, I see fierce eyes locked on mine. My heart stops as I am momentarily stunned, not only by the fact that he knows I am here watching him, but by how devastatingly handsome he is. A burst of energy blasts through my body, bringing me back to the path where I run as fast as I can to the main entrance on the other side of the conservatory. I don't stop, not even once I'm through the doors and back into the ornately decorated hall of the corridor that leads back to the ballroom.

Before entering, I find a private settee and take a moment to rest, hoping to calm my breaths. I simply cannot be seen in this state. I retrieve a handkerchief from my sleeve and blot the perspiration on my neck and face. I wish I could just go home and forget this night ever happened.

I don't know what came over me, why I didn't walk away, why I stayed to watch him, or what happened to my body. A lump forms in my throat as the confusion of emotions overwhelms me. I allow only one tear to escape before regaining my composure. If I walk into the ballroom red-eyed and weepy, the rumors will be flying around town before breakfast is served tomorrow morning.

After ten more minutes of calming breaths, I'm ready to put on a cheerful expression for the crowd that awaits. I stand to shift my skirts and adjust my sash, then turn for the door. It is then that I hear the steady cadence of footsteps against the marble floor of the hallway. The commanding echo triggers my heart to pound once again as my stomach flips, and gooseflesh forms across my entire body. It's him, I know it is, and I cannot bring myself to turn around and face the man that I have seen fully unclothed performing the most carnal of acts.

I move to make my escape, taking only two steps before I hear the deep, accented voice say, "Stop."

I do as it commands, though I keep my back to him. His steps grow closer and closer, the harsh sound ringing in my ears. I sense his proximity and am forced to acknowledge that my hands have begun to tremble as he stops just behind me.

"Turn around." His thick Scottish brogue makes the words vibrate through me.

I don't want to look at him again. I want to keep moving forward and act as if he is not standing close enough for me to feel his body's warmth. But he would think I'm a coward, not worthy of my family's name, and *that* will never do.

I inhale the deep breath I desperately need and hesitantly turn around. Again, I am unable to hold in a gasp, one loud enough to echo through the hall. He's in uniform. "My God, you're a...a...captain in the King's Navy," I hiss as my fingers come up to my lips, holding in words I might regret.

"Aye, I am. And yer a spy." He pauses, arches a brow and smirks. "Or perhaps ye are a true voyeur, in every sense o' the word."

Appalled at his suggestion, my spine straightens as my hands land firmly on my hips. "I beg your pardon! How dare you suggest such a thing?"

He throws his head back and laughs, deep and masculine, and I despise that a part of me enjoys the sound. "Ah, lass. That is humor at its finest. How could I possibly come up with such a preposterous conclusion?" He leans forward, head bowing to look down at me with his blazing turquoise eyes. "I am a bit surprised to find ye are a proper lady. What is yer name?"

I refuse to answer right away, so I hold my ground and return the hardest stare I can muster. How and why did God create a man so physically appealing it makes my hands ache with wanting to touch him? To reach up and trace the perfect outline of his wide lips with the tip of my finger, to run them all through the glossy black tresses that were disheveled, hanging just below his shoulders in the conservatory but are now perfectly combed and plaited at the nape of his neck. A part of me wants to hate him for his perfection, but perhaps more so because of his unwavering confidence in what should be a terribly awkward situation. In a show of courage, I offer him what he asked for, albeit incomplete. "Ella."

His eyes lose all humor as the blue-green color that glows against his tanned skin is almost completely hidden by the black center, like an animal in the night. "Where are yer wings, Ella?" The *R*s roll through his nonsensical question before he pauses to say my name like I have never heard it spoken before. The four simple letters have never sounded more beautiful, more feminine than the way they did when spoken by this man. A man that seems to enjoy playing with me like a cat plays with a mouse.

"That is an absurd question."

"Ah. Then ye don't know the meaning of yer lovely name." He continues to stare at me, as if to study the features of my face. The intimacy of it making my heart race and my body heat up uncomfortably. He reaches up to run his thumb along my jawline, my knees weaken as he explains, "Ella... faerie maiden." Again, his brogue makes the simple words seem special somehow. But his unusual definition of my name, the warmth of his touch, and the spicy scent surrounding him are making my stomach fill with butterflies.

When he pulls his hand away, he stands a little straighter and focuses on my eyes. "I can'na think of a more perfect name fer the ethereal creature that snuck up on me in the conservatory. Although, fer a faerie maiden, ye weren't very inconspicuous." His words and voice are hypnotic as they melt down my spine. "I could sense yer presence. Knew ye were excited to see me. It drove me mad..." He moves closer to me, forcing my head back further. "I could feel ye there more than the sweet lass that was kind enough to pleasure me." He pauses again, continuing the intimate perusal of my face. "Did ye know my compliment was meant fer you, *not* fer her?" His question intrigues me in a way that makes me afraid...afraid of him and the feelings he stirs inside me.

I'm becoming lightheaded. Like this is a dream. Gentlemen

do not talk to ladies this way. It is beyond improper. Yet, he has captured my attention, for I believe that he is telling the truth; he could feel me—for I could certainly feel him— and that notion has my entire body tingling with wanton desire.

"You cannot talk to me this way. You...you can't say such things." I shift my gaze from his and step back, far enough to give myself room to breathe and glance around to ensure no one is near. "As a gentleman, you should know better. This conversation could ruin my reputation." The fear of that reality snaps me out of the trance I believe he has purposefully put me in.

"I would'na let that happen," he responds without hesitation.

"Is that so? Then I shall walk away, and this time you will not stop me. Just standing here talking to you unchaperoned is enough to start rumors that will make it so." Taking another step back, hoping to begin my retreat, I see his eyes drop to my chest. The subtle action makes my breasts seem heavy and tight.

Lifting his chin, he smiles, his eyes clearly locked on the necklace I now regret wearing. "'Tis lovely. It matches yer eyes." His accurate observation makes me shy as I look away, not wanting him to see his effect on me. "Look at me, Ella." He seems able to command my every move as I do as he says, wishing the way his accent on my name didn't cause my stomach to do flips inside me. "They remind me of the clear waters surrounding the Bahamian islands. Ye cannot find a more beautiful shade of blue anywhere in the world." He looks down at the stones resting upon my chest. "The aquamarine is said to be a treasure of the mermaids. It is used as a talisman by sailors to bring them good luck and protection." He reaches up and gently takes hold of the dangling trail of gems, his fingers caressing the skin he should never take the liberty of touching.

My nipples harden painfully, and my breath stops on a sharp inhale. The back of his hand is warm and heavy as he rests it there to rub his thumb across the smooth surface of a stone. My eyes close as I fight against the desire forming in my core.

"Open yer eyes, faerie maiden." Again, I do as he commands. His voice is smooth, like velvet. "The aquamarine is also said to encourage truth-telling." His smirk accompanies an arched brow. "I think we should test the theory."

I don't like where this is leading. My heart is beating so erratically in my chest, he must feel it as his fingers are still resting just above it. I look up at him with a desperate plea to release the hold that his touch, his voice, his scent, *those eyes* have on me. "Tell me, Ella. Did ye enjoy coming undone while ye were watching me?"

Without a second's hesitation, my open hand lands a stinging slap across his perfect face. "You bastard!" The angry word escapes my mouth for the first time in my life. "I will not stand here and allow you to insult me with your arrogant games any longer. How dare you take such liberties with me! Clearly that uniform has been wasted on a lowly *Scot*. The king may try with all his might to refine you barbarians in the north, but I fear his charitable efforts have gone to waste." With haste, I turn for the ballroom entrance, wanting desperately to disappear from this humiliating scene.

"Ella!" My name echoes around me.

I stop just before I reach the door and peer over my shoulder. My heart sinks at the sight of his expression. I don't care. I can't. "Do not ever speak to me again. I am the daughter of the Duke of Somerset, which means *you* are beneath me. It will do you well to remember your place."

Without another word or moment's hesitation, I enter the crowded ballroom.

TWO

Alasdair

T he room is quiet as I sit on the side of my bed, running my fingers through my hair with frustration. I gave up trying to sleep, so I head down to the library. It takes time to adjust to the stillness of land after being at sea for so long. That and the silence. Aboard ship, I become accustomed to the language of the ocean—the loud creaks as she sways, the rhythmic sound of her hull crashing through the waves, the wind as it changes direction and whips the sails until the strong fabric fills with a thundering clap. It's a sailor's lullaby and ensures a peaceful slumber. But here, back on land, my resting mind gets confused by the lack of movement and sound, and my dreams turn dark with fear that something has gone terribly wrong with my ship, and sleep becomes impossible.

Unfortunately, something *has* gone terribly wrong, but it has nothing to do with my ship, and everything to do with the fierce young lady that has taken up occupancy in my mind.

My footsteps echo through the silent halls as I follow the path to my sanctuary. It is the one place I am grounded. Whether in Scotland, aboard my ship, or here in London, my library is where I find peace and comfort, surrounded by a plethora of words, knowledge, and wisdom I have yet to learn. It is the place I can solve any problem, right any wrong, draft a poem to inspire any mind, or make a magnificent woman know that I am more than a first impression.

I light the lantern on my desk before pouring myself a glass of whisky. The small flame gives the oversized room a soft glow, but still leaves every corner as dark as the pitch of night outdoors. I prefer it this way—my desktop as the only focal point in the room, lit up like a beacon in the darkness. It keeps my attention anchored in one place, not on a thousand books lining my shelves, wanting desperately to be read.

While comfortably seated, I fidget with the papers in front of me, not really intending to do anything more than pretend I'm organizing them. My mind is too distracted, too agitated. The more I think about the events of the evening, the more I want to saddle up Magni, ride over to Ella Seymour's home, and let her know exactly where this *lowly Scot's* place is. I'll have to give her credit; she severed a nerve with her parting cut. Just the idea that she looks at me as less than the man I am because I am from Scotland is enough to bring out some ancient berserker that still lingers in my blood. Scot or no Scot, I am a Stewart, descended from kings and queens, the heir to an earldom, two viscountcies, and a barony, as well as a captain in the Royal Navy. She may be Seymour's daughter, but outrank me she does not.

My finger taps a steady rhythm on the glass while my thoughts go back to the conservatory. Cora, the serving maid I was with, was a pleasant surprise after a long journey at sea. Her choice of the garden as our rendezvous location was a bit of a surprise as well, and a pleasant one, still. But Ella's unexpected appearance was something else entirely. I wasn't exaggerating when I told her I could sense her presence. It was as if the air around me shifted, making the hair on my neck stand up. I pretended to not know she was there, only letting my eyes glance over without turning my head. The moon perfectly lit her face, its blue cast glowing against her pale skin, and I was momentarily stunned by her beauty. Never has my heart pounded so hard from simply looking at a woman. But it did when my eyes found her. Remembering it now has increased its tempo once again.

As I take a long sip of whisky, its rich peaty flavor making my mouth water, I continue to relive seeing—*feeling*—Ella as she watched me. I could sense her arousal; I could feel her fight against it and lose the battle. She knew she should leave. What we were doing wasn't for her to see, but she couldn't bring herself to turn away. She wanted to see it to completion, and so she did. From that alone, I would have never guessed she was a proper lady. Yet, when I stood before her, I understood completely as I watched her skin blush, her breath hitch, and her heartbeat's heavy rhythm clearly visible in the shallow dip of her delicate throat. Ella Seymour is an extremely passionate and uncommonly sensual woman. Add to that, wit and tenacity, and it was easy to discern her decision to stay and watch. Though my gut tells me there was something else at play—something neither of us could rationally explain.

I get up to pace around my library, needing to move, to organize my thoughts, to decide upon my next move. One thing is for certain: I will not be following Ella's request to never speak to her again. I may not be the kind of man she is accustomed to, but the more I think about her comments about my Scottish heritage, the more irritated I become. I know Edward Seymour personally, and he's a good man. I cannot imagine he taught his daughter to have a sense of superiority over their neighbors in the north. Her mother—

now that could be a different story. She is the daughter of the Duke of Brunswick, after all.

It doesn't take long for the whisky to relax me and clear my head. Without so many thoughts clashing against one another like the infantry brigade during sword practice, I find I am more thoughtful, more objective to Ella's position. In truth, it is easy to sympathize. She is young and naïve, the daughter of a duke, and has likely never been told the truth about carnal pleasure. She was clearly in shock at what she found in the garden, yet her innate curiosity wouldn't let her leave. When she found herself enjoying what she witnessed, she was likely ashamed. Since I'm a presumptuous arse, I forced her to put up her defenses and give me a well-placed slap and a fantastically executed cut. As I rub the cheek that was the recipient of her aggression, I smile, remembering the fierce look in her crystal blue eyes, complemented by the straightness of her spine. Not only is she uncommonly beautiful and intriguingly sensual, she has an inherent fortitude that would intimidate half the crewmen on my ship.

My laugh echoes through the silence as I pick up my pen and prepare to write something for Ella. A letter, a poem, a story about an enchanting faerie casting her spell upon a sailor. I have decided my next move will be more traditional, perhaps even charming, and give her more insight into who I really am. Maybe then she will be open to a more appropriate introduction. Lady Ella Seymour has gained my attention in a way that is entirely unfamiliar to me, and I fear that I may not ever sleep well again until I can erase the look of contempt or perhaps even hatred in her eyes.

I tap off the excess ink onto the edge of the well, allowing my thoughts to go where they are most comfortable—to the place where letters become words and words become phrases. The contemplations blend, painting a vivid picture; colorful, and filled with emotion. Where the sound of the quill scratching the surface of the paper opens my mind to more words that construct the details and subtleties that make the finished piece poignant, provocative, maybe even persuasive.

The ink's contrast on the paper is harsh as the controlled script of my hand starts at the most basic beginning.

Dear Lady Ella,

THREE
Ella

The door opens to my bedchamber, and Beatrice makes a startled sound at finding me sitting by the window, the drapes pulled back to allow the sun's blinding rays to light up the room. "Why are you not sleeping, child? I would have come sooner had I known you were awake."

Getting closer, she can see that something isn't right, and when she sits down next to me, places her warm hand over mine and gives me a look of loving concern, I am unable to hold in my emotions. Leaning forward, I wrap my arms around her and begin sobbing into her bosom like I did as a child.

"Oh, Beatrice! It's simply awful!" I've barely slept a wink with terrible thoughts about myself swirling through my mind. I am so confused and ashamed, afraid of what happened during my conversation with the captain, and of what happened to me in the conservatory.

"Come, come, dearie. Everything will be all right. Tell me what has you so upset." She pulls me into a motherly embrace, gently rubbing her hand along my back while rocking from side to side like she always has as she hums a sweet melody. It is so soothing and calming, that within minutes I am no longer crying. She places a kiss on the top of my head and gives me a tight squeeze.

"There now. That's better." She pulls back just enough, giving me space to sit up and wipe away the tears that have soaked my cheeks. "I haven't seen you this upset in a very long time, Ella. Do you want to talk about it?"

With a slight nod, I try to swallow another lump that makes me want to cry more rather than talk. "I'm...I'm afraid something has happened—" I stop to take a breath before continuing, "that could ruin me." The tears break through again as the fear and shame take hold. Beatrice has always taught me to be honest with her, no matter what. She knew I would not have that privilege with anyone else in my life and promised she would always be here to talk about anything.

"This sounds very serious. Are you sure it is all that bad?"

"Yes. At least I think it is." I take a deep breath and pray she will understand. "Last night, at the ball, I ended up in the conservatory." She seems puzzled by my statement. "The ballroom was stifling, and I needed fresh air. There was the most splendid indoor garden I have ever seen, truly spectacular. It was immense with winding paths that led from one beautiful scene to another." I smile, remembering how wonderful I felt to walk through the garden, the scent of healthy green plants all around me. "But something happened there...and I...I am very ashamed. Quite honestly, I'm afraid of what I have done."

Beatrice's mouth falls into grimace, showing true concern. "Ella, dear, whatever could you have done in a conservatory, of all places, that would ruin you?"

So, I tell her. I tell her what I found, and that I could not take my eyes off the magnificent man lit up by the moon. Then

I tell her what he was doing and, with my head hanging low, tell her what happened to my body. With the admission, my tears break free.

Beatrice takes both my hands in hers, and her comforting voice wraps around me like a warm blanket. "Ella, I want you to listen to me and listen to me well." She pauses to make sure my eyes are on hers and that she has my full attention. "Yes, spying on the couple in the garden was wrong. However, sometimes our curiosity gets the best of us. It is our mind's yearning for knowledge of things we do not yet know. It is normal. You, as a young woman, are very curious about what happens between a man and a woman. After all, it will be expected of you once you are married."

With that comment, a wave of heat rushes through my body at the thought of doing just that with the captain. I force the thought away.

"Your curiosity got the better of you, and from what you described—" She lets out a laugh. "I almost can't blame you."

I pop my head up in surprise, "Beatrice! Did you actually say what I think you did?"

She laughs harder at my question before responding. "Well, I'm only being honest. I don't think most men are put together as well as the one you saw last night. I'm not sure any woman alive would have been able to walk away from such a scene!"

I am shocked at prudish Beatrice's candor on such a scandalous topic. For a moment, I forget about my shame, and we both cackle and snort with laughter while wiping away the cheerful tears. "Oh my! You have surprised me beyond words. I sat here in fear the entire night, worried about how ashamed you were going to be." As I look up at her, my heart swells with love. "Thank you, Beatrice. There is still a part of me that feels shame, but I'm much better knowing I am not a wanton deviant, deserving of the convent." I bow my head in shyness, still questioning myself. "But...what about my reaction? Beatrice, I did not know there could be a pleasure such as that. Surely that is not normal, is it?"

A slight blush appears on her plump cheeks before she responds, "Well, it isn't something that is discussed so freely. To be honest, most women do not find that kind of pleasure so easily, if they ever find it at all. I think it's best you stop worrying, and know that when you are married and in love, you will truly enjoy the sacred act of love between a husband and wife."

"Do you enjoy it?" I ask with hesitation.

"Yes, actually I do. Although, it doesn't happen as often as it used to," she says with a tender look in her eyes. "but Rupert and I have had a good marriage. We've always been in love, and he doesn't make it only about him. Therefore, it is easier for me to find the pleasure you speak of. I hope one day your husband will do the same for you."

"Thank you for talking so openly with me. I don't know what I would do without your support."

I stand up to pour us each a glass of water, thinking about the magnificent man in the garden, how his behavior contrasted against the arrogant blackguard that confronted me in the hall. I change the subject as I hand Beatrice the glass. "There is one more unfortunate event from last night."

"I'm not sure I can handle any more details beyond what you've already told me!"

"He saw me."

Eyes bulging, she nearly chokes on her water. "What? Ella!"

In a defeated tone, I confirm, "He saw me. He knew I was there and confronted me outside the ballroom."

"Do you know who this man was? Surely he isn't a nobleman."

"Of that I am not certain, but I suspect it is so. When he

appeared in the hallway...I...I was shocked to find...he is a captain in the Royal Navy."

"The Navy? With your father?" Beatrice whispers the last question with the same distress I have felt since I laid eyes on him. "Oh dear. What did he say to you?"

"Actually, I believe he was toying with me more than anything. Which, of course, infuriated me. But it gets better... He's a Scot." I can still hear his deep accent saying my name. The thought sends chills across my skin.

"A Scot? Good grief! Do you know anything about him— well, other than what you already know. I mean, because of what you've seen and...oh, never mind." She abruptly stops in frustration.

"I don't know his name or anything else about him." I walk across the room to distract myself from the feeling of guilt that comes over me every time I think about my parting words. "I told him to never speak to me again because he is a Scot, and that he is beneath me."

"Oh, Ella, you didn't... That is not like you. What on earth would make you say such a thing?" Her sympathy toward him makes me feel far worse.

"He was toying with me. He pushed it too far, and I let him know it shall not happen a second time. My intent was to make him dislike me so that he never speaks to me again. I am keeping my fingers crossed that it works. I can tell you this: my body does not feel like my own when he is around, and I will not have a man controlling me in such a way. Now he knows I am off-limits." I feel somewhat triumphant after that speech. I only hope my wishes are met with success.

My hopes are short-lived as Trudy, one of my favorite maids, enters the room with a look of concern on her face. "A lovely morn to ye, m'lady." She's unusually quiet while peering over at Beatrice, then back at me. "Could I speak with ye privately in the hall, ma'am?"

"Of course," I answer with confusion and undeniable trepidation.

Once in the hall, she turns to look both ways before speaking. "M'lady, someone from the household of Lord Alasdair Stewart just brought me an envelope and package. 'Tis quite heavy, I must say, and he asked to have it delivered to you with haste and discretion. To be honest, I wanted to run in the other direction. It's not my place to receive such a thing, but the man who gave it to me was charming...and...and...good with words, so here I am, doing something I shouldn't be." She stops her stuttering and walks over to the nook just beyond my door, bringing me an envelope and a wrapped gift that is indeed quite heavy.

"You don't know who gave this to you?" I ask, trying to hold back the nausea settling in my stomach.

"No ma'am. I don't know who he was, but I would know him again if I saw him. He was quite...unforgettable."

I'm admittedly perturbed by the sparkle that is obnoxiously evident within her eyes. Not to mention the wanton blush coloring her face a bright ruby red. Whoever this Lord Stewart sent as his delivery man was clearly well-chosen. Trudy is flirtatious by nature, but gullible to the wiles of a handsome, charming man. It must be in the air because the same thing happened to me.

"Thank you, Trudy. I appreciate your honesty. In the future, try not to be charmed so easily." She bows and scurries away, leaving me with more than the weight of a mysterious package.

Once I'm back in my room, I rush to the window settee, bypassing Beatrice. I stare at the letter and gift smuggled to me by a man named Alasdair Stewart. That is a Scottish name if ever I heard one, and my body flushes with heat as I see his masculine script on the envelope.

Lady Ella Seymour

It reads, but somehow, seems to say so much more. Beyond that, I cannot ignore the strange sensation overwhelming me, knowing that the man who stirred desires in me like I've never known, wrote this letter to me. He held the paper in his strong hands, folded it with precision, and sealed it with the proud emblem of his noble family.

Opening the wax seal, I am surprised to find so many words. I glance over its structure, finding it to look like verses of a poem. With another flush of emotion, a slight dizziness overcomes me. I take a deep breath and start from the beginning.

Dear Lady Ella,

I hope this note finds you well as the sun brightens your morning. I indeed hope that your slumber was deep and rejuvenating. For me, sleep did not come easily as my mind was carried away to crystal-blue tropical waters and mythical creatures following me through the forest. It is a dichotomy to be sure. But one so lovely and poetic, it inspired images of a maiden beautiful and ethereal, proud and strong, fierce and tenacious.

I wrote this for you, Ella.

Could God, our creator, be considered an artist?
With a magical brush he dipped into the sea
Creating the crystal blue eyes of a maiden, that sparkle
in the sun,

With unknown depths that capture the curiosity of men.
To use the petals of a rose that stain the lips he shaped
    with precision
Smiling upon only those deserving of their perfection.
To pull the rays of the sun from the sky and spin them
    into shiny golden locks
Flowing in long waves that frame the face of an angel.
He does not stop there
For he is more than a painter, but a sculptor as well,
Giving her the heart of a lioness,
Fearless and proud,
The body of a goddess
Curved and soft, fertile and enticing
The mind of a conqueror,
Sharp and determined and precise.
Let us not forget, God has a sense of humor,
So he made her mischievous, adventurous, and
    unconventional,
Piquing the interest of some and the ire of others.
With his finishing touch, he pulled magic from an
    ancient forest,
From the realm of the Fey, the mythical creatures of
    legend.
With this charm, she surpassed ethereal,
Became an enigma in a sea of what is expected
For he gave her the ability to cast spells
On the unsuspecting hearts of men.
Yes, God is an artist
And you are his masterpiece.

I can't breathe. My eyes fill with tears from an emotion I cannot describe. There is more to the letter, but I keep going back to the poem that is so beautifully written, so generous in its compliments, so kind and thoughtful. I simply cannot connect it to the arrogant man that pushed my anger to heights I did not know I possessed. To force me outside of everything I know is right and proper, then leaving me sleepless with worry and shame and fear, surely this is not the same man. It does not seem possible.

With another deep breath, I finish the letter.

Your gift is from my family's library. It was a favorite book of mine from when I was a boy. The illustrations both inspired me and terrified me, as some of the creatures are kind and some are most assuredly not. But there was always one that I considered my favorite, for she was the most magnificent of them all. You will find her on page 27. She reminds me of you and is the reason I knew the meaning of your lovely name.

Until we meet again.

Fondly,

Lord Alasdair Stewart

I glance up at Beatrice. "Are you alright, dear? Is it the man from last night?" she asks softly.

All I can do is nod.

My hands tremble as I untie the string and remove the soft piece of fabric enveloping this mysterious gift. When I pull it away, I find the most beautiful book I think I have ever seen. It has a dark brown leather cover that is embossed with intricate designs of vines, leaves, and flowers surrounding an oval centered on the front. Inside the oval, outlined with a decorative gold leaf border, the leather is smooth and painted with the scene of a forest. I trace my fingertip along the raised letters of its title, also accented in gold leaf, *The Legend of the Forest Realm – Faeries, Pixies, Elves, Trolls, and the Like.* The cover of this book is like a work of art itself. To even possess such a thing speaks of the wealth that resides in his library alone.

Upon opening the book, I find little embellishments of leaves, flowers, or what look like little flying creatures on every page of text. There is page after page of illustrated scenes from an enchanted forest that only the most creative mind could imagine. Each one is framed in the same decorative gold leaf design as the cover. These images are so defined, every leaf and branch and pebble looks as if you could pull it off the page. But the creatures are so fantastic and realistic, I can truly imagine they are real. Some are in full color and others are the simple black lines of pen and ink, both equally enchanting with personalities emanating from each page. It is no wonder this book captured the mind of a young boy.

Looking down at the bottom of the page, I see the number is 26. Recalling his letter, I know I will find his favorite creature when I turn to page 27, and the thought invites back the insistent butterflies to form in my stomach again.

My breath hitches as the image appears before me. Of all the drawings I've seen in this book, this is truly the most spectacular. It is a faerie walking through the forest, down a path lined with fern, thick and pillowing under the trees. She is tall and beautiful, her long hair flowing gracefully down her back and around her magnificent wings. I feel the heat of embarrassment come over me as my eyes follow the lines of her naked body. His words flash through my mind: *She reminds me of you.* I try to hide an envious smile. If only I were as lovely as this mythical being. I imagine her as free and unrestrained by the rules of society and all that is right and wrong, using her mind and her wit to outsmart the other creatures featured in the mesmerizing tome, to survive in a wilderness filled with wonderment and danger.

My finger comes down to touch her and follow the graceful

lines of her form. Somewhere in the back of my mind, I hear myself speak to her. *I wish you were real. I have so many questions.* But that is silly and just the lingering imagination of the girl I used to be, running through the forest, daring the animals and creatures to show themselves and prove they are real. As my finger continues to trace the details of the illustration, I reach the bottom and that is where I find the small script that gives this fantasy rendition a name. *Ella, the Faerie Maiden.* I cannot stop the joyful smile that spreads across my face as a sense of pride comes over me. Somehow, she has given me a sense of strength and confidence I did not know I possess.

The sudden knock at my door startles us both as my mother swings it open and enters with all the drama of a stage performer. "Ella, darling! I have received a letter from Lord Alasdair Stewart. He has apparently shown great interest in you. Lord Stewart's father is the Earl of Galloway in Scotland, and he is the sole heir to the title—a *very* substantial one." Her excitement is the antithesis of the dreadful knot forming in the pit of my stomach. "Your father was just telling me about the long conversation they had last night at the ball. You caught Lord Stewart's eye the moment he arrived, and when he found out your father is the Duke of Somerset *and* Admiral of the Fleet, he sought him out immediately to make his interests known. He's a captain, you see. Your father says he is very well-respected and will most assuredly be promoted to admiral one day." The pitch of her voice has risen as she rambles on about the man I could not take my eyes off of while he pleasured himself with another woman. Heat flushes through me as I remember wishing it were me he touched in such ways. Then, a cold fear washes over me knowing that same man talked with my father. My sweet father would be so ashamed if he knew the truth behind that scoundrel's intentions.

Mother is still going on, her voice ringing in my ears though I have no idea what she is saying. Finally, she stops. "What is wrong with you, Ella? You look ill. Are you coming down with something?"

"No. I'm fine. I didn't sleep well after a late night."

"Are you not pleased that Lord Stewart is interested? He said the two of you had a delightful conversation and that he finds your charm and wit refreshing and irresistible."

"He said that, did he? I cannot say the same about him," I mumble as I get up to walk off the pounding in my chest that is making it hard to breathe. I cannot believe the terrible turn my life has taken in such a short period of time. Whatever am I going to do?

"Ella! What is the meaning of this letter...of...of this poem? And what on earth is this book? Lord *Stewart* gave you this?" My mother's voice is somewhat shrill as she yanks me out of my cloudy despair. She has the letter in her hand. I didn't even think to hide it somehow when she walked in. Now, she's standing before me with a look on her face that is a cross between suspicion and fear and perhaps a conclusion that reeks of disappointment.

"Mother, please calm down. The look on your face says you have come up with conclusions that are completely insulting. I had no idea this man was going to write me poetry and send me gifts!" My hand waves in the direction of the settee where Alasdair's beautiful gilded book glows in the bright rays of the sun. My eyes will not look away from the magnificent tome that seems to speak to me with its own voice.

"From the sounds of his letter and descriptive prose of you as a person, he has *very* intimate knowledge of you," she snaps, pulling me out of my fantasy. When I look over at Beatrice, I can see that she is reciting prayers under her breath.

"It is not my fault the man apparently has a vivid

ALISON E. STEUART

imagination. I met him briefly last night at the ball. He asked my name, and then he went on to ask me nonsense like where were my wings? To be honest, I was a bit disappointed by his foolishness because he is quite handsome." I finish my rant with a barb that will hopefully distract the rest of the questions I see sitting just under the surface. "And besides, I ended up cutting the conversation short because I simply could not tolerate his insufferable Scottish brogue any longer."

"Oh!" Mother stops and redirects her questioning. "Was it really that bad? With his standing in society, you would think his accent would be more refined."

"Bad doesn't begin to describe it. Every R rolled like a boulder off his tongue, and half his words blended to the point I could hardly understand what he was saying." That's a bit of an exaggeration. If I am being honest with myself, there was something rather appealing about his accent that sent gooseflesh across my body.

"Well, dear, that is a bit surprising. However, his family is quite well off and one of the most well-respected in Scotland. I suppose it could be worse. Though, more than his unrefined speech, my concern lies with how forward this letter is, not to mention how inappropriate it is that he even sent it to you with a gift!"

I almost laugh at the apparent conundrum my mother is in as she mentally thumbs through the pages of *The Book of Proper Etiquette and Maintaining the Highest Standing in Society*. She is weighing the value of a wealthy future earl against the fact that he is clearly no English gentleman. She must have found the page she was looking for, because her eyes widen and her face lights up as she states, "We will put him to the test ourselves. Let us invite him for tea or perhaps even dinner one day this week."

How did we manage to end up here?

"Mother!" My tone is impatient. "Do I not have any say so in this?" The thought of having the man from the conservatory in my home, conversing with my mother and father, is a thought that is so far outside anything my mind can fathom as reasonable or even proper, I think it is making me slightly ill to my stomach. My parents will not know the scandalous, blatantly carnal knowledge we have of one another, but he and I certainly will. I might as well sit down to have tea with them in nothing more than my shift for how uncomfortable I will be.

"I didn't say you had to marry him, Ella. But when someone of his standing shows an interest as keen as his apparently is, you don't snub it, regardless of how forward he might be. It is only proper to at least invite him over for tea. If we are not impressed, we don't invite him back. It's quite simple, dear." Evidently the future Earl of Galloway stands to inherit a large estate with exceptionally deep coffers filled to the rim, otherwise we would not be having this conversation.

"Don't you mean if *I* am not impressed? You and Father are not the ones who would marry him."

"As your parents, it is only fair to assume we are part of the approval process." But her idea of a suitable husband isn't the same as mine. At least not any of the suitors she has pushed me toward so far.

"I am not a ninny, Mother. I feel certain that the man I choose will be met with approval from both you and Father." I'm trying to keep my tone neutral, but this conversation is wearing on my patience.

"Yes, of course you will make a good choice, my love. However, it is my duty to make sure you have plenty of options." With that, she kisses my forehead and turns to make as dramatic an exit as she did her entrance. Before closing the door, she turns and gives me a radiant smile. "I will let you know when Lord Stewart has accepted our invitation and what day we will be expecting him for tea." And with that, she is gone.

I turn to Beatrice, the silent observer. "Please give me one reason I should not leave immediately with a sudden urge to visit family on the other side of the continent? Or perhaps even further. There is an entire ocean between here and America."

"Yes, that is true. But Lord Stewart is also known as *Captain* Stewart, and you know what that means," Beatrice says, pointing out the fact that he probably sails across that same ocean three times a year. "May I see the letter he wrote you, dear?"

Just the mention of it makes my heart beat harder in my chest. Taking it over to her, I say, "I cannot justify this letter and poem with the man I met last night. Surely he is continuing to entertain himself by playing me like a game of chess." I glance down at the beautiful script and even more beautiful words. "I believe I could read this a hundred times and never tire of it."

Beatrice begins to read as I walk back over to retrieve the book of fairy tale creatures. If he is entertaining himself, he's going to a lot of expense to do so. I still can't believe he gave me this magnificent book from his family's collection. It is page after page of original artwork, and I can only imagine how his family came to own it.

"My goodness, Ella. This is one of the most beautiful things I've ever read," she gushes. "I don't think he is toying with you, dear. It is quite obvious you have captured his attention and whether you travel across the country or across the sea, Alasdair Stewart will not be far behind." Her bold statement makes the hair on my neck stand up as a frisson of fear and excitement runs through me.

"As unfortunate as it may be, I fear you are right. However, Lord Stewart will soon know that Ella Seymour is no starry-eyed *lass* that will titter and blush as he lays on his charm. I know the real man under the facade, and I will not be played by him again."

FOUR

Alasdair

I t's been three days since I sent my missive to Ella, but I have heard nothing in response. Therefore, I have taken to pacing the length of my library as a means of coping with her rejection. Try as I might, I can't stop her parting words from ringing inside my head. The need to change her mind toward me is starting to eat away at my patience and possibly my sanity.

Thinking about the poem I wrote her and how easily the words flowed from my mind, a perfect vision of her comes to me. She is breathtaking, and I wonder for a moment if I have exaggerated her appearance in my memory. She possesses a beauty like I have never seen, and I am beginning to think there was some truth to my words—that she is enchanted with a kind of magic from ancient lore. I have not been able to think of anything but her since I felt her appear in the garden. *Never* has a woman taken hold of me, body and soul, the way Ella Seymour has.

The women I spend my time with are uncomplicated. They are either widowed, hoping to become my mistress, married and looking for satisfaction they are not finding in their husband's bed, or unmarried women who only want one night of pleasure. Each scenario is free of attachment and obligation, which is ideal for us both. There have been a few that caught my affection more than others. One in particular, I fancied myself in love with, but now recognize I was young and confused physical passion with a deeper emotion. Still, I feel gratitude toward her for all that she taught me about the erogenous map of a woman's body. I became addicted to controlling her pleasure and found I could not reach climax unless hers came first.

Stopping at the chair in front of my desk, I place my hands on the arched back and drop my head forward to stretch the muscles of my neck. The tension in my shoulders has become painful as the lack of proper rest and overwhelming frustration have settled there. I stand up straight and roll my shoulders, determined to make the rest of my day productive rather than wasting it pacing back and forth conjuring up images of my little faerie maiden.

As soon as I sit down, Ewan, my valet, knocks then enters, carrying the silver correspondence tray. "Pardon me, sir. The mail has arrived."

I notice Ewan is hiding a smile behind what is supposed to be an expressionless face. "Why do I sense ye have more to say, Ewan? Ye have an air of mischief about ye. Go on...spill it."

Ewan possesses a familiarity with me that is typically frowned upon in most households. A *proper* valet is required to mind his own business and never voice his opinion on anything other than attire or schedules. But Ewan's candor and humor are two of the reasons I brought him into my employ as my valet six years ago.

"Well, I could'na help but notice there is an envelope from Lady Seymour," he states as a smile spread across his face. "Ever since I made yer delivery to that house with the exceptionally lovely serving maid, you've been looking at the mail wi' an impatience that's even put me on edge. So, I'm admittedly as curious as a June bride on her wedding night to see if ye got the response ye were hoping for."

I can't help but laugh. "Aye, well, I appreciate yer enthusiasm toward my social life. I admit to being more than curious. I'm downright anxious to know what's in that bloody envelope."

Ewan sets the tray down the tray in front of me and waits as I pop open the wax seal. I'm surprised by the feeling that comes over me when I find the graceful script of Lady Seymour inviting me to join her, Lord Seymour, and their daughter, Ella, for tea tomorrow at three o'clock. It is more disappointing than exciting, though. "Tell me, Ewan, do ye find me to be a man that possesses an overblown ego?"

With a confused tilt of his head, he answers, "Ah, no, sir, I would'na describe ye as such. Confident, to be sure. And rightfully so," he adds with a smirk. "But no' a man of too much ego."

"Thank ye, Ewan. 'Tis good to know. But it does'na justify why I am somewhat offended at having *not* been invited to join them for dinner, only tea. *And* in the company of Lord Seymour, meaning the conversation will surely be dominated by war strategy, the condition of my ship, and whether she can handle a dozen more cannon to be added to her arsenal." I drop the letter down in front of me and rub my hands down my face, allowing my head to fall back against the chair. "Ella does'na want me to call on her. My letter and gift were clearly not well-received. Nonetheless, her mother was obligated to respond because of my family's title. To spare their poor daughter from having to spend her time conversing with a *lowly Scot*, they are embedding her father as a distraction."

Standing up abruptly, I walk over to pour myself a glass of whisky.

"Oh, I dinna think 'tis as bad as all that, m'lord. Ye said yerself that the lass has a little bite to her and that she has the face o' Cleena herself. Ye can'na be expecting her to just give herself away. Aye, if she's truly the rarity ye described, ye need to work fer it." Ewan makes his way over to me and pats my shoulder. "You know it, and I'm afraid she knows it too. However, if ye open yer eyes and look at it through a better light, I think you'll find she's presented ye wi' a challenge that makes her more valuable. She does'na intend to be another one of those women she found ye shaggin' wi' in the gardens. No, she'll be damned before she'd be that, especially wi' you."

I pause to consider his statement. "Ye are young to be so wise, Ewan. I believe there is some truth in yer words. But what do ye mean, 'especially wi' me'?"

"Well, as ye say, I may be young, but I do have the wisdom about me. So, ye can'na tell me a young lass, or any female young or old for that matter, would be uninterested in Alasdair Stewart after seeing him unclothed standing in a garden." He laughs aloud. "I know what ye look like in the skuddie, and ye can rest assured, most men, especially these soft Londonite milksops, do'na look like you. I'd be willing to bet she has thought of nothing else since."

"That's a very interesting and...unexpected observation. I can'na help but ask, have ye seen many Londonite milksops unclothed? Seems a bit unlikely unless ye have interests that I'm unaware of," I say with humor. It is likely Ewan Smith is the most successful libertine in all of Scotland with a list of women a mile long waiting for an invitation.

With heavy laughter, he responds, "Oh, that 'tis verra funny, m'lord. You and I both know ye don't have to see a man wi'out clothes to know his body looks more like that of a nursing mama than that of a true man. By God! Just look at their hands! Soft and supple, free of scars or even the bloody hair that signifies it's attached to a man and *no'* a woman!" He shakes his head with a look of disgust. "I tell ye true, I've seen so many here it makes me wonder if they simply breed 'em that way."

"'Tis a curious thing, to be sure. But I don't think the memory of my naked body is going to change Ella's prejudice against me. I saw the look in her eyes. It is'na something I care to see again." Unfortunately, the image of it comes to me as the muscles in my neck begin to tighten back into knots.

"I will have to disagree, sir. And to prove I'm right, I want ye to make an observation tomorrow when ye arrive fer yer lit'l tea party. When ye make yer proper greeting, kiss her hand. Three things will prove my theory. One, her eyes will turn black wi' desire upon seeing you. Two, the creamy skin on her chest will flush pink and ye can watch it travel up her delicate throat. Then third, she will part her lovely lips in silent invitation." His voice deepens on the last sentence.

"Thank you, Ewan. I did'na realize ye thought I've been livin' under a bloody rock all this time. Now snap out of it. Yer gettin' yerself aroused talking about yer damned theory, and that is'na something I care to witness."

"I'm sorry, sir, I just love women. They're so soft and sweet and they smell so good..."

I snap my fingers in front of his glazed stare. "Out, Ewan," I command. "This conversation is over."

"Aye, m'lord," he replies and abruptly leaves the room, likely rushing off to find relief with one of his many female companions.

As I sit back down at my desk, I look at the invitation again. This is a polite response and nothing more. Nevertheless, it is an invitation that will put me face to face with Ella, and that is all I need. This is a chance to see her again — to see how she reacts to me and how I react to her. I need to know if it is the same as it was the other night. Will I feel her without touching her? Will her scent wrap around me and alter my thinking? Will her beauty inspire more words that need to be written? How long will it take me to convince her that she is mine?

"Bloody hell!" I say to myself, tossing the note across my desk. I lean back in my chair, noticing I am starting to sweat, and my heart is beating harder in my chest. It's as if I have physically exerted myself. "What the hell has she done to me?"

The question echoes around the floor-to-ceiling bookshelves and arched windows. Outside, the sun beams through the parted clouds, and I decide a hard ride on Magni will do my preoccupied mind and agitated body some good.

Before leaving, I respond to the invitation.

Dear Lady Seymour,

Thank you for your kind invitation. I look forward to joining you and your family for tea on the morrow.

Your humble servant,

Lord Alasdair Stewart

FIVE

Ella

"**B**eatrice! Do you think I should wear an old gown that is faded and worn and perhaps pull my hair into a simple bun at the nape of my neck? That would make the point clear, don't you think?" I ask, wishing I wasn't about to have tea with a stranger that I have seen without clothes.

"No, I don't," she replies curtly. "For one, you don't own a faded gown, and two, it is beneath your station to present yourself with such ill regard. Now stop fussing so much about this. My suggestion is that you look better than you've ever looked before and intimidate Lord Stewart with your magnificence."

"I'm not trying to impress him, Beatrice. I'm trying to get rid of him!"

"That simply isn't going to happen, dearie, so you might as well make the best of it," she says, making me wonder if she's temporarily lost her mind.

"Make the best of it? I don't think that's helpful advice. I am dreading this more than anything, ever! How am I going to look at him? What am I supposed to say?" Dropping down

50

onto the stool at my dressing table so she can style my hair, my shoulders sag. "Oh, Beatrice. This is awful. How ever am I to get through it?"

Coming over to me, she begins brushing my long waves, bringing out their glossy shine. "You will do splendidly, my dear. I know you and your wit, plus you've got the spine of a Seymour. I'm sure the thought of how it *might* be is far worse than how it will be. Once the proper introductions have been made, it will be like any other time a gentleman has come to call."

"A gentleman. Hmph. If he were a gentleman, he would have stayed away just as I told him to."

My mind goes back to the poem and the book he gave me. I am admittedly torn. I love them both so much it's hard for my pride to accept who gave them to me. The words he wrote are so thoughtful and beautifully composed, and though they may be bold, they compliment me in such a way that makes me feel powerful, alluring, and even somewhat sensual. But then I remember how he toyed with me outside the ballroom like he enjoyed watching me become flustered by how he talked to me and how he touched me.

I grab a handkerchief from my dressing table and pat my forehead and throat. I hate what happens to my body when I think about him. His spicy, masculine scent made me lightheaded and weak. The way his deep accented voice commanded my attention, whether I wanted to offer it or not. His turquoise eyes complement his handsome face. It's hard not to think he must have been touched by God. *His uncommon looks are not the only thing that was touched by God.* A small laugh escapes at that thought.

"What's so funny? For a moment, I thought you might start weeping, but instead, you are full of mischief."

"Truthfully? I was contemplating the confusion Lord

Stewart has created in my mind. There is a distinct difference between the debaucher that seemed to enjoy playing sport with my innocence and the charming gentleman that wrote me poetry and presented me with a gift of exceptional value and meaning. But unfortunately, whenever I think about him, I think about *all* of him, and, well, this time, I managed to find a bit of humor in it and not the shame or regret I've been living with for days."

"There's your answer then," she states enthusiastically. "When Lord Stewart arrives, just have a little humor about yourself. It is sure to give you strength and if nothing else, a bit of entertainment."

"Considering I cannot avoid this event altogether, I suppose you're right. If I approach the situation with humor, I am less likely to panic." I toss the handkerchief back onto the table.

"I don't think you are capable of panicking, young lady. You and I both know that. Now, let's finish up here and make you so dazzling that Lord Stewart will be the one that is unable to compose himself." Beatrice finishes my hair, then helps me into a gown of pale blue.

Entering the sitting room overlooking the gardens, I find Mother and Father standing by the massive picture windows in a glow of sunshine. It is quite a beautiful scene as he gently touches her face and leans in to kiss her softly on the lips. I do sincerely hope I find that kind of love one day. Yet, a part of me fears that I may not, as it is not as common as it should be, especially amongst the upper class.

Realizing they are not alone, my mother quickly turns away from my father's affection. "Hello, darling! Oh, look at you! What a lovely choice. You brighten the room with your beauty." She pauses in front of me, as she always does, and places her hands on my upper arms, holding me in place while she admires me with a tender look. I wonder if my coming of age has been somewhat difficult for her to accept. As her only child, I suppose it would make sense. I know she longed to have more children, but it never came to be. "Come over here, my sweet." She guides me over to the sofa. "Are you nervous at all?"

"I was, but I am fine now. Just looking forward to it being over," I say truthfully.

"Try not to make it obvious, Ella. Captain Stewart is very well-respected, according to your father. And let us not forget, he stands to inherit an important title and a very substantial estate. I've done some research. The Galloway holdings are quite extensive indeed."

A slight sense of dread comes over me as I see how impressed my mother has become. She was already trying to push Lord Percy on me; now, she is likely to do the same with Lord Stewart.

"Yes, I know, Mother. You wouldn't have invited him for tea, were it not."

"That is true. You shall have a respectable title when you marry, and it is important your children are left a legacy that will carry far into the future."

"And what about love? I thought you and Father decided long ago that you will not choose my husband for me."

"You are correct. However, that doesn't mean you will love him before marrying. You will make a choice that meets the proper criteria and has the *potential* for love. I've told you many times, my dear, that kind of affection grows with time. It is unrealistic to think you will marry for love. That is a thing of poetry and theater. You must be realistic, not foolish and naive."

"Foolish and naive? I have no intention of being either. However, I request that you no longer push Lord Percy as a potential suitor. He may have the *proper criteria*, but there is absolutely *no* potential for love," I state confidently now that she has given me the opening.

"Ella, don't be so harsh."

"I'm not being harsh. I'm being honest."

I'm not able to argue my point any further as our butler, Donovan, announces that Lord Stewart has arrived. My mother is filled with excitement to meet the future Earl of Galloway with his extensive holdings and vast estates. I laugh to myself as I picture the look on her face when she lays eyes upon him. He is handsome in a way that makes you lose track of your thoughts and leaves you staring, wondering if he is truly as pleasing to the eye as your mind is telling you he is. Looking down at my nervous hands clasped tightly together in my lap, I smile and focus my humor on her and not the fear creeping up my spine.

We both stand as Donovan announces the captain's entrance. Staying focused on Mother and the charming smile that lights up her face, I sense the moment he walks into the room. Everything shifts as an invisible force slams into me, causing my breath to catch in my throat and my skin to chill like it did the last time he was near. Mother's smile disappears as her eyes widen, and I have no choice but to turn to him.

Dear Lord! It's more than I remembered. Far more. I do not know how it is possible, but he is so striking as he walks toward us, the man I recall from four nights ago almost pales in comparison. He's more polished, somehow more refined in his deep blue captain's formal jacket trimmed in gold embroidery and polished gold buttons, all of which contrasts against a pale gold waistcoat and the pure white of his breeches, shirt, and cravat.

My heart is pounding in my chest. He is magnificent. His glossy black hair is pulled back, leaving his remarkable face on

THE POWER OF FATE

full display as his turquoise eyes truly glow against the distinct frame of his dark lashes and sun-burnished skin. It is a stunning presentation of uncommon perfection.

His focus is on me and nothing else, pushing my heart to beat faster and grow louder in my ears.

Just breathe, Ella.

The intensity of his stare feels inappropriate as it makes my skin flush with wanton desire. I have a terrible urge to touch him, to inhale the intoxicating scent floating around him and invite his whispering words of sensual promise in my ear. My lips part involuntarily—then he douses everything with cold water as a sly smirk raises one side of his full mouth. The urge to turn and walk out of the room overwhelms me as I realize his games persist. But I rein it in when his attention shifts to my mother.

"Good afternoon, Admiral, Lady Seymour," he says as he reaches for my mother's hand to kiss it properly. If his arrogance didn't so perturb me so, I would have laughed at her response to him. She is completely mesmerized as she struggles to find her voice.

"Welcome, Lord Stewart. I...ah....it is wonderful to meet you. Thank you for joining us this afternoon." Turning to me, she finishes with a proper introduction. "You remember my daughter, Lady Ella Seymour."

I curtsy as perfectly as if I'm being presented to the king. But when I finish, I make sure the look in my eyes is glacial enough to freeze his apparent confidence at ignoring my request to stay away. In an equally cold tone, I say, "Lord Stewart."

His eyes flash as he straightens for a bow that he performs as perfectly as my curtsy. Upon finishing, he keeps one hand behind his back as the other reaches forward in a silent request. "Lady Ella." I have no choice but to offer him my hand; else I will never hear the end of it from Mother about my rudeness.

When his lips gently kiss the tops of my fingers, a tingling sensation travels up my arm, and I have the urge to pull my hand away. He must sense it because his grip tightens, and he doesn't let go as he stands up straight. It is making me terribly nervous that he will make us appear more familiar than I have led my mother to believe we are. Still holding my hand, he looks me in the eyes and says, "Words can'na describe how happy I am to see ye again." A tightness wraps around my chest as my body and mind battle against each other. I fear my body will win as it heats up simply from his touch, his delicious scent, and that accented voice that makes me want to rest my head against his broad chest and listen to him read to me about the mythical creatures that fascinated him as a child. Thankfully, he releases his hold on me and turns to my father. "Yer Grace. It is good to see ye again." He bows before taking his hand in a firm shake.

"Stewart. It is good to see you as well. You haven't been home more than a week, have you?" Father asks in a friendly tone.

"Aye, it will be a week tomorrow. 'Tis good to be home, sir. This last trip was extended a bit. That nuisance in France stirs up more trouble by the day," he responds with ease and familiarity. They appear to know each other quite well.

"That he does, Captain, that he does," my father agrees and places his hand on Lord Stewart's shoulder, gives him a friendly pat, and directs him to one of the two chairs across from the sofa where Mother and I will be seated. "Let us sit and relax, my friend."

Lord Stewart gestures for Mother and me to go first. "Ladies." But his turquoise eyes are locked on mine, and in this light, I see there are streaks of lighter blue close to the black center, and though they are piercing in their sharp focus, they are stunning, so I take the liberty of staring a few seconds too long. Moving toward the sofa, I notice that the room seems warmer than usual, and I am disappointed I forgot to bring a fan.

Once I am comfortable, I glance over at my mother and imagine hearing her voice saying, *Oh my!* Thankfully, she has provided the humor I was looking for to ease my trepidation. Unfortunately, it's so funny that I cannot help but laugh. I try to hold it in, but the pressure of the moment seems to have somehow added to my mirth, and I feel a fit of laughter building up in my chest. I thank God at that moment that my cousin, Mary, is not here, for I would surely have to excuse myself from the room. My mother's foot gently kicks mine underneath my skirts. Apparently, I have become obvious and as I swallow down the burst of laughter that keeps trying to escape, I bring my head up, only to find Lord Stewart staring at me intently once again.

After a few awkward seconds, his deep voice swallows the silence that has blanketed the room, "Lady Ella, although I fear yer humor may be directed toward me, I will admit it does'na matter. For it has lit yer lovely face with a smile that 'tis brighter than the sun." He turns to my father as the smile I didn't realize was stretched across my face disappears and says, "Yer daughter's beauty is beyond compare, yer Grace, if I may be so bold."

My father quickly responds with a smirk and chuckle. "Yes, Captain. She is quite lovely, just like her mother." His eyes turn soft as he glances her way. "But there is more than what you see on the surface. She has a mind of her own, and it is a sharp one."

"*She* is also sitting in the room, listening to you talk about her as if she were not." My annoyance is undisguised.

My father's deep laugh echoes around us. "See what I mean?" he says, almost with pride.

I expect Lord Stewart to take this opportunity to play with me again, yet instead, I find a tender look in his eyes that makes my stomach hurt, almost as if I am falling from a great height. I see kindness, perhaps even affection, and it makes me wish that this was our first introduction. Before I can get lost in this unexpected exchange, Donovan enters with our tea. Distracted, I turn to him and let go of the breath I was holding, breaking the spell of the moment.

A half-hour of forced conversation passes before my father finally gives up his attempt at enjoying afternoon tea and invites Lord Stewart to join him on the other side of the parlor for a drink "that has a bit more character." This is my mother's opportunity to ask the most obvious question.

"Ella! Why did you not mention how handsome he is? My goodness! I fear I was left speechless! A little warning would have had me better prepared."

I laugh as her expression tells me she truly is upset with me. "Mother, I do recall telling you that Lord Stewart is handsome. I believe I told you that he is *quite* handsome even. Do you not remember that part of the conversation?"

"No, I do not. I only recall your lack of interest in him because he is a Scotsman with an unrefined accent, which is entirely inaccurate! He may be from Scotland, but nothing is *unrefined* about his speech. Gracious, Ella! Surely you find *him* appealing enough to allow him to court you?"

Feeling uncomfortable with the pressure closing in on me, I snap at her, "I cannot determine that by looks and title alone, Mother!" The look of shock on her face at the anger in my tone has me apologizing before I can take another breath. "Please forgive me. I fear my patience is a bit frayed by his visit today."

"You are forgiven, my love. I am somewhat frayed myself,"

she says with a laugh. "My word, that man is handsome! And his interest in you is quite keen. Are you sure the other night was the first time you met him?"

I knew his forward behavior wouldn't go unnoticed. "Yes, of course. I would have told you otherwise," I say as the guilt washes over me at the thought of that singular encounter. The hair on my neck stands as, once again, I contemplate if Alasdair Stewart can read my mind. His eyes are on me from across the room, and I could swear that he knows what I'm thinking simply by looking at him.

Before my prayer can be answered, he turns to my father for a brief exchange, pats him on the shoulder with a genuine smile, and begins walking toward me. It seems to take him only a few strides before he stands in front of my mother. With all the courtesy and refinement of a young prince, he asks her if he may take me for a short stroll through the garden.

As Mother fumbles through her approval, I decide that I shall go to the altar this evening and pray for forgiveness. It is clear my penance has just begun.

SIX

Alasdair

A s much as I'd like to stay and enjoy Admiral Seymour's
rant on why we should capture Napoleon and hang him
from London Tower, I am far too distracted by Ella's reaction
to me upon entering the room. It was exactly as Ewan said it
would be, and when her lips parted, speaking truths she did not
wish me to know, I had the urge to steal her away from this
ridiculous gathering and take her to a place where we could talk
freely and be less encumbered by proper etiquette. To make
matters worse, her mind clearly keeps going back to our
encounter in the garden; it is fantastically written on her lovely
face and is distracting the hell out of me.

"Forgive me, Admiral, I am somewhat limited on time this
afternoon. Would it be alright if I took Lady Ella for a stroll
through the garden?" I ask, trying not to sound impatient.

"Oh, well, yes, I believe that would be fine." It's obvious I
caught him off guard, but he doesn't seem to be bothered as a
slight smile lifts one side of his mouth. "I'm sure Lady
Seymour will think so as well." With that, he gestures that I am
welcome to step away and ask. But the glint in his eye says my

concern shouldn't be with him or his wife, but with Lady Ella herself.

Seymour's wisdom proved accurate as I am greeted with the poised elegance of the duchess's lovely smile and the cold disdain of Lady Ella's glare. She's trying to discourage me, sending me what she thinks is a clear message that my efforts will be fruitless. However, I can read her just as easily as I can the book I gave her. The one that captured my youthful imagination and taught me the definition of her perfectly given name. I am as mesmerized by Lady Ella as I was by the illustrated faerie that depicted an ethereal beauty so exquisite, that it seemed dangerous.

"Lady Seymour," I say on a short bow. "Would ye mind if Lady Ella and I endeavor on a stroll through yer garden? The sun is bright, and the air is particularly fresh today—it would be a shame to waste it." The latter part of that statement was directed toward Ella and had enough command in its tone to pique her ire, evident in the straightening of her spine and the slight squinting of her eyes. She doesn't realize that her tenacity only adds to her appeal. If she were typically prim and proper with the naivety of a debutante, I would have forgotten all about her by now.

"Ah, I suppose...that will be alright," the duchess stammers. "Though, it is only proper that you stay within viewing distance of the house," she finishes, hoping that will appease her daughter and make herself feel less like she made the wrong decision.

"Of course, Your Grace," I assure her, then turn to offer my hand to Ella. With a hint of reluctance, she accepts, and the air moves with her as she stands, surrounding me with her scent. Involuntarily, I close my eyes to enjoy the intoxicating aroma. I've never smelled anything like it in my life. My grip tightens as she tries to let go, forcing my eyes to open only to find her confused and perhaps a bit intimidated by my response. "Forgive me," I whisper, hoping her mother doesn't hear and wonder what needs forgiving, before turning toward the doors that lead to the terrace.

Once outside, the cool, fresh air surrounds us, invigorating me on contact, releasing a sense of joy that has comforted me since my youth. I can't help but sense the same excitement in Ella, and it pleases me that we have something else in common. Continuing toward the steps that lead us onto the garden's main path, I ask, "Ye like being outdoors, don't ye?"

Her grip loosens from my arm once we are on the level ground of the path. "Yes. I do." She releases her hold and takes a few steps to the left, putting a defiant distance between us. "Preferably alone." That addition came out as sharp as the edge of another well-honed blade, but I know she is telling the truth.

"Oh? I can't blame ye fer that. 'Tis a lovely display, to be sure. A little solitude in a well-designed garden can be quite inspiring, and for London, this is an impressive landscape."

"I suppose. But I am more inspired by the forests of the countryside. My mother's gardens are quite beautiful, especially so close to town, but they are a tad too perfect for me."

I am somewhat surprised she's offering me a glimpse of her true self, and before I can think of a response, a thousand poetic lyrics begin to dance through my mind, wanting to make her smile again as she did earlier in the parlor.

"I would have to agree. Though a great deal of my time is spent at sea, which is inspiring in its own right, I've always held a particular fondness for the natural beauty of the forests. 'Tis one of the reasons I spent so much time as a boy with my nose in the book I gave ye. I believed that I would happen upon one of those fascinating creatures someday. Although, I must admit —" I pause to laugh at myself, remembering my days as a lad, pretending to be fearless in the face of danger. "I was terrified my wish would come true. Many of them look like they might like to eat me fer dinner." I glance at Ella's profile and see a smile being forced down through tight lips. Yet her eyes can't hide their amusement.

Stopping in the path under a massive sycamore tree, I turn to her. "'Tis alright if ye laugh at me, Ella. Honestly, I would like it verra much if ye did." She doesn't realize the smile she set free is like a spoonful of warm honey, heating me up from the inside and satisfying my need for something sweet.

And then, just like that, it disappears.

"Lord Stewart, why are you here? I specifically recall telling you to stay away." The virulent tone of her statement brings back the memory of her prejudice the last time we parted ways. A flood of anger washes over me as she stands her ground in front of me, protecting herself with a suit of armor fashioned out of haughty disdain. I pause for a few long seconds, giving myself time to maintain control and giving her a few moments to wonder what comes next.

"Why are ye so afraid of me, Ella?" I ask through a low rasp, straining to hold back my anger. There is a subtle shift in her demeanor, perhaps regret. She is back to acting as though I am beneath her, knowing it is completely inaccurate. I wait patiently, staring at her beautiful face marred by the anger of being cornered, knowing there is no way out and, worse, it is entirely her fault.

"Why are you here?" she asks again, her armor cracked, her true emotions more evident.

"Because I can't stay away. That is why."

She will learn that I am not afraid of being honest with her. She will also learn that I expect her to be honest with me.

"Ye feel it, don't ye, Ella?" I continue. "Yer heart beats faster when we are near one another. Yer skin flushes hot."

Her eyes slowly close, and her straight spine relaxes just slightly. "Please stop," she whispers.

"Look at me, Ella." My voice is deep but low, and I can hear my desire resonating through it. Without thought, my hand reaches up, but I force it to stop. I want to touch her so badly, but I can't. Not yet.

Her eyes open, and once again, my body recognizes her desire. "I don't want ye to be afraid o'me, Ella. Though I know ye are. I can see it. I can feel it."

"I'm not afraid of you, Lord Stewart," she states with renewed confidence.

"Oh? Is that so?" There is something about her defiance that I find exceedingly appealing. "Yer no' afraid of the gooseflesh that raises on yer skin at the thought of my touch? Or the sensitive hardness on the tips of yer lovely, full breasts when ye remember me in the garden?"

"Are all Scotsman so lacking in couth, Lord Stewart? Or is it only you that is so unrefined?" she asks as her cheeks turn red with anger and, no doubt, embarrassment.

"I see we have a pattern here. Whenever I bring up a subject ye aren't prepared to discuss, ye turn to insulting my heritage." Taking a step closer, I turn slightly and offer her my arm. "Take my arm. We will continue to walk as I am certain yer mother is watching us. I would'na want her to suspect ye are too familiar wi' a bloody Scot." I made sure to deepen my accent on that last statement.

Fire flashes in her eyes before she reluctantly does my bidding. We continue down the path as it makes its way around the giant tree that hides us from the prying eyes of her overprotective mother. The warmth of her hand penetrates the layers of clothing covering my skin just as the ice in her voice causes my teeth to clench.

"You may see it as a pattern, Lord Stewart, but I see it for what it is. *You* are a Scotsman, the only man of your *heritage* I have ever met. Both times, I have had the unfortunate experience of conversing with you privately, you have talked to me as if I were that maid with whom you had carnal relations in the garden!" She let go of my arm several steps back and has turned to me now, eyes again blazing with anger, yet glossy with hurt. "So don't act as if I am somehow prejudiced or insulting your integrity when you have done nothing but insult my station as the daughter of a duke, not to mention my status as an unmarried woman! No Englishman—or even a Frenchman, for that matter—has ever disrespected me the way you have. Therefore, I'm left with no choice but to question your background. For heaven's sake! You're the heir to an earldom and a captain in the Royal Navy. *You* should know better!"

I can't discern if she realizes the emotion she has exposed during her tirade. Regardless, it's making my chest feel like I've dropped fifty feet untethered. She is the most fascinating woman I have ever met, and she stirs something in me that is foreign yet familiar all at once.

"Well, ye certainly have a way wi' words. There'll be no denying that." She wasn't expecting such a cavalier retort, and the look of exasperation on her face has me throwing back my head as a hearty laugh escapes. "Look at ye! If ye were a cat, I fear ye'd claw my eyes out!" I see the slightest upturn of a smile as her demeanor softens, offering me a chance to put another crack in her armor.

"I believe I'd like to do just that, regardless," she agrees with one raised eyebrow.

"I'm sorry, Ella. Yer right," I say with sincerity through my mirth. "I will ask for yer forgiveness as I have never been a conventional man. I've never been one to abide by the rules of society, rules created by hypocrites and impostors. You'll find I am neither." I pause as understanding releases the tension across her creased forehead. "I can be brutally honest, and I'm sure that isn't what ye are accustomed to. I would'na blame Scotland, though." I offer her a smile and my arm, gesturing for us to continue down the path. Our time out of sight of her mother has lingered long enough. "'Tis simply the way I am."

We walk in silence as I ponder what to say next. There is so much that I want her to know, but she is not ready to hear it. Perhaps I will put it to verse and see if it pleases her. But I have to do something to break through her defenses. "May I tell ye something, Ella? May I be honest?"

She doesn't answer right away, looking down at the path. I do the same, watching the toes of her slippers peeking out from under her flowing skirts with each step, waiting patiently for her to respond.

"I am afraid your simple question is more of a conundrum than I care to admit. I have the urge to tell you not to speak another word for the entirety of our walk so I may enjoy the peaceful sounds of the garden. Also, I would like to ask Donovan to prepare us a picnic down by the pond to appease my curiosity of whatever inappropriate nonsense your mind is conjuring." There is no hiding the mischief behind her admission, and it also has my heart racing with an excitement I have never known.

Just ahead, there is a bench next to what appears to be a butterfly garden situated in the middle of the path with a stone wall around it—a perfect circle overflowing with flowers of all sizes and colors, brightly lit by the sun, highlighting the beautiful artwork of butterfly wings as they flutter around, then pause to drink the flower's sweetness. Gesturing with my hand, I ask, "Would ye like to sit? 'Tis a beautiful presentation, and the sunlight will warm us from the chill of the shade trees."

"Yes, I would like that." It doesn't go unnoticed that this is the first thing she's said to me that isn't laced with venom or vinegar, at the very least.

We take our seats and pause to enjoy the circus before us. From this angle, the sunlight has brightened the color of every flower and highlighted every flying insect beyond the swarm of butterflies flitting about in numbers I have truly never seen. "This is quite an impressive display," I say, somewhat in awe.

"Yes, it turned out better than I had imagined."

I turn to her then and see that glorious smile mingling with pride. "Oh? This was yer idea?"

"It is my one contribution to my mother's garden. I told the head gardener what I wanted, and he delivered more than I could have ever asked. I helped him plant many of the flowers, and he gives them special food to keep their blooms abundant." Her face lights up with joy so pure I can only stare and hope the image is locked permanently in my mind. "Notice there is no pattern; nothing is manicured. It's simply perfect disarray." Ella turns to me, mischief apparent in her eyes. "Perhaps I have attracted one of your faerie friends from the book. They could be watching us right now, debating on which one of us to eat first." A bubble of laughter escapes as she freely pokes fun at me, shattering my resolve to maintain proper etiquette.

The urge to kiss her is so powerful that I forget to breathe.

"Ella." My voice is gravelly and deep. Her smile evaporates as she senses the shift, uncomfortable under its heady weight. "I will speak the truth, and ye may not like it, but I know no other way." I take a deep breath and watch her beautiful eyes dilate with anticipation she doesn't fully understand. "I have thought of nothing but you since last we met. That is no' an exaggeration." I can see the flush of heat as it brightens her color. Her eyes drop from mine to focus on my mouth. She wants me to kiss her, so she bites down on her swollen bottom

67

lip to distract her desire. It's enough to drive me mad. "Ye can'na do that to me," I say as I reach up to gently set it free. "Yer testing my strength and nourishing my weakness."

"I don't understand," she admits through a whisper.

"Aye, I know ye don't. It is another reason I find ye so bloody appealing."

"Lord Stewart!" she admonishes.

"Forgive me. I should have left that thought inside my head."

"Well, at least your choice of words."

I study her face as the sun highlights every detail. Her skin is not as pale as most women of her station. She clearly enjoys the outdoors, and the added color gives her a warm glow that compliments her light hair and eyes. And those eyes...*my God*, I could stare at them for days and never get bored. They remind me of the ocean at midday, when the sun is shining directly above, allowing you to see past the surface and into the depths where the varying shades of blue and green shift and flow with the currents.

Her beauty is classic only in the perfect symmetry of her face and the elegant line of her neck and shoulders. Otherwise, her lips are a touch too full, slightly out of proportion with her small nose. Then her high cheekbones, strong brow, and square jawline are almost masculine in their proud structure. My eyes see her as exquisite.

A cooling breeze passes over us, lifting a lock of hair to sweep across her face. On instinct, I reach up to tuck it behind her delicate ear. "Ye are a masterpiece, Ella Seymour. Quite an extraordinary one at that."

Her breath hitches just slightly. "Your poem."

"Aye. Did ye like it?" I ask, noticing the shyness in my tone.

"I did. Quite a lot, I'm afraid." She turns to look back at the garden.

"Ye sound disappointed. Were ye hoping for something offensive?"

"I was hoping for nothing at all, you know that!" she snaps. "But you didn't listen. Instead, you send me a gift of tremendous value and wrote a poem so lovely; that I could not comprehend that the words came from the man I wanted to hate."

The truth within her words is like a kick in the gut. "Ye wanted to hate me, aye?"

"Yes."

"That was'na a very convincing *yes*. Do ye think there's a chance I could get ye to a very convincing *no*?"

She smiles before lowering her head. "You humiliated me, Lord Stewart. It was wrong of you to talk to me the way you did, and I think you knew that and enjoyed teasing my innocence."

Her proud honesty lands heavily on my chest. "That is why I wanted to talk to ye. What happened that night—I know ye don't wish to discuss it, and yer right, I should'na have been so forward... I'm sorry, Ella. I deserved what ye gave me."

Her ocean eyes soften as she hears the apology she's been waiting for, and I curse myself for being such an arrogant arse. Of its own volition, my hand slides forward to where her's rests upon her lap. The tip of my finger hovers just above its flawless surface, and we both stare at it in strange anticipation. Her breath catches as my fingers wrap around her delicate hand and hold it protectively.

"Ye feel that, don't ye?" I ask her. "That vibration that makes it hard to breathe? There is a connection between us— we cannot deny it, and it is'na something I believe is very common. It has a special meaning, and I need ye to know that I do not intend to overlook it. That would be impossible. After all, I am a Scot, and superstition runs through my veins." She pulls her hand away in denial and possibly a bit of fear. "'Tis the truth, faerie maiden. I have thought of nothing but you since ye shut the door in my face at the ball." I pause to let my words settle in. "Ye cast yer wee spell on me that night, and now I spend my days pacin' the floors trying to conjure up ways to see ye again. And what about you, Ella? Have ye thought of nothing more than me since then?" I ask with a hint of humor, hoping to catch a glimpse of a smile.

She doesn't answer, only stares at me with a look of innocent desire that makes me want to devour her mouth and every moan that tries to escape.

"The look on yer face tells me that deep down, ye will be pleased to know that I intend to begin courtin' you starting today. Although I also know yer mind will tell ye to rebel against it. And that's fine, too. T'will make it that much more fun to change it."

"You are a very presumptuous man, Lord Stewart. And while I will admit there is some intrigue to this connection you speak of, I need *you* to understand that my parents agreed a long time ago to allow me to choose my husband. Now, that may not mean very much to a man like you, but from where I sit, you have a very steep hill to climb if want to win my approval—I might even call it a cliff." Her shoulders square again as she prepares for battle.

"Still looking down on me, aye, princess?" She stands her ground, silently answering my question by lifting her chin, tightening her lips, and attempting to look down her nose at me. "Be prepared. I am an excellent climber."

SEVEN

Ella

We are back at our country estate, not far from London. I am more at ease here without the noise and crowds and confines of the city. There are trees instead of buildings and air that doesn't reek of smoke and filthy streets. I could never understand the appeal of large cities like London. Perhaps for most, it is the social aspect that draws people; there is certainly no shortage of that. For me, it's suffocating and tedious, superficial in a way that wears on my patience. But not here, I think, as I watch a bird fly by carrying a small stick in its beak, landing in a nearby tree. It's building a nest, and I could sit here all day and watch while that tiny creature accomplishes such a great task.

"Ella!" Mary calls, startling me out of my reverie. "You have to tell me this again from start to finish. I cannot imagine that this man, whom you say is a visual treat, not a bloody monkey or a mule—"

"Mary!" I admonish.

"Oh, Ella, it's just the two of us here. You aren't becoming one of our mothers already! You are not even twenty. Surely that offers you some liberty to be improper."

"Oh? And why is that?"

"Because you don't know any better, of course!" She throws her head back and laughs while I wonder at her logic. Mary has always been like a grown woman inside a child's, or now, a young woman's body. She has the carefree attitude and unfiltered speech of a woman fortunate enough to pass the age of seventy-five. However, despite her inappropriate outbursts and tendency to embarrass me beyond words, Mary is a true and dear friend. I trust her in a way that is different than how I trust others, and although it doesn't surpass the trust I have with Beatrice, it is still quite valuable.

Mary sits down next to me by the window and grabs a pillow to hold in front of her, her red hair and green eyes glowing in the bright light shining through the glass. "Now, back to what I was saying. You have a man that has shown great interest in you. He is uncommonly handsome, the heir to an earldom and whatever other titles you mentioned. He's a captain in the Royal Navy, and wrote you that poem that just melted my heart. Yet, you're upset about this...why?"

Without telling her the sordid details of our encounter, not to mention his improper familiarity toward me, she will never understand why I have issues with this man—issues that I fear may never resolve. "Mary, you know I cannot tolerate an egotistical man that cares for nothing more than himself!"

As soon as the words come out of my mouth, Lydia, one of the serving maids, appears with a light afternoon refreshment. My stomach flips as I see she has also brought a small silver tray that holds a single envelope fashioned with the neat handwriting I have already come to recognize as Lord Stewart's.

My heart skips a beat. I stare at the envelope with intense

curiosity mingled with an undeniable blend of anticipation, trepidation, and possibly fear at what may be hiding within.

"Whatever *that* is," Mary says, pointing her finger at me, "that's written all over your face, has my curiosity boiling over. Open the bloody thing, and let's see what he has to say. Because I know that letter is from the subject at hand and not Lord Sweaty Palms." She gives a mock shiver as her face twists in disgust.

Reluctantly, I do her bidding and damn him for playing with my heart again.

Dearest Lady Ella,

You have been in the forefront of my mind since I saw you last. Admittedly, I try to maintain my focus on tasks I am to complete while not at sea—after all, it is my duty. Yet it will all have to wait, for I fear a magical spell has been cast upon me by a mysterious maiden that hides in the forest. She's filled my mind with fanciful notions and whimsical tales as I wonder what she is busy doing now. Earlier today, as I lay on a grassy hill listening to the rhythmic sound of water flowing down the rocky stream nearby, the sun warming me from the outside in, these words came to me, and I rushed home to write them down for you.

Do a butterfly's wings make a sound as it moves from here to there and everywhere?
Distracted by so many colors, too many flavors, to ever stay in one place very long.
"Shhhh," she bids through pursed lips and a slender finger,
"If you know how to listen, you can hear their song."
"Their song?" I question. "The butterfly's or its wings?"
"Shhhh," she sounds again. "Its wings, of course."

Her whisper is soft and soothing to my ears.
I do not ask again, though I long to hear her speak.
She shutters her eyes as the silence surrounds us.
Mine will not close.
Her face is lit by the sun,
Her breathing barely nil.
Her lips slowly spread, then lift at either side.
My heart beats faster,
Then faster still.
My ears do not need to hear the mysterious song to know
    it is real,
For my eyes can see on her lovely face,
Through her smile of pure joy,
That the sound they make is quite musical indeed.

Our visit to your butterfly garden inspired me. The look on
your face as you gazed upon your creation was that of
wonderment and delight, the likes of which I have never seen
before, and I long to see again.
    Fondly,
    Lord Alasdair Stewart

"Are you a slow reader, or is this the third time you've read it? Because I'm feeling my patience wear thin waiting for you to say something."

"Oh Mary, I fear he has done it again." I feel the weight of my shoulders drag my posture down.

"Done what? Is it all that bad?" There is genuine concern in her voice.

"Here," I say, handing her the note. "You may see for yourself."

And so, she does. Her free hand lifts to touch her mouth as a quiet, "Oh dear," escapes on a full exhale. "Ella, why do you

mare as well as a very dear friend. She was a gift from my father, who purchased her by chance one day when he visited a breeder to inspect horses for himself. He walked into the stable and knew the moment he saw her, he would pay whatever price to bring her home because she reminded him of me. "Beautiful light hair shimmering in the sunlight, standing out in the crowd, proud and regal," he said. "She reminded me of the fairy tales you've loved since you were a girl. Isn't she magnificent?"

She and I bonded immediately, touching foreheads together as if we had known each other for a lifetime. I still laugh, thinking about the nickers and neighing as she excitedly stomped her front hoof, creating a cloud of dust around us. She wanted me to ride her and wouldn't calm down until we found a saddle that fit, and I was comfortably seated, easily guiding her to one of the riding trails through the forest. Once I knew she trusted me, I let her instincts guide us, and she took us to my favorite place. That is where she got her name, for the giant willow tree that stands majestically next to the widest part of the stream that runs along the far side of our land. The grass is the greenest green, the water flows in hypnotic swirls that shift and flow in slow motion, and weeping branches drape to the ground and the water beyond, creating an enclosed space of peaceful tranquility from the world outside.

She walked us through the curtain of delicate, bright green leaves and spindly branches into the alcove that could easily fit three more horses and a small group of men. She snorted and whinnied, raising her head up and down, directing me to dismount. We stayed there for a long time. I told her all about myself, my family, my life, what I like about it and what I don't. She knows all about Beatrice and Mary and that my parents are deeply in love. She knows I long for that someday, as well. She understood, it was easy to see, and she didn't judge.

Willow knows all my secrets, even those I don't want to admit to myself. So today, as we meander down a well-traveled path, my eyes adjusting to the constant shifting of sunlight and shade that stripe the path ahead, the patterns reminding me of the strange horse I've seen in books called a zebra, I tell her about Alasdair.

"He is as sweet to the eyes as he is insufferable, Willow. I've never known a man to be so appealing and so offensive all at once. The more I think about it—and unfortunately, I do that often—the more I think he knows how physically striking he is and that it excuses his barbaric behavior. Although I can't say he is completely barbaric—his speech is quite refined, albeit accented, he is clearly a learned man, and he has been impeccably dressed every time I've seen him, well, except the first time...and...well. Oh, Willow! It was awful! Awful in an awful way, and awful in a way that makes me think terrible thoughts I shouldn't be thinking!" Willow's pace picks up as my temper rises. "My goodness, I woke up in the middle of the night, panting and sweating, with a desire that made me wish that man was lying next to me, touching me, the way I know he wants to." With that dreadful admission, I lean forward and push Willow into a full gallop as we exit the forest and fly across the grassy hills and wide-open space.

Willow and I love this; the wind on our face, exertion that forces our lungs to expand, and the sensation of our hearts beating in hard tempos. Up ahead are the obstacles we practice whenever we are alone since Father and the other groomsman would disapprove.

"Here we go, girl!" The fallen tree is coming up fast, so I lift my bum from the saddle. *Swoosh.* We are airborne, soaring like a falcon on the lookout for prey. Everything slows amid the silence, even time, and in that moment, nothing matters but the freedom to spread our wings and fly.

As soon as Willow's hooves land with an echoing thud, time speeds up to its usual pace, and we are galloping at full speed to our next challenge, an odd-shaped boulder that I've always thought looked like a seating bench for a giant. I used to imagine such a creature sitting there enjoying a bright sunlit day. My giant was a friendly sort, and I admit to pretending he was real and engaging in some rather lengthy conversations on the life of a young girl compared to that of an ancient creature from a land long forgotten.

Silence again. Our wings hold us high in the air as we clear the boulder with ease. My legs burn from exertion, but I ignore it as I quickly guide Willow through an S-turn of towering stones that seem intentionally placed in a perfect row. Willow's agility while making sharp turns always amazes me, and I can feel her excitement at being challenged to perform. After a few smaller jumps, we are ready to trot along the shady side of the knoll.

"Well done, Willow!" My compliment is winded as I try to catch my breath. Her hair and skin are wet as I rub along the length of her neck. "You are as fantastic an athlete as you are a rare beauty, aren't you, my girl?" I boast with a few pats of affection.

"The same could be said about you, aye?" That deep, accented voice startles me as it echoes from the forest canopy.

"Lord Stewart! For heaven's sake! Why are you here? You frightened me!" My voice is undeniably shrill, realizing he is here and saw what I was doing, not to mention the dreadful sight I must be with a flyaway mess of hair and perspiration dripping down from my forehead.

"Where did ye learn to ride like that?" Bypassing my question altogether, he cuts directly to the more pressing issue at hand. His authoritative tone piques my defenses as I sit straighter on the saddle.

"Why does it matter?" I raise my chin, hoping to add to the hauteur in my own tone.

"It does'na matter at all. I was just curious if ye had an instructor of some sort. Skills like that do'na tend to come easily to a man, let alone a young woman." He stops to laugh, his face lighting up with that glorious smile that plays tricks on my stomach. "I wish ye could see yer face! Ye've got a ferocity about ye that's bloody intimidating. I'm left helpless, waiting for ye to flay me open wi' another cut from yer wordsmith's sword. What has yer hackles up, lass? Did ye hear what I said? 'Twas a compliment, aye?" His perfect lips hold their position, stretched across his face in unfair perfection.

"For one, Lord Stewart, my hackles are up because you startled me. Two, you are an uninvited, therefore an unexpected, guest. Three, I am entirely unpresentable after such exertion, and it simply isn't proper for me to be here before you in such dishabille. Four, I do not allow, nor do I appreciate spectators when I run obstacles. Five, my faithful horse did not warn me of your presence, which is highly unusual. And six, I am preparing myself for the inevitable lecture on how inappropriate my riding is and that I should be ashamed of myself for such conduct." *Now* Willow snorts, perks her ears, and shuffles backward with warning. No one will ever convince me that my horse doesn't understand everything I am saying.

"Ah, I knew ye would'na disappoint. Let me see if I can somehow get back into yer good graces." I tip my head and raise one eyebrow, stopping him from going further. He acknowledges my unspoken disagreement. "Yes, well, perhaps that was more a figure of speech. May I continue?" I give him a reluctant nod to go on. "First, I apologize for startling you. It was'na my intention to do so. Second, yes, I am unexpected. I came to bring ye a bouquet of flowers from my garden. I think ye'll be pleased to know I arranged them myself. Yer mother said ye had gone for a ride, so I took the opportunity to come say hello." The tender look in his eyes has me turning away in shyness. "Third, at this very moment, ye are more beautiful than I have ever seen ye before. And that is not just flattery, 'tis the truth." Damn this man for his blinding charm. "Fourth, I feel privileged to have witnessed yer riding skills. I'm beyond impressed. Fifth, yer horse is a magnificent creature." Willow, on cue, nods her head, whinnies, and stomps her front hoof. Alasdair throws his head back in amusement, which forces my laughter to escape as well. "And she's fluent in English, I see. The two of you could'na be matched more perfectly. And six, why would anyone tell ye to be ashamed of such mastery? Surely that has'na happened?" I shake my head no in answer. "Good. That would be a shame."

"Is that so, Lord Stewart? You don't think it is improper for me to be riding my horse as a man does and not side-saddle? And what about risking my life making the jumps that Willow enjoys? Women are not supposed to do that, as I'm sure you know." Without waiting for his response, I jump down from the saddle, my tangled skirts swinging out with a loud *swoosh*. I noticed that he eyed the breeches that Beatrice made for me to wear when I go riding. I wonder if he will comment on those as well.

He stays seated upon his horse, a magnificent creature in his own right, black and shiny and a bit intimidating. He is the exact opposite of Willow, and their contrast accentuates each other's distinct beauty. Finally, he dismounts, and my traitorous eyes are drawn to his muscular legs flexing underneath the tight buckskin. My goodness, the way this man is put together ...

"If ye keep looking at me like that, I might start to think ye don't hate me anymore."

Embarrassed at being caught, I quickly shift my eyes to his and find his ego on full display through the mischievous grin with which I am becoming quite familiar. It infuriates me so I don't bother to answer; instead, I simply turn and start walking Willow toward the forest path that will lead us home.

"To answer yer question, yes, that is so. And no, I do'na think the way ye ride yer horse is improper. Neither on the obstacles nor the saddle. And *definitely* not doing it wearing breeches." I hear the delight in his voice as he pokes fun at my unconventional riding attire, but at the same time, he is sincere in his opinions otherwise. Try as I might, I cannot deny how much that pleases me.

"Thank you, Lord Stewart. If you would, please, keep your newfound knowledge of me to yourself. At this stage of my life, I do not like be lectured or reprimanded."

"Oh? And exactly what stage of life are ye currently in?"

"I will be twenty soon."

"Ah, a wise old woman, to be sure."

"You may jest, as you seem to enjoy doing, but you should know that I am…headstrong, let us say. You may not find that very appealing." *I hope*.

"Aye, well, ye may be disappointed to know that I find yer head to be the most fascinatingly appealing thing I've ever encountered. Both inside and out."

Stopping in the middle of the path, I pause as his words sink in. When I look up at him, the affectionate gaze that greets me releases a thousand butterflies through my tummy and up through my chest. "You mean that?" I ask.

"I do. I canna' imagine spending the rest of my life wi' a woman that is soft in the head and needs to be told what to do. A woman that does'na have the will to speak for herself or a sense of humor that ensures laughter in our home. And as for physical beauty, well, I will'na be settling when it comes to that."

"Hmm, there was a conclusion in that statement, Lord Stewart. It's awfully early in this game to be so presumptuous, wouldn't you agree?"

"No." He offers no other retort.

The finality of it creeps up my spine and blossoms, not into fear or dread, but a hot desire that tingles throughout my body. I breathe through it for a moment, then strategically ask, "What is his name? Your horse, I mean. He is quite spectacular."

"His name is Magni, and thank you. He is an impressive beast and loyal to the bone."

"Magni. That is an unusual name. What is its meaning?"

"The Latin meaning is large or great, which is fitting. However, he was named after a pagan god. I read a fascinating book on Norse mythology several years ago. Ye see, we've all learned about the terrible Norseman that came down an' pillaged our lands and did unspeakable things to women and children, but these were a complex, intellectual, and spiritual group of people. I won't bore ye wi' all the details, but let us say, it would take a tremendous amount of time to learn about the many gods they believed in. To add to that, each god has a long and complicated fable about how and why he or she existed. Magni is the god of strength and happens to be the son of Thor, the god of thunder. His mother was a giantess, which explained his size and powerful might. He saved his father's life once and is known to have survived the greatest battle of the gods, Ragnarök."

I am completely enthralled by his answer to my simple question. It is unexpected and fascinating, and I think about Magni's mother, a giantess of all things, sitting upon the bench conversing with my imaginary friend while she tends to her child.

"That is a fantastic story. I would like to know more about these gods. Their stories sound quite imaginative. What did you say the name of this great battle was?"

"Ragnarök." I cannot help but smile as the R's vibrate and roll off his tongue. "Why the sudden mischief, m'lady?"

"I like that word, especially with your accent," I answer in truth.

"Oh? Do ye mean ta tell me ye are no longer offended wi' me speech?" His question is so exaggerated in thick Scottish brogue I could hardly understand him. I try not to laugh, but the exhilaration of this afternoon has me giddy, and it bubbles over with ease.

"No, my lord. I am *no offended wi' yer speech*," I imitate him. Our mingled laughter echoes around us as Willow lifts her head and makes a noise that sounds oddly close to giggling. Lord Stewart and I both throw our heads back as the hilarity of the moment takes hold.

A few minutes pass before he says through winded breaths, "Ah, Lady Ella, ye have a fine sense of humor, but I'm afraid yer brogue needs a bit o' work."

"Yes, I would have to agree. It didn't sound as good as yours." He finds that admission particularly funny. "Lord Stewart? Would you mind telling me more about these pagan gods as we make our way back to the stables? I'm quite interested to know more about them."

"Aye, I'd be happy to." He pauses for a few seconds to gather his thoughts, but something inside me knows his thoughts are not about pagan gods and which story to start with first. Something has shifted between us during this short walk and lively exchange. For whatever reason, I decide not to fight it and find that I rather enjoy being more relaxed around him.

"Ye heard me mention Magni's father, Thor, the god of thunder. Well, Thor is a mighty figure, fearless and strong. He is a dedicated warrior with unmatched skills and is the son of Odin, the Allfather. Thor wields a giant hammer as his weapon. This hammer has special powers and allows Thor to summon lighting and, therefore, thunder."

Our pace slowed as we entered the forest, allowing more time for him to regale me with fascinating tales of the heathens we have recently come to know as Vikings. I believe Lord Stewart enjoyed telling the stories as much as I enjoyed hearing them. When he said goodbye, shortly after our return, he promised there is much more to tell and looks forward to our next walk through the forest to pick up where he left off. I was honest when I told him I look forward to it, as well.

"Ella, darling! You have flowers from Lord Stewart. They are unusual but lovely nonetheless," Mother cheerfully announces.

Entering the sunroom, I stop short as my hand comes up to rest on my chest. My heart feels strange as I see what he put together with his own hands from his garden. A copious array of wildflowers of all shapes, sizes, and colors are densely packed into a large, beautiful crystal vase. I have never seen an arrangement quite like it before. My mother is correct—it is rather lovely.

I pause to wonder how he got such an enormous arrangement here. I am certain he could not have traveled with it on his horse alone, yet I cannot imagine he brought it separately by carriage.

Upon a closer look, I see that he included leaf-filled branches and long blades of grass that seem to anchor this colorful collection of blossoms. I recognize it for what it is: a miniature of my butterfly garden that he knows I love so well. Perfect disarray—he seems to remember everything I say and do, then uses it to create something fantastic and beguiling. Who was the arrogant man I happened upon in the conservatory, who toyed with me and pushed my anger to its limit? He has become a wizard, using his sorcery to change my mind.

A smile spreads across my face as I realize that he has gone to great effort to make this botanical sculpture as real as possible. On the longest stems that reach far beyond the main cluster, right next to three separate purple blooms, he fastened intricately cut paper butterflies. A bubble of happy laughter escapes as I see them move, ever so slightly, in the draft of an open door. Upon closer inspection, I find that their details are not only sophisticated but unique, and I am awed by the precision of each cut.

As I slowly walk around the arrangement, my heart soars with joy and wonderment, I see a slight movement toward the side facing away from me. Quickly, I step around to see what other surprises are hiding within. I cannot stop the joyful smile from spreading across my face as I recognize what he has done... I reach up and touch the whimsical faerie dangling from a fine piece of string.

"Oh...Alasdair," I whisper.

The faerie is even more spectacular than the adept artistry of the butterflies. Her body is drawn onto either side of a cutout piece of paper. I bring her closer so that I can inspect her details. Up close, I see the figure is somewhat rudimentary, yet at the same time, it adds to her charm. But it is her wings that set her apart. They are considerably larger than her body, and their framework is also cut out of paper, outlining the shape of each wing. Yet, every space between the finely cut frames glows and shimmers with the brightest blue feathers I have ever seen.

"Truly spectacular," I whisper to myself.

Curious at how he could have assembled such a thing, I see the underside is framed as well. "How clever you are," I say with a sense of pride I do not understand.

He took a brilliant, iridescent feather and inserted it between the cutout frames he colored black. The end result is what you would think an actual faerie's wing could look like. Alasdair Stewart's mind is proving to be far more interesting than the average suitor.

Once again, the effort and thought he put into his gift do not go unnoticed—or unappreciated. My fingers drift around the arrangement as I study this and that. I can't seem to step away from my admiration of the immense variety that thrives in his garden.

And what do we have here?

I find a small folded piece of paper tucked between the vee of a thick branch.

My stomach flips in excitement. Alasdair has already trained me to anticipate his words. Inside, there are only a few, but their meaning...Oh Lord. Why does this make me so happy?

Ella,
> *You inspire me.*
> *Alasdair*

EIGHT

Alasdair

"Ye've got a lit'l skip in yer step this evening, m'lord. Ye were able to dull the blade o' that sharp-tongued lass ye been pining over, aye?" Ewan asks with his usual candor.

"Is it that obvious, Ewan?" I ask rhetorically. "I believe I may have done just that, and I can'na deny how bloody happy I am about it."

"Oh? So yer efforts wi' flowers and wee paper creatures worked well fer ye, then?"

"Actually, I do'na have the slightest inkling what she thought of that. I forgot all about the damn thing until ye mentioned it just now."

"Weel, something good must'a happened fer ye to forget about that. Ye put a bloody lot of effort into it and 'tis the reason ye went to call. An' let's not forget *I* had to keep the enormous thing from tipping over in yer carriage while *you* rode Magni."

"I suppose ye think it should have been the other way around?" I question with a bit of humor.

"No, no, I dinna say that. I was simply emphasizing my familiarity wi' yer creation."

"I see. And is there anything else ye'd like to say about my creation?"

"Nothing other than the truth, m'lord. 'Twas extraordinary, you ken it as well as I do. Now, are ye going to tell me what has ye chipper as a dandy wi'a new pair o' boots and a shiny buckle?"

I can't help but laugh aloud, "I'll say I'm happier than a dandy wi' a whole new wardrobe! By God! She told me she was looking forward to seeing me again. Ewan, she is...is...bloody hell—she rides a horse like a jockey in the National Hunt Race. Ye would'na believe it!" I ramble enthusiastically.

"I'm a bit confused on how we went from delivering an oversized bouquet o' flowers to jockeyin' the Hunt Race. I fear ye've left out some pertinent details."

"Aye...well, I'll admit my mind's a bit untidy at the moment." I stop my pacing to pour a scotch. After a long draught, I let it rest in my mouth before swallowing. The smokey flavor spreads over my tongue and through my nose as I exhale. My mouth waters, and I swallow again as the flavor shifts to the salty brine of the coast. "Lady Ella was'na there when I arrived with her arrangement. She was out riding and, after a bit of persuasive questioning of the groomsmen that did'na want to be so helpful at first, I was finally pointed in the right direction. When I came upon her, I could'na believe my eyes. She flew over a stone hurdle, landed the bloody thing with perfection, then guided her horse through a maze of obstacles and jumps like a seasoned jockey winning the race. And the best part was when she turned to head in my direction, letting the horse cool down in a steady trot...she had a smile of pure joy, the likes of which I've never seen before. It was the most beautiful thing I've ever seen, Ewan."

"Christ! I don't see how it's possible. Ye can'na jump a horse side-saddle! She'd surely break a bone somewhere in her body!" Ewan replies with unfeigned confusion.

"She was'na side-saddle. She rode like a gentleman, astride, with breeches under her skirts!"

"Bloody hell!" His eyes widen as his mouth gapes open.

"Aye. And as ye can imagine, she was'na too pleased I found out her little secret. But when she realized I was'na there to judge her or reprimand her, that I was bloody impressed wi' her skills, she put away most of the weapons she's had pointed at me since first we met. She put away the rest after we had a few good laughs and a lively conversation about Norse mythology."

"I can barely get a woman to discuss the weather wi' me. Yer Lady Ella sounds like a keeper, m'lord."

I cannot deny that I have thought the same thing on more than one occasion, and I've only just met her. "She is proving to be exactly that, my friend."

After sleeping in due to a rough night of tossing and turning, my mind excited with thoughts of Ella, I'm dressed and ready to attend the Burtons' soiree that I would have otherwise avoided had it not been for the intriguing faerie maiden that snuck up on me unawares only nine days ago. 'Tis a very short period of time to become so enthralled. *Nine days and I can think of nothing more than her.* The thought rotates as I stare out across the gardens.

I know what has happened; at this point, there is no possible way I could deny it, and acknowledging it makes me think of my grandmother, Nanna, God rest her soul, and the lengthy conversations she had with me throughout my childhood and adolescence. The Fey was strong in Nanna, that mysterious clairvoyance and sixth sense that is unusually prevalent within the Scottish people. Nanna would tell me that "the sight" and strong intuition came from our ancestors many, many generations back. She said she could sense it in me, but I never really entertained the notion because I was too busy being a boy and had more important things to do like train my horse, hunt, fish, perfect my sword fight, and anything else that involved me becoming a man. However, as an adult, I never question my gut instinct—ever. It is remarkably accurate, at times astoundingly so, to not only me but my crew as well. That is how I know what Nanna told me all those years ago is true; I can feel it in my gut.

"Ye have an auld soul, Allie," she would say, using the pet name she gave me, her brogue thick through her aged voice. "It has walked the earth many times before, makes ye wise wi' keen instincts, even beyond the Fey. But ye should know, there is another that seeks to find ye. A soul, ould as yers, an' no matter time or place, hers will follow, an' yours shall follow her. Ye belong together...ye always have an' ye always will. 'Tis lovely, my boy, 'tis a lovely thing that ye are so fortunate. You'll understand one day. Nothing compares to the love and passion than that shared by soulmates."

The grounds of the Burtons' estate are some of the most impressive I have ever seen. The lord and lady of the house are the purveyors of several botanical gardens throughout London and the countryside, and they have clearly wasted no effort here at their estate. Lush sycamore and oak trees line the drive along neatly trimmed shrubs with pillowing flowers. It is a fantastic statement for anyone taking the long, meandering drive to the opulent porte-cochere.

When I stop to appreciate the beauty of what they have created, my thoughts go to Ella and how much she will appreciate the Burtons' botanical artistry, regardless of the lack of any sort of natural disarray.

After a brief greeting to the host and hostess—who was uncomfortably forward in the presence of her husband—I am ready to find my sole purpose for being here. After several greetings and a few short conversations, I could not avoid, I am pleased to see Ella has already arrived and appears to be enjoying herself as she freely laughs with her peers. Her golden, ethereal beauty stands out against the crowd of dark-haired young men and women and one vibrant red-haired lass that seems full of mischief even from this distance.

My eyes meet Ella's, and my skin tingles—hers does as well, I can tell by the fear in her expression. My pace is controlled as I steadily move toward her, my only focus. Without saying a word, the circle around her breaks apart as everyone steps aside to give me access. She's frozen, fighting her desire, and everything about it has my own desire on edge. I can see her mind debating whether she is happy to see me, but none of that matters. I can sense that her body has come to the same conclusion as mine.

"Lady Ella." My greeting is traditional, and proper in every way as I wait for her to rest her hand in mine. Reluctantly, she does, and I bring it to my lips while breathing in her delicious scent. I linger too long, as usual, and she tries to take her hand away. *No, my dear. I'm not letting go just yet.* "'Tis good to see ye again. And might I add, ye look lovely this afternoon."

"Thank you, Lord Stewart," she replies as I release her hand a few seconds late. Her eyes are fiery, and I cannot stop the smile from stretching across my face.

To my right, I hear a strained whisper say, "Good Lord...a stallion." Turning to the source, I find Ella's red-haired companion staring at me with wide eyes, a bright mossy green that sparkle with a playful expression.

"Mary!" Ella hisses.

"What?" Mary turns to her with drawn brows.

Ella's only reply is a stern look of displeasure.

"'Tis Mary, is it?" I ask as she offers her hand with unabashed excitement.

"Yes! And you must be Alasdair Stewart!"

"*Lord* Stewart, this is my cousin, Lady Mary Emsworth. Please don't be offended by her lack of propriety. She doesn't get out much." That fiery glare is now on her cousin, and I cannot help but laugh at their familiar banter.

"Very funny, Ella. I get out plenty. I just live by different rules. Nothing wrong with that. Don't you think, *Lord* Stewart?" Mary asks confidently.

"Oh, aye, I can'na disagree. Propriety is'na my strong suit either. Ask Lady Ella. She has corrected my decorum at least once every time I have had the pleasure of being in her company," I say with a wink.

"How charming the two of you are with your lack of gentility. I shall leave you to it." And once again, she turns to leave me stranded, nursing another cut from the blade that replaces her tongue.

With a polite nod, I leave Mary—and her knowing smirk— to regroup with her friends while I make sure Ella does not get too far away.

"I did'na come to this sunny little gathering to spend it wi' yer cousin. I am only here to see you," I say in a low voice close to her ear, avoiding attention.

Her pace picks up before she finally turns to stand on the far side of a massive potted tree, offering the privacy she has clearly been seeking. "I would appreciate it, Lord Stewart, if you would not offer such fodder to my cousin about any possible *lack of decorum* between the two of us. You do not know her, and the fact that she hears and sees everything through the eyes of a secret service spy. God forbid what your comment will stir up in her mind. And let me assure you, whatever it is, she will hound me relentlessly about it!"

"How do ye know about secret service spies?" This woman never ceases to amaze me.

"Have you forgotten who my father is? But the more pressing question is, have you missed my point altogether?" Her hands are on her hips now, she's done that at least once every time I've been around her, as well, and the thought makes me smile. "Why are you smiling, Lord Stewart?" she huffs out with exacerbation.

"Because ye are so feisty, and it's so damned appealing I lose my train of thought."

"Is that so? Does that mean you didn't hear a word I said about my cousin and her inexplicable ability to surmise accurate conclusions with very little information? That little morsel you left her with is going to cause me headaches for weeks to come!"

"I apologize for causing ye such distress. 'Tis not something I would have guessed about her—at first glance, anyway—or I would'na have said a word. But now that ye say it, she does have a keen-eyed way about her, aye. Does yer father know she has this talent? Espionage is'na only a man's occupation. Our female spies are considered our best."

"Please do not tell her that! From this day forward, watch what you say within earshot of Lady Mary. Now, let us mingle about, away from this corner before my reputation gets ruined."

"Yes, of course," I agree, offering her my arm. "Do ye think they will have music and dancing?"

She looks up at me, her blue eyes glowing from the light of the window. "Yes. The music should be starting soon. So, you like to dance?"

"Aye, I do. Did ye forget that I am Scottish, Lady Ella?"

"So dancing is a Scottish trait, is it?"

"Oh, aye. We've got a bloody dance for everything."

"Lord Stewart!"

"Forgive me. I should be more careful with my words."

"Yes, you should. Especially in the presence of a lady," she reminds me, trying to force away a smile.

"Can ye ever forgive me?" I ask as we slow our pace through the crowd.

"Hmm...we shall see if you can redeem yourself." She stops then and turns to face me, her expression coy as she opens her fan to gently cool her chest and throat.

I pause to admire how stunning she is when she's being playful, but before I can articulate a compliment, Admiral Wilfred Buchanan interrupts with a heavy hand on my shoulder as his baritone voice drowns out the noise of the crowd.

"Captain Stewart! By Jove! I wasn't sure it was you. I say, it has been that long since I laid eyes upon you. You must fill me in on your exploits. I've heard stories, but I need to hear it from the horse's mouth." He slowly turns to Ella and acknowledges her *and* the fact that we were in the middle of a conversation— one I wish would continue without interruption. "Please forgive me, ma'am. I must speak with the captain, as we have important matters to discuss. I wouldn't want to bore your sensibilities with the conversations of men."

Everything about that last comment has my teeth clenching. What he doesn't realize is that Ella could likely talk circles around him and leave him wondering if he knows as much as he thinks he does.

Apparently, Lady Ella agrees. She leaves Admiral Buchanan bumbling and snorting, trying to regain his footing after elegantly snapping her fan closed right in his face and turning away, performing a silent cut that slices damn near as deep as those in her verbal arsenal.

Ready to defend his pride, chin pulled back into the pillow of fat that hangs from his jaw, he begins, "Well, I say...she..."

"Before ye make any harsh judgments about Lady Ella that ye will regret, let me educate ye—her father is Admiral Edward Seymour." His yellowing eyes bulge. "Yes. *That* Admiral Seymour."

"Oh, I see. Yes, she has certainly grown since the last I saw her. What a lovely young lady, quite lovely indeed. Tell me, Lord Stewart, I heard about a scuffle in the Mediterranean with the Spanish fleet. Nelson says he's not sure victory was ours without your skill in battle. That is quite a compliment, you know."

"Aye, Admiral Nelson is a good man. And he would never admit that his compliment is indirectly one to the man himself. After all, I've been a captain in his fleet for many years, and I've learned more about battle strategy from him than anyone. Although, skill or no skill, there are times when numbers outweigh all. 'Twas good we arrived when we did."

"Come. Let us go find the gentlemen and the whisky." I watch as his belly bounces in time with his laughter and wonder what he finds so funny.

We make our way through the crowd, stopping for a casual greeting here and there, I see Ella on the far side of the room talking to a mealy-looking young man. He certainly isn't any sort of competition, but it doesn't change the fact that his presence makes me uneasy. Just before she is out of my sight completely, I see them exit through the French doors to the terrace beyond.

Apparently, we found the gentlemen and the whisky because I now find myself in a room filled with both. And a bloody lot of pipe and cigar smoke. Lord Buchanan is in his element, joyfully introducing me to everyone who passes by, regardless if I am already acquainted with more than half of them.

The further into the room I get, the more stifling the air becomes. It gets worse as I become trapped by Oliver Adams, who insists on a conversation about the potential for another war with France so that he can bet accordingly on its outcome. Thomas Webb joins in with a complaint about all the money he lost last month and that the betting books are "nothing more than a fraudulent scheme." His clear lack of understanding of the concept of betting explains his loss of money, and I have the urge to tell him so, but that would extend my time here in this rather obnoxious place.

Through a well-timed interruption, I managed to separate myself from Adams and Webb and gradually make my way closer to the door, so I could seek out Ella again. I have an uncomfortable impatience eating at me that is growing worse the longer I am trapped in this overcrowded room. Finally, Lord Canton gives me the opening I was looking for, and I slip out the door.

The cooler, fresher air is a welcome relief as I skirt along the wall, away from the crowd. Once I am on the terrace, I look for Ella but do not see her amongst the mass of oversized hats in every shape and size, and my gut tightens with apprehension. Something isn't right, and my first instinct is to look for her in the garden that, from this point of view, looks like a damned labyrinth.

My pace is quick without running as I enter. Once I am

no longer in view of the guests mingling on the terrace, I am in a full-out run as I try to navigate through the manicured shrubs, massive trees, random statues, fountains, and enormous planters overflowing with more flowers. Coming to a fork in the path, I stop, looking both ways hoping to see Ella safely walking in either direction. Yet instead, over the sound of my winded breath, I hear a cry, and I know it's her.

What I find when I round the corner at the end of the path turns my vision red. The man has her pressed hard against a column inside the towering white gazebo. She is fighting against him, repeating the words that echo under the canopy, "Stop! Please stop!" But he doesn't abide.

Without thought, I fly up the steps and, in one swift move, alter their positions, slamming him against the column, the point of my dirk pressed hard against the soft underside of his jaw.

"Ella, stand down on the path and wait fer me." I don't want her to witness what I am about to do.

"Alasdair! Please. Don't kill him. Please, let us just leave." The terror in her voice has me pressing the blade further into his pale skin, breaking the surface. He flinches, eyes squeezing tightly as the sting of the cut makes them water. I want this man to suffer. I want him dead.

"Ella. Do as I say."

I can hear her scurry down the steps behind me, still calling to me, "Alasdair! Please!"

He's trembling under my grip, useless fucking bastard. "Open yer eyes." He doesn't—he only squeezes them tighter as he whimpers in fear. My hold tightens on his throat as I press harder. "Open. Yer. Fucking. Eyes." He does this time. "What is yer name?"

"I...I..." He makes some unintelligible sounds before

answering, "L...Lord...Wes...Weston Percy." He has a rancid stench about him that goes beyond his fear.

"Lord *Weston* Percy, do ye feel the warmth slowly traveling down the skin o' yer throat? Aye, 'tis yer blood, and there's plenty more where that came from. A slight twist o' my wrist and just a wee bit more pressure is all it will take. You'll lay here as the light fades on your sorry existence, yer blood permanently staining the white marble beneath. A testament to where yer pathetic soul finally left this earth and made its journey straight to hell where it belongs. From what I've seen, 'tis an unpleasant experience to know yer death is inevitable an' there isn'a a bloody thing ye can do about it."

I can hear Ella down on the path crying, still begging me to leave him here. To not kill him the way my instincts are telling me to.

His blood is spilling over and seeping under my hand, making my grip slippery against his throat. "Today just might be yer lucky day, Weston. Can ye imagine that? All ye have to do is answer one question properly, and yer free to go. I will'na kill ye." He responds with a strangled squeak but doesn't move his head for fear of deepening the cut that is hiding the tip of my knife in his gullet. "Will ye ever come near Lady Ella again, intentionally or otherwise?"

Panicking, he gurgles out, "N-no."

"Good. That was the correct answer. Now let me fill in a few holes fer ye. If I find that ye've gone back on yer word, yer a dead man." My grip tightens. "If I find that ye've tried to communicate with Lady Ella, through yer own pitiful mouth or someone else's or even through written fucking word, yer a dead man. Have I made myself clear?"

"Mmm...mmm...y-yes." His face crumbles in pain from the movement of his jaw, pushing the blade deeper into raw flesh.

"Good. Now get yer worthless arse out'a here and pray we

never cross paths again." I remove my blade and shove him over the edge of the gazebo's foundation with the hand gripping his throat. He lands on his back with a loud thud, choking and gasping for air as the wind is knocked from his lungs. I turn and calmly walk to the trickling fountain in the middle of the large pavilion to wash his blood from my hands, disappointed a spot of it stains the cuff of my white shirt.

Back on the path, I don't see Ella, but I can hear her weeping. I rush toward the sound, finding her on a bench tucked into a carved-out section of the thick hedge. I kneel down in front of her, running my hands around her face, inspecting for injuries, and moving her disheveled hair away as it sticks to her tears.

"Are ye alright, lass? Tell me where yer hurt." Seeing her like this is tearing me apart and taking every bit of strength I have to refrain from going back and finishing what my gut tells me I should have done.

"I'm fine, I...I'm just shaken up. I don't...he just... Oh, Alasdair!" She grabs onto me, burying her face in my shoulder and cries harder. I hold her, letting her release the pent-up fear. Eventually, her sobs ebb, and she relaxes in my arms. "Alasdair, I've never been so afraid. I don't know what came over him. I kept trying to go back to the party, and he insisted on showing me something. I...I...knew something wasn't right, but I never imagined..." She lifts her head from my shoulder and looks at me in earnest. "I didn't do anything to provoke him, Alasdair, I swear."

The thought that she thinks I would blame her or think that she had a part in the bloody pervert's actions is like a kick in the gut. "Look at me, Ella. Look in my eyes. What happened was'na yer fault, and I would'na ever think otherwise. That is a sick man, and I can assure ye, he will never come near ye again. Ever. Do ye understand?"

"Yes," she whispers.

"Good. Now, do ye trust me?"

She hesitates for only a few seconds. "Yes. I do."

I wipe another tear away, this time, with my lips. "I want to erase the memory of what just happened to ye," I say against her wet skin, then move to her other cheek and open my mouth to taste the salt, to kiss away the fear. "It will only take a few minutes, and ye will feel better."

"Alright," she whispers again.

"Give me yer hands." She does, and I gently pull her. "Stand up." I give her a moment to steady her legs before bringing her body to mine, wrapping one arm around her back, cradling her face with the other. I study her beautiful features as she stares up at me, eyes swollen. I will not let that bastard ruin Ella's passionate nature. Her sensual desires will not be extinguished by that loathsome man. I sweep my thumb across her lips. "I'm going to wipe away everything that bastard did to ye. You'll never be touched like that again." I pause and kiss her forehead gently, resting my lips against her soft skin. I move to kiss the corners of each eye near her temples. I linger, warming the chill with my mouth. Her body continues to relax in my arms. Instinctively I pull her closer as my other hand drifts to cradle the back of her head. I move down to her cheek, crooning to her in Gaelic, "Mo leannan...tha thu sàbhailte a-nis."

The closer I get to her mouth, the more erratic her breathing becomes. "Ella, I'm going to kiss yer mouth the way it deserves to be kissed. May I?" She nods. I want her to feel what this is meant to be, not the fear and grotesque force that vile man used against her. When our mouths connect, she turns into it with a hunger I wasn't expecting. I must tighten my grip on her as the force of her kiss makes us unsteady. When her hands reach up and grab onto the back of my head, then my neck, then up to my face, I let her lead our mouths and tongues through their primal dance that speaks a universal language.

My God! This woman is like nothing I ever knew possible. With this kiss, she has ignited a fire in my blood that makes me want to conquer the world. Yet, at the same time, all I want to do is cradle her like a babe, rock her to sleep, and let her know she is safe with me.

She is devouring my mouth like she's been craving this for a lifetime, her full lips warm and soft as they move around mine, her tongue sweeping through to caress my own, shooting a bolt of desire straight to my loins. I feel myself losing control. Our mutual need for each other is visceral, and I cannot help but think of the potential in our passionate connection.

Holding her head with both my hands, I slow our pace, though I wish it never to end. "Ella." I'm breathless against her mouth, my lips pressing into hers—small kisses, gentle sucking, licking, a tender bite. "I only want ye to remember what we just shared, only this kiss. Tell me it is yer first."

"It is," she confirms on a heavy breath.

"Good." I lean down and take the liberty of a chaste kiss as my heart explodes from the smile that lights up her face. "From this moment forward, when ye think of a kiss, when ye think of a man kissing a woman, this, what we have shared, is the only thought that comes to yer mind, aye?"

"Aye," she agrees with her mock brogue, and we both laugh, lifting some of the weight off her shoulders. I continue holding her. Truly I do not want to let her go. "Are ye well now?"

"Yes. Thank you. I cannot bear to think what would have happened had you not been there."

"Then don't. I've given ye something far better to think about."

"I certainly cannot disagree." She looks away in shyness, but I place my hand under her chin and tilt her face back up to mine.

"Do'na be ashamed of the kiss we shared, nor the pleasure it brought ye."

"I won't," she replies with blushing cheeks. "Is Lord Percy dead?"

My body tenses at the thought. "Unfortunately, no. I did'na want ye to carry any more burdens from this day. But I will tell ye, it was'na easy to spare him. I've never wanted to end a man's life as much as I wanted to end his."

We stay a while longer, holding each other, contemplating everything that has happened in such a short time. Everything has changed. She knows it as well as I do.

NINE

Ella

"Did you forget that I'm riding in this carriage with you?" Mary startles me out of my daydream.

"What? Oh, I'm sorry, Mary. I didn't mean to ignore you. I'm just a bit tired today." Distracted is more like it. But I can't tell Mary that yesterday was the worst and best day I've ever had. Alasdair was right—the kiss we shared has completely overridden the awful fear Lord Percy left me feeling. The warmth and strength of Alasdair's arms around me and the indescribable desire his kiss ignited inside me has been in the forefront of my mind ever since.

"Are you going to attempt to convince me that dreamy look on your face has nothing to do with you and Lord Stallion disappearing from the Burtons' yesterday?"

My head turns to her abruptly, only to find her tittering behind her fan. The humor I see in her eyes is contagious, and I can't help laughing at her play on his name. "Well done, Mary. Lord Stallion. I hope that doesn't slip off my tongue in his presence. I would be mortified!"

"Why should you be mortified? It's the truth, and don't think for a minute he doesn't know it! Did you see his shoulders? Broad and set perfectly square, not sloped and droopy and weak. He likely has a body like the men in those paintings at the museum that Mother doesn't want us looking at."

She stops then and studies my face. "But you already know that his body looks like skin stretched tightly over thick muscles, don't you? How do you know that, Ella?"

"Mary! I have never seen *any* man unclothed, and certainly not Lord Stewart! I should be offended by such a suggestion."

"But you're not." She pauses to fan her face and eyes me a bit longer. "Something happened. Nothing so far as losing your maidenhead before your sweet papa has given you away, but *something*."

"No. However, I will not deny...the *thought* of him unclothed is very intriguing and is certainly worthy of a blush or two."

"Did he kiss you yesterday?"

This could be my opportunity to steer her away from the truth, which she seems hell-bent on getting me to confess, and this is surely the lesser of all evils. "Yes. Are you happy now?" It almost feels good to say it, to get it out in the open.

"I knew it! Oh, please tell me it was as fantastic as I imagine it would be. He is simply swoon worthy! You are so lucky."

"Mary, it was absolutely amazing and almost completely overshadows his insufferable ego." A very true statement.

"How did you ever get away from Lord Slimy-and-Gross long enough to get a kiss from your thoroughbred? I felt so sorry for you when Percy approached. He was acting more oddly than he normally does."

"Thankfully, Lord Stewart scared him away so we could

take a stroll through the garden." I still can't make eye contact with Mary.

"Well, I am truly happy for you, Ella dear. We must pray that another stallion comes from a land far away and sweeps me off my feet. Now that I know it is a possibility, I cannot settle for less. Oh! We are here!" Mary finishes her statement with a squeal of excitement.

The carriage slows as it approaches Sylvie's dress shop. It's a quaint storefront painted white with big display windows that feature colorful paintings of ladies in ornate gowns. The canvases are surrounded by ceramic pots, big and small, filled with flowers fashioned out of a kaleidoscope of fabrics. They must be from remnants of all the dresses she's made. It is a fantastic display, and I wonder if Sylvie created them all herself.

"Well, this certainly is charming," Mary says as the footman helps us out of the carriage.

"Yes, it is. I'm excited to see her inventory!"

As we stop outside to admire the display windows, I glance over at a group of women nearby pointing at us and talking in hushed tones. I ignore them, yet I cannot help but notice the chill that comes across my skin.

Inside, Mary is overjoyed as she goes from fabric bolt to fabric bolt, and trim displays that are too numerous to count. Finally, Sylvie comes from behind the curtain in the back of the store and gleefully greets us.

"Ladies! You've arrived. I am so happy to see you!" Her French accent is thick through her enthusiasm. "Come here, my darling," she says to Mary. "My goodness, you are lovely. Look at dis coloring! You are a dressmaker's dream!" Mary is practically purring like a kitten, no doubt wondering what ideas the apprentice to the famous Rose Bertin has in store.

This place is like candy to a woman's soul, and I am so

happy we planned this visit to Sylvie's shop. The quality of her fabrics is the best I have ever seen, and her artistry could very well be beyond that of the master under which she studied. But I am a little unnerved that two other women, with whom I am acquainted, have come in, looking at me with an abnormal degree of shock, then left as though I have the plague.

Something has happened. That is blatantly obvious, and the longer I stand here, the bigger the rock becomes that is weighing heavily in my stomach.

"Are you alright, dear?" Sylvie asks with sincere concern.

"I don't know. I suddenly feel like I am the focus of something untoward, but I do not know what that could be."

"Come here, my darling. Come." Sylvie pulls me to the back of the shop, behind the curtain that hides her workspace. "Sit right here," she says in a comforting yet commanding way. "I know too much. Ladies are vipers, and society is their breeding den. You are a good woman. I know dis because I know what people are made of. I learn dis so I survive. A rumor has spread...it is malicious. I have seen dis before. Someone wants to harm your reputation. Say you have been in action like that of a whore with a Scotsman."

I think I'm going to faint...or vomit. Everything is spinning, and I'm trying to balance myself, so I don't topple out of this chair. "This cannot be happening. Please tell me this is not happening."

Sylvie kneels in front of me and grabs my face. "Look at me! You look in my eyes. Trust me when I tell you, it could be worse. I know who you are and where you come from. You are far more protected dan thousands of other women. Your family will see to dat. Now we must be hopeful dis man will honor you with his hand in marriage."

His hand in marriage? This cannot be real. I have only

walked into a dress shop, and somehow my life has been yanked out from under me, and I am to be married?

"Ella! What is going on? You look awful! And why is everyone looking at us like we have stolen the king's crown?" Mary's voice is shrill with desperation.

"Come. Sit with your friend."

"She's my cousin."

"Well, good. Someone is trying to ruin her reputation. Day say Lady Ella has had carnal relations with a Scottish captain. I hear dem saying it dis morning." Sylvie comes over and wraps me in her arms, humming the sound of a sweet lullaby. "I have seen 'dis too many times. The ignorant lies the haut ton craves to make their days more interesting. They never lift you up... only drag you down. You must be stronger than 'dat. Never let society get the upper hand." She is rocking back and forth, rubbing my back firmly. "Strong, little dove. Be strong...stay strong."

Listening to the conviction in her voice is making me want to cry. Not only for the ruination of my reputation—that my poor mother held sacred—but for Sylvie and her country and the murderous terror they have had to endure.

"I cannot believe this has happened." My voice is barely a whisper.

Mary comes over to sit in front of me. "Ella, dear. Look at me." She takes my hands in hers. "Lord Stewart will make this right by you. He will not let you be ruined." The sympathy in her voice makes the tears spill over.

"I know he will. But that does not change what has happened. It does not change why we would be married. It shall be tainted with scandal forever. My mother's—oh God, and my father's—hearts will be broken." I look up at Mary. "Will they ever be able to trust me again? I could not bear it if they don't."

I stand up abruptly, anger replacing the sadness and fear. "It's that bastard, Percy. I know it is. He forced himself on me yesterday, and Lord Stewart let him know, quite convincingly, that it will never happen again! This is his revenge."

I look over at Mary, her eyes shiny with emotion. "Please don't overthink this, Mary. I didn't want to worry you unnecessarily. Lord Percy is a demented man, and I am now fearful of Lord Stewart's retaliation. I literally had to beg him not to kill him yesterday after what Lord Percy did."

The emotion is welling over, and now Mary is the one consoling me. She gently rubs my back as I fall into her arms. "I knew something was amiss with that toad. Thank God Lord Stewart was there to protect you!"

I can't help but wonder about his reaction to the rumor that has spread through London.

"Mary, I think I want to go home. I'm sorry to have spoiled your day."

"Nonsense. This is not your fault."

"Ladies, I will put together an ensemble for each of you and have it delivered. I know what will look brilliant on you and bring out your magnificence." Sylvie puts her arm around my shoulders. "You go home and rest, child. If I hear any more talk of dese lies, I will diffuse them as best I can."

"Thank you, Sylvie. You have been so kind."

The ride home was somber. Mary did not force any conversation on me. She let me be quiet and stare out the window, wondering what my future will hold. More than anything, I dread telling my parents what has happened.

"We're here," Mary announces quietly. "Do you want me to stay?"

"I would love that, but I need to face my parents alone. Thank you, Mary."

The footman helps me out, and Mary gives me a hug and a

few more words of encouragement. Donovan greets me at the door with his usual welcome, but the look in his eyes belies the truth in his words. He is giving me a warning that the rumor has arrived before me. With a slight nod and a deep breath, I acknowledge his silent message.

My poor mother. She must be beside herself. I wish I could simply run upstairs to my room and cry in Beatrice's arms. But, that will never do, for I am no longer a child.

When Donovan reaches for the polished doorknob of the sunroom, a wave of anxiety washes over me. There is another voice mingled in with my parents, it is deep and accented, and the meaning of its presence sends a chill across my body. I open the door and all I see is Alasdair. He is stunning, standing there with undisguised confidence, dressed as if he were going to be presented to the king. I am torn between a spark of happiness —this incredible man is here to ask for my hand—and intense indignation, freely choosing my husband will not be my liberty.

Lord Stewart is the first to speak. My parents are clearly distraught and must not know what to say. I see my mother has been crying; her eyes and nose are red, her mouth drawn down in a devastating frown.

"Lady Ella, may I speak wi' ye in private?"

My spine straightens.

"It would appear that *no* is not an option."

I look at my father, who offers a half-smile and nods his head. I trust him implicitly, so I take Alasdair's proffered arm and allow him to escort me to the terrace.

The clouds are thick overhead, casting a gloom that seems to mirror the sense of dread that is making it hard to breathe.

"The first thing I want ye to know is that Percy will pay fer what he has done. He will be paying fer a very long time to come."

"How have you ensured that? What have you done?"

"I have only followed though wi' my word. As fer now, he will be enjoying a long tenure aboard a pirate ship, captained by one of the most ruthless men I've ever encountered."

"What does that mean, Alasdair?"

"That he will suffer."

I turn away from him and lean against the banister. I know Lord Percy deserves punishment. But I can't help feeling uncomfortable with the ease at which Lord Stewart delivers it.

"He deserves worse." The anger in his voice does not go unnoticed.

"Yes. He has managed to alter the state of my life rather abruptly. But why are you here, Lord Stewart?"

"Ye know why I'm here, Lady Ella." I can hear the frustration in his voice. He should have known I would not make this easy for him. "I told ye the night we first met that I would protect yer reputation. We are to be married."

"Are we? Just like that? And I suppose you thought I'd be overjoyed with this news, no doubt." I cross my arms firmly over my chest, glaring in frustration at this beautiful man. "What will you do if I tell you no, I will not marry you?"

"I will tell ye that the fierce glare in yer eyes and the conviction in yer voice makes me want to marry ye even more. It makes me want to take ye in my arms and kiss yer lovely mouth and make you not regret having yer choice taken away from ye." Damn him for knowing how that will affect me. "I know this has ye in knots...Christ! It has me in knots as well. It was'na supposed to be this way, the choice being forced upon ye."

He stops then to let us both have a moment to absorb our reality. Reaching up, he puts his hand under my chin, gently nudging me to look at him. "Ella. Let me protect ye. I promise ye will'na regret it."

My eyes close as the tears overwhelm my vision. "It's too much, too fast. Yesterday...yesterday you saved me, and then... the kiss we shared... It was all so much to take in. But even still, I was looking forward to seeing you again."

"Were ye, now? Tell me a bit more about that. I believe my fragile ego might enjoy the boost." His lopsided smile creates an endearing dimple in his tanned cheek.

"Hmph! There is nothing fragile about your ego and well you know it!"

"Aye. Ye may have me there."

His jesting changed the tone of our conversation, easing some of the tension.

"I don't know if I'm ready," I say with all seriousness. "What if we are not a good match? I know quite well how insufferable you can be."

He throws his head back in laughter that echoes across the terrace.

"I'm a man and a bloody Scot, of course I'm insufferable. But you...ye are strong and sharp of mind, tenacious and fearless. That's why we are such a good match. Ye are sure to keep me in line."

The severity of our reality creeps back upon us as we stop and simply stare at one another, picturing our future, a life together as husband and wife. How has this happened? Is this the right thing?

"Do ye believe in fate, faerie maiden?"

His question and the smooth tenor of his voice send a chill up my spine. I don't know that I have ever given much thought to the notion of fate. I certainly never intended to give up control to anyone or anything. Yet, look at the turn my life has taken since I happened upon this man in the conservatory. I was determined to despise him, to rid the glorious image of him from my mind. But here I stand before him, expected to take his hand in marriage, every alternative far less appealing.

"Well, Lord Stewart, I suppose I do, albeit reluctantly. However, you may not be so pleased to know I have no intention of making this easy for you."

"Lady Ella, I would expect nothing less. But more importantly, ye've just agreed to be my wife."

TEN

Alasdair

I suppose I should be thankful my conversation with Ella went as well as it did. I will not deny that I was a bit nervous talking to the duke and duchess as I waited for her to arrive home. Unfortunately, I was the one that had to inform her parents of the rumor that bastard Percy had spread. I assured them it wasn't true and that the man who started it was acting out of jealousy. They seemed to understand and take my word as truth, though it didn't change the reality of the rumor's damage.

Ella had been in town shopping, so it was my suspicion that she got word of what had happened while she was out. How she would react, I could only imagine. All I knew was that I had to make it right, and I had to do it fast.

"Capt'n Freeman seemed a mite pleased takin' in that wee bastard Percy. The look in his eyes did'na bode well fer his new recruit," Ewan announces with humor.

"Aye. That was the point. And Freeman owes me, although I had hoped to never have need of callin' the favor. Keeping him in my pocket relieves me of potential headaches when I'm at sea. He's a ruthless bastard, but one that keeps his word."

"How the hell did ye end up in that man's good favor?"

"I saved his life."

"Saved his bloody life? Seems like that would call fer more than one favor, would it not?"

"Aye, it would. But I have no expectations beyond this one. That would be foolish."

"An' out of curiosity, how'd ye save the life of a ruthless pirate like Freeman?" Ewan asks, ever the curious valet.

"It was in the Caribbean. We were playing poker. It was a rather diverse group of players, ye see. I was hopin' to gain information about a fleet of Spanish ships rumored to be planning an attack. Freeman and I were doing vera' well and continued to play long into the night, sharing some good laughs and decent wine. Toward the end of the evening, an oriental-looking fella sat down, and I knew right away it was'na because he enjoyed the game. So, I watched his every move. Time went on, nothing seemed out of sorts, but when his hand dropped to his side, and his lithe fingers pulled a weapon out o' the cuff of his sleeve, I had little time to react. When he brought it up to throw it at Freeman's throat, I stuck his hand to the table wi' me dirk. His weapon tumbled across and came to a stop in front of its intended target. Freeman picked up the strange-looking blade and examined it. It was perfectly polished to a mirror's shine and looked like a star, each point as sharp as a razor's edge. I'd never seen anything like it. Then, wi'out hesitation, Freeman sent it flying across the table, a shiny blur, the sound of it like the hum of a bee...it hit its mark with the precision of a master. The little man bled out within seconds, the burnished star protruding from his jugular."

"Bloody hell, m'lord. Ye have'na told me about that. I've

never seen one o' those wee men from the East. Sounds like a damned hornet!"

"Aye. A dead hornet. An' as ye can imagine, Freeman was grateful fer my keen eye and quick reflexes. He got up from the table, shook my hand, and said, 'I'm in yer debt. Ye know how it works.' And then he was gone."

"Ye live an exciting life, m'lord, and ye've got bollocks the size of boulders."

I laugh at Ewan's crass metaphor. "Aye...well...If ye don't, yer a dead man, and I prefer not to be that until I'm old and weathered."

"I can'na disagree wi' ye there, sir. So...how do yer bollocks hold up to yer...*eh em*...fiancé? She seems a bit more formidable than the pirate that scared the bloody hell out o' me today."

"Ella Seymour is exactly what I never knew I was looking for. Ye know I can'na tolerate a simpleton, and I knew when the time came to choose a woman to be my wife, it would'na be fer sport nor a contract made to appease anyone other than the two of us. Percy may have expedited the inevitable, but either way, fate has brought me to my perfect mate, and I must tell ye...I'm damned happy about it."

"An' I'm happy fer ye, m'lord, I truly am."

Ewan leaves me to my correspondence, and I spend the next hour writing letters and scheduling appointments for the week to come. I find I rather like this time of solitude, focusing on specific tasks, and getting matters tended to without distraction. Of course, there is always the sound of my quill scratching across the paper and the clink of its point on the glass well as I tap off the excess ink. It's a therapeutic melody that eases away any tension and opens my mind to the plethora of words that can be combined into simple responses, from responding to the letters before me—*Thank you, I'd love to attend*, or *Perhaps we should discuss this in person*—to imagining detailed descriptions of the pleasure I look forward to bringing my bride and putting into verse—*when I taste the sweet evidence of your release; the sensation of your taut nipple between my teeth, and your cry of pleasure as I add more pressure.*

"Pardon me, m'lord," Ewan interrupts my erotic fantasy. "Ah, Lady Ella is here to see ye. Should I bring her in, or would ye like me to escort her to the parlor to wait fer ye there?"

A strange feeling swirls through my gut at the thought of Ella walking through the door while my mind is occupied by visions of her in ecstasy. "What a strange coincidence," I mumble to myself. "She's here alone?"

"Ah, no, sir. She brought her lady's maid as a chaperone. But she has requested to speak wi' ye alone," Ewan explains with trepidation.

"Then, by all means, escort her here."

"Aye, sir."

A few minutes later, she walks through the door, her posture and presence as regal as ever.

"Lady Ella," I say, reaching for her hand as I bow. She offers it, and I hold it longer than is proper. "This surprise is welcome beyond words."

"Why do you do that?" Her terse question spikes my desire.

"Do what?" I feign curiosity

"Bow with my hand to your lips far longer than is required?"

"Because ye smell like something I've been craving fer a thousand years," I tell her honestly.

She doesn't respond right away. The bluntness of my reply seems to have come as a shock to her, but she doesn't realize that I know it is also piquing her desire as well. I can see it in the sudden blackness of her eyes, the subtle opening of her mouth, and the lovely flush of her cheeks. I reach up to gently caress along her jawline and take a few small steps toward her. "The urge to kiss ye is overwhelming. Yer spell seems to become more powerful by the day."

"You want to kiss me?"

"Aye, I do. More than I want to take my next breath."

She moves closer now, wrapping one hand around my waist as the other comes up to cradle my neck. "Then please do."

Without hesitation, my mouth is on hers, and God save me —it is incredible. Her lips are full and soft, yet firm like perfectly ripened fruit—its sweetness ready to be savored. My tongue and lips move around hers, sucking, licking, trying hard not to bite. I can't resist. My teeth scrape across her full bottom lip just before I devour her again.

I pull her to me, needing more. She moans, and the sound of her longing hardens my cock to a full and painful erection.

"Ella," I say, my lips firm against her mouth. "My God. What ye do to me. I can feel yer desire, and I swear to ye..." I pull away. Her lips are wet and red and swollen. My thumb sweeps across her mouth, and I press gently. "Open yer mouth." She does, and I push my thumb inside. "Close yer lips around me..." Before I can tell her to suck, she does it on her own, full lips wrapped around the base, her warm tongue massaging the underside. When her eyes close and her head falls back, her mouth opens and she licks all the way to the tip.

"Christ!" I pull away fast and lean hard against my desk. "Where did ye learn how to do that? Are ye tryin' to kill me?" My chest heaves, breathlessly. When she glances down, eyes widening, I realize my hand has a firm hold on the erection threatening to tear through my breeches. I release my hand and apologize. "I'm sorry. My desire for ye is like nothing I've ever known."

She's still looking at my cock, perfectly outlined behind the thin material. If she doesn't stop, I may release simply from her wanton need that is about to swallow me whole. "I did that to you?" she asks, and I suddenly fear for her virginity.

I groan out a strained "Yes."

"And your thumb...in my mouth. Is that...is that what you want me to do with this?" When she reaches forward to place her delicate hand on my rigid shaft, I damn near explode.

"Ella!" I grab onto her upper arms to hold her at a distance. *Bloody Hell!* Her sensual innocence is more erotic than anything I've ever experienced. I'm using every bit of restraint I can muster not to take her upstairs and teach her everything there is to know about carnal pleasure.

"I'm sorry." Her voice is sad as she pulls away.

"No, no, Ella, do'na be sorry. It is I that should apologize." I stop to bring her closer, tipping her chin up so she can see the truth in my eyes. "You will understand more after we are wed. You'll know that yer touch drives me mad, in a good way, and the pleasure we will share will be like no other."

"Did I hurt you when I touched you there?" Her eyes are glossy with concern.

"God no! The only thing that hurts is making ye stop!" We both smile at the vehemence behind that declaration. "We must do this properly. I will'na dishonor ye, Ella. I do'na ever want ye to have regrets about our marriage. It's bad enough that it has been forced on ye. 'Tis a shame, ye know. I was truly looking forward to charming ye senseless with all my gallantry until ye finally gave in and agreed to be my wife."

I reach down to take her hand in mine. It's cool to the touch, soft. I lift it up to my lips, wanting to kiss the creamy surface. I pause to examine our contrast. Her hand is so small and elegant compared to mine that is battle-scarred and bronzed by the sun. I have a profound and sudden urge to protect her, not just now, but for eternity. I rest my lips on her skin and inhale a slow breath, letting her scent infuse my soul.

"That is what I came to discuss with you." She snaps me out of the fog.

"Oh? Have ye changed yer mind about being my wife?"

"No, I have not. However, my mother insists on a rather large wedding ceremony, and that takes a tremendous amount of planning, which means it takes a great amount of time."

"Aye, it does. But I am sure yer mother has been looking forward to this day since ye were born. I don't believe I'm inclined to take that away from her. After all, I am hoping to be in the good graces of my future mother-in-law."

"How wise of you, and yes, she has been planning for this event my whole life, and if the ceremony is large and traditional, it will look less like a marriage born in scandal." It does not go unnoticed that Ella is becoming somewhat coy during this roundabout explanation.

"I'm afraid I'm missing something here, my dear. Where does the problem lie?"

"I don't want to wait. Though you tend to test my patience with your overblown ego." She stops to raise a brow at me. "I... I like the way you kiss me. I like how my body feels when you're near—when you touch me." Her head drops in shyness. "I've been dreaming about you touching me. And I do not wish to wait any longer." She brings her eyes back to mine, her face flushed with desire.

Bloody fucking hell! My fated mate may end up bringing about my early demise.

"Lady Ella, I will do everything in my power to expedite our wedding *and* appease yer mother's dream of giving ye away properly. But I must be honest; I am suddenly afraid of what ye will do when we are husband and wife, free to test the boundaries of our passion, and ye fully understand the power ye have over me."

"I think it sounds fun," she says with a grin and leans into me with surprising familiarity.

"Aye, it does. But bear in mind, my version of fun will push yer limits beyond anything you knew possible."

ELEVEN

Ella

I t's been two months since I told Alasdair I didn't want to wait to be married. Two months was the best he could do to push things along without offending my mother. If we had waited for her, we would still have to wait another month, possibly more. But we didn't, and here I sit as Lady Ella Stewart, wife of Captain Alasdair Stewart.

Beatrice should be here any minute to help calm my nerves. I can't thank her enough for coming with me to Alasdair's London townhouse. As lovely and spacious as it is, it's not the home I am accustomed to. Having her here makes it seem like everything will be all right now that I am married.

There it is again. That swirl in the middle of my stomach every time I think about walking down the aisle toward Alasdair. He was so striking I had to remind myself to breathe. There he was, a regal air about him, standing proudly before the many that came to witness our union, regardless of how it was forced upon us.

He chose to wear the formal attire of his homeland instead

of his captain's dress uniform. For whatever reason, that struck me as poignant, though I can't say for certain why. Perhaps it is because I had never seen him wear a kilt, only the stylish breeches or pantaloons worn by every man in England, and I suppose the Lowlands of Scotland, as well. Or maybe it was because it reminded me of the vicious cut I left him with when we first met. Was that his way of letting me know he has not forgotten? Or was he showing everyone, especially me, that he is proud of his heritage, of his name, and that neither history nor prejudice will sway his true loyalty? Whatever his reason, he was more stunning than I had ever seen him before, and I must admit, his kilt—patterned in the red tartan of Clan Stewart—was a powerful statement that gave me an unexpected sense of pride.

His cravat and shirt were whiter than freshly fallen snow. They contrasted sharply against the pure black of his tailored vest and jacket that complimented the black thread crosshatching the bright red of the tartan. His hair was neatly pulled to the nape of his neck, eyes glowing against the warm darkness that is his coloring. I felt a jolt of girlish excitement just seeing him standing there, waiting for me.

Before my father and I had started the long, slow walk down the aisle—that poignant transition of leaving the only life I knew to a new one that is completely unknown—he held my hands and told me that he loved me, that he is proud of me, that he knew Alasdair will be a good husband, and that he will miss me more than words can say. We both cried—not so hard that it would be obvious to the crowd that had gathered beyond the ornate doors that kept us hidden, but more than we were able to hide from each other. He wiped away my tears, and I wiped away his. As the music changed, we took our deep breaths and followed the cue to make our way to the altar.

When my father offered my hand to Alasdair, he took it graciously, thanking him with a humble shyness. He stopped then, not caring that we had an audience, and said, "Ella, ye are a bride so lovely, I fear my heart will never be the same. I am a lucky man, and I will'na ever forget it."

After the preacher delivered the numerous prayers and had us repeat our vows, committing ourselves to one another till death do us part, Alasdair asked for permission to say his own vows before family, friends, and God. He turned toward me with a slow smile spreading across his face.

My heartbeat fluttered as he began.

"Handfasting is an age-old tradition in Scotland. 'Tis a simple but meaningful ceremony where a man and woman stand before a holy man, hands held together, wrapped in a sacred cloth, and declare their intention to be wed in exactly one year and a day. When the time finally came, and they found themselves in front o' the preacher again, he would give them a choice: did they want to marry, or did they want to call it off? After all, the couple may have found during that year that they could'na stand each other." Soft laughter echoed around the massive hall. "Since you and I will'na have that choice, I am making a commitment to ye, here in front of God and witnesses." He stops then to get down on one knee, taking both my hands in his, that beautiful face so striking in masculine perfection, eyes blazing with sincerity. "I vow to ye, Ella, that when a year and a day has passed from this day, ye will be happy, and ye will know we've made the right choice. And if I fail ye, an' the sun does'na shine bright in yer heart fer the overbearing Scot ye find yerself married to, yer free to go, an' I will'na stop ye."

His words, the integrity with which he spoke them, and the unfeigned depth of his stare that left no doubt he spoke the truth made my stomach do flips inside me. I knew that Reverend Matthews and my parents were likely in a bit of shock at what Alasdair had just avowed in front of more than a hundred peers, but I could not stop the smile that spread across my own face. The sense of freedom overwhelmed me, but more than anything, I felt gratitude. He knew how much it meant to me to choose my own husband, a privilege stolen from me. But with that one noble statement, pronounced there, of all places, gave me back what I had believed would be mine for as long as I could remember. In doing so, Alasdair stole a little piece of my heart, right there at the altar, on the day we were wed.

"Thank you," I whispered, too emotional to say more.

A light tap on the door startles me away from my thoughts.

"'Tis only me, dearie. How are you feeling?" The tenderness in Beatrice's tone makes me nostalgic for a time far less complicated where I knew who I was and what was expected of me, and everything around me was familiar and comfortable.

"I'm fine. Well, as fine as can be expected," I say with a huff of laughter.

"This is a nerve-wracking evening for all brides, but you're one of the lucky ones. Not only is your husband as handsome as the day is long, but he's also thoughtful of you and your needs, not just his own. The same can't be said for most men."

I smile because she speaks the truth, but also because my nervousness is based more on excitement than fear. "Is it improper of me to be looking forward to consummating my marriage?"

Beatrice's plump form bounces with her laughter. "He is a fine specimen of a man, and after what you described finding in the conservatory, I can't blame you for your eagerness. 'Tis going to be a special night, my dear."

Even through the humor, I can sense the emotion she is experiencing as well. I'm like a daughter to her, and what I experience has an impact on her. The poignancy of it all has put a lump in my throat, but I refuse to let myself cry, especially tonight.

I jump up from my seat and twirl around to show off my nightgown and robe. Mother gave it to me a few days ago when she—very lamely—tried to educate me on my duties in the bedroom. It is the most luxurious silk I have ever felt, thin and smooth and soft like perfectly warm water without the wetness. The color is a soft white, and there is delicate lace trimming along the hem. When I looked at myself in the mirror, I wondered if my mother noticed it is somewhat transparent. The darkness of the tips of my breasts was provocatively apparent. Something about that made me feel more beautiful, the kind of beautiful I want to be tonight.

"You look lovely, Ella. Your husband is receiving a gift tonight, and this gown is a perfect reminder of its purity." With that, she walks over and places her hands on my shoulders, eyes shining bright with emotion, "I love you more than words could ever justify, Ella dear. You have been the light of my life, and my heart is filled with joy and broken all at once. My sweet darling isn't a child anymore, and though it is time to set you free to live as a woman and learn as a woman, it doesn't mean I will not be here whenever and wherever you need me."

"Beatrice! You sound as if you are leaving me. I thought you were going to stay with me as my lady's maid" I grab onto her and hold her to me with all my strength. "Beatrice, are you staying? Please tell me you will stay." My eyes are spilling over.

"Yes, dearie of course. I will always be here for you in whatever capacity you need. But everything changes for you today." She stops to pull away and wipe away the fat tears she is all too familiar with. "You are the lady of your own house now.

You have a husband who needs your attention and homes that need managing. I will be here, but you will be living a different life. And that is alright, it is wonderful—your duty—but it will never be the same as it was before. Your innocence will be gone, and our relationship will change with its passing. Yet, that does not mean I won't miss that sweet little girl or that brazen adolescent or this anxious young woman." Her hands squeeze harder on my arms. "All the stages of your life have made my life more joyful and meaningful than I could have ever wished for. I've had to adjust before, and I will adjust again as you enter this new stage, but for me, it represents a passing of time I wish I could slow down."

Her smile forces the deepening of the wrinkles that fan out from her eyes, a visible reminder that her youth has long passed. "Well, now that I am married, there is a good chance I will be with child soon, and you get to start the whole process over again."

Her eyes pop open, and her mouth forms a perfect circle in surprise. "Lord help me! Let's not get too ahead of ourselves."

We both laugh, happy to shift to more jovial banter.

"Well, dearest, I should leave. Your husband has likely worn a path in his bedchamber floor by now." My hand covers my mouth to hide a giggle. "I will stop there to let him know you are ready."

I hug her tightly one more time, the girl in me not wanting to let go. "Thank you, Beatrice. I love you."

"I love you more, Ella." And she pats my face, her mouth quivering, and quickly turns to leave.

I am suddenly at a loss as to what to do. Should I get in bed and lie down or sit up with pillows stacked behind me? Do I sit at my vanity, brushing my hair with nonchalance? Stand at the foot of the bed, dutifully waiting?

Without thinking, I walk over to the window and pull back

the heavy curtain. I cannot see much in the darkness since my room faces the garden, but the moonlight is sparkling on the surface of the fountain in its center, capturing my attention.

"Is it possible fer ye to be more stunning right now than ye were walking toward me this afternoon? I will hire an artist to paint ye just like this."

My breath is caught in my chest. I try to swallow, but I can't. There is something different in his voice that has my skin tingling. But more importantly, he has entered my room shirtless, wearing only loose pants meant for sleeping. I swear I have never seen anything more spectacular, more appealing, more beautiful than my husband's natural form. *My God!* The desire that has taken over my core is all-consuming, and the only word I can muster is a whispered "Alasdair..."

He walks slowly toward me. I don't even look at his face. I'm too fascinated by the subtle movements of his sinuous body. When he is finally standing directly in front of me, I am lightheaded, my knees weak.

He reaches forward and tips my chin up. "Touch me, Ella. I am yours now. I never want ye to be afraid to touch me."

"I...I don't know what to do."

"Follow yer instincts. Ye have already proven they are quite keen." The smirk that accompanies his comment accentuates that dimple on his cheek.

My trembling hand comes up to touch his chest. The hair is coarse and springy, and I like the way it feels under and between my fingers. But the taut skin over hard muscle is so enticing that my other hand comes up to join the exploration. I notice that his nipples have raised and hardened like mine do whenever he touches me. I know the ache of wanting I experience when it happens, and I wonder if it is the same for him. Bringing my thumbs down to rub them around his hard pebbles, I get the answer I was looking for.

"Christ, woman! Yer curiosity will be the death of me," he says on a harsh inhale.

"Does that feel good?"

"God, yes, it feels good!"

His answer pleases me. Pulling my robe to the side, I look down to see my own nipples protruding harshly through the thin material. "I want you to do it to mine."

When I look up at him to make sure my request is acceptable, I find the eyes of a hungry beast, nostrils flared, a signal he is ready to pounce.

"Give me this," he commands as his warm fingers come up to pull my lip from between my teeth. Once again, I didn't even know I was biting it, distracted as I was. He brings me close, arms wrapped around me, mouth almost touching mine. "You and I are going to have a verra blissful marriage." Then he devours my lips and tongue with his own, and I become lost in the barrage of sensations that have me wanting to beg for more.

The kiss goes on, just as I had hoped it would. From the first time he kissed me this way—in the garden after he saved me from Lord Percy's attack—I have craved it. We managed to sneak a few more in, here and there, before our wedding, but then he wasn't standing before me shirtless and ready to take my virginity as my husband. That knowledge alone has taken my desire to new heights.

As his hand lands firmly on my hip and slowly glides its way up my side, pausing at the heavy weight of my full breast, I fear I will lose my ability to breathe altogether. But when the palm of his hand moves over my nipple and circles firmly, then takes it between his thumb and finger, a warm wetness releases between my legs, and my knees give way.

His firm hold keeps me floating against his body and free to focus on the combination of his strength, his ravaging kiss, and his masterful hand building the same unbearable pressure in my most sensitive and private place as the first time I saw him hidden in the darkness of the conservatory.

Without warning, he pulls away, breathing heavily and still holding me upright.

"Ella." His breath is hard against my face. "We must slow down. I do'na want yer first release by my hand to be wi' ye standing here after only a few minutes of kissing." He cradles the side of my face, his thumb gently massaging. "Let me see those beautiful eyes." He draws up my shy attention. "Tonight, is about you. Yer pleasure is my highest priority."

He guides me toward the bed. The room is large, so it takes several paces before we stop at its side, enough time for me to regain some of my composure. Intimacy with Alasdair Stewart is like a drug, and my mind can only imagine where this night —and our marriage—will lead.

We kiss again because it seems that neither of us can do otherwise. When the tempo of our passion slows enough for him to speak, he gives me a polite warning. "I'm going to undress ye now. I want to see my wife the way God created her." He kisses my lips gently as he slips the robe from my shoulders, my gasp catching his attention. "What is it?"

"I just... it felt different, the robe gliding across my skin."

"Was it arousing?"

"Very much so." I laugh in response.

"Good." His voice goes low as his accent thickens. "'Tis what I want to hear." The rolling of the R vibrates down my spine.

He takes the time to gently caress my shoulders before untying each of the laces holding up my gown. It falls down my body in a wistful flow that washes me in a cool draft, landing at my feet in an elegant puddle of shiny white silk. I stare at it, wondering at all it represents, then say a silent goodbye to my former self—to my innocence.

"Ella." Alasdair's voice is gruff with emotion. "I have'na ever laid my eyes upon anything more lovely than you right now at this moment. I need ye to know that is the truth. It is no exaggeration that ye are a work of art, a true masterpiece."

No expensive gown, no fancy piece of jewelry, no fashionable adornment has ever made me feel more beautiful than the look in Alasdair's eyes as he gazes upon my naked body. His desire for me is undeniable, and through it, I feel my sensuality blossom.

"Thank you," my ingrained propriety replies.

"Ye are most welcome, Lady Stewart. But I am the one that should be thanking you." He pulls me back to him again and kisses me with a different kind of hunger. Instinctively I know what he wants, though it is nothing I have ever given myself the liberty of contemplating.

"Lie down."

I do, then spread my legs, hoping he will focus his attention on the aching pulse that is begging to be brought to the surface. Of its own volition, my hand roams across my slick surface, pausing to rub that sensitive nub I have only become familiar with since my introduction to this man.

"Don't stop. 'Tis a beautiful sight to see ye pleasure yerself."

He moves to the bed, leaning over to place his hands on either side of my waist, the mattress dipping from his weight. He kisses along my hip, teeth scraping with gentle pressure. "Tell me, Ella. Have ye done this before, touched yerself this way while ye thought about me doing this?" His mouth opens wider as he sucks my tender skin just next to my hipbone, his deep moan vibrating through my lower body.

My back arches as I try to respond. "Yes, Alasdair."

"And were ye able to fully release?"

"No," I reply, forcing myself not to beg him to make it happen.

He kisses his way up my side toward my breasts. Once there, he drops to his elbows, his massive body pushing my legs wider apart, leaving little room for me to continue massaging myself. Both of his large hands come up to grab hold of either breast, and the heat returns as more wetness leaks from my core.

"I think I must have been a verra good man in a previous life fer God to have gifted me a wife wi' mounds on her chest such as these. I have dreamt of having them in my hands, in my mouth, since we first met."

He smiles at me, bringing his tongue to my hard tip to play with it before sucking it deep into his mouth. I cry out as the throbbing under my hand becomes too much.

"Alasdair!" I need more. Now.

"Dip yer fingers into yer wetness. Then bring it up to my mouth."

I do as he says, though I am shocked at the request.

My fingers are shiny as I sweep them against his full lips, but when he opens and takes them across his warm tongue, sucking as I did with his thumb so many weeks ago, I feel the dam beginning to break.

He pulls away quickly, bringing himself completely upright onto his knees, his glorious naked body on full display, hard erection jutting out from the dark patch of hair.

My God! How is this real?

When he strokes his rigid cock once, then twice, I know I am about to release. My husband looks at me then, stating in a hurried growl, "I'm going to make ye cum now, Ella." Then he takes my hand away, drops down, and devours me with his hot mouth.

The pulsing pleasure shoots through me with such

intensity I scream aloud, my hips pumping toward his face as he draws out my climax, forcing it to become stronger and stronger.

Hands gripping the sheets, I fall into the abyss and let Alasdair lead the way.

TWELVE

Alasdair

T he sounds she's making are almost as delicious as the taste of her release. I slow the pace of my tongue, wanting to leave some of this orgasm intact so my entry is less painful. I don't want her to focus on any potential discomfort, only the fullness I know she craves. My beautiful wife doesn't realize her next climax will far exceed this one.

I glance up from my position to gaze across the softness of her abdomen to the abundant mounds of her breasts; hard nipples raised high. Dear God! She is magnificent with her head thrown back as she calls my name, her beautiful throat exposed and begging to be marked.

I flatten my tongue and slowly lick up the full length of her, ending with a delicate flutter on her swollen clit. I am rewarded with the throaty sound of another moan, its vibration music to my ears. She lifts her hips when I stop, an involuntary display of her natural desire and sensuality. Tonight, is an exercise in self-control, as my own desire has me wanting to drive into her hard and fast as I devour her screams through my kiss.

"Ella," I breathe as I lick my way up her body. "Are ye ready? I want to be sure that ye are—that yer ready for me to truly make ye my wife." I finish by taking her erect nipple between my teeth and sucking it up into my mouth, where my tongue massages its tip.

"Alasdair! Please...please...I need more! My God, I need more!" she begs as her hips press up against me.

I release her nipple and taste her neck, selfishly marking her, though low enough to remain hidden from society, driving her closer to the edge before fully taking her mouth in an all-consuming kiss that borders on violent.

My hardness presses against her entrance, and she pushes toward me again.

"Ye are mine now, Ella," I say against her mouth as I enter her in one fantastic thrust that blurs my vision and ignites both familiar and unfamiliar feelings of possession and belonging and a need to protect I didn't know existed within my selfish soul. I thrust hard again as I hear her scream my name. I know I should be more careful; I felt the tension of her maidenhead break and wonder how painful it had been. But I swear she is about to climax, so I continue driving into her as she wraps herself around me, legs held tightly around my waist, arms locked as she scratches my skin and pulls my hair.

"Alasdair! Oh God! Alasdair!"

She's up on one elbow now, the other locked around my neck bringing her back up off the bed as she pushes her hips toward my pounding thrusts. She's cumming hard around me, kissing me with such hunger and ferocity that it reaches down like warm, sensuous tentacles, wrapping around my heart.

An intense flash of light overtakes my vision.

I am suddenly thrust into the forest. The damp coolness in the air is heavy on my skin, infused with the green scent of nature.

137

I can hear my footsteps along the path on which I am walking. I am looking for someone—someone special. Through the sounds of shifting leaves, distant birdsong, and the crunching of gravel and debris beneath my feet, I hear singing floating toward me on the breeze. It's her! I pick up my pace and run toward the sound. When I exit the shade of the forest canopy, the sun is shining brightly along the shoreline, and I squint my eyes in the sudden light. The singing is clearer now, and I can see her, beautiful even from this distance, pale blonde hair sparkling in the light. She is sitting by the water's edge, washing something in a methodical, almost rhythmic fashion. As I get closer, her beautiful song surrounds me, her voice angelic in its perfect pitch, ethereal in its unique tone. I pause to watch her for a moment and realize she is washing in time with her music. At closer inspection, I see it is a long piece of fabric, freshly dyed dark blue—she is rinsing it clean as it changes the surrounding water to an unusual shade of dark green. I take a few steps closer, wanting to see her face. I've caught her attention, and she stops singing, turning toward me. My heart stops as I gaze at her. It's the same stunning beauty of my wife, but different somehow. Her face lights up with a smile that stops time, and she says, "Well, hello again!"

Another flash...and I am back with Ella, driving hard into her as she throws her head back in ecstasy. I pull her to me as my orgasm explodes inside her, growling out her name and latching onto her neck as an indescribable feeling comes over me. It is primal, animalistic as if the strength of an ancient god has possessed my soul.

As my climax ebbs to a slow pulse, gooseflesh raises the hairs on my arms, creeping its way up my back and neck. This was no ordinary coupling, no simple consummation. This was the reuniting of two souls whose eternal destiny will not be denied. The power of fate has proven itself to be almighty. I have a sudden and profound urge to tell her that I love her, but my conscious mind says it is too soon.

"Ella." The sharp exhale lifts the hair next to her temple. "Are ye alright?" She is limp in my arms, eyes closed, but the corner of her mouth lifts, speaking a thousand unspoken words. I rest my lips against the subtle smile and say, "I'll take that as a yes." Her full mouth stretches wide beneath mine before I roll onto my back, taking her with me. That glorious smile is now beaming down at me, a curtain of shimmering hair tickling my chest as she straddles my waist.

"You can most assuredly take that as a yes, Alasdair." Her smile disappears as she gazes upon me with something new in her eyes. It tightens my chest, and I'm suddenly desperate to know what she is thinking. "I had no idea...no idea it could be like that. It felt..." Her eyes turn away in shyness.

"Tell me, Ella. I want to hear ye say it. I want to know if I pleased ye as well as I had hoped to."

"Everything felt so good. Even looking at you made my insides tingle." Her fingers dig into my skin, just slightly. "But the building of pressure—it was almost unbearable at times." She pauses to run her fingers through the hair on my chest. "But then, when it finally came to the surface, it literally exploded with a pulsating sensation that made me feel like...like I was coming undone, but with pleasure and not pain."

I can feel myself getting hard again. Bloody hell, that was a fantastic description. "Aye. 'Tis exactly what I want to hear. And yer eloquence adds to it quite nicely." I can't resist raising my hips to press my stiffening shaft against her round arse.

"Oh!" she exclaims through a shy giggle. "Are we to do it again?"

Reaching up to caress the soft skin of her cheek, my hand glides into her golden tresses. I wrap it around, tugging ever so gently. "Aye, we are...and frequently, but not just yet. Come lie against me, lass. Ye need to rest, and I canna' express how badly I've wanted to simply have ye naked in my arms."

A deep moan escapes as she tucks herself next to me, her head on my chest, one leg draped over mine as if she'd done it a thousand times before. "Can I tell you something?" Her breath is warm across my skin.

"Of course. Ye always have a voice wi' me, Ella." I want to know every thought in her magnificent mind. I can't imagine snuffing out such brilliance, such curiosity. I swear every word she speaks inspires me to write, to create, to memorialize everything about her into something tangible that will stand the test of time and pique the imagination of the fortunate souls that read my prose many generations into the future.

Her hand is roaming the terrain of my abdomen and chest. Every so often, her fingers stop to swirl through the thick hair above my cock, the simple, innocent motion making my breath halt in my throat. "I've wanted this, too. To lie like this, touching your beautiful body without so many layers between us. Skin to skin, the scent of you surrounding me." She pauses then to shift so that her chin rests atop her hands as they lay flat over my tight nipple. She's disheveled in the most beguiling way as she continues, "Do you realize how good you smell? It's been somewhat maddening to me since first we met. It's quite distracting, I'll have you know."

My God, how will I ever get enough of her? I'm suddenly at a loss for words as my mind conjures up all the ways I can devour her; her kisses, her skin, her wetness, the air she breathes. "Ella, there is nothing that compares to the hypnotic scent that follows ye everywhere ye go, yet after tonight, after I have smelled and tasted yer sweet cunny, I know fer certain we were made fer each other." With that declaration, her expression shifts from playful to yearning as her leg comes further up and over mine. "Did ye just press yerself against me, my little faerie bride?"

"Yes." Her reply is a heavy whisper. Then she does it again.

"Ye like what I said, don't ye, Ella?" I dropped the tenor of my voice to test how well its command will be received. Will she become aroused or defensive? The darkening of her eyes confirms my suspicions. My bride is going to enjoy learning the art of letting go, of allowing me to control her pleasure so that I can bring forth its full potential.

"Yes." Her right hand moves to continue its perusal.

"Ye want me to say things that aren't proper. Ye like it when I talk dirty." It wasn't a question. But she answers anyway.

"I think so."

"Press into me again." Her hand tightens on my side as she does my bidding adding leverage for extra pressure. "Do it again, but this time watch my cock when ye do it. Watch how ye make me swell."

I can hear the hitch of her inhale as the blood fills the veins of my shaft, a simple example of the power she has over me. Another push of her hips against my thigh, and I have a full cock-stand, ready to please her.

"Alasdair." She doesn't say more, though I know she wants to.

"Take it in yer hand, Ella. Explore my body. I never want ye to be ashamed o' yer desires. Ye are a verra sensual woman...et's beautiful." My accent has thickened along with my cock. I try to offer more encouragement but choke on my words as her delicate hand wraps around me and hesitantly moves up then down. *Dear God!*

"Like this?" Why does that innocent question make my heart and my manhood feel as if they will both explode?

"Aye. Like that," I struggle to answer coherently.

She continues to stroke up and down, testing the strength of her grip, squeezing tighter and then loosening so her fingers can play around the head. When I tear my gaze away from her unwittingly deft masturbation of my shaft to look at her face, I almost lose control and ejaculate all over both of us. She is completely aroused by the effect she has on me, enthralled by the control she wields. What a gift this is, to literally watch this magnificent woman's power blossom, her confidence, and sensuality, her curiosity and desire, each one like a delicate petal, slowly opening to create the most bewitching flower known to man.

"Alasdair," she whispers again.

"Tell me what ye want, Ella. I know et's there. I can see et on yer face." The words roll out, unrefined, deep and commanding, yet strained with desire.

She explores a little longer, then turns her gorgeous eyes to me and asks, "Do you want me to put my mouth on it like you did to me?"

God help me!

"The question is, do *you* want to put yer mouth on it?"

"Yes." Her reply is a heavy whisper as her eyes lose contact with mine. "But...I don't know what to do. I...I want to please you the way you pleased me."

"Give me yer eyes, Ella." She does without hesitation. "I am presently more pleased than I have ever been in my entire life. So do'na worry yerself over that. Remember what I told ye before. Follow yer instincts, and you'll do just fine." At this point, I'm more concerned about my composure than I am hers.

"Alright." She agrees and moves to position herself between my legs.

"Here, let me move to the edge o' the bed. T'will be more comfortable fer ye." She slides down until her feet hit the rug.

"On yer knees." My cock swells with the command. She is so bloody beautiful right now. Creamy skin and full breasts, nipples tight with expectation, eyes wide with curiosity, yet glazed with arousal, full lips parted with wanton need.

She reaches up, taking me in her delicate hand again. Stroking up and down, studying her subject, learning from the reactions she induces. Then, as I notice the corner of her mouth lift in an almost triumphant smirk, she leans forward and takes the head into her mouth, warm and wet, and damn near too much for my determined resolve.

"Christ! That feels good, Ella."

She likes the compliment, and she takes more of me in. Hand at the base, she's fully moving her head up and down, letting me go deeper and deeper as she adjusts. Fuck! I don't know how long I will last.

"Yer mouth is perfect. Ye look so damn beautiful right now, Ella." She starts moving her hand in time with her mouth, spreading the wetness along my full length. "That's et, my love." I bite down as I fight against the tightening in my stomach. I'm about to lose the battle when she loses her rhythm and pulls back to take a breath. My breath halts in my chest. She is the most alluring woman I have ever seen, on her knees, mussed hair, swollen mouth, hand still stroking my erection. She is reveling in her desire, the power of that desire that *she* has over me. It is an exquisite example of feminine sensuality.

"Ye like this, don't ye?" I move my hand down to join hers.

"Yes," she replies as her eyes follow my movements.

"You could make me climax like this. Is that what you want?"

Her features soften. "Yes, Alasdair."

"Then do it."

She lowers her mouth to me again, this time taking a

moment to fondle me with her lips and tongue. Her eyes shut as she opens and closes her mouth, erotically kissing the head, letting her tongue come out to lick around the hard ridge and slide down the sensitive underside. Good God! This woman's instincts! I always thought this act was a learned technique. But Ella, my beautiful wife, has an innate gift that goes well beyond her natural sensuality.

She's enjoying herself. But when she starts taking me deeper, I see her hips start to rock back and forth, and then she moans.

God...damn...

I don't have time to warn her before the simmering pulse I'd kept at bay breaks free in an explosive orgasm that releases with such force, I fear it might choke her. Quickly pulling it out, I aim it down toward her breasts and watch as the remaining essence pumps out and across her full mounds.

I make a strangled sound as the intensity starts to ebb. Good God! What just happened? I haven't lost control of myself since I was a lad. When I look up from the unholy mess I made on my wife's bosom, I see her licking her lips and wiping her chin with a slender finger.

"Did ye swallow it?"

"Yes. Was I not supposed to?"

I almost laugh as her expression says she would have done it anyway. "There is no right or wrong. It's whatever you prefer."

She looks down at her chest and runs the same tainted finger through the spew I marked her with. "I like both."

She looks as if she's taken a dram of laudanum with that black-eyed daze and subtle sway in each direction.

"Come here, love." I take her hands and lift her to stand with me. I use my foot to quickly lift my pants off the floor and clean her chest, then pull her to me. I kiss her softly, then turn around to gently lift her onto the bed. "Lie back, relax, and spread yer legs. Ye need to release after that, aye?"

"Yes, please, Alasdair." Her back arches with the reply.

"Good. This won't take long. Then ye can rest."

I lean down to kiss her swollen cunt and see it gently pulsing, tightening, then relaxing, her lubrication flowing with each contraction. I could simply blow on her clit and make her cum, but she deserves more than that, and I'm far too greedy. I suck on the inside of her thigh as I spread her lips and push two fingers in. I feel her tighten as she cries out my name. My tongue moves down to play with her clit while she rocks her hips harder toward me. The wet sound of my fingers fucking her is testing my will to let her rest and not keep her up for the next two hours, gallantry be damned.

I tamp down my greed and stand upright to watch as she comes undone.

Just as her canal tightens, I curl my fingers up to rub along her firm ridge as my other thumb puts pressure on her sensitive nub. Her climax immediately erupts, turning to clear liquid in my hand.

Bloody fantastic!

It's hard to believe that Ella was a virgin when this night began. Her eager willingness is like that of a worldly woman. But then I think about the night she snuck up on me in the garden. I knew then there was a connection that could not be easily explained; after tonight, I understand that connection more clearly.

I move up onto the bed and pull her to me, holding her in my arms. She curls into me, humming a contented sigh. Before I can tell her goodnight, she's fast asleep, so I kiss her forehead, pausing to breathe in the luxury of her scent. As I relax further into the mattress, surrounded by soft pillows and blankets, my lovely bride asleep in my arms, my grandmother's words echo in my mind, "There is another that seeks to find ye."

Chills rise on my skin like they did when first Nanna told me. Yet, this time, there is another reason. My thoughts go to the vision I had and the young woman sitting by the water, whose smile reminded me of Ella's. She seemed to glow with her pale coloring and bright eyes, her song like that of an angel, penetrating deep into my soul. She was familiar in a way that made my chest hurt, leaving me with a sense of urgency, of yearning. *Who was she?* It is likely I will never know for certain. But as I let my imagination ponder the possibilities, an immense sense of joy blankets me in comforting warmth.

She found me.

THIRTEEN

Ella

I can hear Mary excitedly making her way down the hall to my new bedchamber. A minute later, the door flies open. "Ella!" She's almost out of breath, "This place is brilliant!" She stops to take in the opulence of my room, slowly turning in a full circle, mouth agape.

I smile to myself, thinking my reaction was the same. It is nothing less than spectacular. Pale blue wainscoting adorns the walls halfway up around its entirety. Everything above that, including the ceiling, is a hand-painted mural that starts with the leaves and stems and blooms of various native blue flowers: delphinium, morning glory, blue poppy, and an occasional cluster of wildflowers. Just before the ornate crown molding at the ceiling, the scene takes the natural progression to a blue sky, wispy clouds, and birds are playfully flying about. It is reminiscent of a perfect spring day. No matter the circumstances of a previous day, I doubt there will be a morning when I wake in this room and find my mood to be sour. If only we were living here, at Alasdair's London townhouse, for more than a few months of the year.

"This mural is fantastic!" Mary says, head titled back to admire the clouds and birds and the yellow glow of sunshine that fills the entire ceiling. "This must have cost a bloody fortune."

"Mary!" I admonish.

"What? I only speak the truth."

"Yes, you do. But with the tongue of an ill-mannered scamp."

"Oh Ella, don't be so dramatic. And besides, when have you ever known a scamp to be mannered?" Her inquisitive expression makes me laugh out loud.

"Come here, look at this." I walk over to the wall by my dressing table and point at a cluster of leaves. "The artist added little caterpillars and ladybugs. Then over here is a butterfly." I look around the expanse of my chamber and gesture with my hand, "I may never find all the treasures hidden in her work." I turn to Mary and smile, the notion of a lifelong treasure hunt lighting a spark of happiness.

"Well, look at you." She pauses with her hands on her hips as if noticing me for the first time. "Somehow, I doubt that glow on your face has much to do with the little creatures hidden in this mural. I want all the details of the *dreaded consummation*." Her voice lowers in theatrical doom, and we both laugh at her silliness.

"Mary Elizabeth, you know we aren't to discuss those things. It isn't proper!" I respond automatically, knowing full well that I want to tell her everything about the most wonderful night of my life. I simply can't, though. I fear even Mary would be scandalized by what I did.

"Ella, dear, are we to be in our sixth decade before you realize I don't care about what is *proper*? My curiosity is too preoccupied with all that is *improper*."

I have to turn my eyes away from hers. She has a way of

pulling information out of me with just a raised brow and tilted head.

"All I can tell you is that it was far better than I expected. So much so, I blushed when he bid me good morning, and I could barely make eye contact at breakfast though my eyes yearned to stare at him, and my voice yearned to beg him to do it again."

Mary's eyes are round. "You wanted him to do it again?" She knows that for me to divulge that much information, it must have been exceptional. "Oh, please set aside your prudish upbringing and tell me everything! How am I ever to know what the possibilities are, should I be so fortunate to marry a man who knows how to perform as apparently, *your* husband does?" She pauses in thought. "You know, we should be allowed to—how should I say this—put our suitors to the test. Try them on for size, per se."

We both cover our mouths at the same time as the bubbles of laughter overflow. A few minutes later, Mary elaborates on her ridiculous idea. "Can you imagine? 'Lord Stanbury, might you remove your breeches so that I may see your tallywag?'" I must sit down because I'm laughing so hard as she acts out her interview with shameless exaggeration. "'Hmmm...I'm not entirely sure I like the looks of that. Next!'" She can't hold back the giggles as she pretends to wait for her next victim. "Ah, the Earl of Weston."

"No, no, no!" I protest. "Not the Earl of Weston! I simply cannot have that vision in my head."

"Yes. You're right. He probably hasn't even seen his *thing* since 1765! He is apparently more interested in food and wine than he is in creating an heir to the earldom. The poor fellow is going to have to pass it on to a distant cousin, so I hear."

Still laughing, not only at her jesting but the fact that Mary manages to know everyone else's business. "What about

Graham Knightly? He's not titled, but he is very handsome and very wealthy," I say.

"Ah yes, Graham Knightly. He is a striking figure indeed. Even his name is appealing! I cannot deny a daydream or two about him, and if I were allowed to try him in for size, I wouldn't hesitate for a second! However, let us not forget that title is more important than money, according to my mother, that is. And, as we know all too well, *she* is the one making all the decisions here." Mary sits down, rather ungracefully, and sighs. If ever there was a woman that should choose her own husband, it's Mary. Her mind, wit, and beauty are too powerful and too unique to be handed off to someone who won't fully appreciate her.

A sudden knock on the door echoes through the room and startles us both. There is only one person in the house that could command such attention with a simple knock. My heart beats faster in my chest as I await my husband's entry.

"Come in."

The door opens, and I hear Mary whisper, "Oh my."

As always, he is impeccably dressed, a model of masculine appeal. Face freshly shaved, hair pulled back, dark and shiny, bright ocean eyes glowing against tanned skin complemented by a perfectly tailored dark emerald-green jacket, polished knee-high brown boots, and pale breeches that show the full definition of his strong legs. Legs that draw my eyes upward to the bulge that reminds me of last night, then cause heat to flush through my body and involuntarily make me tighten and release as subtle pleasure pulsates between my legs.

"Ladies," I hear him say as I bring my eyes up to his.

"Hello, Alasdair." I see Mary snap her head toward me and realize my voice must have sounded strange to her, too. I didn't mean for it to come out that way.

"Lord Stewart, it is nice to see you again," Mary says.

Standing up, she offers a polite curtsy and her hand. "The ceremony was quite lovely yesterday. I must be honest, your little handfasting speech got me all teared up."

Alasdair releases her hand, then reaches for mine. "Hello, my dear," he says with a smile before responding, "Thank you, Lady Mary. I rather enjoyed giving that little speech."

"Yes, I'm sure you did. Although I'm not certain Reverend Matthews enjoyed hearing it, but that's neither here nor there. Isn't that right, Ella?"

"Isn't what right?" I'm not certain what Mary just said. All of my attention is directed toward my husband as I contemplate if I will ever tire of looking at him.

"It's of no mind, dear," he replies and winks at Mary. "I came to let ye know we are almost ready to travel. We have two carriages, one packed with yer belongings, and the other is for us."

"Oh. I thought I was to ride Willow, and you are riding Magni."

"Ye are correct. But we will not be riding them fer the entire journey, 'tis too long. They will need to rest and can do so in the horse trailer. Furthermore, we need a comfortable place to travel when the weather is unfavorable."

A wave of sadness comes over me at the reality of leaving my home, family, and friends. It must have been obvious as Mary tries to lighten the mood.

"Cheer up, Ella. At least Galloway Castle isn't located in the Highlands."

Alasdair laughs, exposing that beguiling dimple that contradicts the sharp lines of his face. "Aye. Ye could add a fortnight to the journey, maybe more. Fortunately, we'll only endure half that if all goes well."

An entire week traveling with strangers to a land that is as unfamiliar as they are—I do wish Beatrice was joining us, but she and Rupert must settle things here first and won't be arriving for a few months. Alasdair has assured me that they will have a lovely home of their own not far from the manor. That Rupert will have land to grow crops and a workshop to build furniture and cabinetry. Knowing I will have them there, living a normal life, makes the suddenness of our leaving a little easier to bear. Saying goodbye to my parents is something my mind has avoided since Alasdair informed me that we must make haste to Scotland as he has gotten word that his father's health has taken a turn for the worse.

"We shall make it an adventure, isn't that right, husband?" I cheerfully ask, trying to change the subject in my head.

"I detect a challenge in that question, dear wife. Ye aren't plannin' to race me to the Firth o' Clyde, are ye? I've seen ye ride, and I'm no' ashamed to tell ye you'll likely win."

"Don't tell Magni that. You'll hurt his pride."

"No, he and I have already discussed it. Don't forget, Magni was there that day. He thinks Willow has invisible wings."

Alasdair and I both laugh before Mary chimes in, "You've seen Ella riding her secret course? Even I haven't witnessed that. I was starting to believe it was a myth."

"Oh, aye, I have. And it's a sight to behold. Yer cousin rides better than any man I've ever seen." He turns to me then. "I think you and Willow are going to be verra pleased wi' yer new home. The land surrounding us is quite spectacular. It'll be hard to decide which trail ye want to ride, and I can already think of two places that would make excellent challenge courses."

The look in his eyes is so tender, so sincere like he truly knows how much that means to me and how happy it will make me, that it will drown out some of my sadness. That's when it hits me, that sudden shift inside me, deep within my chest. A tickle, maybe tension, an expansion of powerful emotion, a swirling of something I've never felt. I fear I know what it is, but it's far too soon for that. Mother always said it is foolish to have high expectations for love. It doesn't come easily, if it ever does at all. *Don't be naïve about your feelings, Ella. They can make a fool out of you, and that is never acceptable.* I shut down my emotions before I get carried away.

"Thank you, Alasdair." I don't say more because I'm too distracted. I haven't even been married a full day—how could I possibly have emotions that should take years to establish? I turn to look out the window, wishing I were alone. I suddenly feel naive and immature like my inexperience is making me vulnerable, making me a fool. There is no way Alasdair feels that way about me. He has too much experience to misinterpret his emotions.

"Aye." He pauses to wait for me to look at him. When I do, the look of concern I see there constricts my stomach. "I will leave you ladies to finish yer goodbyes. We are scheduled to leave at one o'clock. I will have the carriage ready for ye shortly so that ye may go and bid yer parents farewell." With that, he offers a polite bow and walks out of the room.

I turn back toward the window again and wait for Mary to interrogate me. She doesn't waste a second.

"What just happened there? Everything was sweet between the two of you, and then suddenly, you turn sour. Did I miss something?" Mary is genuinely confused, and frankly, so am I.

"I'm fine, Mary. Really, I am."

"No, you're not. Spill it, right now. I'll not have you leaving me here worried sick about your happiness." She sits down next to me and waits.

"I don't know what has happened. But I have only been married a day. I barely know him, and...*ugh!*"

"Take your time, dear. Just say what is on your mind

without all this angst. Surely it isn't all that bad. For heaven's sake, look at your husband! I will be honest; the envy I have for you is worthy of a whole sermon by Reverend Matthews." At that declaration, I throw my head back and laugh.

"Thank you for your honesty, Mary. The truth is, he stirs something in me that I don't recognize. I *become* someone I don't recognize when he is near. And...and..." Why am I so flustered now? I don't even know what I'm trying to say, and I'm getting ready to leave with this man, to Scotland of all places, to live with him as his wife. After last night, I should be ecstatic, but that isn't what has me suddenly so insecure.

"I'm sure you don't want to hear this because I do remember a time not so long ago—as in barely two months ago—that you despised Lord Stewart for even existing."

"Get to the point, Mary."

"You're in love with your husband."

"No, I am not!"

"Yes, you are. I could see it when he walked in the room."

"Well, you're wrong. I've only been married a day. It takes time for those sorts of emotions to develop."

Mary laughs before responding. "Says your mother! Listen, dear, love doesn't have a schedule or a timeline. You could fall in love with a person upon a first meeting and certainly within a day."

"That is preposterous, Mary Elizabeth."

"Hmm, the use of my middle name says otherwise." Her retort accompanies a sly smirk. "And the fact that you still won't tell me the details of your introduction to Lord Stewart tells me there is far more between the two of you than you are willing to admit." Thankfully, she doesn't press that subject. Reaching over to take my hand, she finishes, "Ella, if you are in love with your husband, it honestly eases my mind. It makes me happy to know that you will be happy in your new life. We can write to each other all the time, and you can brighten my days with stories of your loving marriage. You know how much I love romance. I still read Mr. Burns at least once a day. *Oh, my love is like a red, red rose that's newly sprung in June / Oh, my love is like a melody that's sweetly played in tune...*"

"You do know that it is written with a rather pronounced brogue, don't you? I believe that's what made it so popular."

"Yes, of course I know that! And I've tried to read it the way it was intended, and I simply sound ridiculous. Therefore, I don't do it. The words are still just as lovely in proper English."

"Indeed." I don't say more as I look down at my hands fiddling with the lace of my gown.

"What is it?" Mary asks.

"I'm going to live in Scotland now, and I fear being a complete outsider; the only person to speak with a proper English accent. What if nobody likes me?" My head drops as my throat tightens with emotion.

"Ella, don't do that to yourself. I happen to know how endearing you are, so stop giving yourself more reasons to be sad. Truth be known, Galloway Castle will never be the same after you enchant it with your charm. Everyone will love you, not to mention every deer, rabbit, bird, and butterfly within thirty kilometers will likely be there to greet you for the sunrise every day!"

To that facetious comment, we both laugh as I think about how grateful I am to have such a wonderful friend. "I'm going to miss you so much, Mary."

"Well, I've already cried enough tears over you leaving, so please don't get me started again. I will be up to visit before you know it, and maybe I'll finally find a man I want to marry. And when I do, he and Alasdair will become fast friends, and we can all live happily ever after!"

"That sounds perfect! Now I have something to look forward to."

I don't let Mary see the tear that slipped away as we hug farewell. I don't say more about my feelings for Alasdair and how they scare me. I simply let her know that everything will be fine, and in my heart, I can only pray it will be so.

FOURTEEN

Alasdair

"Ewan, finish packing, so there are no delays. I want to leave at precisely one o'clock," I say, impatiently pulling out my pocket watch.

"Aye, sir. But, if ye don't mind me askin', why the sudden change in yer demeanor? Not an hour ago, ye were hummin' happy tunes from the homeland like a wee lad who just got his first kiss. Now yer acting as if ye whacked yer thumb wi' a bloody hammer."

I stop my pacing and turn to him. The questioning look on his face should make me laugh, but Ella's sudden change in mood earlier today has me on edge, unwilling to even crack a smile.

"I apologize. I did'na mean to be so curt. I'm concerned about my father, I've got a full week of travel ahead o' me, I am now a married man, and my lovely wife has turned from a starry-eyed lass to an uninterested snob. I honestly don't know what happened. She seemed damned well pleased to see me when I entered her chamber earlier, but it all turned off when I told her of all the riding trails she and Willow would enjoy at

Galloway and that she'd even have a few places to set up challenge courses. One would think that would make her happy." I finish my rant with my arms thrown into the air as I restart the pacing that has taken over my life.

"Oh, I see. So, it's easy fer me to assume Lady Stewart enjoyed her first evenin' as yer wife, am I correct?"

"Aye. Verra' much so."

"Weel, I doubt she was expectin' whatever it was ye gave her, and it's easy fer the lasses to attach affection to pleasure. In certain situations, that can complicate things. But here, the will o' yer bride will'na be swayed wi'out a fight."

"What the bloody hell are ye trying to say, Ewan? Yer damned philosophy comes out in riddles sometimes, ye know?"

"'Tis true, m'lord. I can'na disagree. What I'm trying to say is yer wife will'na be the first one professin' her love. She'll be guardin' that wee trinket wi' her life."

"So yer saying Ella has fallen in love with me?" For a brief moment, I imagine her saying the words and meaning them. My heart beats faster as a sense of joy and comfort comes over me. The feeling reminds me of the vision I had last night of the young woman by the water's edge. I have a sudden urge to see Ella, to be near her, to reassure myself that everything is alright. Perhaps read her through the eyes of a poet, not of a skeptic.

"Oh, aye. She likely has been long before now. She's only just now realizing it."

Why does that make me so profoundly happy?

"You, on the other hand, fell in love wi' her the first night ye found her sneakin' around the garden."

My head snaps toward him, brows drawn as I disagree. "I beg yer pardon, Ewan. I think yer getting ahead of yerself."

"No. I'm not. These things are easy to see from the outside lookin' in, m'lord. But do'na fash yerself. Ye married her yesterday. Think o' all the unlucky bastards of yer ilk that had no say-so in who they marry and ended up wi' some beastly-looking lass wi' bad teeth and smelly parts."

"Bloody Christ, Ewan! I'll stick wi' being in love wi' my wife if ye promise to go no further."

"I'm only speaking the truth. Did ye see yer neighbor, the viscount's wife? One o' the staff said it was an arranged marriage. Poor fella did'na have a choice. 'Tis a curious thing, m'lord, because they also said she may be wi' child, an' I can't help but wonder how he was able to get a cock stand to do the job. I can assure ye that Fergus would'na wake up to perform for that woman."

"Who's Fergus?"

"Aye. Et's what I named my cock."

"Ewan. Please finish packing. I'm going to find my wife."

I don't bother requesting Ewan leave my office. I take the liberty of exiting before I have to hear more information I'd rather do without. Though, I cannot stop the quiet laugh that escapes as I make my way down the hall. If ever there was a man that would name his cock, it'd be Ewan.

Feeling slightly winded after climbing two flights of stairs, I approach Ella's bedchamber. I don't hear any voices inside, so I assume she is alone. My stomach swirls with unfeigned excitement as I lightly tap on her door.

"Come in." The directive is distant and muffled. When I enter the room, I find her seated on the opposite side by the largest window overlooking the courtyard. She's surprised to see me but not displeased. I must admit, it makes me happy, but the deepening color in her cheeks as I approach is making my fingers twitch with wanting to touch her and my mouth water with the need to taste her.

"Hello, my dear. How was yer visit with yer parents? I know that must have been difficult."

"It was. I am sad to be leaving, more for them than for me,

I think. But it eases my heart to know they have each other."
She pauses and looks away. The disconnect from earlier is still
there, yet now I see it as a forced maneuver and not the haughty
disinterest from our early days.

"Ella." Her eyes meet mine, sparkling blue in the light.
"Give me yer hand." She hesitates, no doubt skeptical of the
tone in my voice, but waits only a few seconds more before
placing her delicate fingers on mine. I give her a gentle tug.
"Stand up." And she does.

I hold on to her hand and take a moment to gaze upon her
exquisite face highlighted by the bright sunshine.

"Is everything alright, my lord?" she asks, nervously, as I
pull her closer.

"No. But it will be." My hand comes up to cradle the side of
her head, thumb gliding across her soft cheek. Those seductive
lips part and I feel my cock jump with a surge of arousal. "I can't
seem to do anything but think about you. And now that yer
standing before me, even lovelier than the last time I saw ye, all I
want is my mouth on yers, tasting yer lips, full and sweet. Kissing
ye slow and gentle before I devour yer moans like a starved beast
that knows no bounds." Her breath hitches. "Would ye like that?"

"Yes," she whispers.

"Then say it." Her eyes widen at the force of my command.

"Alasdair."

"Ye are my wife now. I am yer husband. There are no
barriers between us. Whatever ye have learned from society
about what we are to do, how we are to act, how we are to *feel*,
has no place here. If ye want me to kiss you, ye are free to
request it. If ye want me to touch you, all ye need do is ask. If ye
want me to *fuck* you, ye simply make yer desires known, and
from there, ye can rest assured, ye will be sated."

"Alasdair. You shouldn't..." Before she can reprimand my

choice of words, I pull her toward my mouth, letting my lips gently caress hers as I speak.

"I should'na what, Ella? Use that kind of language?" I press my lips harder against her, taking hers between mine before speaking again. "I should'na tell ye how good it feels to fuck my wife?" My arms tighten around her as she opens her mouth and moans through the next kiss. I let her take my mouth a few minutes longer because it feels so damned good to kiss her—to be kissed by her. I pull away to latch onto her neck, biting, sucking, the vibration of her cries tickling my tongue. "I should'na tell ye that I will never be the same after being inside you? That ye were made fer me and that I want nothing more than to lift yer skirts and bend ye over that chair an' fuck ye till yer screaming my name while yer wet cunny milks my cock dry?"

"Alasdair!" She devours my mouth again as her arousal bursts into flames.

"What, Ella? Say it. Bloody tell me what ye want." Both hands are on her, holding her steady, keeping her mouth a fraction away from mine. "Say it, Ella."

Her eyes are round with the fear of being pushed passed her boundaries, yet black with desire and need. My thumb firmly glides along the smooth skin of her jaw as I pull her lips to mine, letting my tongue reach out to gently tease them. "Say it," I whisper against her.

"Fuck me, Alasdair! Fuck me, please, just like you said... lifting...lifting my skirts. That's what I want." She finishes with a whisper, her lashes wet with emotion. I should feel guilty, but I don't. I want to reward her by making her cum harder than she's aching to. Forcing her to understand what I'm capable of providing her. Forcing her to become familiar with who she really is and to not be afraid of her desires, but to let them soar, let them fly free from the cage of society, of propriety, of standards set by others.

"Verra good." She looks away. "Keep yer eyes on mine, Ella. Understand this—there is no shame in our passion. No shame in our carnal desires. There is no shame in how slick yer cunt is with anticipation. I will teach ye to crave that anticipation." I stop to kiss her again, hard and deep. She relaxes, letting go, allowing me to pleasure her the way fate intended. I scrape my teeth across her swollen lip as I pull away. "Look at me." Her eyes slowly open. "There is no shame in how we feel about each other, no rules that dictate our marriage, only trust. Ye can always trust me, Ella."

She gently nods her head in agreement as I reach down to lift the flowing layers of fabric that hide her beautiful body. Once I meet the soft silkiness of her chemise, I know I am close, as does she, eagerly spreading her legs to receive my touch.

"I'm going to tease fer a bit," I say as my fingers glide slowly up her inner thigh.

"No, Alasdair, please," she begs as she pushes herself toward my hand.

"Yes, Ella. T'will make yer release come easier. We do'na have much time as we are to leave in less than an hour."

She whimpers as I get closer, leaning further into my other arm wrapped around her back. My fingers slide through the wetness on her leg, then meander up, spreading her just enough to massage her clit.

"Oh God!" she cries, already close to the edge. Her ability to cum with such ease is a potent aphrodisiac that has my cock throbbing with the need to please her.

"Not yet, Ella. Do'na let yerself cum." I push one finger in to take her closer, another to test her limits, and a third to ready her for my entry. I pump only twice before I feel a gentle pulsing, then remove my hand and turn her around in one swift move as I throw her skirts up. Once she's bent over the chair, the creamy white skin of her bum glowing in the light, I rip my cock from my breeches and enter her in one powerful thrust. She screams out in pleasure and pushes back toward me. I cannot stop myself from landing a loud smack across that perfect skin, and a second later, her cunt is swallowing me whole, pulling my shaft deeper and deeper with each contraction. My orgasm explodes inside her as a guttural sound escapes my throat. My movements become labored, almost impossible, as my muscles lock with the intensity of my release.

I lean forward, one hand on the chair, the other holding her hip. I look down, her face turned to the side, eyes closed. She is beautiful! Her mouth is open in supplication "—*Don't stop!*" her panted moans convey. She's still pulsing around me so I continue to drive into her, though my momentum has slowed.

She's fully relaxed now and likely getting uncomfortable, so I stand up, my flaccid cock easily slipping free, and bring her with me to lie on the floor.

"Come here, love. Rest wi' me for a while." She does without protest, lying in my arms, head on my chest, a puddle of ornate fabric blanketing us as we come down from a fantastically intense release. "Are ye alright?"

"Mm-hmm," is all I get in response.

"Good." I rub her back softly as she falls asleep, her slow breathing like a gentle melody. My eyes close, and my mind drifts back to what Ewan said—that I fell in love with Ella the first night I met her. As I lay here, sated in a way that I have only felt with this woman, I can't help but think that maybe he is right.

FIFTEEN
Ella

The first two days of travel were less than ideal. I opted to ride in the carriage for our departure as I was sore and physically drained after Alasdair came to me and coerced me into saying and doing things I had never before contemplated, let alone acted upon. I try to ignore the shame that Alasdair said has no place in our marriage, but the young woman I used to be is still there, holding onto all she has ever known. She was unconventional in many ways, though very few people knew that; however, I know for certain she did not have the intense desires she has now. They have only come to life since I met Alasdair.

My mind is constantly filled with thoughts of how he and I come together as husband and wife. How he kisses me, touches me, how he likes to *tease* me—as he says—and how he likes to... oh dear God, I can't believe he said that to me. That, *I* said that to him! The thought escapes again through the clatter of the carriage and the steady rhythm of horses trotting on wet pebbles and mud.

I close my eyes and take a deep breath, the cool, damp air

stinging the inside my nose, and pull the wool blanket Alasdair gave me tighter around my shoulders. Once again, my self-reprimanding leads me back to the truth, and I am forced to acknowledge the sensations that run through my body when I think about his ungentlemanly approach to our coupling. The heat that flushes my skin, the hardening of my nipples, the sensual contractions between my legs. I even want to take his shaft in my hand, stroke its hardness, bring it to my mouth again. *Stop it, Ella.*

Just as I sit forward to stretch my back and move my legs and do anything other than constantly think about my husband's manhood, the sun breaks through the clouds in a blinding glow through the carriage window. I pray it will last and that I can finally get out of this container.

Alasdair said it was best for us to push through the inclement weather that has persisted since shortly after our journey began, allowing his men and the horses to rest only when necessary. He has joined me in the carriage on several occasions, but he prefers to ride Magni so that he can patrol the surrounding areas through our progression. He said he trusts all the men in our travel party, but when it comes to protecting me, he trusts himself the most. Of course, when he said it, looking me straight in the eye, sincerity attached to every word, I felt the same emotion swirl through my chest that scared me the day after we wed. I felt it again when he rode Magni next to the carriage and caught my attention through the window. He stared at me with a hard intensity, then the corner of his mouth turned up, and he offered a flirtatious wink that made my stomach flip with girlish excitement. I bit my lip to hold on to the smile his charm coaxed free, still feeling the need to appear unaffected by the long list of reasons I should adore him.

As the carriage slows down, I see the sky has become a cloudless blue, and a burst of excitement runs through me.

Coming to a complete stop, Alasdair dismounts Magni and walks toward me. He is disheveled, hair falling free from its tie, face darkened with thick stubble, his clothing wrinkled and wet. Living somewhat of a sheltered life, I haven't seen many gentlemen in such dishabille, yet on my husband, I find it rather appealing.

"The look on yer face says yer happy to see me," he says as he opens the carriage door. "Or perhaps yer simply happy to get out into the sunshine an' stretch yer legs?"

"Hmm," I playfully contemplate, "Perhaps both."

I hear a low chuckle as he helps me down. "Well, yer going to be very happy wi' me in about a quarter-hour. Come here, let me grab this bag. We're going fer a walk." From the second carriage, he pulls out a rather large travel bag and throws it over his shoulder, then turns to find me standing where he left me. "Ye look nervous."

"Not nervous. Only curious," I correct.

He comes to me, standing close and tips my chin up with the side of his finger and asks, "Maybe a bit nervous?" then places a small kiss on my lips.

"Truth be known, I'm always a *bit* nervous around you."

His dimple appears before he responds, "Good." Then he takes my hand and walks me into the surrounding woods.

The scent of leaves and moisture surround me, and a spark of alertness refreshes my mind. It reminds me of so many days when I would stare out the window, waiting for the dreary weather to pass so I could escape the confines of the indoors. After days of smelling candles and wood smoke and everything in the house that was a hundred years older than me, I would become melancholy and start losing interest in anything but my craving for sunshine, fresh air, and a brisk ride through the forest with Willow.

"Feels good to be out here, aye?" Alasdair asks.

"You must be a mind reader. I was thinking exactly that. But I'm still curious. You seem to know where you're going, and I don't see much of a trail."

"Aye, I do. I've stopped here many a time. Just a bit further, and you'll see why."

We continue for another ten minutes until I notice a distinct drop in temperature, the sound of rushing water, and the clean aroma that is only created by a waterfall. My pace quickens out of instinct. I regularly visit all the water features on my family's land, but I have to sneak over to the adjoining property to enjoy an actual fall. I love anything that has to do with water, from the smallest trickling creeks to the lakes that seem as big as the sea, but there is something different about a waterfall beyond its mesmerizing beauty. A special sort of sensation, like a vibration that makes me feel more alive, forcing me to take deeper and bigger breaths while engaging all my senses.

The sound is louder now, and unable to wait a second longer, I run ahead of Alasdair. When I round the wall of stone, I am stopped fully in my tracks.

"Oh my goodness! Alasdair, this is spectacular!"

"I knew it would please ye. I had hoped the weather would clear so ye could enjoy it."

I walk closer to the edge of a pool surrounded by huge gray boulders scarred with ancient cracks and painted with bright green moss. The water is crystal clear, allowing me to see the kaleidoscope of colored pebbles and stones that line its floor. I stand staring at this natural mosaic, mesmerized by the way the sunlight shifts and dances across its surface. There is something about a pond that is as clear as glass that fascinates me. It's as if I'm looking through a window into another world, and my curiosity has always wanted to explore what is on the other side.

A random droplet of water lands where I am staring, and I smile as the perfect circles drift outward from its center. The distraction pulls my attention to the waterfall that will not be ignored. It is magnificent. Truly awe-inspiring. All of the waterfalls I have seen flow down the rocks and into a stream. This one is unique in that it flows off a massive flat stone that juts out from the wall that supports it, creating a curtain of water that lands in an adjacent pool.

"Alasdair, I can't believe how beautiful this is. I've never seen anything like it." A lump forms in my throat, as it always does when I am presented with something exceptional that nature has created; from a multicolored butterfly's wing to a burnished orange sunset, my emotions seem to get as excited as my mind and my eyes well up with tears.

"Aye. It is one of the most beautiful falls I've ever seen. It's hard to tell from here, but ye can walk behind it, and I will tell ye, that is an experience ye will never forget."

I turn to him in excitement, "Will we do that today, right now?" I can't even imagine doing such a thing.

"Oh, aye. But first things first," he says with a devious smirk.

"Why am I suddenly nervous?"

Alasdair throws his head back and laughs. "Try not be nervous, my little faerie maiden. And keep an open mind. Ye will be happy ye did." He pauses then and walks closer, reaching up to touch the side of my face. "But most importantly, ye need to trust me."

My body heats with the thought of us coupling out here, in nature. "Are we to...um...here?"

"From the look in yer eyes, ye are quite pleased wi' that notion. But, no, I would'na do that here wi' all my men waiting fer us. However, ye can plan on it when we get home." He stops then to kiss me, slow and sensual. I've missed this over the past few days, and now I desperately wish we had more time. Making love to Alasdair, here in this magnificent place, is like a fantasy I could beg to become a reality.

He slows the kiss, letting his lips meander around mine, melting my resolve to not change his mind. Pulling away, he looks down at the ribbon keeping the front of my gown closed. His right hand comes up to pull the bow loose, and then the left joins in to work the rest of the lacing free.

"As ye can see, I'll be removing yer gown. When I'm done, I'll remove my clothes as well." He says this with complete focus on the task of unclothing me. I feel things happening to my body that I can't control.

"And we are not to..." I whisper.

"No. We are to bathe."

"To bathe?"

"Aye. T'will be a bit cold. But I can assure ye, the rest of our journey will be far more pleasant because we did."

He is able to remove the top portion of my dress easily and is now working to free me of my petticoats. I look down to see the hard points of my breasts protruding through the thin fabric of my shift. A few minutes later, it is the only thing left covering my naked body.

Alasdair steps back to remove his clothes now. It seems erotic to stand here in this state of undress, watching him do the same. When his upper body is completely exposed, I feel gooseflesh tickle my skin. He is so incredibly sculpted, like nothing I ever imagined seeing with my own eyes.

He removes his boots and breeches next, and I cannot ignore the tightening of my chest and the tickling sensation in between my legs. His manhood isn't erect as it has been every other time I have seen him unclothed, but it looks as if it wants to be. It is hanging and swollen, not quite as defined as when we come together, but still as enticing. I see it jump and become firmer, startling me as I gasp a small breath.

"Ella, ye can'na look at me wi' such wanting. I will'na be able to control my cock stand knowing how badly ye want it." His voice strains through his explanation.

"I'm sorry. I...I just... I'm sorry." I turn away, embarrassed by my brazen behavior.

"There is no need to apologize, Ella. Ye can'na imagine how good it makes me feel that ye want me so freely." He comes to me then, holding my face in his warm hands. "But we must at least try—" He laughs and kisses me playfully. "to maintain control. Though it be a mighty tall order."

"Well, shall we get on with our bath? I am both excited and dreading how cold that water will be."

"Aye, as am I. But that is what makes it so damned invigorating."

He walks over to his travel bag and pulls something out. Turning back to me, he says, "Now, remove yer shift."

The command makes my stomach twist in raw desire while my ingrained propriety is screaming, *"Absolutely not!"*

"Take it off, Ella. There is no one here but me, and I'm sure ye have'na forgotten, that lovely body is mine."

Why does that make me want him to change his mind about us coming together, here, now, potential spectators be damned?

"Alright," I agree and slowly begin lifting my shift up and eventually over my head.

"Stay like that. Let me look at ye," he almost begs as I turn to hide. "There are no words to describe how magnificent ye are standing here in the light of day. Ye are the most beautiful woman in the world, Ella."

My throat constricts at his compliment. I know he has traveled the world. I know he has been with other women. So, to witness his sincerity, unmistakable in his expression, stokes a sense of confidence not only in my sensuality but in my femininity. It's as if I have become someone I've longed to be for a thousand years. I can't explain what has happened with the simple act of removing my shift under a patch of sunlight next to a hidden paradise, with a man that is masculine perfection. I can't stop the tear that escapes as my emotions soar with a special kind of joy.

"Are ye alright, Ella?" he asks as he wipes the tear away.

"Yes, Alasdair. Quite alright."

I take his hand and walk toward a break in the rocks that creates a perfect path for us to enter the pond. Alasdair moves in front of me to get in first, then turns to take my hand. My breath catches as my feet touch the water.

"Come. 'Tis better to just get it over with. The more ye hesitate, the harder it is."

He leans back and falls into the glassy surface of the pond, back stroking to its center, then stopping to go completely under. A few seconds later, he comes up and stands in the waist-deep water. He is stunning. The next thing I see has me tipping my head in confusion. He actually is bathing, with soap!

"You brought soap? I didn't know you had that."

"Aye. I cut a small piece off and had it in my satchel. Ye'll be pleased to know it's lavender."

"That is my favorite!"

"Yes, weel, ye won't be enjoying any of it unless ye get yer naked arse over here wi' me so I can bathe ye."

"Fine," I declare, slightly perturbed at being coerced. "You seem to like challenging me, dear husband. Don't think it has gone unnoticed."

"Aye, I do," he agrees with a laugh. "It's damn good fun to watch ye get all flustered."

Not one to ever pass up a good challenge, I take a deep breath, lower my entire body underwater, then swim the whole way to him, rolling onto my back to swim around him again, relishing the stunned look on his face.

"That was verra good, Ella. Yet another thing ye do better than most men." He lowers himself down into the water and reaches for me, pulling me to him. "Wrap yer legs around my waist." And so, I do. He doesn't say more, only looks at me with a peculiar expression and begins to wash my back and neck, then slowly moves around to my shoulders and chest. He is serious now, focused on the task of bathing me, but not as if it were a mundane chore—it's like he's worshiping me. He's so tender yet methodical, his big hands moving in slow circles across my skin. The coarseness of the soap scrapes gently, its strong scent surrounding me with that unique mixture of flowers and pine.

"Stand up," he says.

He washes my breasts and my stomach, then turns me around to wash my lower back. He stands then, wraps his arm around my chest, and pulls me to him, his mouth resting against my ear. "Yer beauty drives me mad, Ella." His voice is low and raspy, but he doesn't say more, only lowers his hand further down, gently cleaning between my legs. I swallow the whimper lodging in my throat just as he turns me around to face him. It feels too good when he cleans me from the front. I almost beg him to stop since I know he will go no further.

"Et's too much fer ye, aye?" he asks, reading my mind, again.

"Yes," I whisper.

"Here. Take this." He hands me the soap. "I've been looking forward to this fer three days." His dimple is deep with his admission.

I don't talk as I begin to bathe his sinuous body. I take my time exploring every curve and valley, the coarse hair as it thickens and thins in various areas of his form. I understand why he took his time with me, why he became quiet and focused. I feel like I'm worshipping him now. It seems spiritual, sensual, and natural. An image comes to my mind, inspired by this moment and a book I read from Father's library. It talked of the ancient people of this land who worshipped nature: the trees, the water, the animals. I can't help but wonder if this was a ritual for them. Cleaning your mate in an icy pool of crystal-clear water while the mist from a waterfall floats through the air.

Alasdair takes the soap from my hand, what little is left of it, and finishes washing himself. "It does'na seem respectful to have ye clean some parts of me." His wink makes me laugh as he dips down into the water to hide while he finishes the job.

Once he is done, he pulls me to him again. "Let's rinse off and go see yer waterfall."

"Wait." I wrap my arms and legs around him like before. "Thank you," I say against his mouth before taking him in a deep and sensual kiss. I stop before it can get too heated. "This was a gift, Alasdair. One I will never forget."

SIXTEEN

Alasdair

W hat I want to tell her is that *she* is a gift. One I thank God for every night I go to bed and regularly throughout the day. As I am right now, watching her take my hand to help her navigate a boulder we need to climb to get to the waterfall. She's still naked, though she's wrapped in one of the linens I brought for us to dry off. She protested about not getting dressed before starting the short hike, but she'll understand why once we're there.

Her hand grips tighter on mine as the rocky path becomes wet from the splash. It's loud now, the sound almost heavy, a whirring hum, unique and mysterious. We approach the entrance, and I stop to let Ella look through the opening to see the wonder that's in store. Her eyes widen, and her hand covers her open mouth.

"Alasdair!"

My heart beats faster with her excitement. I step in first to make sure there are no unwanted surprises, then turn to guide her in with me. Once we are fully inside the cavern, the light changes to an elegant shade of blueish-green, and it's bright enough for me to see that Ella's eyes have welled with tears. She is staring at the wall of water, lit brightly by the sun. Through it, you can see the blue of the sky and the green of the trees, but everything is an abstract blur that creates a magnificent piece of art, alive with movement and sound.

I reach down to take Ella's hand and bring it toward the fall. She watches the slow progression, and when her fingers finally part the liquid glass, her face lights up like a child seeing her first shooting star. It is a joy so pure; I cannot only see it, I can feel it. In this moment, I realize I truly am in love with Ella. I stare at her as the truth is set free inside me and if I'm being honest with myself, the intensity of it is almost painful.

"What?" Ella asks with concern.

I reach for her and pull her into my arms so that I can hold her. She wraps her arms around me and asks, "Is everything alright?"

I move closer to her ear. "I...I..." The courage to tell her my true feelings vanishes. It's too soon. "I knew how much ye'd love this. I can see it on yer face. It makes me happy to see ye so pleased." I kiss her temple, then finish, "Though our marriage may be new, Ella, ye are verra special to me."

She pulls away to look into my eyes, perhaps wanting to confirm my sincerity. She finds what she's looking for. "Thank you, Alasdair." Her chilled hand rests on my face, the gentle caress speaking more than her words.

She opens the linen that is protecting her from the cool, damp air and brings it with her arms as they wrap around me, creating a cocoon that protects us from the mist of the waterfall. Our bodies touch, flesh to flesh, her head resting on my chest. We stay this way, each of us staring out through a window that seems as if it could take us to another world, another time and place where the rules of society don't weigh so heavily.

I wonder if she can hear the beating of my heart. Does she know that it beats for her, that it always has? Can she feel the connection of our souls? I want to tell her what Nanna told me all those years ago; I want to know if she believes it could be true. That we found each other, as Fate had intended.

Her arms tighten around me as one hand slips free to roam around my chest. She slows to play with the thick hair, nails gently scraping as her fingers curl and uncurl, sending gooseflesh across my body, then moves lower, tickling the ridges along my side. I can sense the shift in her body as her hand finds my hip. She wants me, and I don't know if I am able to refuse. The feelings that have freely risen to the surface are so much more intense than simple carnal desire, so when the linen falls free and she takes my fully erect shaft in her hand, I know I will not have the strength to deny her what she craves.

My hand comes up to grab her hair, gently pulling her back enough so that I can see her eyes: black, only a small ring of pale blue behind the glistening surface.

"Ye test my will beyond its limits."

"I'm sorry, Alasdair. But being here, in this place, with you..." She releases my erection and places both hands upon my shoulders. "And the way you just looked at me..."

My mouth is on hers, devouring the temptation she knows I can't resist. *I love you, Ella.* The words echo through my head, loud and desperate to escape. My grip tightens as she kisses me in return with unbridled passion, her moans vibrating across my tongue. *I love you, Ella.* My hand comes down to massage her full breast, kneading its firm roundness before taking the hard tip between my thumb and finger. I hold the pressure as I pull my mouth away from hers.

"I told ye I did'na want to do this wi' my men so close by. But ye insisted otherwise." I lean down and take her tight nipple into my mouth, sucking it deep as I tease it with my tongue. Her legs go weak, and she cries out. Letting it go, I finish, "I will give ye what ye want, but we are to be quick about it. We've already been gone too long." My hand moves down to the slit between her legs. It's slippery and swollen, and my cock swells with appreciation. "Listen to me, Ella. I'm going to be aggressive, I'm going to try and bring ye to climax, but I don't want ye to cum yet. Understand? Do not cum until I tell ye to."

"Alasdair, why? I want to."

"And ye will. But since I can'na take my time, I'm going to make sure it's worth it fer ye."

My fingers move faster across her lips, coating her with the sweet essence. I increase the pressure, slipping in and out of her entrance, and feel the slight contractions of her orgasm building. She can barely breathe through the onslaught of my kiss. When I set her mouth free, she sucks in the cold air, creating a rush that I know will intensify her high. Her head falls back as I bite onto her neck, pulling the tender flesh into my mouth.

"Alasdair! Please!" She's close now.

"I'm going to lie down, and ye will mount me, but do'na release until I tell ye to."

She nods her head through panting breaths while she strains not to cum from the efforts of my hand. I let go and move to lie on the wet ground. My view from here is spectacular; the waterfall on one side, bright, moving, and energetic, highlighting Ella's beautiful form. She is a goddess, like those painted on canvas.

"Come here."

She steps over me, placing one foot on either side of my waist as I've guided her to do.

"On yer knees."

She drops to her knees, falling forward, hands braced on

my shoulders. I reach down to take my cock in hand and guide it to her entrance.

"Take me, Ella. Take what ye want. But remember what I told ye."

She doesn't hesitate to lean back so the head glides easily, past her slippery layers to the opening that is pulsing and ready for release. My hips jut forward on instinct, slamming my stiff shaft into the warm softness of her canal. Ella's scream mingles with my growl that echoes around us.

"Not yet, Ella," I grind out through gritted teeth.

I'm fucking her hard now, my abdomen tight and burning from the strain. Her breasts bounce in time with the pounding contact. When I know my orgasm is about to explode, I grab her hips, tip them forward, and grind her clit into my taut muscles.

"Now, Ella, now!"

She tightens hard around me, squeezing and pulling me deeper. Her head is back, eyes closed, mouth open in a silent scream. I grab the back of her head and pull her face to mine.

"Open yer eyes." My voice is ragged and crazed.

They stay closed a few seconds longer, hard breaths escaping with each thrust. When her wet lashes finally lift, I find the ringed onyx of desire has been replaced with a blue so bright, so unusual, it glows in contrast to her and everything around us. My confusion is replaced with a sudden blast of renewed arousal as my bollocks tighten and I swell inside her.

"Alasdair!" she cries out, sitting up straight with her back arched, riding me harder as her hips roll on me in a perfect, steady rhythm.

"Look at me, Ella!" I want to see her eyes again—blue, luminous, like that of a mythical being.

Her hands land hard on my chest as she braces herself to receive the revived momentum. Her damp hair is draped around her shoulders, a few tangles hanging long, tickling my skin as they sway. When her eyes open again, I am pleased to see it wasn't all an illusion. They are still bright, like when the clear sunlit water surrounding a tropical island meets the purple-gray of a wicked storm, an impossible crystalline aquamarine.

She calls my name again as the contractions begin, triggering an orgasm so powerful, I can barely move. The jerking, fractured thrusts are purely involuntary as my body is taken over by a pleasure so intense my vision fades as I try to stay focused on her stare. Then her eyes close, and she falls to my chest as my arms lock around her in a protective vice.

"Ella, are ye alright?" I constantly feel the need to make sure it isn't too much for her.

"Yes. I just need to rest."

Her body relaxes as our breathing ebbs from panting exertion to a meditative calm.

She's asleep, twitching every so often as she falls deeper into her slumber. We should have joined the travel party by now, but I want to let her rest. I wasn't anticipating the intensity of what just happened; it wasn't even supposed to happen at all. But I'm weak when it comes to fulfilling her desires, and after this session, I'm more than fascinated. Whatever that was, it created a noticeable shift not only in her, but in me as well. I have never had an erection swell like that so soon after climax, and I have never had an orgasm release so forcefully it bordered on painful.

There must be a connection to Nanna's premonition, and I am now anxious to get home to my library, where I can do some research. I've been collecting books on the mythical beings of lore since I was a boy, some of which are very old. My gut tells me I will find clues to satisfy my curiosity in the pages of the timeworn text of centuries past.

Less than ten minutes pass before I wake my faerie maiden. It's too cold and wet to stay here unclothed for so long.

As Ella stands before me, she appears weak and tired on her feet.

"Give me yer hands." And she does. They are cold, but their grip is strong. "Ye need to wake up if ye want to ride Willow and not go back in the carriage." I laugh as her eyes widen, and she shakes her head in protest. "Turn this way. Hold tight. I'm going to let ye drift back into the waterfall. I will'na let ye go."

"Are you sure?" she asks, but when she looks at the water, there is excitement in her eyes, though her trepidation overrides her voice.

"Aye. I'm sure."

She lets me turn her back to the fall as we both tighten our grip. Her smile lights up her face right before she leans back into the clear wet curtain of water. My God. She is glorious! I pull her back so she can take a breath. Her face beaming bright again.

"Oh Alasdair! That was wonderful! I had no idea it would feel like that!"

"Yes, well, I had no idea ye'd look like that."

"What do you mean?" she asks with a creased brow.

"I mean that was one of the most beautifully erotic things I've ever seen in my life. The way the water flowed over yer lovely face and down onto those magnificent breasts...bloody hell, Ella! Ye keep casting spells on me at every turn."

She laughs at the jest, though it was stated with little humor.

"I want to do it again!"

"Of course, ye do," I say under my breath.

She goes under three more times before I stop her to rinse myself clean and get us heading back toward the road. Her love of nature and newfound hunger for sex has completely altered my schedule.

A few minutes into our trek through the forest, she says, "I still can't believe you had a clean gown and my riding breeches in that bag—not to mention linens and lavender soap. That was a completely planned event, wasn't it? You had it all set up before we even left London, didn't you?"

"I did. Although, there were some details about that *event* that were'na planned. Ye are devious when it comes to taunting my weaknesses. I'm afraid ye've become familiar wi' yer power over me a little sooner than I had expected," I offer her the truth with a raised brow.

She laughs aloud, and the sound of it causes a tingling inside my chest. "Power over you? Don't be ridiculous."

"I'm not. It's the damned truth, and ye know it. You've had control over everything I do since I first laid eyes upon ye."

She stops then to look up at me. "Do you mean that, Alasdair?"

"Aye."

Her eyes soften when she replies, "I'm sorry."

It's my turn to laugh now, "Don't be. Right about now, I'm feeling like I've been blessed by God a thousand times over." I pause to tilt her chin up toward me and give her a tender kiss on her full lips, the urge to tell her how much I love her resting on the tip of my tongue, "Ye are perfect, Ella Stewart, and ye are mine. Please don't ever be sorry fer that."

SEVENTEEN
Ella

I can see the facade of Galloway Castle through the trees as Willow and I trot alongside Magni and Alasdair. We entered his family's lands over an hour ago, and the long ride here has been nothing less than spectacular. The forest is a rich green, dense with a wide array of plants and trees, some of which are enormous. I simply cannot wait to explore these woods, and I have told Alasdair exactly that at least ten times so far.

The sun is blinding as we exit the canopy of trees, making my eyes blink and water. When my vision finally adjusts, my heart flutters with excitement as I take in the opulence of my new home.

"Alasdair! This is so beautiful. I never imagined..."

"Aye. It was built in the 1500s by my great-grandsire many times over. A few others added to it over the centuries, but maintaining its integrity has been the utmost priority of my family for almost three hundred years." I can hear the pride in his voice.

We dismount when the groomsmen arrive to take Willow

and Magni to the stables. I take a minute to talk to her, bringing my nose to the long bridge of hers. "Thank you, Willow. That was more fun than we've had in a long time, huh, girl? Although Magni might be a bit moody for a day or two, he'll get past it soon enough." Willow knickers and nods her head in response.

"Ah, ye do know that was loud enough fer both of us to hear, aye?"

I can't help but laugh, and I swear Willow does the same. "Was it?"

"Yes. It was. An' I suppose you and yer magic horse are never going to let us live it down, hmm, Lady Stewart?" I see the corner of his mouth lift into a charming half smile.

With a hardy laugh, I look at Willow, patting her side, "Did you hear that, girl? Alasdair thinks you are a magic horse!" She whinnies and stomps her front hoof, making Alasdair and me burst into laughter.

"Weel, aren't you two the happy couple. Found yer wedded bliss so soon, aye?"

The raspy brogue startles me, and I turn to find an elderly man leaning on his cane and wearing a rather charming grin.

"Hello, Father," Alasdair calls out, then takes my hand. "Come. Let me introduce ye, and do'na worry, he only looks like a grouchy ol' curmudgeon."

"I heard that," his father says before gasping on a cough.

After a short flight of stairs, we stop on the landing at the grand front entrance of carved, dark wood double doors, guarded by two noble lion statues.

"Father, I'd like to introduce my lovely wife, Lady Ella Stewart."

His father reaches for my hand, shakily bowing down to offer a proper kiss. His breaths are heavy with a rattling wheeze.

"Ella, this is my father, Callen Stewart, Earl of Galloway."

"Yes. Well, not fer long. I'll be dead any day now. But at least I got the chance to meet yer bride. She is lovely indeed." He is interrupted by another coughing fit, and I can see the concern in Alasdair's eyes.

"Ye should be resting inside, Da. Ye did'na need to push yerself fer a simple greeting."

"That's kind of ye, son. But at this point, it does'na make a difference. Therefore, I do what I want." He finishes his statement with a wink in my direction and a half smile that reminds me of Alasdair. I feel my own sadness set in knowing that I will not have the time to get to know this man as well as I would like.

"'Tis a fair point, and we are glad yer here. Shall we go inside? I know Ella is excited to see her new home."

"Ye should be," Callen says succinctly as he shuffles toward the door. "It's an impressive manor. The only problem is that it's too damn big. It's a bloody pain in the arse to get from one end to the other."

Alasdair and I laugh as the footman holds open the door. Once inside, my breath stops on a sharp inhale. "Oh my! Lord Galloway, this is impressive indeed."

"It'll be Callen to you, my dear. When yer knocking on death's door, formalities seem a waste of time." He stops then to catch his breath as the servant brings over a chair on wheels.

"Please, sir, sit here. I'll take ye to the parlor," the man says to Callen.

"Fine, fine, thank ye, Douglas."

Callen sits down in the well-worn chair and closes his eyes as Douglas pushes him through the foyer.

I turn to Alasdair. "I've never seen a chair such as that. What a brilliant idea."

"Aye. There is a local craftsman that is a very skilled wheelwright. We had him fashion wheels for Da's favorite chair. He did'na use it much at first, but as his health has declined, he has a renewed appreciation fer it."

We follow Douglas to the parlor, walking to the right of the grand staircase that starts wide from the marble floor of the foyer, then branches in either direction from the landing that is big enough to accommodate two enormous floor vases that stand on either side of a beautiful tapestry depicting the forest where it meets the craggy coast. The walls of the hallway reach high to the tall ceiling and are lined with portraits of the Stewart family, each one framed with ornate moldings of dark wood.

The parlor is no less beautiful. As always, I am drawn to the oversized picture windows. They overlook a vast expanse of green that is completely unblemished in its consistency. To the right, I see a pond a fair distance away, and next to it is a weeping willow that may be even larger than the one I frequently visited at home. I am suddenly anxious to go for a walk and visit that majestic tree.

"'Tis quite peaceful, is it no'?" Callen asks as Alasdair brings him close to the window.

"Yes, that is a perfect description," I agree.

"I sit here often. 'Tis a great place to contemplate." He pauses to clear his throat. "With so few obstructions, it's easy to see the wildlife that pass by to graze across the moor. Red deer are very common, as are pheasants. I have seen several badgers over the years and a wildcat once or twice. Those are the two ye need to look out for; they can be a bit ornery. Especially if they're nursing."

"I am quite the lover of nature, so don't be surprised if you find me sitting right here on a regular basis."

Callen laughs. "'Tis good to hear."

My first several days were busy while getting settled into Galloway Castle. Alasdair proudly showed me around. Callen was right, it is quite an effort to get from one side to the other. Fortunately, it is designed for more than one family to live here with a fair amount of privacy. Alasdair and I have our own wing that is larger than his London townhouse. There is also a full staff, each going out of their way to make me feel welcome and at home.

We have separate bedchambers that share a common sitting room that overlooks the Firth of Clyde and the rocky cliff that outlines the shore. It is a perfect place for us to enjoy tea in the morning, to read a book or correspondence, or to converse over a glass of claret after a long day. Although, for me, there is nothing quite like the view of the sunsets as they paint the sky pink, then orange, and eventually a slate blue-gray as the day transitions to night. I find the comfortable ease of our time together in that room to be reassuring and pleasantly domestic, as if we'd been doing it for years, not less than a fortnight.

Though our sitting room is my favorite, Alasdair's office and library is a close second. It is his domain, and it speaks of his character and personality—stately, refined, worldly, educated, curious, masculine. The ceilings are high, painted emerald green with carved moldings that match the rich, dark wood of the paneled walls. One side of the room is lined with oversized arched windows that mimic the framed arches of the floor-to-ceiling bookshelves that take up most of the other walls.

I felt the urge to cry when I first saw his collection. The crowded shelves create their own elaborate decoration in the room, one of color and texture, but more importantly, one of knowledge, influence, and an understanding of time long past.

I lightly tap on the door, hoping Alasdair is working at his desk. I haven't seen him for the past two hours.

"Come in," he says in a distracted tone.

Upon entering, I find him standing by the window, focusing on the book in his hand. He turns the page, brows drawn, before looking up, almost startled to find me walking toward him.

"Ella, dear, I did'na know it was you. Ye do'na have to knock before entering." He closes the book and places it down on his desk with a loud thump, then leans down to give me a soft kiss.

"I didn't want to be rude and interrupt in case you were doing something important. Though, from the look on your face, whatever you were reading was of significant interest."

He offers that charming smile that tickles my insides. "Aye, that it was. But what is of more interest is how beautiful ye look standing here in the sunshine. Did ye know when the light shines on yer eyes, they sparkle like a faerie pool at midday?" His hand glides along my cheek.

"No, I'm afraid I have no way of knowing that since I don't know what a faerie pool is. But I thank you for the compliment, nonetheless," I reply with coy flirtation. The way he looks at me wakes up the butterflies in my stomach. It's different than what I've become familiar with these past several weeks. There is a yearning that goes beyond physical desire, like he has something to say but can't find the words.

"The faerie pools on the Isle of Skye." He pauses again, leaving me curious as to what is going on in his mind. Something is there. "They are truly something to behold. Little waterfalls that make the gentlest, almost delicate sound. Like a lullaby sung by the sweetest angel. And the color...'tis something that can'na be replicated by man. 'Tis only a thing that is created by the magic that is nature."

My heart beats faster with every word. A dam is forming in

my throat as his words evoke emotions that are foreign, yet familiar.

"I see it in yer eyes, Ella."

"What? You see what?"

"Magic."

My eyes burn as I fight off tears. He is so sincere, and I know there is still something he hasn't said.

"What is it, Alasdair?" I brush my thumb across his full bottom lip.

"I want to show ye something. Let's go fer a walk? I know ye've been anxious to see the forest."

"Oh, Alasdair! That would be wonderful!" The burst of excitement makes me giddy. "Are we going right now?"

"Aye," he replies with a laugh. "Come here, faerie maiden." He pulls me to him and kisses me hard with unfeigned hunger. When the momentum slows, he says against my mouth, "Yer genuine enthusiasm fer the outdoors has become quite the aphrodisiac."

"What is an aphrodisiac?"

"Never mind. Let's go fer that walk."

EIGHTEEN

Alasdair

I t has taken me a few days of research to find answers to the questions that have been nagging me since Ella and I came together under the waterfall. I was somewhat familiar with the legends and stories for which I sought, those of the faerie People—the Fey. They were said to possess exquisite beauty beyond ethereal. It was often irresistible to humans, or it was a dark magic created by the devil to lure innocent humans to the depths of hell—a clear indication the church did not approve.

I found two very detailed descriptions of the Fey. Their physical characteristics were human, and most of the illustrations depicted them as such. Yet, what differed were their natural gifts or abilities, many of which the average human did not possess: the "sight," the ability to look into the future, to know things before they happened; their healing abilities, extensive knowledge of the plants that cured each disease and a healing touch that could be powerful enough to knit bones back together in a day; their extraordinary beauty with an inhuman, intriguing aura about them; their connection to nature, gaining strength and vitality when outdoors surrounded by trees and plants and water and clean air; and their sensuality, which ensured their health and wellness and a long joyful life.

It was said that coupling with a Fey, male or female, was dangerous because the pleasure was so intense that nothing could satisfy your desire again, and your life would turn to despair as you withered away, longing for what you could not have. But there were also stories of happy endings, lifelong love and partnership, even marriage, where a Fey and a human mated for life and inevitably had children. These Fey-human offspring were said to carry many of the gifted traits of their mythical parent and, more interestingly, have handed them down through countless generations, a truly fascinating concept.

It was in the last book, the one I was reading when Ella came into the library. It had a brief mention of what I was looking for: the story of a traveler who got lost in the forest for weeks. One day, he came upon a couple making love under a willow tree, next to a stream. He was surprised to find people that far into the wood, and though he wanted to leave and give them their privacy, he was transfixed by their glamour and unbridled passion.

She rode him, controlled the momentum with the rolling of her hips. Their pleasure was palpable, reaching outward like a vibration in the air until finally when they reached the pinnacle together, she opened her eyes and they glowed with a blue so bright, I wondered if she was blind. But when the man opened his eyes, I saw the same glow, and when they both called out, the unmistakable sound of sexual climax, a soft light haloed around them. I felt like I was witnessing something sacred. I became overwhelmed with a sudden urge to cry and found the strength to run away.

Even though it is the recollection of only one individual, it is enough to reassure me that what happened at the waterfall was no coincidence. If my theory is correct, my wife is more extraordinary than I already knew, and the more I think about it, the more it makes perfect sense. Her uncommon beauty, that genuine connection to nature, her innate sensuality, and the connection between us—all seem to be scripted by fate.

The temperature drops as we enter the forest, the sound shifting to the subtle voice of the trees as they mingle with the plants and the breeze, occasionally highlighted by the call of a bird or the scurry of a rodent.

I sense Ella's excitement even before she speaks.

"Oh, Alasdair!" She stops to turn a full circle, eyes bright with emotion. "This is incredible! It's so different than anything I've experienced. It even smells different. You are going to have a hard time keeping from this place." She declares as she turns to me, her face brightened by a smile that knocks the wind out of me.

My God! How I love you, Ella Stewart. I could never imagine this kind of emotion to be real, the love I'd read about a thousand times from the fanciful minds of a poet or playwright, an author with fictional ideas of what love should be. What I feel for Ella goes well beyond that.

"*Tapadh leibh Dia,*" I whisper as her smile fades.

"What does that mean?"

I pause to silently debate telling her the truth. "It means 'Thank you, God.'"

"Oh. What are you thanking God for?"

"You."

We don't move or say another word. Just look at one another, letting the threads of our connection continue to weave the tapestry that is us.

"Come. I want to show ye something."

We continue down the well-worn trail in silence, the heavy weight of curiosity surrounding us, each wondering what the other has on their mind. The newness of our union and the lingering tension from our introduction leaves us both unwilling to speak our hearts, and it is creating a maddening frustration within me.

"Here. We are stepping off the trail fer a bit. If ye continue going that way, ye'll come to a clearing that overlooks the Firth of Clyde from the high perch of a clifftop. 'Tis quite stunning, but first, I want to show ye this."

After wading through and around the pillowing ferns of the canopy floor, we come to one of the older oaks on this side of our land. It is a proud historical relic that knows the secrets of the forest and likely those of man. This is the perfect place to test the rest of my theory.

"Alasdair, this tree! It is magnificent!"

"Aye, it is. Something else I knew ye would appreciate."

"I love old trees!" She walks up to its trunk and places her hands on the rough surface. "You will think this is strange, but I feel something when I am near them. It's like a tightening in my stomach, and then my hands and feet feel cool and light. Then, my throat fills with the urge to cry, but with joy, not sadness." She pauses to stay with it for a moment longer before turning to me to say, "That's silly. I'm sorry, you must think I am addled."

"Stop. Look at me."

She does, and I watch as she tries to blink away her tears.

"There is nothing strange or silly about what ye feel, Ella. And ye will'na shy away from being open about yerself wi' me. Understand?"

"Aye," she replies with a hint of brogue and a mischievous smile.

"Ye've no shortage of charm, Lady Stewart, and ye've got a

damn good sense of humor," I say as I grab onto her arm and pull her to me, "Now come here and let me taste it."

Our mouths come together with the leftover zeal of our earlier kiss. Our physical desire for one another is insatiable, but she needed a break these past two days to recover physically. If she is not fully enjoying herself, I cannot enjoy myself. But she is eager now, as I knew she would be.

Pulling away from the kiss, I look down at the front of her dress and begin untying the ribbon. Her breathing is heavy, and concern is written across her face.

"Do'na worry. No one will see us here. I want to give ye what ye want, Ella."

"This is what I want?" she asks through panting breaths.

"Aye, it is. I think I know you better than ye know yerself."

Her dress falls to the ground, the ties of her petticoats are next. Within minutes she is clad only in her shift, the breeze pushing it close against her skin, making my mouth water as her dark nipples appear through the thick fabric.

I begin to take off my own clothes and watch as her arousal ticks higher with the removal of each piece.

"Ye like watching me undress, don't ye, Ella?"

"Yes," she whispers.

"Take off yer shift." It's the same as before. She waits for me to instruct her, then she takes her time exposing herself to me fully. She has a natural ability to be erotic that she is completely unaware of.

I bring my hands down to caress her breasts—full, soft, flawless creamy skin. I lift them slightly, pleased with their abundance, as I rub my thumbs around the rigid rosy points. She sighs as her head falls back, exposing the irresistible skin on her throat. I bring my mouth to it, licking up from her collarbone to the tender flesh below her ear. I pull it into my mouth, gently at first, teeth scraping, tongue tickling. The vibration of her moan drives me to suck harder.

"Alasdair!"

My arms are around her now, holding her close as she becomes heavier with relaxation. I release her neck and pursue her lips—I cannot stay away from them for long. She doesn't want me to stay away from them, begging without words, and when she gets what she wants, she rewards me with a kiss in return that drives my desire to maddening heights while it speaks to my soul, confirming I belong to her.

"Lie down."

I guide her to the grassy floor and lie next to her. My hand glides over her soft skin, following the moving highlights that shine brightly between the shadows. I will write about this moment, though it is more beautiful than words will ever justify. Ella and I were meant to be together. I can sense it deep within my soul and perhaps beyond, in the realm of past lives, intuition, and our sixth sense. Maybe it doesn't have a name, but whatever it is, it knows that we are home.

I move lower across her stomach and through her coarse fur. She spreads her legs and sighs as my fingers find her slick with desire. My cock swells to a full erection, instinctively preparing to give her what she needs. I play with her for a while longer, teasing her clit and preparing her entrance with my fingers. Wanting more, she pushes her hips harder toward my hand, so I keep them deep inside her as the heel of my palm massages her swollen nub. She almost cums when I take her nipple in my mouth and roll it between my teeth, but I stop before she does.

A cool breeze drifts by, raising chills on her skin while the shadows of the ancient oak's leaves and branches dance across her body. I move to cover her with my own, taking position between her welcoming legs. I kiss along the side of her neck, then bite along her jaw before taking her mouth again. She's pushing against me, moaning, yearning. When I bring myself to her entrance, the sounds become louder, and when I enter her in a controlled thrust, resisting the urge to drive hard and fast, she cries out my name.

I take my time, building our momentum slowly, gliding in and out of her tight sheath, savoring her pleasure as it vibrates in the air and pulls me deeper.

"Look at me, Ella."

Her eyes open, and my heart pounds harder in my chest. There it is—just as I suspected it would be—the glow of blue that seems otherworldly. But only when we make love out of doors, somewhere in nature, does this phenomenon occur. Each night and two mornings since our arrival at Galloway Castle, we came together in either her room or mine, and never did her eyes become bright with a crystalline glow that matches the pale blue sky as it approaches the blazing sun. It is only when she is allowed the freedom to experience what her ancient ancestors thrived on.

Her hips are pushing against me as my thrusts become harder and faster. I feel her tightening around me as she cries out my name.

"Alasdair!"

Neither of us can hold back now, the pleasure too intense, and we both fall into the ecstasy that seems only possible between us. It is blinding, all-consuming, it tears us apart and puts us back together, and each time it does, it reconnects us to who we once were, ensuring that, eventually, our souls become one.

We slowly come down, holding tight to one another, neither wanting to let go. Her body relaxes as it yearns to rest. But I don't want her to sleep just yet. I need her to know.

"Ella."

She opens her eyes as her mouth lifts in a soft grin. They are back to their stunning blue, the black center large with sated desire. I stare at her for a moment longer, relishing this special moment.

"I love you."

Her eyes widen on a small gasp, but she doesn't say a word. She doesn't need to. The single tear that escapes her glassy eye says all I need to know.

$\mathcal{Ella}$

U nfortunately, the afternoon sun is hidden behind a blanket of clouds which is casting a gray hue across the typically bright green expanse outside the parlor window. I've been sitting here for the past thirty minutes, watching a small herd of deer graze along the edge of the forest. It is calming to witness their slow migration, heads popping up occasionally to check their surroundings or identify a sound. It's a sort of entertainment, just as Callen had suggested.

However entertaining it may be, it cannot distract my mind long enough to put me at ease. Yesterday, when Alasdair told me he loved me, I felt something open inside me. Like he found the key to a chest that had been locked closed for millennia, its lid finally lifted, releasing emotions I never knew existed. It was profound and thrilling and made me happier than I ever dared dream possible. But I did not voice my feelings. They are still stubbornly lodged in my throat, controlled by fear and the ego of my former self. That proud Seymour girl who will not be molded or manipulated or taken for a fool. Yet I am nothing more than a fool as I realize my silence may be a heavier burden.

Am I in love with him? Or am I truly naive and only enthralled with how he makes my body feel? After just a fortnight of marriage, I fear I will never be able to do without the pleasure he so easily brings to the surface, the touch of his skin, his masculine scent, the way his turquoise eyes speak to me in their own compelling language. My stomach suddenly drops with a fearful ache at the thought of being without him. Perhaps that is the answer to my question.

Before I can contemplate further, Callen enters the room in his wheelchair, Douglas dutifully guiding him toward me by the window.

"Good morning, Ella." His voice sounds weak and raspy.

"Good morning, Callen. How are you feeling today?"

"Terrible. But, after ye've felt terrible every day fer a year and a half, the word loses its potency and simply becomes what is." He stops to clear the phlegm from his throat. "How I feel is of no mind, though. The important question is, how do you feel?"

I laugh at his frank dismissal of himself and reply, "That is very sweet of you, but you will never get me to be more concerned with myself than with you." I wink at him. "I am doing quite well. I've been watching a herd of deer graze alongside the forest. There are a few young ones and one very large one with antlers."

"Aye. The stag is a sacred animal in Scotland with many ancient stories and folklore." He moves his chair closer to the window and watches as the herd makes its way back into the trees.

"How interesting! I would love to know more about these stories."

"Weel, I'm no' a verra long-winded man these days, but I can tell ye that yer husband has an extensive library wi' no shortage of books on everything ye need to know about the legends of that magnificent creature. Especially the legend of the white stag. I'd be willing to bet that'll be yer favorite."

"That is wonderful, Callen! Thank you so much for the suggestion. I want to know everything I can about this lovely place I now call home."

"That pleases me immensely, Ella."

Just then, Ewan politely interrupts, "Pardon me, Lord Galloway. M'lady, yer husband would like to speak wi' ye in the library."

My stomach drops again as something in his tone and expression leaves me with a sudden sense of dread.

"Of course. Thank you, Ewan. And thank you, Callen. I am going to look for these books right now."

"Good. I look forward to hearing all about what ye've learned." The sparkle in his eyes confirms he speaks the truth.

A few minutes later, I walk into Alasdair's library, finding him by the window with his back to me. His hands are gripped tightly behind him. He is tense, I can sense it as soon as I enter the room and I'm suddenly afraid to know what is wrong.

"Alasdair, is everything alright?" I ask as I walk up behind him, placing my hand on his shoulder. He doesn't speak or look at me, and the firm set of his jaw tells me that he is not pleased.

"No. Everything is not alright."

He turns to me then, the stern look of disappointment glaring from his eyes. Is it something I have done? Does this have to do with yesterday?

"I have received a missive. I am to leave immediately and assemble my crew to set sail as quickly as time will allow. It seems our never-ending conflict with France has reached a boiling point once again, and I am needed to help bring about England's victory."

I feel like the floor has been yanked out from under me—my heart is pounding out of my chest, and my head is light and dizzy. He cannot leave so soon. We have only just wed, and I cannot picture myself here without him.

"Here, sit down, Ella. Ye do'na look well."

He guides me to the closest chair, and I collapse into it.

"I'm sorry, my dear wife," he says softly, kneeling in front of me. He takes my hands in his. "I had'na planned it this way, leaving so soon. I wanted to ensure ye were properly settled here at Galloway, comfortable in yer new role. Not to mention my father—it will'na be long now." He pauses as that horrible reality settles in, that he won't be here to say goodbye. "But more importantly, I—" He stops again, the tenderness in his eyes squeezing my chest painfully. "I do'na want to leave ye."

He lets go of my hands and abruptly stands to walk back over to his desk, where he picks up the paper that holds his directive. He stares at the words, jaw ticking with pent-up anger before he slams it back onto his desk. "Dammit!" I hear him say under his breath while he rubs his hands down his face, then places them flat on his desk and leans forward, head hanging low. A few minutes pass before he lifts it and looks me in the eye.

"I'm leaving tonight. I've no choice."

No...

My eyes sting with tears. *I don't want you to go!* I hear myself scream inside my head. Do I say it? Surely, he already knows. I need to say something, but if I speak now, I will cry, so I turn to look out the window instead. I take a few breaths, blink my eyes, and swallow down the painful lump. I watched my mother do this many times with poise, grace, and emotional dignity. I must be capable of the same.

One more breath. "That is certainly unfortunate news," I say, feeling weak as I stare at my lap, where my hands fidget with one another. "But it is your duty, and duty comes first. I am the wife of a captain in the King's Navy. Therefore, it is my duty to support you and pray for your safety, that you find victory, and that you may have a speedy return."

I cannot tell from his expression if he is angry with my response or the situation itself. But he has a predatorial vibe as he walks around his desk toward me.

"Stand up, Ella." The gruff command tingles through my body, settling between my legs.

He lifts my chin and smiles down at me. "Ye are a stubborn creature, faerie maiden. I think ye've got a bit o' Scots hidden somewhere in yer family tree." He rubs his thumb across my bottom lip as his face turns serious. "Are ye going to miss me, Ella?"

My stomach tightens. "Yes."

His thumb presses harder on my lips, commanding them to part and when they do, my tongue instinctively comes out to tease the tip, forcing a hiss to escape his firm mouth.

"Do ye want me to leave?" he asks through gritted teeth.

I shake my head in response as my lips release his thumb.

"Say it." His tone startles me.

"I don't want you to leave, Alasdair."

"Why not?" His hand wraps around the back of my neck, his grip tight as he pulls me closer.

"Because...we...we've only just got here...only just been wed. I...I like spending time with you."

"Yer sure there is'na more?"

He brings his mouth close enough to touch mine, but he

doesn't kiss me. My body is trembling with anxiety, fear, sadness—and intense arousal.

"Alasdair...please," I whisper.

He steps back and looks down at my gown, obviously pleased with his observation. "I want ye to go upstairs to yer room and undress completely, then stand at the foot of the bed, back to the door, close yer eyes and wait fer me. When I enter the room, keep yer eyes closed and do'na turn around. Understand?"

"I...ah..." I stutter incomprehensibly.

The only reply I get from Alasdair is one raised brow and a challenging glare.

"Alasdair..."

"Do ye trust me?"

"Yes."

"Then go."

And so, I do. I turn and walk out of the library, closing the door behind me with a gentle click. I scurry down the hall and up the stairs, nervous I will not be ready by the time he gets there. After only a few weeks, he has introduced me to so many ways a man and woman can come together, all of which I have thoroughly enjoyed, but just now, his demeanor was so different, and his command has me confused about what he has in store.

Regardless, I do his bidding and find myself standing at the foot of my bed naked, the cool air drifting around my body, tightening my nipples. I'm staring at my bed, trying to imagine what he will do to me there, then remember he said he wanted me to close my eyes. When I do, I find it is easier to imagine his masterful hands and beautiful body bringing me the ultimate pleasure. The cool air seems to fluctuate more, the silence of the room now heavy around me; my awareness seems to be blossoming, and the anticipation is overwhelming.

Just then, I hear the faint echo of footsteps in the hall outside my room, and my heartbeat ratchets higher. They get louder with each ticking second, their cadence controlled, measured, distinguished. My body flushes with heat, pooling with desire between my legs. The footsteps are louder now, echoing in my ears, making me shiver with need. When they stop, right outside the door, my head falls back, and I almost beg him to open it and come inside.

Finally, the latch opens, then closes, the sound bouncing across the walls and high ceiling. He waits before walking toward me, again building the anticipation that is ready to burst from my veins. Ten steps, each one like an erotic touch, and then he is behind me. He's not touching me, but I know he's there—his warmth, his woodsy scent, his arousal.

"Ye have no idea the gift ye have presented to me, Ella," he says next to my ear. "I will take it wi' me on this journey and know that my love is waiting fer me to return."

His words make my chest tight with emotion. I want to turn and put my arms around him, beg him not to leave. But I don't.

He taps the inside of my foot with his own. "Open yer legs."

He still doesn't touch me, but I can hear that he is taking off his clothes, slowly, letting each piece drop onto the floor next to me.

"Ye are a mouthwatering sight to behold, Lady Stewart. I can sense yer arousal wi'out even a touch. 'Tis making my cock stand painfully hard."

"Alasdair...can I see you, please?"

"No. Do'na move."

I stay still, happy that he is close to me again, his radiant heat warming my back. When his lips find my shoulder, I gasp in surprise. But I nearly collapse when his hand suddenly appears between my legs and his teeth bite down on my neck. *Oh God!* The pressure is building. I won't be able to hold back.

"I can feel how much ye like that, how you pulse around my fingers. But do'na let go, Ella. Ye need to wait."

He releases me then and abruptly turns me toward him, taking my mouth in a devouring kiss that steals my breath and keeps me close to the edge of release. He deepens the kiss, a desperate hunger taking its fill, knowing it may be its last, and the longer it endures, the more it connects with the emotions he set free when he told me he loved me.

Slowly, he walks me backward until the backs of my legs meet the bed. He pulls away from my mouth, holding me close.

"Let me see yer eyes, Ella."

What I see when I open them confirms he spoke the truth yesterday, and I wonder if he sees the same in me. I have learned through this extraordinary man that there is a difference between the lust-filled eyes of carnal desire and the tenderness in the eyes of one who is enchanted by love. The words are trying to break free, fighting their way through the dense bramble of my insecurities. But before I can give them assistance and say what I know needs to be said, Alasdair speaks first.

"I would like to introduce ye to a different kind of pleasure."

He stops then and brings up an instrument that looks like a riding crop with short strips of leather in place of the usual flat pad. My breath catches hard in my throat as he glides it across my breast and circles it around my nipple. No words can escape as a barrage of emotions take over my body: fear, excitement, embarrassment, curiosity, intense arousal. My fear says it will hurt, but the wife of Alasdair Stewart says that whatever he does will be ecstasy like I have never known. With that knowledge, the pulsing between my legs intensifies, and when he speaks, heat flushes through my body.

"Do'na be afraid, Ella. I am going to teach ye how to find pleasure in pain," he says as he continues to circle the hard point of my breast. "'Tis something I have been craving to share wi' ye since I felt ye orgasm while watching me in the conservatory."

"Alasdair..." I whisper, not wanting him to talk about that night.

"Shhh. Ye said ye trust me. Was that true?"

The continuous circling of the tassel around my nipple is driving me mad.

"Yes, I trust you."

"Good," he says, right as he brings the crop back and snaps the leather fringe on the tip of my aching breast.

"Ahh!!" I cry out as the stinging sensation spreads like lightning through my body and ends as a warm wet release between my legs.

He teases with a few more gentle circles, then snaps the leather again, this time a little harder than the last. I don't know if I like it. It's startling and painful, stinging in a way I've never felt. But when he leans down and takes my burning nipple into his warm mouth and massages it with his tongue, gently sucking deeper, moaning with deep vibration, my legs give way as an orgasm that I am unable to control ignites.

"Oh God!"

He releases my tender bosom and wraps his arm around my back. His mouth takes mine in a deep and violent kiss as his other hand slips through my wetness so he can fuck me with his fingers, pushing my climax higher while I grind into the pressure. It feels like it will never stop, and weakness takes over as he lays me on the bed.

He removes his hand to rub my essence across the

ALISON E. STEUART

throbbing nub of my breast, then brings his tongue down to lick it clean. My breath stops as my body jumps from the erotic sensation on his tongue.

"Ella, darling. Ye were'na supposed to cum so readily," he reprimands, standing before me in glorious arousal.

"I'm sorry, I didn't..."

"No. Never apologize. 'Twas I who should've known that would happen. Yer ability to enjoy the delights of the flesh knows no bounds." He holds out his hand to help me stand, then kisses me softly before continuing, "Prepare yerself, my faerie. We are not done."

He turns me around, again facing the bed, and places a blinding veil over my eyes. When I protest, he hushes me quiet and kisses my temple. Once it is fastened, he guides me a few steps over and brings my hands up over my head to place them against the bedpost.

"Hold on to this, and do'na let go."

He coaxes my feet to the proper position, slightly open and back. I am completely exposed, and in this darkness, I can sense his desire to inflict this new kind of pleasure, knowing I will want as much as he can give. He knows me better than I know myself, and with that knowledge, I can wrap myself in the protection of our mutual trust.

"Oh..." I whisper as he tickles the length of my spine with the gentlest touch.

"Ye are so beautiful, Ella. I will dream about ye every night I am gone."

His words make my heart swell with happiness, shutting out the sadness of his sudden departure. There is no chance to think further because the next sensation is the soft tickle gliding up the inside of my leg. It feels so good, I spread my legs more and lift my bum in hopeful greeting. But instead, I receive a stinging snap of the leather in the center of one unsuspecting cheek.

Oh my God!

It hurts, but I don't have time to think about it as the next one lands on the other side, then another directly after that. Heat flashes through me as confusion takes over my brain. I know there is pain, and I know there is something about it I do not like, but the sensation that is without equal, that incomparable pleasure, blurs the edges between the two.

He gently sweeps the tassels across my hot skin, then moves to whip me again and again and again—my thighs, my bum— the heat blending, and I hear myself begging for more. Alasdair growls something in Gaelic and drops the crop on the floor. When he spreads my cheeks and buries his face in my cunny, I know I cannot stop the second orgasm from releasing, so I push myself to him, desperate for more.

"Bloody Christ!" I hear him yell as he grabs my arms from the post and throws me onto the bed. He is inside me before I can think, driving hard and fast, slapping my hot skin with his hand, digging his fingers into my tender muscles.

"Harder!" I hear myself scream as he falls to my back and latches his teeth onto my shoulder. My climax has yet to subside, and I feel myself going numb as he pounds harder and harder with each thrust. The sounds echoing around us are violent as we are ravaged by our need for more. It is a driving force that neither of us can control.

Then suddenly, I am floating, drifting in a pool of ecstasy as I listen to the echo of his cry, distant and haunting, an agonizing release.

I fight it, but there is no stopping my fall into the abyss. I call to him, but I do not know if he can hear me. *I love you, Alasdair, I love you!* I fear my voice is only in my head.

When I wake to the darkness of a moonlit room, I sit up and try to clear the fog from my mind. I look around, confused. Then, reality hits me directly in the chest. The wrenching sobs rip at my throat. It's too late.

He's already gone.

TWENTY

Alasdair

I've always loved serving Great Britain in her esteemed Navy. Even before I was promoted to captain, I took pride in my service and a job well done. My family was proud as well, though my mother was fearful for my safety, and my father would have preferred I come home to be groomed and polished for my future position as the Earl of Galloway. After my brother's death, I should have done so, but I felt a distinct obligation to my country and my comrades, and I cannot deny the adventure and excitement of captaining a magnificent Navy ship is a powerful force.

Yet, from the moment I walked away from Ella, sleeping in her bed, sated and content, I have regretted the choice to continue my career in the Navy. It was gut-wrenching to leave her, painful in a way I didn't know possible, my body filled with a fury that craved destruction. I was a stranger to myself, and the tension of keeping it in caused a nauseating pounding in my skull.

The long journey back to London and the ten days it took to gather my men and ready my ship was spent in a malaise. I want to be with Ella, to protect her, enjoy her new discoveries at Galloway, watch her face light in pure delight with each new experience. I want her to walk into my office and make my stomach swirl with youthful excitement like it does every time she enters. I want to watch her smile and giggle at the letters she receives from her cousin, Mary. I want to sleep with my head on her chest so I can hear her heartbeat and know she is alive and well. I want to kiss away the tears that well over when our pleasure is so intense. I never wanted to part from her and didn't realize how much so until I was left with no other choice.

I made sure to write her a note before departing and left it on her vanity so she could find it easily in the morning. I wonder about her thoughts upon reading my words.

My Dearest Ella,

I feel a sense of disloyalty when I think about your sentiments on my unexpected call to service. You said it is my duty and that duty comes first. I certainly cannot disagree, and it is something I have lived by my entire adult life, but that was before I met you. That was before you enchanted me with your ethereal presence, beguiled me with your clever wit, charmed me with your breathtaking smile, and stole my heart with your passionate soul. Now my own heart says that my duty is to stand by your side, to protect you, to provide for you, to make sure you are happy and joyful every day, that you are pleasured and fully sated, that you are loved deeper and more completely than any man has ever loved another woman. Is this treason, my loyalty, now owned by you? It is of no mind, for only you and I will know the truth.

Rest assured, I will find victory for my king, for my country, and above all, for you.

I will write to you often, as you will constantly be on my mind. Instead of writing in return, keep a journal of our time apart so that I may enjoy your adventures with you when I return. The thought that one of your letters could be lost and never arrive weighs heavy on my heart.

Please know that I will bid you good morning every day when the sun rises in the east and good evening when it sets in the west. I will bid you good night just before I close my eyes, and I will speak the words of my heart...Lady Ella Stewart, I love you.

Your loving husband and humble servant,
Alasdair Stewart

"Pardon me, sir," Lieutenant Harris interrupts my reverie. "I have correspondence from Admiral Nelson."

"Thank you, Lieutenant."

I break the seal and find the distinct upright and somewhat unrefined script of Lord Nelson's hand. After last year's unfortunate battle wound and subsequent loss of his right arm, my dear friend is now forced to write with his left hand. Although I can see his technique is much improved over the past many months, there is still evidence that he struggles.

Fortunately, he has not lost his sense of humor.

Dear Sir,

I hope this letter finds you well and aboard ship, sailing in the direction of my fleet. Please accept my sincerest apologies for interrupting your honeymoon. However, I must point out the irony that ultimately, it was your father-in-law that requested I do so. Perhaps you did not make a proper impression with our esteemed Admiral of the Fleet.

Forgive me, I digress. I've been tracking the French for months. They took Malta, as I suspected they would, and I fear Egypt is next. Their mission is to disrupt trade with

India, and if they are successful, it could be devastating for Great Britain.

I am heading back to port in Naples. We shall rendezvous there to replenish supplies and meet with the captains to finalize our strategy. The French will be most unhappy when we arrive.

Have a safe and swift journey, my friend.

Very Respectfully,

Admiral Horatio Nelson

I fold the letter and place it in my pocket, taking a moment to look out across the sea to the perfect line of the horizon. Weather and time permitting, I prefer to spend my time on deck where the air is fresh, and the stench of unwashed men isn't thick in the air. So far, this journey has been blessed with blue skies and calm seas, a steady wind, and no distractions. Nevertheless, it is not where I want to be, and I need to find a way to get my head focused on the duty of captaining this vessel and making sure my part in assisting Nelson ensures victory.

Twelve days later, we arrive in port, and it is an impressive sight. Nelson's fleet is amongst the multitude of merchant and privateer ships, creating a sea of masts and sails. I've always thought sailing ships were works of art; even as a boy, they fascinated me. But to see this number and variety in one place has always been a source of excitement and inspiration. It speaks of the power and ingenuity of man; the creativity of design, the desire to seek new worlds, to protect a nation, or gain wealth through the transport of goods. Once man was able to master the sea, the world became less vast, and progress advanced at a faster pace as the thoughts and ideas from other lands were easily shared. These ships are magnificent, and they articulate so much more than simply a vessel that sails across the oceans.

The noise aboard ship is louder now as we prepare to anchor; the echoing flap of collapsing sails, heavy ropes coiling on deck as the sails are lowered, and the mingling calls from the lieutenant's orders on each deck. It all comes together to give me the motivation I've been desperately seeking.

"Sir! The men are readying the skiffs to sail ashore," Lieutenant Harris bellows through the noise.

"Thank you, Harris."

Within half an hour, we are rowing across the harbor to the docks where my transport awaits to take me to Nelson. Along the way, we approach his flagship, *Vanguard*, an impressive seventy-four gunship of the line.

Harris whistles through his teeth before saying, "That sure be a fine-looking vessel."

"Aye, that it is, Lieutenant," I agree.

Everyone on board our skiff looks up to admire the ornate carving on the stern over the captain's quarters, depicting two Roman soldiers standing guard at either end while cherubs float through the clouds above. It is freshly painted, the dominant bright red standing out against the black hull, white trim, and two bands of yellow gold that follow the line of the gun flaps. As we pass the bow, we see another Roman soldier taking charge as the figurehead of the ship, wielding his shield and sword.

At the docks, we find the expected crowd of men busily gathering supplies and completing their shore-bound duties before setting sail, as well as the plenitude of whores offering the wares to lonely sailors. It's loud, and it reeks of the stench of too many people and an unfortunate lack of sanitation.

My liaison, Mr. Wickham, picks me up and takes me to the tavern where Nelson has planned our meeting. It is further inland, away from the hustle of the port, a detail that pleases me immensely. Before parting ways, I hand Mr. Wickham a stack of letters and a shilling.

"Thank ye for the comfortable ride. If I may impose further, would ye please find a ship departing for Scotland? If there is'na one, England will do. I need these delivered as soon as possible."

"Yes, m'lord. I know of one leaving this afternoon."

"Good. Much obliged."

It's dark upon entering the tavern, but my eyes quickly adjust, and I see the admiral seated across the room with two other men.

"Good day, gentlemen," I say as I approach.

"Ah! Stewart, you finally made it!" Nelson says with a firm pat on my back as the other men stand.

"Gentlemen, may I introduce you to my friend and esteemed compatriot, Captain Alasdair Stewart."

"Josef Wagner. A pleasure to meet you, Captain Stewart," the taller man says, reaching for a handshake.

"Likewise," I reply, noticing he has a slight accent.

The other man is a bit older and quite familiar.

"Hello, Captain Stewart. It's been a while."

It hits me then. "Bloody hell! William Davies! 'Tis been far too long. I almost did'na recognize ye."

"Yes, well, age does tend to play tricks on your appearance. White hair, furrowed skin, and a potbelly are an excellent disguise." He laughs, and the sound brings back memories of my early days captaining and long nights of cards and spirits.

"Ye look well, my friend. Wise and well-traveled as we all hope to be."

Davies is a tradesman and, at times, a privateer for the British. He makes his way around the world rather efficiently and has always been a reliable source of information, as well as a damn good poker player.

"Have a seat, gentlemen." Nelson offers. "Captain Stewart, you already know that Davies has always been a valued ally of Great Britain. Well, Wagner here is considered the same. He is Austrian by birth but lived much of his life in England, or perhaps I should say at sea, as he is very proficient captain of a rather large merchant ship." Wagner chuckles and nods his head at Nelson's clarification. "These fine men have come to me with the same information: the French are going to invade Egypt and are setting up a naval blockade at the Port of Alexandria in the Aboukir Bay. I heard this same intelligence weeks ago, yet when I arrived, the bay was empty. There wasn't a French ship within sight. But Davies and Wagner have assured me that the French fleet, commanded by Admiral Brueys, is currently there, while Napoleon's army has already left Malta and is heading to Egypt. Needless to say, we must make haste."

"How many ships are in Brueys's fleet? Do we know?" I ask.

"Thirteen," Wagner replies. "Said to be almost 1200 guns."

"The French Navy does have an impressive line of ships. It is unfortunate for them that many of their most talented admirals and captains were all banished during the Revolution," says Nelson.

"That'd be a fine example of cutting off your nose to spite your face," Davies adds.

"That it would," Nelson agrees. "Now, Stewart, so you know, by the time the rest of the fleet arrives, we will have fourteen ships, though we will be shy, maybe a hundred guns. That is never a concern for me, though, as strategy is what wins a battle." He raises his ale so that we can all toast our agreement. "Davies and Wagner will be on standby to help deal with the injured, make any emergency transports necessary, and relieve us of some of our prisoners to take back to England. In the meantime, we will finish supplying our ships and prepare our men." He pauses to look me in the eye. "And to pray. This is going to be a bloody battle."

TWENTY-ONE
Ella

I started my walk a little earlier today. I find it is my best distraction from the worry and waiting that eats away at my sanity. When I married Alasdair, I knew the time would come for him to leave for duty, that it could happen at any time, and he would be gone for extended periods. I was accustomed to it, having a father in the Navy. But waking up over a fortnight ago to find him gone, with no chance of telling him my true feelings, has been haunting me day and night. What if something happens and he doesn't return? He will never know how much I love him or how much he means to me. He requested that I not write, and in truth, I don't want to distract him from his duty, but more so, I want him to hear me say the words as he looks into my eyes, knowing I am sincere.

"Oh God," I whisper as the tears burn my eyes. I quicken my pace as I approach the entrance to the forest. This is my sanctuary, the only place I can find any sort of internal peace.

There it is—the shift in everything around me as I enter the forest canopy. The cooler temperature that carries a dewy dampness, the clean scent of living plants and rich soil, and the sound that floats around you, pretending to be silent, but, is filled with a harmonious convergence of a thousand voices—the air, the water, the plants and trees, the animals, the insects—each with their own sonance that combines to create the most fascinating melody. Even my hurried steps down the path make a pleasant addition to the composition.

Before long, I am exiting the wood at the clifftop that overlooks the Firth of Clyde, an extensive body of water that is dappled with islands of varying sizes in the distance. This is my routine, to come to this clearing to sit upon the flat boulder overlooking this spectacular vista and pray for Alasdair's safety, then I visit our oak tree where I always feel closer to him.

I get comfortable, relax my shoulders, and take a few deep breaths, then close my eyes. A few minutes pass with the sounds of the wind, the small waves on the gravel shore echoing up the cliff wall, and the sea birds that sing in their own special voice. It is easy to let go in this place, to focus only on my prayers, and they always start the same. I ask God to watch over Alasdair and his men, to keep their ship sound in battle and free of disease for their journey. I ask for forgiveness should Alasdair take anyone's life and the strength to forgive should anyone take his. I ask for his speedy return home and for the patience to endure the wait. I pray for his father's soul as his time ticks nearer with each passing day.

I open my eyes and swallow the emotions that always emerge when I pray, especially now. The sunlight is glittering across the water as it accents each wave and ripple. I wonder if Alasdair likes looking out across the sea to watch the sunbeams dance across the surface. It saddens me that I don't know the answer, but I assure myself that I will very soon.

"I'm sorry I did not say the words you were hoping to hear," I say to the wind and hope it carries it to Alasdair. "I say it every day. I bid you good morning and good night and know in my heart that you do the same. It comforts me as I wait for your return." I pause to wipe away the tear that escapes. "I am sorry to say that your father is not well at all. I spend as much time as I can with him, but he prefers to be alone when the coughing becomes too much. I can honestly say that I am going to miss his company and the blunt conversation and humor I have come to love. It hurts my heart that I will not get more time with him. He loves you; you know. Quite a lot, I might add, and he is very proud of the man you have become. That all probably helps me to love him even more."

I stop again to wipe away more tears. It has been hard watching Callen enter his final days, but his strength has been a support to me. Yesterday, after Douglas gave him his breathing treatment, Callen spoke to me through labored breaths, while I sat upon his bed, holding his hand. He said, "There is so much about life that 'tis overlooked or taken fer granted. The small things, maybe a few more significant. I miss mi' wife. God rest her soul. That is one thing I never took fer granted. Lilith was a happy woman. I made sure of it. I loved her wi' all my heart. But I did'na pause enough to take in the freshness of a clear spring day or the beauty of a violent storm thrashing the Firth as she wanted me to. She wanted me to follow her through the forest and see the wonders of its magic. She said there were faeries in that forest, said they were her friends. She was always a fanciful girl and no less as a woman. Now that she is gone and my life is almost over, I wish I had taken the time to experience what made her so happy. Even if it were'na true, I could have made pretend."

A tear streaked his weathered cheek as I squeezed his hand. "Callen, you will be with her soon. Take comfort. She is waiting for you."

"Aye. That does bring comfort, as do you. Thank ye, Ella."

I smile, remembering our exchange as I re-enter the forest.

The drop in temperature feels good after the bright sun of the clearing had become too hot through all the layers of my clothing. It makes me think of the day before Alasdair left, and he had me undress under the ancient oak before we made love. It somehow felt liberating and natural, and I cannot deny there is a part of me that would love nothing more than to remove all my clothing and walk the entirety of this trail back to the entrance. I laugh at the absurdity of my imagination and turn off the main path to make my way to my favorite tree. Once there, I sit down and adjust my skirts as I cross my legs underneath them. I am comfortable here. Everything about it assures me that my new life as the wife of Captain Alasdair Stewart is a gift I could have never imagined, especially considering his arrogance when first we met. I laugh, cringing at how much I wanted to despise him.

"Well, he was ridiculously full of himself, not to mention rude," I say aloud just as the sun catches one of the flying creatures I've seen every time I've been here. It is not a butterfly, and it's far too small to be a bee moth, but it flies in a similar fashion. Whenever they appear, I feel a burst of happiness come over me as the whimsy from my childhood comes to the surface. Perhaps it was the same for Lilith. Either way, I do find it a bit strange that they seem to be as interested in me as I am in them.

"Hello again," I say to it. "We are fortunate to have another bright summer day. I can get used to all this sunshine." I stop to pick a wildflower and roll it between my fingers, admiring its lovely purple hue. "I had another restless night's sleep. I tossed and turned with dreams that confused and scared me. I can't remember all the details, but they were dark and made me anxious." I look up to see there are more of them flying about now. I seem to have attracted an audience. "I decided that would not do, so I got up and lit a candle and read Alasdair's letters again. I thought I would bring one today since you seemed to enjoy the last." I giggle as they appear to get excited, flying in loops and twirling around each other. "This one is sure to please, for it includes a poem."

My Dearest Faerie Maiden,

"I love it when he calls me that," I say with a smile.

I hope this letter finds you well and comfortable at home. I am well, though less than comfortable. Everything is fine aboard ship—the crew is healthy, the weather quite favorable—but I am not as content here as I used to be. You know the reason why—you cast a spell on me, and I am no longer the man I used to be. That is not a bad thing, you see, for the man I used to be, did not know such happiness existed as what you have brought into my life. I wonder if you feel it, too. You have turned this once-cavalier man into a lovestruck lad who daydreams of only you and your unmatched beauty.

I spend a lot of time on deck where the air is fresh, and the view inspires thoughts of you. I wish you could be here to see all the wondrous things that I see. I know how much you love the beauty of nature on land—the trees and plants of the forest, the perfect disarray of a butterfly garden, the brilliant colors of flowers in bloom, but you would love the beauty of the ocean, as well. You can feel its depth beneath you; you can see through its surface as creatures swim by, some small, others enormous. It can be calm and kind one day, then show you its power the next, but it always demands your respect.

On a particularly fine day, I was inspired to write this for you.

The vista before me
Monochrome is its theme,
Hues cool and bright,
Barely differing in tone,
Though separated with distinction:
One accented with sparkles of light,
The other with thin wisps of white.
What is this color,
As far as the eye can see?
It can only be one,
for no other could it be.

I look up and laugh, "Any guesses?" I ask playfully, knowing my question will not be answered. Then, to my utter shock and surprise, a blue sparkle of light flashes from one of the flying creatures. My heart pounds in my chest. Was that simply an odd coincidence? Surely, whatever that is, it did not just answer my question. I decide my only option is to go with it, otherwise, I will appear horribly rude. What a humorous notion.

"Very good. Aren't you the clever one?"

It does not go unnoticed that it appears pleased with my compliment as it loops circles through the air. Could I be losing my mind?

"There is a little bit more to the letter."

I'm sure you know the answer... It is the color of your eyes, though yours have an elegant touch of green. You probably don't know this, but they change color when you are excited, a crystalline blue like that of a rare gemstone, and it is befitting for the rarity that is you.

I must go now. But I will be writing you again soon.

Your loving husband and humble servant,

Alasdair Stewart

"He is quite the charmer, isn't he? Though I'm not sure about him saying my eyes change color. I believe his mind is always thinking in verses of poetry. Perhaps that explains his reasoning." I chuckle at the thought as I get up and straighten my skirts. "I shall be off now, but I will return tomorrow if the weather allows."

Back on the main path, I think about what happened after reading Alasdair's poem. It was unmistakable that a blue sparkle flashed from that...creature. Yet, how is that even possible? I have always had a fondness for the whimsical fantasy of folklore, but it was always just that—fantasy. However, I keep going back to what Callen told me about Lilith and her love of this forest. *"She said there were faeries in that forest, that they were her friends."* It gives me chills thinking about it now, whereas before, I thought it charming for a grown woman to be so imaginative. Perhaps I should be open-minded, be more imaginative. It seems as we age into adults, we lose the ability to let our minds wander to a place where anything is possible, where pixies and brownies and faeries play about in the forest, creating magic and mischief. What if these fantastical things *are* real and only the open mindedness of a child allows them to be seen? I am certain I will never know the answer, but I can make a choice—colorful or mundane. It seems a waste to choose the latter.

Outside the forest, the breeze is strong across the open meadow, and carried on it is the distinct sound of a horse galloping toward the manor. Excitement bursts through me, and I run to see if Alasdair is home. When I round the tall shrubbery on the east side of the castle, I can see that it is not him, and I am once again blanketed with the horrible dismay that has followed me for weeks.

The young man on horseback comes to a stop before me. "Good day, ma'am. I have yer mail delivery."

My heart swells with excitement as I pray there are letters from Alasdair. The young man hands me a small stack of letters for everyone at Galloway Castle.

"Thank you so much. Would you like a refreshment before you leave, or perhaps you'd like to take your horse to the stables to rest?"

"I thank ye, m'lady, but we refreshed at my last stop, and I need to get back to town before sunset."

"Very well. Thank you again, and safe travels."

He tips his hat and says goodbye.

I quickly climb the front steps and am greeted by one of the footmen at the door. I scurry through the foyer and down the hall. Once I'm in the parlor, I quickly sort through the stack of mail. To my heart's delight, I have two letters from Alasdair.

I get comfortable by the window and break the seal on the first letter.

My Dearest Ella,

As always, I hope this letter finds you well and happy. My crew and I are all well and are preparing to arrive at the port in Naples by midday tomorrow. There, I will meet with Admiral Nelson to determine our next moves against France. It is likely we will go to battle.

Please do not fret. My ship is quite able, and my crew is second to none. Furthermore, Nelson will have assembled the best Great Britain has to offer as his fleet. We have fought side by side before and always ended in victory.

I will return home to you, though currently, I cannot say

when that will be. It is a day I look forward to with a yearning I have never known. That's what happens when your wife carries a secret magic in her arsenal of charm and beauty. It traps your soul and holds it captive for all eternity —a sentence I will happily accept and indeed view as a rare gift of immeasurable value. I often wonder at my good fortune and why I am so deserving of it, but then I stop and simply focus on my gratitude and offer thanks to fate for ensuring our union—or perhaps I should say our reunion.

I know I will not have an answer until I return home, but I think of my father often. I do not expect him to be alive when I return. He is a good man, a good father, and husband. Imperfect, to be sure, but courageous and strong, righteous without arrogance, yet proud with uncompromising wit that forces you to laugh at yourself and the world around you. I hope you have gotten to know some of those characteristics. No doubt he has made you laugh on many occasions and taught you things you never dreamed of knowing.

I must bid you farewell. Always know you are forefront in my mind, morning, noon, and night.

Your loving husband and humble servant,
Alasdair Stewart

After reading this letter, I have a windstorm of emotions colliding inside me. My heart beats harder with worry knowing he sees an inevitable battle ahead. Is this a battle meant to intimidate our enemy where only a few cannons fire, or is this going to be a full-scale conflict with fire, explosions, black billowing smoke, sunken ships, and far too many deaths? I wish I had never seen those paintings, the ones depicting various battles where England was victorious. For me, it didn't matter who won. When I looked at the details so vividly portrayed, I could hear cannons firing, the cracking of wood, gun shots by the thousands, and the horrible screams of men inflicted with unimaginable pain. I've often wondered if it was the same for others when they looked at these works of national pride.

I stand to move closer to the window, feeling too upset to sit still. I take a deep breath and look to the sky as a small flock of sea birds swoop and play around each other. Their grace and agility conjure a smile, and I think of Alasdair's ever-flowing endearments and the girlish butterflies they wake up in my stomach. I love how he still refers to me as his faerie maiden as he did that fateful night. Now I carry secret magic that is holding him captive. I laugh out loud at his fanciful charm.

Once I'm seated again, I reread the letter and my eyes burn with tears of sadness for his father. Alasdair is right in his expectations.

Not wanting to cry again, I put that letter aside and open the next.

My Dearest Ella, Faerie Maiden,

As I sit at my desk, the ship swaying with its steady progression, charting our course, and journaling the necessary notes, I am distracted by thoughts of my lovely wife. You are everywhere. Your eyes are in the sparkling water on which I navigate. Your clean scent is on the fresh breeze across the waves. Your tenacity is in the sails whose uncompromising will advance my ship across the sea. Your smile shines brightly within the rays of the sun, and your lips are in the extraordinary design of a seashell, one that is lined with the most exquisite shade of pink.

You would not know this, but I have an extensive collection of seashells that fill the voids of the shelves that line the walls of my private quarters. They are wonders of nature, their artistry so fine, their beauty singular with shapes and colors and textures as diverse as they are similar, yet clearly, the ocean is their domain. There is one in particular I have always considered to be my favorite: the queen conch and it is prominent throughout the Caribbean. The tip of the shell shows the perfect outward rotation from its center, accented with smooth points that gradually get larger until it eventually fans out to a wide opening. It is here that we find its most appealing characteristic. The inside of its chamber is a perfect pink, a mixture of an elegant pale rose in full bloom and the high clouds of a summer sunset contrasted against a darkening sky. Try to imagine it in the drawing I attempted for you.

Not only is beautiful, but the snail that resides in this surprisingly large shell is an important food source for the people of the islands. They prepare it in numerous ways; sometimes raw, sometimes cooked, but always quite delicious as the meat is mild in flavor with a subtle sweetness that is easily complemented by other ingredients. Someday, I will take you to the islands so you may taste it for yourself.

I think you would love the Bahamian islands, in particular. They are, by far, my favorite. The water is crystal clear. The sand is white with a slight pink hue, and the islands are covered in coconut palms that stand tall with long fronds that sway in the wind. It is warm and humid, with bright sunny days, often interrupted by fierce squalls that drench the land and cool the air. You can comfortably swim in the water, for its temperature is like a luxurious bath. It is everything you would imagine a tropical paradise to be, and I think what you would love most are the seashells that wash in on the beach. In my mind, I can see you walking along the shore, collecting the treasures that you find. I imagine you amassing an impressive collection of your own, and the notion warms my heart.

I will bring home a few for you to admire. Rest assured, that will be soon.

Your loving husband and humble servant,
Alasdair Stewart

Before I can contemplate the idea of visiting a tropical island any further, Ewan enters the parlor.

"Pardon me, m'lady. But Douglas is requesting yer presence wi' Lord Galloway."

My chest tightens from his grim expression. "Of course."

We hurry down to Callen's bedchamber where the air is thick with the stench of illness and oncoming death. I go to the window and pull the drapes, then let in some clean air. The cool draft lifts my hair, and I breathe in its freshness.

As I'm looking across to the forest that Lilith always wanted him to visit, a thought overwhelms me.

"Douglas, please tell me you have a litter here in case of emergency."

"Yes, ma'am, we do."

"Good. Go as fast as you can and bring it here. We are taking Callen to the forest."

"But...m'lady..."

"Please hurry, Douglas."

Before long, we are entering the forest and making our way to a clearing covered by purple, white, and yellow wildflowers.

"Bring him over here." I direct Douglas and Ewan to set Callen down in the shade of an elm tree with a fantastic view of the flower patch brightly lit by the midday sun.

I situate myself by his head and gently lift it so that it can rest in my lap. His hair is damp and heavy as I brush it from his face.

"Callen, we are here in Lilith's forest." I see the corner of his mouth lift in acknowledgment. "Open your eyes, look upon the place that she loved." His eyes slowly open, taking time to adjust to the light. "I can picture her sitting right here, enjoying the beauty of the wildflowers as the butterflies fly about. Can you picture that too?" He nods his head ever so slightly. "Perhaps if we are lucky, her faerie friends will appear," I say with a slight giggle as my hand gently rubs his forehead. He smiles again, gazing upon the flowers, trees, and underbrush. It simply could not be more beautiful than it is right now. The flowers are glowing in the light, contrasting against a sea of green.

I catch something swooping through the flowers, distinctly different from the butterflies. It moves fast, then slow, stops, disappears, and reappears. To my delight, another joins in, and then another and another. Minutes later, a strange sense of joy overcomes me, and a presence I have yet to feel before.

"Callen, they are here. Can you see them?"

He nods again.

"She was telling the truth. There *is* magic in this forest."

A tear falls from Callen's eye; he blinks, and another follows the same wet trail. My own eyes sting with emotion:

sadness for saying goodbye but also happiness knowing Callen and Lilith will be together again soon.

"Callen, I think Lilith is here with us. She is waiting for you. She's ready for you to join her."

Tears run down my cheeks as I try to hold back the sobs. I wipe them away as the air shifts and a sudden breeze gusts hard around us. I glance around, expecting to find clouds moving in, but the skies are clear. Callen's head turns, and his eyes widen as if he sees something. Slowly, he raises his hand, thin and frail, fingers opening as if to take hold of another. My heart beats faster as his breaths rattle in his chest.

"Go, Callen," I whisper.

His hand falls, his eyes close, the air becomes still...and he is gone.

TWENTY-TWO

Alasdair

"Alasdair, wake up." Ella's voice is smooth and sultry, her hand warm as it glides across my abdomen. "I need you," she says, her lips kissing a trail from my chest to my neck, ending with a gentle bite on the lobe of my ear. "I need you to fuck me, Alasdair." Her whisper is hot, her tongue wet as it teases me. My cock is painfully hard. I need to be inside her.

"Ella..." The gravel of my voice echoes in my head.

Her leg comes over my hip so she can straddle me, her long hair soft like silk sweeping across my skin. My hands grab onto her hips and guide her to my throbbing shaft. She moans as the head breaches her entrance...

I jolt out of my heavenly slumber to the sound of the sails snapping as they catch the shifting wind. "Bloody hell," I say aloud while I try to calm the pounding of my heart. That dream was more realistic than any I can recall, and my poor cock isn't accepting the fact that it was just a dream.

It doesn't take long to relieve it of its tension, but my longing for Ella becomes greater still. Perhaps longing isn't the right word; it seems too gentle, too tender. This is more like a ravenous hunger that leaves a gnawing pain in my gut while my mind tries to accept the terrible reality that satiation will not come any time soon.

I drudge through my routine of ablutions before heading to the quarter deck to check with the lieutenant and confirm that we are on schedule. I slept for most of the morning after a late night of navigation planning and ship's log entries, as well as routine checks with the lieutenants overseeing the various decks and gunner stations. If the French fleet is in Aboukir Bay on the coast of Alexandria as we expect them to be, the battle will ensue without delay. The French will not be expecting such aggression upon arrival, especially so close to dusk, putting them at an immediate disadvantage. Nelson has been combing the Mediterranean for months, looking for Admiral Brueys's fleet; once he finds them, he will not hesitate to engage, hopefully bringing us to victory that much sooner.

The horizon is clear with minimal haze, ideal conditions for a battle at sea. I look around and see the rest of the fleet in full sail, moving at the same steady clip. It is an impressive sight: thirteen ships of the line, massive hulls lined with gun ports, every sail filled with wind, the ocean thrown aside in a splash of white water as the bow carves its surface. Napoleon's admirals will be rather displeased when they see our fleet coming up the coast. Surely, they are expecting some show of force, considering Bonaparte is trying to block our largest trade route. It is hard to fathom they can be that naive, yet in the past several battles, they have proven to be just that.

"Lieutenant Fernsby," I greet on approach.

"Captain Stewart." He nods. "We are moving ahead of schedule. Aboukir Bay should be in our sights in little more than two hours."

"Excellent news. I'm glad I didn't sleep through it," I jest, wishing I could go back to sleep and finish the dream that was sadly interrupted. Tension creeps up from my gut and lands in my chest as I think about Ella. This is the side of love I'm finding difficult to deal with—the desperate longing to have her in my arms again, to hear her voice, to see her smile. *I will be home soon, my love.*

I take my leave to do one last inspection. After checking on the upper decks, I quickly descend the steps to the first gun deck. It is important that I make these rounds before battle, not only to encourage my crew as they face an imminent battle, but I may not see many of these men after today.

"Listen up, gentlemen!" I shout through the echoing chamber and watch as everyone stops their duties to stand at attention. "Once the French are in our sights, battle will ensue immediately. Admiral Nelson will give us the signal, and our job is to sink as many French ships as possible in the shortest amount of time." The echo of my steps is intentionally loud as I walk slowly down the line. "Remember, should we take prisoners aboard this ship, we will treat them with respect. These men are doing their duty just as you are. Soldiers don't start wars—kings, queens, and conquerors do." I stop to look into the eyes of the men before me. I wait a moment longer to let the silence grow heavy before proceeding down the center of the deck lined with men and battle-ready cannons. "God forbid if any of ye parish during this fight. Should that be yer fate, I will personally ensure that yer family receives enough compensation that they will not have to turn to the streets to survive." I've done it before, and I will do it again. My men fight harder and with more faith knowing I will not let them down. "We've been here before, we've fought together before, we always find victory. And why is that, gentlemen?" I shout the question louder than the previous statement.

In unison, they all answer, "Because victory is the only option!"

"That is correct. When victory is the only option, ye do not lose."

I turn back for the stairs, my pace quickening. Once there, I make one last announcement.

"On behalf of King George III and the blessed country of Great Britain, I thank ye for yer service. I appreciate ye being a part of this crew, and I trust ye to help keep the *Orion* above water. Godspeed." I offer a salute and head to the next deck.

Fernsby was right. Two hours later, after skirting the Egyptian coast, we arrive at Aboukir Bay, where Napoleon's fleet is anchored off its shoals. I take out my telescope and count thirteen ships with the flagship *L'Orient* guarding the center. It's an impressive vessel, much larger than Nelson's *Vanguard*, but I notice the ships flanking it are not nearly close enough to properly protect such an important asset. I know Nelson sees this as well, and as soon as I turn the scope toward his mast, I see his signal—*enemy, in sight.*

As if God had given his approval, the wind picks up from behind us, pushing the *Vanguard* directly at the enemy fleet in swift and dramatic fashion, no doubt sending terror throughout the thirteen French ships. Admiral Nelson's charge is a clear message that an attack is underway, leaving Brueys's men with little time to prepare.

The rest of our fleet follows the *Vanguard* as we begin to take our positions to surround the anchored fleet. *Goliath* and *Zealous* are the first in battle as they each race separately between two enemy ships, firing perfectly aimed cannons directly through their center from stern to bow and vice versa. It is the most vulnerable shot a battleship can take, and in this initial move, our fleet has already severely damaged four ships.

Horatio positions *Vanguard* on the seaward side, and I command Fernsby to round their first position and bring us to the landward side.

"Bring us close, Fernsby! I want to finish the ship Captain Foley just hit!"

Fernsby deftly maneuvers *Orion* within close enough range to keep us out of the shoals and to completely disable the ship with chain shot.

"Destroy the masts!" I yell to the closest lieutenant, who then sends the message down through the gun decks.

In that one pass, we finish what *Goliath* started; the ship is destroyed. I hear men screaming as smoke billows and flames crackle, and I pray for their souls and that many will escape.

"Stay away from the shoals, Lieutenant! They want us grounded!" I yell as the setting sun darkens the waters, and we approach another target. "Lieutenant! Take out that frigate!"

My command is drowned out by the thunder of cannon fire, both ours and theirs. I hear the splintering of wood and feel the floor jolt beneath my feet as we take a significant hit. Regardless, my crew has peppered the frigate with twenty-five-pound shot, destroying its hull. Within minutes, the ship is sunk. One more down.

Further down, I can see that *L'Orient* has taken a battering from one of our ships of the line, *Bellerophon*, but the French flagship is now retaliating with full force, and Captain Darby has very little space to maneuver away.

"Bloody Christ! Someone must get over there to help Darby!" I yell to anyone that can hear.

The skies are darkening now, and the thick smoke that fills the air glows with the light of fire. Orange and red mixed with black, moving like a surging mass that swells, then rolls into itself like a serpent monster from the furthest depths of the sea. Every breath makes my throat choke on the stench of gunpowder, burning wood, and death. There is never a moment that isn't littered with the sound of cannon fire and musket shots. It goes on and on, an endless tempo, but there is a rhythm, the steady beat of victory and defeat, that is both devastating and encouraging—the sound of war.

Time passes though it seems to stand still. More ships down, more damage to my hull, more death on the decks of the *Orion*, but she is still afloat and still fighting with a mighty force.

I hear Fernsby yell from his station at the ship's wheel, "The flagship's ablaze, Captain!"

I squint my eyes and look between two French battleships toward the last location of *Vanguard* on the seaward side of the fight. Praise God, Nelson's ship has not been destroyed. I don't see flames, though I do see significant damage. The smoke drifts through to block my view but leaves an opening on the opposite side that shows *Bellerophon* completely demasted and set adrift. I say another prayer for Captain Darby and his men and that they do not drift too far so they may be found when the fighting has ended.

The sky becomes bright with the blinding light of an inferno, and I turn to see that Fernsby was right, only it is *L'Orient* and not *Vanguard* that has caught fire. The ship is massive, a floating fortress with at least 120 guns, surrounded by three of our own, relentlessly showering the flames with more cannons.

"Do ye smell that, Fernsby? 'Tis bloody turpentine! Good God! That ship is going to blow!" I turn and run to the edge of the quarter deck and yell to Harris, "Drop the anchor! Drop the anchor!" We cannot get any closer, or the *Orion*'s sails will be vulnerable to the blast.

We stumble to the side, and I grab the rail as the force of the anchor taking hold stops us short. The entire bay is lit bright, and we watch as the crew of *L'Orient* begins jumping ship in desperation.

"Harris! Keep pounding the two in front of us. They are

almost sunk. Lieutenant Croft! Blast the shore with thirty-fives! It sounds like we're in a bloody swarm of hornets; so many bullets are coming our way!"

No sooner does the vessel to my right start to sink from our relentless barrage than the wind is knocked out of the entire bay from the explosion of Napoleon's prize flagship. Fernsby is thrown across the deck, and I am slammed into the rail behind me. I fall to my knees and cover my ears as the reverberating booms continue to blast through the night sky. It is a deafening sound, loud enough to shake the bones in your body. Once I've caught my breath, I crawl over to the lieutenant, who lies face down and completely still. I roll him onto his back and find him covered in blood. My hand automatically looks for a pulse in his neck. It's light, but it's there. Thank God.

I sit down then lie on my back and wait while my vision, hearing, and breathing adjust. My chest feels bludgeoned, and my hearing is muffled. I blink several more times and see the sky is filled with the burning debris of the explosion raining down on the bay. I get up on my hands and knees and slowly rise to stand and get my first glimpse at what's left of *L'Orient*.

"By all that is holy," I whisper through the dryness of my throat.

I have never seen such damage to a ship as what I'm witnessing right now. Its whole center is gone, and what is left is still ablaze. The cannon fire is still echoing around us, but without the might of the prized *L'Orient*, the volume is noticeably diminished.

Turning back to the rail, I see Harris and a few other crewmen scrambling to put out fires from falling embers. The two ships we had in our sights are down. It's time to change position.

"Harris! I need a medic on the quarter deck! Fernsby's down! Pull anchor! We're moving position!"

While looking out across the line of the French fleet, it is easy to assess the outcome of this battle.

"When victory is the only option, ye don't lose," I say to myself, just as a sharp pain lances the back of my head and everything turns black.

TWENTY-THREE

Ella

I have received word that Beatrice will arrive tomorrow afternoon, and to add to my delight, Mary decided to travel with her. Apparently, she has found London to be a bore without me there. To add to her woes, the past three potential suitors her mother invited for tea made her lose all hope for the future. *A change of scenery is what is needed,* Mary wrote. *Actually, a change in my social status is what I need, but that will not happen unless I fall into some mad, passionate love affair and end up with child, eventually giving birth to the sweet bastard that saves me from the chains of an unwanted marriage.* Mary tends to be dramatic, but at this point, I wouldn't put that scenario past her—she's that desperate.

"Oh! Hello, Douglas. Is everything prepared for our guests' arrival tomorrow?" I ask when I pass him on my way to the library.

"Yes, m'lady," Douglas answers.

"Wonderful. And how are you doing?"

"I am fine, ma'am." His forced smile says otherwise.

"Please take the rest of the day off if it suits you," I offer and gently pat his arm.

"I prefer to stay busy, but I thank ye nonetheless."

Douglas had a hard time saying goodbye to Callen. He had worked for him since he was a boy, but he has been his valet for the past twenty years. They became friends during that time, and when they each lost their wives only a few months apart, their friendship was an invaluable source of support and understanding that most others could not give.

When Callen passed away in the forest five days ago, Douglas sat next to a nearby tree and cried. Ewan and I left him alone to release his sorrow privately, but later that evening, he came to me and thanked me for taking Callen somewhere close to Lilith to take his last breath.

That evening, Douglas and I stayed up late into the night, talking about his dear friend. It was wonderful to hear so many stories I may have never otherwise known. It touched my heart to know that Alasdair's parents had a loving marriage, as did my parents, but apparently, they fell in love when they were barely adolescents. Callen spent years courting Lilith and making sure no one else caught her attention. They were finally married but soon faced tragedy when the first-born son died at only a week old. A year later, they were blessed with another son, Alasdair's older brother Rory. Sadly, he succumbed to illness at the age of twenty-three. Rory was said to be wise, always showing himself to be responsible and respectful so that he could proudly follow in his father's footsteps one day. On the other hand, Alasdair was mischievous and playful as a child, always pushing the limits. Douglas said Lilith doted on Alasdair even though he gave her fits with his antics. He said the four of them were a very close family and that the bond of the remaining three helped heal the wound of losing Rory so young. When the sad day came, Alasdair and Callen were there with Lilith when she passed away, holding her hands when she left to be with her sons.

I cried myself to sleep that night. I cried for my father-in-law, whom I barely knew, but loved as if I'd known him for decades. I cried for Lilith and Callen and their loss of two children, for Alasdair losing his brother and both parents. I cried for Beatrice and her warm, comforting embrace, for my father's ever-constant support, and my mother's persistent worry over propriety and proper etiquette. And I cried because Alasdair doesn't know how deeply I love him.

We buried Callen next to his beloved Lilith and their two children the next day. He requested no ceremony at all, but I would not have it. He deserved beautiful prayers, hymns that renew your faith in heaven, and words that spoke of the man he was here on earth and the respect he earned from those around him.

I took a long ride through the forest that afternoon. Willow and I ran free through the trails and found a few jumps that lifted our spirits. She knew I was down and did her best to make me forget, even for just a few moments. The goodbyes, the tragedies, the regrets, and words unspoken, so many things over which we have no control. She pushed me past my melancholy, forced the wind through my hair, and invigorated my resolve to find happiness beyond the pain.

We ended up on the northern ridge and a clearing that was more purple than green. "Have you ever seen anything so beautiful?" I asked Willow. "It simply doesn't seem real, does it, my girl?"

It truly didn't. It was a sea of color blanketing the entire clearing. Up close, I could see the small flowers that cluster at the end of each branch, but in the distance, they blended together, creating a field of solid purple.

"Absolutely breathtaking," I whispered to myself as I looked around the expanse.

Something in the sky caught my eye; a bird soaring in slow circles. Once my eyes adjusted, I could see it was white and rather large with wide wings tipped with black feathers. Its wings stayed wide as it searched the ground below, riding the air with elegant grace.

"What a lovely creature you are," I felt compelled to say.

He seemed to appreciate the compliment as he cried out a piercing call. It echoed over the purple landscape, and I was overwhelmed by an unexpected sense of nostalgia. He sent another call across the moor, then another as he swooped nearby.

"Do I know you?" I asked, laughing at his obvious grab for our attention. Two more circles above, and he swiftly moved toward the woods behind us, landing on a low branch in the nearest tree.

"Well, hello there," I said, admiring his stature.

His feathers were a powdery white, brighter on his chest and tinted with gray along his shoulders and head. His wings were decorated with a soft pattern of stripes and patches, and the black tips were tucked neatly behind him. Sharp, shiny black talons curve from his toes where they rested on the branch. But the most impressive feature on that magnificent bird were his eyes. Their focus was fierce, almost penetrating as they stared me down. Their bright, golden-yellow hue was a perfect match to his beak, also tipped in black.

He let out a loud screech, as if to offer a greeting in return, then lifted all his downy feathers and stretched his wings. I laughed at the casual display and thought it must feel good for a bird to do such a thing.

"I'm glad I happened upon you today. It is quite lovely

here. I've never seen so many flowers in one place. It's like a purple sea, for heaven's sake!"

He let out another loud reply, then turned his head around to call into the woods. Looking back at me for several long seconds, he called one more time, then flew away. I watched him go and felt a jolt of sadness come over me. When I looked back at the forest, wondering if he had called to a mate, my breath caught short in my chest. There, maybe twenty paces away from me, standing in the thick of the wood, was a white stag.

"Dear God," I said, holding onto my chest.

He stood there, staring at me with unfeigned interest. He seemed enormous, his pale coloring contrasting with his dark surroundings. Yet, it was his aura that intrigued me most. The beast that stood before me was composed, focused on me with a dominant air, yet I felt unthreatened. He seemed distinguished, and the more I stayed in his presence, the more I sensed his importance. He was no ordinary beast of the forest —he was regal, a prince, perhaps even a king.

"Hello," I said, not knowing what else to do. "I've read about you. I feel very fortunate to be here with you. I understand it is not common...seeing you, that is." I was both nervous and excited. From what I read, this was a very sacred animal in these lands, its mystery and mythology thousands of years old.

Startling me, Willow nudged me from behind, pushing me toward the stag, offering a low muffle of encouragement. I turned to her and asked, "Go to him?" And she raised her head, then lightly tapped her foot in agreement. Even Willow's movements were subdued, as if showing proper respect.

I turned back to find he hadn't moved, but I could sense his patience, as if he were waiting for me. So, I followed Willow's instruction and slowly walked around the low-lying plants and the trunks of a few young trees. When I finally stood before him, looking at his handsome face, I felt a strange tingle run through my body. I smiled, because I was happy, very happy, as if I were being greeted by an old and dear friend.

"Thank you for letting me come to you. This is quite a privilege. May I touch you?" I asked with a sudden familiarity.

He hesitated for only a moment, then lowered his head enough for me to reach up and pet the bridge of his wide nose and admire the massive antlers branching out high above like a splendid crown of nobility.

"What a wonderful day this has turned out to be," I said as I gently caressed his snow-white fur. "I have been very sad as of late. My dear father-in-law has just passed, you see, and my husband is at sea fighting in a war. I feel very alone in this new place, though here in the forest, I feel like I make a new friend every day. I never got to meet my mother-in-law, but she thought this forest to be gifted with magic. She was right. I have seen some extraordinary things, and now look at me!" I said excitedly, a genuine smile spreading across my face as I continue to pet along the side of his nose to the protruding mound of his jaw muscle. "Petting the legendary white stag of the forest. I believe I will keep this our secret. How does that sound?" His shiny, long-lashed eyes blinked, and I felt my own eyes sting with the poignancy of the moment.

We stayed in each other's company a while longer. I told him a bit more about me and relished the awareness that he truly seemed to be listening and was interested to know more. But the clouds began to move in, and I knew it was time for us to part ways. He had been so generous with his time, I didn't want to take advantage, though I believe I could have stayed in his presence for many hours more. I felt renewed, invigorated being near him, petting his coarse white fur.

"I have to go now," I said with a little sorrow in my voice.

"Thank you for spending time with me. I have enjoyed it immensely, and I do hope to see you again someday."

He kept his regal composure and stared at me for a moment before dropping his head down toward me. The only thing I knew to do was lean forward and kiss his forehead, then rest mine against it in silent communication. When I lifted my head, he stood tall again, eyes sparkling with an ancient wisdom and turned to leave. Before he was out of sight, he stopped and looked back, watching as I wiped away the tears that spilled from my eyes.

"Goodbye, my friend," I said through a choked voice and watched as he bowed his head in reply.

Willow and I took our time going home. I didn't want to be in the confines of the manor, especially after such a profound meeting in the wood. It was all so surreal, the clearing of purple heather, the white bird of prey, then the white stag, both of which seemed to have as much interest in me as I had in them, something that seems strangely common in this place. I felt like I had been brought here on purpose, and I was starting to feel like I belong here far more than I belonged in England. Perhaps Alasdair was right—I should believe in fate and trust in its guiding hand.

About ten minutes from Galloway Castle, I was struck by a recollection from my research on the legends of the white stag. Some myths say that an encounter means a great change is coming into your life, while others say it is a deceased loved one that has come to visit. My first thought was that maybe it was Callen. He had only just passed, but maybe he wanted to reassure me that everything would be well. But then I thought about the familiarity I had with that mysterious animal, and it made my stomach sink in terrible fear. What if it was Alasdair? What if he had been killed? "No..." I said aloud as my hands began to tremble. "It simply cannot be."

I rushed home, pushing Willow hard to get us there quickly so I could check the day's mail. Though anything that I received would already be weeks old, it was always reassuring to see his prose in the beautiful script of his handwriting.

I was left disappointed that day and every day since then. Plenty of mail has come to the manor, and I was beside myself with excitement when I got word that Beatrice and Mary would be here soon, but the consistent letters from Alasdair have stopped. I didn't want to taint my special meeting with the stag in the forest by filling my head with dreadful thoughts, but the longer I don't hear something from Alasdair, the harder it is to stay calm.

In his office, I sit down in his chair and lean back relaxing my shoulders. I come here often because it makes me feel closer to him. I close my eyes and see his face, those gorgeous eyes, that flirtatious dimple. Oh God, how I miss him. He will return to me, and we will have a whole life to live, long into the future. We will have children and grandchildren...

A tap on the door startles me.

"Come in."

Ewan enters with the correspondence tray, and I can see it holds at least three letters. I say a silent prayer that at least one is from my husband.

Mother and Father.

My aunt, Mary's mother.

Our neighbor to the east.

Nothing from Alasdair.

"Thank you, Ewan."

He nods and leaves the room.

"Please, Alasdair, dear God, please still be alive," I whisper to myself and pray for it to be true.

TWENTY-FOUR

Alasdair

"Good afternoon, Doctor. What is the update on Captain Stewart?" I hear someone ask the question, but it is so muffled in my head, I cannot discern who. I want to stand up, open my eyes, and leave this darkness.

My crew...*Orion*...the battle...

I continue to ask myself the same questions, day after day, but I never find an answer.

Where the hell am I?

Nausea...it won't go away.

My arms are heavy.

I can't move.

I'm floating again, but there is nothing here.

Nothing.

Only darkness.

Ella...

⌇

"A musket ball grazed his head...fell to the deck...hit hard, it appears."

More muffled talk.

"Will he make it?"

"I don't know yet."

Get me out of here...

~

"Alasdair! Where are you? Please! Alasdair, help me!" Ella's voice is desperate.

"Ella! Can you hear me? Where are you? I can't find you!"

I feel like I can't breathe. Where is she? I hear her, but I can't see her, I can't see anything.

"Ella!"

~

"Everything will be alright, son," my father says, his voice deep and smooth. He's strong, free from illness.

"Father! You are well?"

"Yes, Alasdair. I am well, as are Rory and your mother. She sends her love."

My God, he sounds so young, and Mother...how can that be?

"Where is she? Can I see her?"

I wait, desperate for a reply.

"Father! Can I see her? Can I talk to Mother?"

~

There is noise, someone in the room.

Can you hear me? Please! Get me out of here!

The noise continues, but still, no reply.

Hello! Can anyone hear me? I need to get out of here!

I hear a door shut, and I am left in silence once again.

I know I haven't been captured by the enemy, but I'll be damned if I don't feel like I have been. I'm confined to the darkness, and I can't escape. For all I know, I've been here for days, maybe weeks. In and out of consciousness. I haven't moved, yet I'm exhausted.

Ella, my love, I pray that you are well. I pray that we will be reunited soon. I pray that I will leave this dark and dreary abyss and return to your loving arms. I will return to you, Ella. I promise.

TWENTY-FIVE

Ella

"Words truly cannot do justice for how happy I am that you are here, Beatrice. But I fear I am having difficulty expressing it since I'm carrying this heavy burden everywhere I go. Please forgive me."

"Well, dearie, I think you forget that I know you better than you know yourself, so there is nothing to forgive," Beatrice replies with a motherly pat on my shoulder. She and Mary arrived two days ago and brought the comforting hugs and familiar conversation I had been missing.

"Yes, you probably do. I just know I would feel so much better if I received a letter from Alasdair. I have myself in knots with worry. How did Mother do so well? I don't ever recall her fretting over Father's absence."

"You know your mother...she wears a stoic facade better than anyone. Her upbringing didn't allow otherwise. She was likely in knots, as are you, only unable to express it. Be glad you don't have to hide it. 'Tis better to let it out." I relax, listening to her soothing voice offer words of wisdom.

"You are right. I don't see the Duke of Brunswick allowing

his daughter to show emotion of any sort. I can't say I've ever seen the man smile. Can you imagine my poor mother's childhood?"

"Let us not forget the Duchess of Brunswick. I was a grown woman, and she terrified me. It didn't go unnoticed that your mother did not shed a single tear when she passed away."

The door flies open, and in enters Mary, "Good morning, ladies!" She practically glides over to the settee and does a dramatic spin before sitting down. "I feel quite special being here in this exquisite castle. Like I'm part of some fairy tale. Ella, your letters did not do any justice to this place. Wouldn't you agree, Beatrice?"

"She did say it was lovely, though she didn't mention its size."

"Precisely! *Oh, it is quite nice here at my new home. It is so well-appointed, and everyone here is kind and welcoming.* There was no mention of it being a fortress fit for the king!" Mary finishes with her arms waving around my admittedly quite opulent room while Beatrice giggles at her imitation of me.

"Is my voice really that annoyingly high-pitched, Mary?"

She throws her head back and laughs. "No, darling! You know how I love to exaggerate. Now tell me what I am dying to know. What is it like being married to a stallion?"

Beatrice and I both laugh before she says, "I will leave you young ladies to enjoy that conversation without me. I still have a lot of unpacking to do. Do you need anything else, dear?"

"No, I am fine. Please take as much time as you need to settle in," I say, and add another hug to the multitude I've already given.

Mary doesn't waste any time getting to the point when Beatrice closes the door, although the point she makes is far from the one I was expecting.

"Oh, Ella, something has happened, and I...I don't know what to do."

I'm so taken aback, I don't respond. The change of subject accompanied by her tone along with the tears welling in her eyes has me completely thrown. Mary is usually not this serious, and I don't think I have ever seen her at a loss as to how to handle a situation. Before I can swallow my surprise and ask her what is wrong, she continues.

"Remember when we joked about Graham Knightly?"

My heart is beating faster, for I fear what she will tell me. "Mary, what did you do?"

"Well, I still have my maidenhead if that's what you're worried about."

"Oh, thank God!"

"Don't get too ahead of yourself. It's a wonder I didn't lose it!"

"No! What happened?"

"It started weeks ago when we danced at the Fairfield ball. Ella, he looked so handsome, and he kept watching me all evening with this look in his eyes that had me all flustered. By the time he came over to talk to me, I swear I was completely aroused!" Mary is clearly out of sorts as she gets up to pace around the room.

"My goodness, Mary. What did he say to you?" I can honestly tell myself that I am dying to know where this story leads. Graham Knightly is an exceptionally handsome man and much more distinguished looking than most of the titled men her mother keeps pushing on her.

"First, he took my hand and greeted me with a proper bow. I could feel the softness of his lips on my fingers—he made sure of that. When he stood, he just stared into my eyes for what seemed like many long minutes. He was trying to jumble my thoughts; I know he was. And it worked!" She continues her pacing with added huffs of frustration. "Ella, I am never at a loss for words, but when he told me that I was the most beautiful woman in the room, I literally forgot how to say thank you!"

"I understand completely. Alasdair left me in that same stupor on more than one occasion, and I was not happy about it." Though, at this moment, I would love nothing more than for Alasdair to stand before me and fluster the words right out of my head.

"Well, I finally got my wits about me and told him he had excellent taste. But, before I could turn and walk away, hoping to save my dignity and not get tongue-tied again, he asked me to dance."

"Clearly, you didn't say no."

"No, I didn't. I danced several dances with him. Thankfully Mother wasn't there, or she would have had fits. I was definitely over the limit for not *seeming too familiar*," she says, exaggerating the last part. "What a preposterous rule! I rather enjoyed dancing with him. He is quite good, you know. Not to mention the bantering back and forth—that was more fun than I've had in years."

"Mary. You seem to be taking the long way around this story. What happened between you and Graham?"

"There is a lot to it, but if you want to get straight to the point, fine." She hesitates for a moment, and I notice her cheeks turning red. "I went to his townhouse."

"Unchaperoned?" I say, aghast.

"Yes."

"Surely you knew that was a bad idea."

"I did, and I didn't care. I had argued with Mother because she was threatening to choose a husband for me, and I was tired of her trying to control everything I do. But more than anything, I wanted to be alone with him. He had kissed me the day before, and I thought I had died and gone to heaven, and I wanted to feel it again. So, I told Mother I was going shopping, and I went to Graham's house instead. Now I have a terrible dilemma on my hands." Her voice is thick with emotion.

"You've fallen in love with him, haven't you?"

"Yes," she whispers and falls into a fit of tears.

"Oh, Mary, it will all work out," I console her while guiding her to come and sit next to me by the window.

"No, it won't. My family will not allow me to marry an untitled man, no matter how wealthy he may be."

"Have you spoken to your mother about it?"

"Somewhat. All I know is I will be disowned and considered a disgrace to the family name." I help her wipe the tears away.

"It is hard to imagine your parents doing something so extreme. Perhaps she is bluffing, and if not, it's *your* life, not hers. If she's more concerned with your status than your happiness, it's her loss." I say, knowing if I were in her shoes, it simply wouldn't be that easy. "What about Graham? Has he made any declarations?"

"Oh yes! He most certainly has, one being that he will not tolerate a rejection based on the shallow mindset of the haut ton where title is the determining factor."

"He told you that he wants to marry you?"

"I suppose you could say he did, although it may have been more of an indirect approach. I believe his words were, *'When you are my wife, you will quickly learn that I judge a man by his character, not by the lineage of his family.'*"

"Oh my. Either you gave him a clear reason to make that statement, or he is arrogantly presumptuous," I reply with a raised brow.

Mary looks away, avoiding my eyes while another flush of pink brightens her cheeks.

"Look at me, Mary." She waits only a few seconds, then brings her eyes to mine. "The choice has already been made, dear cousin. I can see it in your eyes. You are simply having a hard time coming to terms with what that means because if your family truly does disown you, you will not have them to fall back on should things not go well with Mr. Knightly. It is a bit of a gamble, but if you are sure your love for one another is true, and in your heart, you know he is an honorable man, then I think you should let him know your answer is yes."

Her face lights up with a contagious smile. "Thank you, Ella. It has been awful pretending that everything is well when I've been ready to collapse with the weight of this burden. I'm so happy I decided to make this journey to visit you. I knew if we talked about it, you would help me make the right decision. Now all I must do is figure out how to tell my parents. For all they do, especially my mother, I love them and would be heartbroken if they never wanted to speak to me again."

"Yes, that is something I cannot imagine. Perhaps I can talk to my father," I offer. "I know he will listen, and maybe he can help talk some sense into your parents." If Mary's parents disown her, it would be devastating to our family.

"I don't know that it will help, but it is certainly worth trying."

A knock at the door interrupts our conversation, and I turn to find Douglas entering with a folded letter in his hand.

"Hello, Douglas." My heart ticks higher at the thought of finally getting a letter from Alasdair.

"There is an urgent letter from the garrison, m'lady."

"Oh." I suddenly don't feel well. My hands shake as I take the letter from him. I break the seal and unfold the crisp paper, and my stomach sinks as I read the words that blur as my eyes fill with tears.

"Ella, what is it? Is everything well?" Mary asks with obvious concern.

"No." A sob breaks free. "No. There was a battle. I...don't know, but it says that Alasdair is on the list of wounded and deceased." I'm going to be sick. I know I am. Oh dear God, no. I don't want to live without him. I cannot live without him.

"Give me the letter, dear," Mary says, leaning forward to take it from my lap where it fell. She begins reading aloud as I lie back and close my eyes, hoping to stop the room from spinning.

Dear Lady Galloway,

It is our duty to inform you that news has arrived in Great Britain that a battle has been fought in Aboukir Bay off the Alexandrian coast between the French and British fleets. We are receiving conflicting reports as to whom shall claim victory, but at this time, the number for France outweighs those for Great Britain.

Of greater concern for you and the estate of Galloway is that Lord Alasdair Stewart's name appears on the list of wounded and/or deceased. These are very early reports we have received, so they are subject to change. With that, there is hope. We will continue to pray for your husband and our esteemed comrade, Captain Alasdair Stewart, Earl of Galloway.

Any news we receive will be forwarded to you forthwith.

Your most obedient servant,

Colonel Neil Hughes

I feel the warmth of my tears streaming down my face, turning cold just before they drip onto my chest. Alasdair is gone. He is gone before we can live our lives together...before we can grow old together. It *was* his spirit that came to me in the forest, the magnificent white stag was the vessel he chose to visit me one last time. It was an excellent choice—he knew how happy it would make me, and it did. I was overjoyed to be in its presence, albeit confused by the sense of familiarity. Yet now, it makes sense.

I must go. I must go to the purple meadow and find him again, tell him how much I love him, and that for as long as I live, I will never love again. He must know, somehow, that the short time we spent together as husband and wife was more meaningful than I ever knew possible, and I will thank him for that joy every day for the rest of my life.

But most importantly, I will let him know that his legacy will live on through the child growing inside me.

TWENTY-SIX

Alasdair

"If my head did'na hurt so damn bad, I'd throw that bloody doctor over the side of the ship."

Nelson laughs, then tries to calm my ire. "Settle down, my friend. The poor fella didn't know you can't handle your laudanum."

"I fell and hit my head. I did'na get a leg amputated." I stop, realizing the slip of my tongue. "I'm sorry, Nelson. That was insensitive of me."

"Don't be sorry. You're right. When they amputated my arm, I had enough laudanum in me to keep me out for a week. But in the doctor's defense, that musket ball left a nasty gash, you lost a lot of blood, and apparently, you weren't making a damn bit of sense when you tried to talk. I suppose he was forcing you to rest so you could get your wits about you again."

"Aye, well, it does'na change the fact that I don't like being drugged, especially wi' laudanum. Makes me sick to my stomach, and I feel trapped inside my own head. I've lost an entire week of my life that could have been spent accomplishing a long list of tasks and preferably making my way back home to my wife."

I've been on edge for the past two days after realizing the doctor was dosing me with that godforsaken drug. I spit it out and wouldn't let him give me more. It may have been painful as hell, but that would have been better than where I was. Now I'm dealing with not only the after-effects of a blow to the head, but my body is craving more medicine, making a bad situation worse. I'm weak and starving. My clothes are hanging on me, and a lingering fog clouds my every thought. But the one thing that has been clear this entire time is that I desperately want to get back to Ella.

"We leave tomorrow. The prisoners have all been dispersed amongst the ships, and we've captained anything that floats. The repairs to *Orion* should be completed today," Nelson assures me.

"Yes, Harris came by earlier with the updates. I was happy to hear Lieutenant Fernsby finally woke up, but it appears he may be blind in one eye." Again, I look at Admiral Nelson and wonder if I've touched a nerve knowing he has suffered the same injury.

"We take a beating out there, and then we get up and fight again. It is our duty. No matter if you're the king or a crofter, you stand for what is right and protect what you love, using your strength of mind and body as sword and shield."

"Aye, 'tis true. Though what is right, and who or what ye love is subjective, else we would'na constantly be fighting these bloody wars," I note through the persistent throbbing in my head.

"Indeed, you are correct. Makes you wonder if it will ever stop or if we will always be at war with someone, somewhere near or far."

We both stay silent for a while, contemplating the notion

of never-ending battles. Of life and death, the celebration of victory, and the pain, anger, and fear of defeat.

"You and I both know the answer to that. 'Tis why it is good to always appreciate the pleasures of life, be them big or small. Delicious food, expensive whisky, a full moon resting above the horizon, the bright sun of a cloudless day, and the woman ye love lying next to ye, warm and sated in yer bed." My chest tightens at the thought of Ella's skin touching mine.

"You have a love match, then?" Nelson asks with a smirk.

"Aye, I do."

"What's it like, being married to the woman you love?"

Though the question seems odd coming from Nelson, I answer without hesitation. "Indescribable. I've never known such happiness, never believed it was real. I am enthralled by every move she makes, every word she speaks, the way she smells and tastes. I did'na know the pleasures of the body could ever feel so good that they change who ye are from the inside out. I've loved this woman in another life, I know I have. I can feel it in my bones. That is why I pray the wind is hard at my back the entire way home."

Nelson waits, taking in my words that are more than I've told any other man.

"Perhaps that is what has happened to me."

"Oh?" I question, sensing that he is not referring to his wife, Fanny.

"There is another woman in my life, and I cannot sleep or eat or fight a bloody battle without her being in the forefront of my mind. I believe she served me a potion the first time I had dinner at her husband's estate." He shakes his head. "He's an old man, and she is young, beautiful, quite sensual. She cannot be satisfied with him in the sheets." He stares across the room for a moment. "From the moment I saw her, I knew something was there, an attraction I've never felt before. She charmed me all evening and wouldn't allow my attention to be anywhere but with her. It was exciting. I was young again, a virgin taunted by the flirtations of a girl who knew her innate power over me. I read her signals clearly and made sure she and I found a moment to be alone. Once we kissed, I feared I would never be the same again."

I am surprised by my friend's confession, but more so, I am surprised by the sheen of tears that have glassed his pale blue eye. His feelings are true for this woman, but she is not his wife. Yet, I see something else in the layers of emotion he is not hiding on his face. Longing—not simply for this woman that has captured his heart, but maybe a life that is less dictated by duty and expectation, by life aboard ship, one that is shrouded in loneliness and monotony—where weeks and months of confinement with the same men and the same routines can play tricks on your sanity. But Horatio Nelson is a man of honor and integrity and extreme ambition, so no matter the depth of his longing, he will do what is right for King and country.

I feel a bit of sadness for him. "Perhaps it is the same for you and this woman, that you were meant to love one another. But you must handle it with care, for the reputations of many could be harmed by the actions of one. It is a slippery slope that needs to be navigated with extreme caution and the utmost consideration."

"I appreciate your honesty, Alasdair. I have much to consider, for I fear I do not have the strength to stay away."

"I understand. If I had wed another and happened upon Ella by chance, I would have a similar dilemma on my hands. Whether right or wrong, my soul will not let me be without her."

∾

We departed as the sun rose the following morning. Our progress was slow through most of the Mediterranean, but now that we have rounded the tip of Portugal at Cape St. Vincent, my prayer has been answered, and the wind is steady at our back.

I've been busy reviewing the ship's log to get a clear understanding of what happened while I was down. Twenty-nine men were wounded, most of who are recovering well, but we lost thirteen. My eyes drift to the stack of letters I've written to their families, thirteen pages lined with words of sympathy, gratitude, and encouragement. I love to write, it is my passion, but I hate writing these letters to families. Their loved one is gone, and nothing I write can bring them back. The words seem empty, so I fill them with the security of knowing they will not starve and that a roof will always be over their heads.

I dip the quill again just as the boat sways, causing the black ink to drip down the side of the well and gather around the bottom, a pointless addition to the existing stain that darkens the surface of my desk. I stare at it for a moment, watching it slowly fill the tiny void between the glass and wood. That list should have been fourteen and the letters written by another hand. A musket ball grazed my head. The difference between life and death was likely determined by a fraction of an inch. I can't help but wonder why. Did fate protect me, and did she do it because of Ella? It gives me chills to think about it, and it makes my yearning for Ella that much stronger.

I stare at the blank paper before me, then to the point of the quill saturated with ink. Words come to my mind as they flow from my soul. I sort them out, play with the verses, then set them free.

My eyes have seen beauty,
so glorious and true,
Flowers and their petals
Red, pink, orange, blue,
I've seen these colors paint the sky
The artist's brush so free,
An abstract work of brilliance
For who could disagree.
This palette doesn't shy away,
No bias will you find
From stones to leaves to rainy days
And wings of every kind,
Lo, there is another,
more than glorious, you see
No red or pink, orange or blue
Can match its reverie.
It's made of bone and flesh and blood,
Its structure is divine,
The softness of her lovely curves.
Her posture so refined.
That silken hair that shines like gold,
The flawless skin so fair,
A face so well appointed,
She's an angel, you would swear.
And on that face her eyes behold
The truth within I see,
Your soul is mine and mine is yours
Throughout eternity.

I cannot wait to have her in my arms again. It is maddening, this wanting that digs at my gut, harder and harder with each passing day. I dreamt of her again last night, her hands tied with white silk, her creamy arse cheek bright red from my attention, her begging for more. I've obsessed about how well she took to that kind of play, how she trusted me to show her the pleasure in pain, how much she truly enjoyed it, and how hard it made her release. My cock swells from the images in my mind, awakening the throbbing ache that has followed me for months. I rest my hand on its length and gently squeeze. I will not take myself in hand again this close to home; I want my wife.

I wonder at my fierce attraction to her and the unusual connection I detected from the first moment she was near. I know now, through the help of Nanna's clairvoyance, that we were meant to be together. Yet, even without that knowledge, it is clear through a simple touch or gentle kiss.

The beautiful young woman from the vision I had, the night Ella and I first came together as husband and wife, comes to my mind. I wonder if that is when our souls first met or was that just one of many lives we've enjoyed together. I feel an exhilarating flush come over me at the thought of loving Ella through various lives in various times throughout history. How did we become so fortunate? I try to imagine the original love that created such a bond—one so deep and true, so passionate, and all-consuming, that they would not be denied eternity in each other's arms. Is there magic involved? Does this have something to do with the Fey? Does faerie blood flow through Ella's veins and mine as well? It must, for it has explained so much already.

My skin tingles, remembering Ella under the waterfall and the ancient oak, enthralled with passion and pleasure, her eyes changing to the translucent blue that is reminiscent of gemstones held to a flame and tropical waters lit by the sun. It is the most mysterious trait she has exhibited. In truth, the idea that Ella has an ancestor that is a being of legend excites my imagination; I am awed by it.

On the last night of my journey back to Britain, my dreams are once again filled with Ella's passionate cries of release. They play out so vividly I could swear they are real, and when I wake with the sun, my arms and bed empty, I know my day will be tainted with the foul mood of a starving man. But today, I will be on land, making my steady progression back to my wife. That knowledge alone makes the pangs less sharp.

I make one last round through my ship to thank my men and bid them farewell. It is always a bittersweet goodbye when some of our comrades are not here for the handshakes, pats on the shoulder, and well-wishes.

The hustle on the docks buzzes around us as the boat is tied off. The air is still and reeks of population as I stand at the top of the gangway looking out over the crowded pier. My heavy steps echo down the side of *Orion* as I make my way to the dock, and I feel a spike in my mood, knowing I am that much closer to Ella. No sooner does my foot land on the weathered wood, I see a boy squeezing through the busy crowd, his familiar smile bright with excitement through the filth covering his face.

"Captain Stewart!" he calls enthusiastically. "What can I do for you?"

I toss him a coin, which he catches deftly in his right hand.

"Bring me my horse."

TWENTY-SEVEN
Ella

I'm finding it difficult to keep any food down. My stomach was uneasy before I got word from the garrison, but now food is of no interest to me, so when I do eat, it makes me feel worse than when I don't. Perhaps I simply prefer the sharp pang of an empty stomach to that of the heavy churning of nausea.

"Ella, dear, you must eat more. If you weren't expecting, I'd feel less concern, but with the babe, you must find a way." Beatrice rubs my shoulders.

"I know. I have terrible guilt over it, over everything. I was only married for a very short time, and somehow, I've managed to acquire more regrets than from my entire unmarried life." I swallow a painful lump in my throat. "I let so many things get in the way of simply loving my husband the way he deserves. I doubted my emotions and kept them hidden inside, not letting him hear the truth and never realizing how selfish I was being. I thought I had time. I was waiting for the courage to simply speak the truth in my heart."

I should have never let the ideas about love that my mother

and society instilled in me rule me the way they did. They limit me from being my true self, even when Alasdair was pushing me to simply be who I am. He died knowing he had the love of his family, likely everyone here at Galloway Castle, his friends, and his crew, but not his wife.

I think about the baby growing inside me as I sit here in a fog of despair, and I make a commitment that I will not let my child live with the restricted emotions of the gentry. When his time comes to wed, or even before, the true feelings in his heart will easily be spoken. Our child will grow into an adult who isn't burdened with doubt but confident in the way he expresses his love—just like his father.

"Ella, my darling, you mustn't commit yourself to the idea that he is gone. There is no certainty at this point. I don't understand why you insist upon being hopeless. It simply isn't like you. You have reason to be afraid and even to doubt, but why you are insisting that he died in that battle is beyond comprehension. You must always have hope, my love. Especially now."

"I have my reasons, none of which would make sense to anyone. You might think I have lost my mind. But regardless, they overpower all sense of hope I have left."

"I won't push any further, but I will hold on to hope for both of us. Now, let's go downstairs and visit with Mary a while longer before she leaves."

"Yes, let's do that."

My body aches with fatigue and the weight of my sadness. I need to go for a walk, preferably a long one, to breathe fresh air and move my body. But I am so tired, I'm not sure I can make it across the moor to the forest edge, let alone to the clearing by the sea.

Entering the parlor, we find Mary sitting on the sofa reading a letter. Whatever it says has her full attention because she doesn't even notice that Beatrice and I have walked in.

"Is everything well, Mary?" I ask with true concern.

"Oh, hello, ladies. I apologize...I'm...yes, everything is fine," she fumbles.

"That wasn't very convincing, cousin. Who is that letter from?"

Beatrice and I sit across from her, and I can't help but notice the mixture of emotions clear on her face.

"Well, I wrote a letter to Graham and have received one in return. But I have also received one from my mother." Her eyes remain focused on the papers lying on her lap.

"Can we start with your letter to Graham? What did you say?" I ask.

She hesitates for a moment. "I told him the truth. That I have made up my mind, that I cannot ignore my feelings for him, and that I will no longer be pressured to only pursue a man that is titled. If that means my family will have nothing to do with me, then so be it. I will not live a life of misery simply to please my mother and father." Her voice strains with the last sentence.

"And what was his response?"

Her smile widens, and her eyes sparkle with mischief before she answers, "You must understand that Graham loves to taunt me with his arrogance. He knows I have a mind of my own—he's rather charmed by that notion—and he loves to play sport with my ire. So, his message was short and to the point." She picks up his letter and reads it word for word.

My Dearest Lady Mary,

I have received your letter and am pleased to know you have accepted my hand in marriage. It is fortunate that you are currently so near Gretna Green, and your journey to meet

*me there will be short. I will bring my finest carriage so that
once we are wed, your journey with me to my estate in
Lancaster will be pleasant. There, we will enjoy ourselves and
begin our married life together.*

Consider yourself affianced.

*I will see you in Gretna Green on the 2nd of September
1798.*

Your soon-to-be husband,
Graham Knightly

"My goodness, Mary. That is awfully fast. Are you sure this
is what you want?" Beatrice asks, not knowing as much of the
story as I do.

"Not only fast, but presumptuous," I add, raising a brow.

Mary throws her head back and laughs. "Well, he is that.
But he will also be perturbed when he has to follow me around
Gretna Green, trying his damnedest to get me to agree to be his
wife. Though, just between us, I think he'd be disappointed if I
did otherwise."

That sounds more like the Mary I know, but she is in love
with Mr. Knightly, that I can see clearly. My heart aches at the
thought of falling in love and how good it feels to come
together as husband and wife. I feel the emotions welling up
inside me, but I will not take away from Mary's excitement, so
I swallow it down and rejoin the conversation.

"What did your mother say in her letter? Surely, she knows
nothing about this," Beatrice says.

"According to this letter, she doesn't know. But her
patience has worn out, and she has apparently chosen a
husband for me. She expects me to be home within the next
fortnight so that I may be introduced to him and start the
engagement proceedings."

"Does she mention who this man is?" I ask.

"Lord Adam Chapman, Earl of Dalton," she answers succinctly.

"I've never heard of him."

"Neither have I. And it matters naught—because he will not be my husband." She puts her mother's letter down and looks at me. "Enough about my never-ending saga to find a husband. How are you doing today?" She reaches over to take my hand.

"The same as yesterday, perhaps worse. My stomach is terribly unsettled, and I can't stand the thought of food. But I am going to have some broth and go for a walk. Maybe that will lift my spirits." I look down as the tears spill over, and I quickly wipe them away.

"Ella. Look at me." She waits with patience for me to bring my eyes to hers. "Alasdair will come home to you. You must believe that in your heart. You must never give up hope."

"I will do my best, Mary, I promise."

"I don't have to leave, you know, even though it appears my schedule has changed a bit." She shrugs her shoulders and offers me a wink. "Graham can wait. It will only make him want me more."

I laugh because that is very likely a true statement, but honestly, I want to be alone for a while as I come to terms with the drastic turn my life has taken.

"Thank you, but no, dear. You must go and meet Mr. Knightly if that is truly what your heart desires. Just promise me that you will be careful and that you won't go through with it if it feels wrong. Trust your heart."

～

I take my time walking to the forest. Before I left, I ate some buttered bread and drank a mug of broth, which settled my stomach and gave me a noticeable boost in energy.

There is a breeze coming in from the sea, carrying the scent of brine. The occasional gust pushes against me, lifting my skirts and sneaking under the layers of fabric that cover my body. The cool, humid air touches my skin and awakens my senses.

Once I am under the forest canopy, I stop to rest and just listen. There are no voices, no questions asked, no answers given, no doors opening and closing, no tablecloths snapping open as they are set in place, no carriage wheels or horses' hooves, only the pleasant sound of the forest. I close my eyes and fill my lungs with fresh air. I do it again and again. And each time I do, I feel a little bit more of myself coming to life. I've always felt more at home out of doors than in. I love beautiful gowns and opulent homes, that is all I have ever known, but the simple act of standing in the forest, breathing the air of the trees and plants and animals, is more exhilarating than any fancy ball could ever be.

My eyes open, and I look above at the beautiful mosaic of leaves and light and branches. I hear the hum of trees, young and old, birdsong that no musician's instrument could ever replicate, the air that is moving, yet blind to the eye, its scent is every shade of green. Two more breaths, and there it is. Serenity.

Can she feel it too, my baby? Surely, she can. I smile, thinking about how my mind goes back and forth between a boy and a girl. Each day passes with a different certainty, and I wonder if I will drive myself mad with curiosity until the happy day finally arrives. My thoughts shift. Will it be happy? If Alasdair truly is gone, giving birth to his son or daughter will undoubtedly be a blessing and will fill me with joy, but my heart will break again knowing my child will never know her amazing father. And what if the child looks like Alasdair? Will a part of my heart hurt every time I look upon her...or him? The idea makes the nausea return, so I throw the thought away and continue down the path.

Halfway to the clearing, I see a rabbit hopping along the side of the trail. It is adorable with its plump little body, long ears, and a face that is the definition of cute. He stops to nibble on the grass that grows between the stones, his tiny mouth working quickly as the blade completely disappears.

"Hello, little fellow! You're the first bunny I've seen here in Scotland. You have a beautiful home. This forest is my favorite place to be."

He pulls off another blade of grass and devours it as readily as he did the first. I'm quite close now, and he doesn't seem as though it bothers him, so I kneel and take the liberty of rubbing his forehead with my finger. A burst of happiness bubbles in my chest as he nudges his head up toward my finger, wanting more, a clear sign that he trusts me.

"You like that, do you? Well, you certainly are the most adorable thing I believe I've ever seen," I say with genuine delight.

Just then, something whirs past my ear, loud and swift, startling the rabbit and me. I stand up and see it quickly fly away until it stops abruptly over the ferns some distance ahead. I stand here for a moment staring at it, in shock that it seems to be doing the same to me.

"Were you trying to get my attention?" I ask through a laugh, feeling that nervousness in my stomach that I always feel when my little flying friends' actions seem premeditated. No matter how many times I tell myself to let go and have the open mind of my youth, it doesn't change the fact that this seems to defy all logic.

In answer, it loops in circles, then darts off in the direction of the oak tree I always visit when I am here. Once again, I cannot be rude, regardless of whom or what is offering an invitation. In truth, I want to avoid that special place—my heart is too tender right now—but I alter my plans and head toward the oak.

My stomach tightens as I approach the place where Alasdair made love to me. It was the second time he had me undress outside the confines of my bedchamber, and I still wonder at how good it felt, how natural it was to be naked, standing under a massive tree in the middle of a forest or inside that magical cavern created by mountain stone and a wall of water. Each time was exhilarating, feeling the ultimate pleasure through the masterful techniques of my husband while also feeling connected with a part of myself that had been buried so deep that I didn't even know it was there. Yet, once I tapped into it, I felt free and powerful, beautiful and sensual, healthy and vibrant.

I sit down next to the trunk, leaning against its rough surface, then close my eyes so I can concentrate on its subtle vibration of hundreds of years of existence. My shoulders relax, then my neck. I'm able to slow my breathing and just be in the moment. Within that peaceful space, an image comes to my mind: our baby, healthy, happy, smiling. I see myself holding the swaddled infant; I can sense the joy in my heart. But then I see Alasdair gazing upon his child with fatherly pride. He is so handsome; it makes my insides swarm with excitement and my heart swell with love as I focus on the tenderness in his eyes. I tell myself that this can be real, that it is my future. I want to feel the truth in my words. I fear so much will be missing from my life if it is not.

I stay with it for a moment longer, then take a deep breath of forest air and open my eyes. They are here, as I knew they would be. I count six but feel certain there are more.

"I've had a difficult time lately," I begin, wanting to get some of this heaviness off my chest. "Word has come that Alasdair has either been injured in battle...or worse." I don't let the dreadful word leave my mouth. "I'm trying to stay strong and not lose hope, but I saw a white stag in the forest last week, and I was able to approach him and pet him. He was not afraid and acted as if he knew me, and now I have convinced myself that it was Alasdair's spirit visiting me, just as I read in the books."

I stop to wipe the tears from my cheeks, and when I look up, a shallow gasp catches in my throat. There are at least twice as many members in my mystery audience, and they are all hovering around the same height above the ferns. *Good Lord.* I believe I have upset them as their usual whimsical flitting and swooping has come to a halt. "I didn't mean to trouble you, truly. I was only venting my woes. You see, I have told no one of my encounter with the stag for fear they would question my sanity. I know I certainly have. But I do have good news, very good news. I am going to have a baby!"

I watch them fly excitedly around one another, dipping and diving under and over the plants, and the laugh that escapes me is loud and invigorating. I rather enjoy coming out here to be surprised and entertained by these little mystery beings. Alasdair's mother called them faeries, but I don't think I'm quite there yet. Perhaps after I've lived here a while longer, that will be a notion that is easier for me to fully accept.

Standing up, I adjust my gown and look around at the scene before me. It truly is that of a storybook, the emerald forest where the princess is saved by a handsome knight, where hidden in the thick foliage are mythical creatures whose mischievous antics somehow teach important life lessons to the children fascinated by their mystery. I imagine bringing my own child to this forest, where the magic of folklore seems real and how it will inspire her imagination to soar with possibilities.

"I'm so glad I came here today. It has lifted my spirits tremendously. Thank you," I say sincerely and wave goodbye.

Back on the main trail, I decide to go home to eat a normal size meal. For the first time in days, I have an appetite unaccompanied by terrible nausea. I pick up my pace, suddenly excited about the idea of food.

The breeze has calmed quite noticeably as I exit the forest. There must have been a storm nearby earlier as the sky is considerably brighter. Perhaps I will enjoy my meal outside, as it seems a shame to waste this precious sunshine.

Looking down, I notice that I have worn a trail through the grass of the moor that surrounds the manor. I smile, thinking of how prominent it will become as the years go on. I should line it with stones and flowers. I could plant a tree part way through, and when it grows big enough, I could put a bench under it, where we can sit and enjoy the fresh air coming in off the water.

I look toward the castle, wondering where I might plant the tree along my landscaped trail when I see a man walking toward me down the same path. I stop abruptly as my eyes adjust. I try to pull in another breath, my heart begging for this to be real.

"Alasdair," I whisper as my fingers come up to cover my mouth.

It's him. His dark shiny hair, his beautiful face—severe and unsmiling, his tall stature and broad shoulders. Am I imagining this? The cadence of his walk says I am not, as it speaks with its own commanding voice: *I am alive, Ella, and you are mine.*

I'm frozen in place. I fear if I move, I will fall to the ground and weep an endless flow of gratitude for what I see before me. Alasdair is alive!

My hands cover my face as the sobs break free. My knees are weak, and my head feels light. I want to sit down, but I can hear each footstep now.

He stops, close enough for me to feel the heat of his body. The sobs are wracking through my chest now as the fear, sadness, and regret all flee the confines of my heart where they were determined to break me. There is so much I want, I *need* to say, but there is no room for words as my emotions continue to overwhelm me.

"Come here, lass."

The sound of his voice and its comforting familiarity forces the air from my lungs as he pulls me into the comfort of his arms.

Thank you, God. I repeat the prayer repeatedly as his warmth seeps through my skin and releases that terrible hopelessness my mind had latched onto.

The tears finally ebb, and I move my hands from my face and wrap my arms around his waist, my head resting on his broad chest.

"I must be honest, I knew ye probably missed me, Ella, but I had no idea it was to this degree."

I can hear the humor in his voice, and I swat his back before reprimanding him, "Alasdair, don't. I thought you were dead." The words are strained as I bury my face further into his shirt.

"Oh? Why would ye think that? I assured ye I would return, did ye not believe me?" Although his tone carries the noticeable sympathy of concern, it is still laced with humor.

"Your name was on the wounded and deceased list from the garrison, and I...I had seen a white stag in the forest a few days prior and..." I stop, embarrassed to go any further.

"Look at me, Ella."

I wait a moment, then take a small step back so that I can wipe my face and adjust my hair. When I do look up at him, I can't help noticing the prominence of his cheekbones and jaw. My hand comes up to touch his cheek, my thumb naturally gliding across his full mouth. His turquoise eyes blaze with emotion.

"Ye saw a white stag, did ye? Well, I don't know if ye are aware, but that is considered a good omen, no' a bad one."

"Yes, I know. But it is also said that when you see a white stag, it is a loved one that has passed away and returned to visit you. And I was able to approach him, even touch him. I talked to him for quite some time before he eventually turned to go. But, even then, it seemed he did not want to."

Alasdair reaches up to stop a few more tears. "And...?" he questions, raising a brow.

"I convinced myself it was you, your spirit." I put my head down, embarrassed by how wrong I was. "Why else would he have been so familiar with me? His eyes, they were so kind and knowing. I felt like he was communicating with me somehow, but I didn't know what he was trying to say." The pitch of my voice rises as I try to explain.

"Ye have an old soul, faerie maiden. Perhaps he was simply there to visit you."

That thought never even entered my mind. Could that be true? It would surely make me happy if it were. I only wish I had thought of it then and saved myself weeks of grief. Before I can express my thoughts, Alasdair reaches up, grabbing onto my head with both hands, my jaw perfectly cradled in his palms.

"I will be kissing ye now, Ella."

And so, he does, with all the passion and skill and hunger that I have been craving. My fingers dig into his back as he pulls me closer, hard against his body. I moan as his tongue sweeps across mine, forcing that tickling pleasure to blossom between my legs.

"Christ, Ella!" he growls as his teeth bare down on my bottom lip. "I have dreamt about ye every night." He kisses around my mouth and face, down my neck. "I kissed ye just like this and made ye cry out in pleasure. It saved me from going mad. I swear to ye it did. But having ye in my arms again, flesh and blood, yer taste and smell, the sound of yer moans... There is no pleasure or sensation that will ever compare. My God, woman, I have missed ye."

The sincerity in his eyes, the love I see, warms my heart. I will not wait a moment longer to say the words I've wanted to say for so long and feared I'd never have the chance.

"I love you, Alasdair," I say, looking him in the eye. "I love you with all my heart and soul. I have since the day we wed. You are everything to me, and you have made me happier than I ever imagined possible." I stop to kiss him again, to show him, not only through words, how much he is loved. "I have shed so many tears of regret for not telling you that before you left. I feared if something happened to you, if you did not come home, you would never know how much I love you. And for that, I would never forgive myself."

He stares at me, his smirk deepening that dimple I have missed so much.

"That was a lovely little speech, my dear. I am truly pleased to know I have made ye so happy and that I am loved so well, but I already knew that before I left." He winks and gives me a gentle kiss.

"What? How?"

"Well, ye must have told me a hundred times the last time we made love. It was quite a beautiful thing." His smile is enough to melt my heart, regardless of the mischief behind it.

"Alasdair, I have no memory of that."

"I can assure ye 'tis true. Though ye were in quite a state." He gets serious then, rubbing his finger across my cheek. "That can happen when the pleasure of carnal play is that intense. Yer mind stops thinking and lets ye simply be with the pleasure. It's like an escape from yer conscious mind."

"But I was so distraught from the moment I opened my eyes and found you were gone. It has plagued me for months, Alasdair, thinking you didn't know how much I love you. It was awful!"

"Rest assured, Ella Stewart, I know what is in yer heart. It was yer love that brought me home."

TWENTY-EIGHT
Alasdair

"I could stand in this field and kiss ye fer days, but I must be honest, I'd much rather do it in yer bedchamber," I say with a soft kiss on her lips.

"That sounds wonderful, but Alasdair, your father..." Her eyes are tender, and her voice is rough with emotion.

"Aye, I know. But 'tis not something I want to discuss right now. I don't want to cloud this moment wi' sadness. I'm sure ye understand," I tell her truthfully.

"Then let us go inside. I would very much like to change into something more comfortable. I'm afraid I got my gown a little soiled during my walk," she says with obvious flirtation.

Her arms are wrapped around my neck, and her smile is so joyous and sincere that my stomach clenches with desire while my heart overflows with love. We stay like that, holding on to one another, gazing through the windows of our souls. It feels so good to look upon her again, I don't want to take my eyes away, and neither does she.

"Ye are a sight to behold, faerie maiden," I say, tucking a

delicate curl caught by the wind behind her ear. "Such a rare beauty."

She offers a delicate smile. "Thank you. You may not know this, but for a man, you are quite beautiful as well."

"Oh? Beautiful, am I?"

"Especially now," she says, bringing her hand up to caress my cheek. "But I must say, they did not feed you very well. I will have to tell Margie she needs to fatten you up." Her sweet laugh sends a tickle up my spine.

"Yes, well, she'd be very pleased wi' those instructions, and I've got a strong appetite about me, but it does'na compare to my hunger fer you." I pull her closer.

"Then let's go inside. These past months have been long, and I feared we'd never be like this again." Her voice stops short with emotion.

"I'm here, love. Just as I promised."

I tap lightly on Ella's door, and her soft voice bids me to enter. The latch clicks open, then closes, and I slowly turn around. What I find knocks the air from my lungs.

"Ella…" Her name is carried on a harsh exhale.

She is standing at the foot of the bed, naked with her back to me, the same as I requested last time we made love. Knowing this is her choice speaks volumes and reinforces that unique desire that only she controls. My steps are slow and measured as I make my way to her, a reality that seems surreal after months of pining over this singular moment. When I am close, I smell her sweet, exotic scent, and my body ignites with a feral hunger that makes my mouth water.

"There is not a greater welcome ye could have given than this, faerie maiden." My hand comes up to her shoulder and slowly glides down her back and side, then around her hip to her stomach and up to her full breast resting atop her panting lungs.

I stop.

"Turn around," I say with deep and unexpected sternness.

When she does, my heart pounds harder in my chest.

"Ella?"

"Yes?" she questions with concern in her eyes.

"Ye are...ye are wi' child?"

The tenderness in her eyes confirms her answer before it leaves her lips. "Yes, Alasdair, I am."

I see it now, the rosy glow in her cheeks, and I smile at how it adds to her ethereal beauty. I glance down and almost growl in pleasure at seeing the evidence of my planted seed. Her already full breasts are noticeably more abundant and heavier, but the slight roundness below her naval is enough to clog my throat with emotion.

"I'm only just now beginning to show. I didn't think you would notice," she says quietly.

"My hands have yer body memorized, faerie maiden. There is nothing about ye that will ever go *unnoticed*. But I am curious, when were ye going to tell me?"

She doesn't answer right away, and I sense she is debating on whether to tell me the truth or not.

"After...after we...um..."

"Fuck?" I finish for her.

"Yes," she whispers and drops her eyes.

"Look at me, Ella." She waits a moment, then brings her eyes to mine. My cock swells when I see them black with desire. "Why were ye going to do that?" I feel the side of my mouth lift as I read her mind.

"I thought...I was afraid that you wouldn't..."

Again, I help her fumbling words. "Play as hard."

"Yes." Another whispered reply.

There is something charmingly innocent about her logic in holding back such important information, yet the reason she has done so is irresistibly arousing. I tip her face back up to mine and kiss her full mouth with enough force to be both a punishment and a reward. I don't stop for many long minutes, and when I finally do, she pulls away on a desperate gasp of air.

"What ye need to understand," I say, reaching forward so that I can hold the weight of her swollen breast in my hand while my thumb rubs across her sensitive nipple, "is that knowing ye are pregnant wi' my child, that yer body will become full and round as it grows inside ye, is arousing to everything that makes me a man. I've claimed ye, marked ye as mine, planted my seed." I kiss her lips softly. "Now yer beautiful, healthy fertile body will make us a strong lad or a bonnie lass. My God, Ella, it makes me want ye even more."

"I love you," she whispers against my lips before devouring them in a kiss that speaks louder than words. I grab the back of her head and pull her to me. When she moans, I bring my other hand down to slide between her sensitive folds and find she is drenched with arousal.

I stop abruptly.

"Lie down on the bed."

She does, and my hands slip under her arse to lift her off the bed, bringing her sweet, wet cunny to my mouth. She cries out as I ravage her with the force of a starving man. A growl escapes as I feast on the essence of my mate, pulling her hard to my face while I fuck her with my tongue, listening to her cries of pleasure echo around the room. She's about to cum, I can feel it, so I drop her onto the mattress, pull her to the edge, and drive my rigid shaft home. A guttural sound escapes my throat, and my eyes shut tightly as the pleasure of being inside her again overwhelms me. I thrust once, twice, then smother her screaming mouth with mine as her orgasm forces my own to explode.

It seems like time stands still while we float in the ecstasy of our release. I lean forward and place my hands on either side of her, slowly moving in and out as the last of our climax fades. Her eyes are fixed on mine, blinking every so often, heavy with the weight of exhaustion.

"Are ye alright?"

"Perfect," she answers with a smile.

"That ye are, mo ghràidh," I say and lean down to offer her a soft kiss. "Scoot up a bit. I want to lie wi' ye. I need to just have ye in my arms, listening to ye breathe, surrounded by yer warmth."

I get comfortable, and she tucks herself next to me, head on my chest and one leg draping over mine. God, how I've missed this. My arm tightens around her while my fingers roam gently across her skin. There is no more peaceful place than where we are right now, and in this content state, I wonder when it was that my seed was planted. I know it doesn't matter, but a part of me hopes that it was when we made love under the old oak in the forest. It's likely the poet in me that would hope for such a thing, but truthfully, the notion is quite poetic, so I play with the words in my head.

Upon these ancient lands
Sits a forest by the sea.
It knows the tales of many
From age-old history.
Its eyes have seen the battles.
Its ears have heard the song.
Its heart has sadly broken
For many weak and strong.
Yet, hidden beneath its surface

The roots of life abound.
The trees,
The plants,
The animals,
The treasures never found.
It's here the seed was planted
By love that's unsurpassed.
A passion few will ever know
Through time it will outlast.
Not only do you share the blood
Of your mother and of me,
You share the spirit of this land
And the forest by the sea.

I will write it down for her and leave it somewhere for her to find, the settee by the window or her dressing table, perhaps upon the bookshelves she's always perusing to appease her curious mind. I imagine her smiling as she reads it and decide to make that a tradition in our home, leaving her poems here and there to brighten her days. I will do whatever it takes to make sure that she knows how much my heart loves her; my body craves her. How she inspires my mind, and that my soul needs her.

I feel her arm pull tighter around my waist, and her body press harder against me.

"Ye must be reading my mind."

"Oh? If your mind is filled with thoughts of gratitude, and love, you'd be right." She brings her body up and over mine to lie between my legs, placing her chin on her hands that are resting on my stomach. "Thank you for coming home, Alasdair. I was so scared. What happened? Why was your name on that list?"

I explain everything that happened in the battle, detailing

the fights, my injury, and the week lost to laudanum before I could make my way back to her.

"Alasdair, I cannot believe you were shot in the head! How do you feel now?" she asks, now sitting upright before me.

"Perfectly fine. Especially sitting here looking at my naked wife wi' her body filling out from the bairn that's growing inside her. I swear on my life, Ella, I love ye more with each day that passes. I'll likely burst with it by the time I'm an ould man."

She leans forward to put her hands on the bed by my waist and crawls toward me with a smirk on her face. I feel my cock surge with anticipation.

"You like the idea of my body being abundant with child?" she asks right before she licks my lips then pulls them into her mouth for a kiss that speaks of what she's craving.

"Ye can'na fathom how much I like that idea." I stop to caress her lovely face. "Yer soul is mine, faerie maiden, and mine is yours. No man has ever loved a woman as much as I love you. And to see that lovely glow about yer skin, that sparkle in yer eyes, and the full round belly that signifies the fertility of our union—aye, it nourishes my strength and will to survive, my need to protect and provide, to guide and teach, to love."

Our eyes stay fixed on one another, each of us seeing the truth that lies within. My hand comes up to push her long hair over her shoulder.

"The eyes are the window to the soul. In yers, I see eternity."

"That is very poetic," she says as she bends her head down to kiss my chest.

"'Tis true. We have loved before in another life. And we will love again after this one. Our souls are fated to be together forever," I state matter-of-factly, then pull her to me.

When I finally release her lips, she asks, "How can you possibly know this, Alasdair?"

"I suppose ye could call it speculation. After all, I do'na have definitive proof. But there is something between us that is different, unusual. I know ye don't have much to compare it to, but I do. Ye clearly know I was'na a virgin when we met."

"Alasdair," she reprimands.

Through a laugh, I continue, "Well, 'tis the truth, and it's a factor in the equation."

Ella sits back on her knees and places her hands on her hips. "Oh? How so?"

God, she is perfect. "Look at you." I sit up and reach forward to pinch her nipple. "Are ye jealous?"

She swats my hand away. "It is certainly something I do not wish to think about."

"Well, I can't blame ye fer that. But I do have experience where you do not. And I can assure ye, what we have between us is'na something that is common between lovers, married or no." Her eyes turn tender with the conviction in my words. "But there is something else, and ye may find this to be a little harder to believe. You see, my grandmother—Nanna, we called her—had a powerful sixth sense, she was a seer. In Scotland, they call such a gift the Fey, but that's another story entirely we can save for another day. Nanna and I were very close, and she loved to talk to me about my old soul and how that made me special, though she may have been a bit biased." That jest earns me a smile. "When I was old enough, she explained to me that there was another soul that sought to find me. She said this woman and I had loved in a previous life, that our souls were meant to be together, that fate would not allow them to be apart, and after this life, they will find each other and love again and again."

"Alasdair, that is beautiful. My God, could that really be true?"

I move closer and sweep my fingers through her hair. "Tell me, what did ye feel when ye saw me fer the first time, in the conservatory that fateful night?"

She hesitates, then replies, "You were...I couldn't look away. You were so beautiful it didn't seem real, and my insides constricted with a tension I'd never felt. I wanted to touch you so badly I could weep. The intensity confused me so much, and then I could feel the pulsing pleasure blossom between my legs."

I feel a surge of blood fill my cock.

"When I noticed you weren't alone, I wanted to run away, but I couldn't. I had to stay. I wanted to see what you would do to her with your body, your manhood. But when you did, when you touched her, I was torn between intense desire and sickening jealousy. I wanted you to touch *me* that way, not her." She pauses then, eyes black with desire, face flushed and heated. "When you spoke, hearing your voice...it made the hair stand all over my body and my heart pound in my chest. Then you took her, hard and fast, and I thought I would choke on the emotion and pleasure that was overflowing inside me. But when you pulled away and took your shaft in hand, milking yourself across her back, I could feel you inside me, filling me with your essence, and I was unable to hold back any longer and...and my climax broke free."

Her voice breaks a little as her head falls in shame.

"Come here," I growl and pull her body to mine, my cock rigid with wanting to satisfy her.

I lift her face to mine and take her mouth as my tongue dives deep to feed her desire. We are both on our knees, pressing hard to one another, hands gliding across fiery skin, touching, squeezing, scratching. Her moan is muffled through the force of my kiss as I push her further and further. When I pull away to suck on her neck, she gasps, but when my hand finds her cunt dripping with her slippery wetness, she cries out my name and begs for more.

"I told ye before that I could feel ye there, knew yer presence before I could see ye." My fingers slide into her tight channel, and my teeth latch onto the meat of her shoulder. "I was confused as well, couldn'a grasp what was happening, and then I saw ye, and just like that, I felt as if I turned into a wild beast, almost like a rage came over me. You were mine...and somehow, I knew it." I pause to bite down on that irresistible bottom lip. "I was mad wi' desire, and I wanted ye so badly. In my mind, I was fucking you and not the maid. 'Tis why I could'na last. I knew you could feel it too. I felt yer climax building, and it was too much; my cock exploded in release." She's grinding herself against my hand now, panting out my name. I put my mouth against hers. "I was angry. Could ye see it in my eyes? When ye looked at me, could ye see the mad desperation to have ye?"

"Yes."

"Were ye jealous of the woman?"

"Very." Her voice is gravelly.

"That's because I am yours. From the day I was born, I belonged to you."

I remove my hand and bring my fingers up to my mouth, licking away her sweet potion. My other hand pulls her closer, and she joins me with fervency. My bollocks tighten as she mimics my play, licking with her tongue, sucking with her lips. It's erotic, bloody fantastic, and she loves it, so I push my fingers into her mouth and kiss along the edge of her lips while she sucks them deep and teases them with her tongue.

"Lie down. I've been too long wi'out ye, and I can'na handle the wiles of that exceptional mouth," I pant, guiding her to her back. Looking down, I remember how desperately I wanted her. I brush the stray hairs away from her face, then lean down to press my lips against hers. "You heard what I said. I belong to you."

I enter her with ease, relishing the warm softness that surrounds my rigid shaft. My skin tingles with tiny bolts of lightning as my body is strengthened by our union and weakened by the mind-numbing sensation of being inside her. Her legs wrap around my waist as my arms slide under her back to hold her close. I need as much contact as possible. I need to feel her skin against mine as we move with one another, a perfect momentum that feeds the passion to nourish the pleasure that, with her, is more than God intended.

"Alasdair," she says against my ear, her panting breaths teasing my orgasm closer to the surface. She moans as I squeeze her tighter, then she takes the lobe between her teeth, biting down just enough, before teasing it with her tongue. "Alasdair..." Her fingernails dig into the sweat-covered skin of my back, forcing my hips to grind harder against her. The pitch of her cries grows higher with the added pressure.

"Cum fer me, Ella," I command, knowing how much she loves being pushed beyond the boundaries in which she was raised. She tightens around me, driving me to push harder.

"Alasdair!"

My thrusts are labored through the pulse of her release, unmistakable in the contractions that pull me deeper and the sound of her cries that sing to my soul.

I squeeze her tighter, pulling her face back toward mine so I can take her mouth while my orgasm paralyzes my body with its force. But her body knows I'm not done, so she pushes herself against me, taking over the thrusting for me, gifting me with a longer release than I would have otherwise enjoyed.

We stay that way, connected not only to each other but to

the moment, gently riding the ebbing tide of our release. How is it that this feels just as good as the pinnacle? In some ways, more. To lie with my mate, my ethereal wife, sated by the pleasure only our love can create. Her eyes are dreamy as they stare into mine. They speak to me, an inexplicable communication that tells a story of love that is so deep and so profound, it knows no end.

"Ye are an exquisite woman, Ella Stewart. My heart beats fer you, and I will spend the rest of my life offering thanks, not only to God and to fate, but to the lovers that connected our souls fer eternity."

She sighs in reply, a lazy smile lifting her cheeks. "I love you, Alasdair."

TWENTY-NINE

Ella

"Good morning, dearie. How are you feeling?" Beatrice asks. It's the same question she's asked me each morning for as long as I can remember.

"I feel wonderful, Beatrice! How could I not? Alasdair is home, and he is well. Can you believe it? I keep pinching myself to make sure I'm not dreaming!" I reply with giddy excitement.

"I knew he would come back to you, love. Now, tell me what he said when you told him he's going to be a father."

My stomach swirls with butterflies when I remember him discovering the truth before I could tell him. I truly did not know I was showing enough for him to notice, but clearly, I was wrong.

"Well, he sort of...found out without me telling him." I laugh at Beatrice's confused expression. "Apparently, I'm showing more than I thought I was."

"Ah, I see."

"But, to answer your question, he is beside himself with excitement. He doesn't care if it's a girl or a boy; he is simply thrilled beyond words that we will soon have a baby. Though I must say, it certainly brought out the...how do I say this... manly side of him." I laugh at the thought. "If you can imagine a more manly side to Alasdair Stewart! He was very pleased with himself, having *planted his seed*," I boast with an exaggerated brogue.

Beatrice and I fall into a fit of giggles, not only from my sarcasm but because there is so much to be happy about, it is easy to laugh freely and soak up the joy of the moment.

Just then, an abrupt knock sounds at the door, and in walks the subject of our humor.

"Good morning, ladies." Alasdair pauses and lifts one brow. "Why do the two of you look like ye've been conjuring up mischief all morning?"

Beatrice almost chokes on her embarrassment as she turns away from Alasdair's inquisitive glare, mumbling and coughing as she makes her escape through the opposite door.

"That was a blatant admission of guilt if I ever saw one," he says through a glorious smile that tickles my insides.

"Yes...well, you may have just caught the cat with the canary."

"Aye. And something tells me you fed it to her," he retorts with another raised brow.

Laughing aloud, I agree. "You'd be right, again, dear husband. But, not to worry, we were only discussing how manly you are."

"Is that so? And do I need to blush the next time I see Beatrice?"

I give him a small peck on his lips. "Maybe a little."

"So ye've been tellin' yer lady's maid how I please ye in the sheets, have ye?" he asks, then teases me with a deeper kiss.

"Perhaps. But it had more to do with how pleased you are that I am pregnant. I don't know if you are aware, but it seems to bring out a different side of you—" I pause to kiss him again. "a side I must admit, I like very much."

"'Tis good to hear, faerie maiden. You seem to bring out my baser instincts, turnin' me into a feral beast wi' yer wicked spells." His accent thickens, and he nips at my neck playfully, making me laugh harder.

"Stop! That tickles!" I say through the giggles. "Is this why you came in here, to torment me?"

"As much as I'd like to say yes, simply because I love to hear the sound of yer laughter, I actually came here to say thank you." His tone becomes serious with his admission.

"Oh? What are you thanking me for?"

"Come, let us sit," he says, guiding me to the sofa in our sitting area. Once we are comfortable, he begins again. "I just had a meeting wi' Douglas. He told me what ye did fer my father."

"About taking him to the forest?" I ask.

"Aye. He said it was a beautiful gift ye gave him. He believes my mother was there to guide him home." He stops then as the emotion thickens his voice and glosses his eyes.

"She was. I could feel her presence. I think your father could see her, Alasdair. It truly was quite beautiful." I stop as my own emotions overwhelm me.

Alasdair leans forward and pulls me into his arms, holding me tightly. I can tell he's crying, so I squeeze onto him to let him know that it's alright to let go. We stay that way for several long minutes until his arms loosen and he pulls away.

"I can'na thank ye enough for that, Ella. It does my heart good to know that is how he left this world. She was everything to him. He loved her since he was only a lad, and he was never quite the same after she died. Not only did my heart break because I had lost my mother, but it broke for my father, as well." He stops to wipe the tears from his eyes.

"They are together now, with my brother. That is what matters."

"That's right." I reach over to take his hand. "Your father and I talked quite a lot before he became too ill. He told me so much about Lilith and how he adored her. He told me about you and the joy you brought them, about the children they lost, and how they overcame heartbreak. Their love story was quite remarkable, and I cannot tell you with words how much I loved that time with your father. He made me laugh and cry, and he taught me so much in just a short period of time. He was my friend, and I miss him terribly."

"Ye are a good woman, Ella. Thank you fer looking after him so well."

"You're welcome," I reply, squeezing his hand a little tighter. "Can I ask you something?" I ask with trepidation.

"Of course."

"Callen told me that your mother spent a lot of time in the forest, that it was her favorite place. She used to tell him there were faeries there and that they were her friends." I stop as Alasdair's smile spreads wide across his face. "You knew about this?" I ask.

"Oh, aye. She used to take me with her fer long walks to the cliffs and back. When I was just a lad, she would tell me fantastic stories about faeries and goblins, maybe a troll and sometimes the kelpies. She's the one that gifted me wi' so many of the books I've got in the library, some of which are verra old. She swore there were faeries in the forests surrounding Galloway Castle, said they were watching out fer us, that they were our friends."

"And did you believe her?"

"I did. I did'na have a choice," he answers with a laugh. "She was very convincing, you see. She would insist that we leave them gifts so that they knew we could be trusted and that we were their friends. So, every now and again, we would leave a token of some sort, maybe some honey or sweetbread. She said they loved anything shiny, so she would leave them little metal trinkets, always something small. In return, they would leave her a flower or a sampling of herbs. She kept them all, pressed them in her favorite book of plants after she identified them. I still have them in the library." He stops then, obviously contemplating our unusual conversation. "Ye probably think that's strange, and I suppose it is, but if ye knew her, ye'd think it was charming more than anything."

For whatever reason, the idea that there is some doubt in his mind about his mother's beliefs and affection toward the faeries she admired makes me sad.

"No, I don't think it's strange at all," I say, looking him in the eyes. "I've seen them, or at least I've seen something. At first, I thought I was crazy, but after talking to Callen and hearing that your mother experienced the same thing, I decided it couldn't be a coincidence."

Alasdair's smile fades, only a little, but his eyes squint in obvious curiosity. "Ye've seen them?"

"Yes. Haven't you?"

"Well, 'tis been a long time. But I remember seeing something, then telling my ma that it was only insects flying around, and she told me that I better not let *them* hear me say that." He laughs, and I can't help but join in, picturing Alasdair as a boy teasing his mother. "Truthfully, I was a little afraid of the notion that something from the books she gave me could be real. Boys can be brave, aye—just don't let their imaginations get carried away. That's when we turn into complete cowards."

His dimple is pronounced with his slanted smile, giving him a hint of the boy he's jesting about, and I am struck with a sudden longing for a little boy just like Alasdair. Dark hair, light eyes, and an adorable smile.

"Where did yer lovely mind drift off to? Yer expression turned tender and sweet, and that bonny smile is enough to make my heart beat out of my chest." He reaches up, the backs of his fingers sweeping gently across my cheek.

"I was picturing you as a boy, and—" I stop, my hands naturally resting on my stomach. "I wonder if we're having a boy. If so, I hope he is just like you."

"Careful what ye wish for," he says with a smirk and taps my nose. "My mother swore I made her hair turn white and put wrinkles in her forehead."

"I do wish I could have known her."

"Yes, well, the two of ye could have sat around telling stories about the wee faeries to yer heart's content." He stands up then. "Come, let us go fer a ride. No jumpin' hurdles and flying through the air, of course. Willow will be alright wi' that, won't she?" he asks, offering his hand to help me stand.

"Yes. In case you haven't noticed, we are quite in tune with one another."

"Oh, I've noticed. But in tune wi' one another is'na what I'd call it. Ye bloody taught yer horse to understand English, and now I've got to watch what I say around her."

"It's a good thing she can't *speak* English. She knows all my secrets."

A few hours later, Alasdair and I are entering the wood on the opposite side of the estate from where I usually go. The north side of the property that leads to the cliffs overlooking the sea is, without doubt, my favorite place to visit. I know my familiarity with it is certainly a factor, but it is also comforting that I feel a strong sense of nostalgia being there, so it is easy to let myself wander in that direction when I feel the need for fresh air and the company of trees and plants, birds, and rabbits, and—who knows—maybe a faerie or two.

"My mother loved it here," Alasdair announces as we pass through the proud regiment of tall trees, most of which are many decades older than me. Beneath them, the ground is free of the pillowing ferns and undergrowth of the northern wood, leaving instead the densely packed earth that exposes the entirety of each ancient pine. It is a magnificent scene of repetition and grandeur, distinctly highlighted by the sunlight that breaks through the high branches.

"This is beautiful, Alasdair. It is so different from the north side of the estate."

"Aye. 'Tis quite lovely, and it would make an excellent challenge course. Not far ahead, there are a few hurdles I think Willow will be pleased with."

"That'll be a bit of a tease since she won't be riding like that any time soon," I say, patting Willow along her neck.

"Oh? She won't jump the hurdles wi'out ye?"

"No. You see, part of the fun for each of us is knowing how much the other is enjoying it. I know for me, feeling her strength and agility, sensing her pride and gratitude, makes the whole event worthwhile. Isn't that right, girl?" As always, Willow replies by nodding her head and muffling out a few snorts.

Alasdair laughs before saying, "Well, nonetheless, I think ye both will enjoy the stream that is nearby. 'Tis quite large and exceptionally beautiful."

"Really? That sounds wonderful! Can we go faster? You know how I love being near the water." My excitement causes Willow to pick up her pace.

"Of course," he agrees, pushing Magni into a slow gallop.

Following Alasdair down the worn path that weaves around the tall pines, I am struck by the magnificence of not only this regal forest but of my husband. The way he rides his powerful horse with such ease and grace, steering him and guiding him with the slightest movements of subtle communication. His strong muscles are flexing with exertion through the thin fabric of his shirt and breeches, mimicking those of Magni. I see his hand reach back to release the tie that was holding his hair at his nape, and I feel my chest expand as I watch his dark wavy tresses fly free, the sunlight accentuating its movement as it flows with the wind. This is an image of Alasdair Stewart in his element, and I am suddenly reminded of the poem he left for me on my settee.

Not only do you share the blood
Of your mother and of me,
You share the spirit of this land
And the forest by the sea.

Seeing him now, I know the same can be said about him. He is a part of this land—it is a part of him. Its knowledge and wisdom, its history, its fertility all are woven into the fibers of the man before me, and I am hit with a deep sense of comfort and love for my husband and for Scotland. I realize I never had this connection with England; I certainly felt out of place there. Is it my love for Alasdair that draws me in, or is it something deeper, like he spoke of yesterday, of us loving in another life? Maybe it was here, upon this land of mystery and beauty and magic, where it all started. I cannot deny that the thought brings a sense of contentment, of truly being home.

Up ahead, I can see the sparkle of moving water through the trees, and I must force myself not to go faster as excitement wells inside me.

"Oh, Willow! There it is!" I say with delight.

A minute later, Alasdair is exiting the forest ahead of me, the bright light of the sun making him glow in contrast to the shaded wood.

"'Tis been a while since I've been here. I did'na realize how much I missed it until now." He looks out across the stream that seems more like a river.

"It is amazing! I can't believe the size of some of the boulders," I say, looking with wide eyes at the moving water, its edge lined with rocks, boulders, and the thickest moss of bright green I've ever seen.

"Aye, they create deep eddies that the trout love to rest in. My father and I used to fish here all the time before I joined the Navy." There is sadness in his tone.

"Well, that will be you and your son soon enough," I say encouragingly.

He turns to me then, the serious look on his face making my stomach stir as I wonder what he is thinking. He abruptly dismounts and walks over to help me get down.

Still holding onto my arms, he says, "Ye have no idea how much I love ye, Ella." And then he kisses me, not with the force of his passion, but with the tenderness of his love.

I don't want it to end. I feel as if I'm floating, though my feet are firmly on the ground. There is something different about this kiss, the emotion of it palpable, encompassing us in its warm embrace.

His hands are still cradling my head as his lips release mine. I open my eyes to find his painted in the true sentiments of his heart. It is a mirror of my own, the deep and profound love I only dreamed my heart would know, yet here I am.

"I think I may have some idea, Lord Galloway. After all, my heart is overflowing with love for you as well."

"Aye, 'tis true. I have no doubt of yer affection fer me. It speaks to me through yer eyes, yer touch, yer kiss." His lips touch mine again, soft and warm. "But I love ye even more than that."

"Is that so? This may be an ongoing debate for some time to come."

"'Tis very likely, and it is one I will thoroughly enjoy." He kisses my forehead and turns back to Magni. "Let's sit by the water fer a bit. I brought a blanket."

"You did? You are always thinking ahead. Did the Navy teach you that? To always be prepared?" I ask, watching as he shakes the blanket open in one big swoosh.

"No. It was my mother. She was a MacAlister, ye see. They're a sneaky bunch, always plottin' and plannin' something, trying to stay one step ahead of everyone else, friend or foe. Sometimes it panned out in their favor, and sometimes it got 'em hanged. So, it's not hard to imagine they always needed to be watchin' their backs. My mother said ye always need to be prepared because ye never know when yer situation could change and ye need to flee. She had satchels packed with necessities hidden all over the bloody castle." He stops to laugh at the memory as we get comfortable by the water's edge. "Thankfully, there were never any emergencies that required us to leave wi' such haste. Regardless, we never left the house without water, dried meat, and a wool plaid. And I can tell ye, I was thankful we had them more often than not."

"Your mother was a MacAlister? I'm assuming that's where you got your name?"

"Aye. She was very proud of her heritage, as are all Scots. Alasdair Mór is our descendant father, so as ye can imagine, there are a bloody lot of Alasdairs coming down the family tree."

"Ah yes. Just as England has its fair share of Edwards,

Williams, and Georges. We must commit to being more original with the names of our children, unless, of course, you were hoping for an Alasdair Gavyn Stewart II," I suggest.

"Well, 'tis the Scottish tradition to name the first son after my father and our first daughter after yer mother. The pattern is the same for the second son and daughter wi' the grandparents. I don't get an Alasdair Gavyn II until son number three." He holds up three fingers, wiggles his eyebrows, and offers me a charming wink. "And if ye ask my grandmother, we are obligated to do so, or it's bad luck fer the family."

"She's the clairvoyant that told you the sweet story of our souls?"

"Aye. Not only was she a seer, but she held wisdom that seemed to be gifted to her from heaven. We could talk about anything fer hours, and it never got boring. She was my mother's mother, born and raised on the Isle of Skye. She married a MacAlister, but her blood is of Clan MacLeod," he explains.

"You cared for her very much, didn't you?"

"I did. She was more like a friend than a grandmother. When I was young, I would go to Skye fer the summer and stay wi' her. 'Tis a beautiful place steeped in the myths of ould Scotland. There are more mysteries and legends than ye can keep up with."

"More so than here?" I ask playfully.

"Well, let's put it this way: On Skye, if ye told yer neighbor ye saw a faerie in the forest, they'd smile, pat ye on the back, and tell ye you'll be havin' good luck fer the rest of the day," he answers with humor.

"So, Scotland is overrun with faeries, is it?"

"Apparently so. And not just the wee sprities that ye've seen flying around the ferns and trees. There is the legend of the Fey

Folk. They look like humans but possess an unnatural physical beauty and are gifted seers and healers. Legend has it that way back in the MacLeods' history; there was a chieftain that fell in love wi' a Fey princess whose beauty was beyond compare. They wanted to marry, but her father, the Fey King, only allowed them to be handfast fer a year and a day. They did and lived happily, even had a son, but when the day finally came, they had to part ways, and both were left brokenhearted. The child stayed wi' the MacLeod chief, and his faerie mother was said to sneak in the babe's window to console him if he cried, and she could be heard singing to him from afar. 'Tis a very sad story, is it not?"

"Yes, Alasdair," I agree, blinking away the sting in my eyes. "I hope it's simply an exaggerated tale passed down through time."

"Well, I'm not so sure about that. The MacLeods are in possession of a relic that is said to be a gift from the Fey princess. 'Tis an enchanted cloth they call the Faerie Flag that, when waved during times of peril, will grant the clan a wish to turn the tides in their favor. They are only allowed to use it three times and have already used it twice. Nanna was adamant that this tale was true as she had seen the relic with her own eyes. Said she could sense its authenticity and could not contain the urge to weep at simply being in its presence." He pauses, and I stare at him in fascinated wonder. "She was a damned convincing storyteller, so I never doubted it was true."

"That is truly fascinating! Suppose it is true." I stop and laugh a little to myself. "Of course, I am a bit of a romantic, so I suppose I'm somewhat gullible when it comes to stories of the heart."

"I would'na feel gullible. I have read plenty a' tale about a human and a Fey falling in love, even marrying as the MacLeod did. There are stories that venture many generations back in time. They speak o' the children born of these couples. Some say 'tis where the gift of the Fey comes from—faerie blood."

I stare at my husband, so handsome and masculine yet, so at ease with the notion that these legends could be true. At this point, after everything I have seen and experienced here at Galloway, it is rather easy for me to accept this sort of fantasy is real and, truly, there is something about that freedom of thought that makes me very happy.

"If that is true, then you must have faerie blood flowing in your veins," I say with a jesting tone, then lean toward him and offer a quick peck on his beautiful smiling lips.

"Considering my family tree, 'tis very likely. However, it's you that exhibits more Fey traits than me. Ye had a bloody white stag greet ye in the forest, and he let ye pet him! I've never heard of such a thing, only read about it."

That comment startles me, and I sit up straighter. "What do you mean...you've read about it?"

"Well, the white stag is a rare beast, and as ye know, there are many legends that follow its history through time. But one says that the mystical white stag is a friend of the faerie folk, the Fey. Some say it's because they are faeries themselves, shifting to the form of a stag so they can live at peace with nature and not be encumbered with the routines and responsibilities of their more human-like counterparts."

"I fear I will never be able to keep up with all these stories, legends, and mysteries. Growing up in England, I only recall learning how to be a proper lady in society. Though I was fortunate to learn reading, writing, and arithmetic—my father made certain of that—but I had to make up my own fantastical stories as I looked for adventure in the forests."

"Not to worry, faerie maiden. Yer ould soul has likely roamed these lands many times before, so it's in there somewhere. It won't be long before yer a fine storyteller yerself wi' a mind full of tales you'll be sharing with our children and grandchildren." He pauses to push my hair behind my ear. "The thought of seeing ye with our bairns, telling them stories of old and even those of new, makes me so happy, ye might find me praying the Lord blesses us wi' ten or more." His eyes sparkle with humor.

"Ten or more? Good heavens, Alasdair! Is that even proper for a lady?"

His hearty laughter blends with the sound of the water rushing over and between the rocks. "Perhaps it is not, but society will'na be determining the size of our brood. That will be a decision made by you and me." He gets up on his knees and moves toward me. His arm wraps around my back as he coaxes me to lie down on the thick wool blanket. He situates himself next to me, our bodies comfortably pressing into one another, his hand roaming across my chest and neck and face. "I will be kissin' ye fer at least the next hour. I hope ye did'na have other plans."

Butterflies swarm in my stomach as I look up at him, the light of the sun shining behind him, creating a bright halo, a perfect contrast to his black hair. My fingers gently follow the outline of his smiling lips, my thumb circling that ever-intriguing dimple, before my hand reaches to the back of his neck and pulls him to me.

"No, Lord Galloway. My afternoon belongs to you."

THIRTY

Alasdair

The soft feather of my quill tickles the underside of my chin as I sit contemplating the arrangement of words in my head that speak of the feelings in my heart. Watching my beloved wife over these past many months fully blossom into the glowing flower of fertility has been an eye-opening experience, to say the least. If I thought I loved my wife before, seeing her body change as our child grows inside her has compounded those emotions with a different kind of love. This love isn't signified by passion, hunger, or need; its foundation is based on gratitude in its purest form. With every day that passes, as her body nourishes our babe, that love grows, weaving in and around the affection and devotion that owns my heart.

Ella is going to be a wonderful mother. When she doesn't know I'm watching, I find her singing to him or telling him stories while her hands gently roam around the full mound of her belly. I say "him" because she has grown so much that I can't imagine a girl would take up that much space—unless, of course, there are two. That was suggested by one midwife, but the midwife that is here now is adamant that there is only one and likely a "fair-sized" healthy lad.

The words start falling into place as I see her in my mind. Everything that I love about her is enhanced by the glow she wears so well. Before my quill touches the paper, I say another silent thank you to our souls that loved before, wherever, and whenever that may have been. I will forever be grateful to be a part of, what appears to be, an eternal romance.

Has there ever lived a woman as beautiful as thee
Whose skin is pure,
Whose hair does shine,
Whose eyes reflect the sea?
Has there ever lived a woman as powerful as thee
With strength of mind
And depth of heart
And uncommon bravery?
Has there ever lived a woman as feminine as thee
Whose grace is poised,
Whose curves are soft,
Who glows with fertility?
The answer is resounding:
Not ever has there been
A beauty or force of nature
A woman so feminine.
For you, the center of my heart
Are simply beyond compare.
But add to that the seed that grows
That will become our heir,
Safe and swaddled within your womb.
'Tis wondrous to see.
Yet what I've learned from watching you
Along this long journey

There is no mother ever lived as exceptional as thee.

I put the quill in its station, dust the shiny ink, and wait for it to dry. My eyes roam across the words as the tickle of excitement flutters in my stomach. It will be any day that labor will begin, and Ella and I will finally lay eyes upon the child created by our love.

A knock at the door interrupts my reverie and announces the entrance of Ewan.

"Pardon me, sir. Breakfast will be served shortly. Lady Galloway has requested it in yer private parlor upstairs."

"Thank ye, Ewan. I'm starved."

"Aye, I bet ye are. 'Tis common fer a pregnant woman's mate to take on the same intense hunger that she is experiencing. That's why men tend to gain weight when their wives are wi' child," he explains nonchalantly.

"Is that so? Ye never cease to educate me on the nuances shared between a man and a woman. Ye are quite the plethora of knowledge. And might I ask, does it appear that I have gained weight?" I know that I have but wonder if it has become noticeable to others.

"Oh, aye. That is fer certain. But it's easy to understand considering the size of the seed ye planted. Yer sweet bride has a ferocious appetite, and you do as well."

I feel my head tip to the side, and my eyes squint slightly as I try to decide if he means what I think he means. "The size of the seed I planted?"

"Weel, you would clearly know more than I, but 'tis impossible not to notice that yer lady is carrying a rather hefty-sized lad in her womb. And, as I'm sure ye know, there are plenty more seeds where that one came from, but it's no' guaranteed that the others will be the same. The next seed ye plant could be a scrawny lit'l fella if it's even a boy. But this one

—oh aye, ye'll be lookin' up at him one day," he finishes with a laugh.

"Simply out of curiosity, how do ye know i'tis a boy?"

"It's as obvious as the glow on Lady Galloway's lovely face, m'lord, if a may be so bold. The babe is sittin' low in her belly," he explains while his hands mimic holding onto the underside of a large belly. "That's how the lads lie in the womb. The lasses sit higher, ye see." His hands move to signify his explanation. "'Tis a simple formula and quite accurate. I've never been wrong, not once, in determining the sex of a wee bairn before it slips out o' the chute and is suckling its mamma's teat." He finishes proudly.

"Well, ye certainly have a unique way of explaining yerself, Ewan. And I have no doubt of yer accuracy, as the midwife is of the same opinion."

"Thank ye, m'lord," he says with a genuine smile. "I must say, I'm as excited as a kitten that caught his first mouse about havin' a lit'l one in the house. Gonna bring new life to this ould castle, an' I can't wait to spoil the wee lad. He's gonna love ol' Uncle Ewan, teachin' him all about mischief and how to give his da gray hair." With that comment, his smile turns from genuine to devilish.

"Ye'll do nothing of the such, ol' Uncle Ewan," I assure him.

"Ah, I'm only teasin' ye. You know I'll be keeping an eye on the little bugger, makin' sure he does'na get *into* mischief." He pauses for a moment. "Yer going to be an excellent father, m'lord, and the lad will grow to be as admirable as you."

"I thank ye, Ewan. I must admit, I'm damn excited to meet him and even more excited to watch him grow. And his siblings too," I add with a wink.

Ewan laughs, then pats me on the shoulder as we head toward the door. "Before we know it, there'll be wee lit'l

Stewarts runnin' all over Galloway Castle, givin' us all gray hair."

~

Arriving in our parlor, I find Ella already seated, putting butter on a small piece of bread.

"Good morning, dear. How are ye feeling?" I ask, leaning in to kiss her forehead.

"Oh! Hello," she says, seeming somewhat startled. "I am fine. Although I thought I was famished, now that I am sitting here in front of food, I'm not so sure."

"Are ye sure yer alright, then? Perhaps ye should lie down," I suggest, feeling a twinge of concern.

"No. It's fine. I am not comfortable sitting or lying down at this point, and I keep having those false contractions that are terribly uncomfortable. I don't think it will be long now, Alasdair." The fatigue in her eyes does not go unnoticed.

"Is there any place that is comfortable fer ye to get some rest? Perhaps the settee by the window in yer room wi' a few extra pillows to prop ye up? Ye'll be needin' all the rest ye can get if the bairn is arriving soon," I suggest, walking over to grab the bed pillows.

"It's alright, Alasdair. Truly."

I prepare the settee, regardless, and encourage her to come lie down.

"Come. Let's get ye comfortable so ye can rest fer a while," I say, taking her hand and helping her over to the settee. She is noticeably slower on her feet, and her gait is wide and awkward. Once she takes a seat, I help her lean back against the soft pillows and watch her eyes instantly close as a content smile widens her mouth.

"You were right. This feels amazing." Her eyes open. "Thank you. I think I will rest for a while."

And so, she does, instantly falling into a deep slumber with her hands resting atop her round belly. I eat breakfast slowly, happy to watch her sleep and taking the time to memorize how beautiful she is at this moment, knowing that she will soon be cradling the babe in her arms.

I hear the door open and see Beatrice come in. I wave to her and put my finger up to my lips so she knows to be quiet and have her follow me out to the hallway.

"She thought she was fine and did'na need to rest until I got her comfortable. She was asleep in less than a minute," I tell her through a chuckle.

"I'm sure she was. Poor thing hasn't been sleeping well. 'Tis the way it always is at this stage of the pregnancy, though. I haven't experienced it myself, but every mother I know has said the same thing—in the last few weeks, the baby takes up so much room you can barely walk, sit, lie down, eat, or even take a deep breath!"

"Well, I'm glad to know 'tis all normal. I've been concerned the bairn is too big," I admit, hating the thought of her labor being worse than it already would be.

"It is obvious the child is large, but she's not the first woman to give birth to a big baby. She'll be fine, Lord Galloway. Try not to worry, though I know it is hard not to. I've spent most of my life worrying about that girl."

I can see the glistening of her eyes, so I try to change the subject somewhat.

"The midwife is in residence now, correct?" I ask, though I already know that she is.

"Yes. She is the best in southeast Scotland, and Ella seems to like her very much."

"That is good to hear. Personally, I've made sure my

inventory of whisky is in good supply. By God, I know I'm going to need it," I say as we both laugh and turn to head down the hall, leaving Ella to rest.

"Yes, you will, m'lord. Birthing is a nerve-wracking event, to be sure."

Just then, we hear Ella cry out from down the hall. We both turn and run back to her room. I throw the door open and find Ella holding her belly and panting while she tries to speak.

"Ella! Are ye alright? Has yer labor begun?" I turn to Beatrice and instruct her to bring the midwife immediately.

"Yes, my...water has broken. The...contractions are...much stronger now," she struggles to say, holding tightly onto my hands.

"The midwife will be here verra soon, my love. She and Beatrice will help ye deal wi' the pain. I'm afraid I have no idea what to do other than tell ye how much I love ye and that I'm proud of how strong ye are."

"Yes, well, that is kind, but..." She doesn't finish as her face winces in pain.

I can feel the tension tightening all my muscles and constricting my chest. Finally, the contraction stops, and she can relax enough to catch her breath.

"Christ, Ella! I do'na think I can stay fer this. To see ye in such pain...I feel so bloody helpless. I don't know what to do." I can hear the desperation in my own voice.

"Alasdair, my sweet husband." She puts her hand on my cheek as I kneel in front of her. "I don't expect you to do anything but wait patiently for me outside this room while I deliver you a healthy son."

My throat thickens before I say, "I love you so much, Ella Stewart."

My lips rest gently against hers until she pulls away as

another contraction begins. She looks at me, trying to maintain herself through the pain. "Go, Alasdair. I love you."

I stand to leave, but something in me won't let me step away. I feel anxious and strange inside my gut, and for the first time throughout her pregnancy, I am afraid. Acknowledging it makes my heart pound in my chest as I remember Nanna's words: *The fey is strong in you, Allie. Your ould soul gives ye powerful instincts. Always trust your gut.* I notice my hands are sweating as I clench my fists. I don't know what to do. I can't stop what is happening, and as I continue to watch Ella struggle through another contraction as nausea forms in my gut.

"It's time for you to go, Lord Galloway," Beatrice's calm voice announces from behind me.

"What? Oh, aye..." I fumble, looking back to see the midwife enter, hands full of the supplies she'll need for delivery.

I need to leave, but I can't move my feet. It's as if they are stuck to the floor. What if I walk away and I never see her again? I can't do that! That cannot happen!

"M'lord? Are you alright? You look like you don't feel well," Beatrice asks in concern. "Everything will be fine. Go to the study and wait. There is nothing more you can do than that. Yours is a tedious job. Waiting makes time slow down, but rest assured, your boy will be here soon." She pats my shoulder and nudges me to leave.

"Ella," I say through the gravel in my throat. "Ella, I..."

"I know, Alasdair. It's fine. He will be here soon. Go. I love you."

"I love you," I whisper and force myself to leave.

Once I am outside her bedchamber, I run down the hall to the stairs, where I scale them three at a time. The footman doesn't have time to do his duty as I throw the door open myself and run around to the side of the manor, where I proceed to vomit the contents of my stomach next to the hedge. I try to level my breathing and lower my head so that I don't lose consciousness. I dry-heave again, wishing something more would come out as the forced motion is making the nausea worse. I stand slowly, then walk to a nearby tree where I sit down and lean against its trunk. I close my eyes and let my head rest against it as I try to regain my composure.

I force the terrible thoughts from my head, convincing myself that everything will be well. Ella and our child will be fine. *They are healthy and well...they are healthy and well...* I keep repeating it over and over in my mind. I tell myself that this is no different than Ella believing me dead after seeing the white stag in the forest. It's simply my emotions and superstition overriding my logic.

"Bloody Christ, man. Look what ye've done to yerself," I say to myself after several long minutes of chanting what I want to believe.

I stand abruptly, needing to brace myself on the trunk of the tree as the lightheadedness follows me up. I breathe through it and turn to leave, glancing at the evidence of my weakness. I cannot let that happen again. Ella expects me to be strong for her and our son. So that is what I will be, regardless of the anxious fear that has settled in the pit of my stomach.

Once I have reached the solitude of my study, I pour myself a glass of whisky and drink it down in one burning mouthful. The distinct sensation of heat leaves a trail down my throat and spreads throughout my empty stomach. My mouth waters as the flavors mingle and dance across my tongue. When I finally release my breath, the salty brine of Skye gives an incredible finish that anchors my soul.

I pour another glass and stand by the window overlooking the south vista of the estate. I envision riding toward the pine forest with my wife and our son. I see him riding with her as she proudly teaches him how to guide Willow with the reins. *She is such a good mother*, I think to myself just as I notice the cool wetness on my face. My fingers quickly reach up, hoping not to find the evidence of tears, yet knowing they will, and there it is, puddled on the tips of my two middle fingers.

"Damn it," I say under my breath and move to the bookshelves where I can find something tangible to distract myself with.

Thankfully, that occupies three hours, during which time I consume far too much whisky and end up prostrate on the sofa for the next five, unable to worry myself into any more knots than I already had. But Beatrice interrupts my coerced slumber, startling me with a nudge to the shoulder.

"Wake up, m'lord."

"What? What is it? Ella...is she alright?" I ask, sitting up straight, still feeling the effects of the spirits I drank.

"She is resting. It...it was a difficult labor, you see. The babe —you have a son, Lord Galloway. Come, let us go see him."

It is then that I see the fatigue and worry that has replaced her usual glow and never-ending smile.

"Beatrice. Is Ella truly alright? You...seem distraught." I ask, grabbing firmly onto her shoulder.

"She appears to be fine now, m'lord. But she struggled for many hours—he is bigger than expected, and...she seems to have lost a lot of blood. She will need round-the-clock care to ensure her recovery," Beatrice explains through a quivering lip and fat tears.

"My God! I must see her at once!"

I don't wait for Beatrice as I run to Ella's bedside. What I find knocks the wind out of me. Her bed is covered in bloody linens that the housemaid is hurrying to remove. Ella is propped up against a stack of white pillows that her skin now closely matches. Gone is the radiance of the past nine months, and in its place is a body, pale, sheened with sweat, and still as a corpse. I feel the bile churning in my gut, only this time, my logic is at the helm, and I am drowned in a flood of terrifying fear.

"Dear Lord," I whisper.

"Sir...pardon me," I hear from behind me and turn to find the midwife holding my swaddled son. "Ye have a verra healthy lad here. Would ye care to meet him?" she asks.

My head turns back to Ella, limp and lifeless, and I feel as if I've been kicked in the gut. I quickly turn back to the midwife carrying my son. What do I do? I need to know that Ella will be alright, that she will live. The sense of panic that has come over me dictates my voice.

"Please, can ye tell me that she will be alright? She does'na —" The dam is breaking. "She does'na look well." My voice cracks and my face crumbles as the sobs break free, wracking through my chest while my worst fear seems to be my reality.

"Lord Galloway," I hear her say, though it is only faintly through the screaming inside my head. "Lord Galloway!" she says again, louder this time. "Look at me!" she commands.

I hold my breath and squeeze my eyes shut to stop the crushing pressure of my fear. The sobs win the battle for minutes longer until I can finally stop long enough to look at the midwife. When my eyes open, I find her expression to be severe with warning.

"Listen to me, Lord Galloway. Yer wife had a verra difficult labor. This lad is not only brawny, but he was breech." That last bit of information was laced with sadness and disappointment. "I tried to turn him before he entered the birth canal, but he was too big. Yer wife is one of the strongest women I've ever seen, but she lost a lot o' blood, and she is completely exhausted, not only from the effort it took to deliver but from the pain. She will need time to recover, and I pray that she does. I know it looks bad now, but she does have a chance to make it through this. I've already sent fer the doctor from town to come and make sure I have'na overlooked anything."

I hear her, and I can see her mouth moving and the worry in her eyes, but it's like a dream, like this isn't really happening. If only that were true. I look down and see the bairn in her arms. He looks like me. My heart pounds harder in my chest as I gaze upon my son, plump and healthy and full of life. Then I turn toward Ella and could swear that I am looking at her corpse.

I rush to her side, needing to feel her warmth, her pulse—anything that will let me know she is still here. But she is cold and clammy, and I want to shake her back to life. I don't realize that my hands are on her shoulders, firmly gripping her until she whimpers and moves her head.

"Ella! My God, yer alive! Can ye hear me? Ella, ye must stay strong." I sit down next to her and take her hand in mine. "Listen to me, Ella. Squeeze my hand if ye can hear me." And she does, only very slightly. "Oh, thank God." I bring her hand to my lips and kiss her freezing fingers. "My love, our son is healthy and well. I do'na want ye to worry. I need ye to focus on you. Ye've lost a lot o' blood, and ye need time to heal...ye have to heal, Ella." My voice cracks again as I cry against her hand. I feel her weak fingers try to squeeze mine. "I'm sorry, I'm sorry. I'm just afraid. Ye know how much I love ye, and I can'na lose ye. *We* can'na lose ye, Ella. Ye are so deeply loved. Please stay. Do'na leave us, Ella. Please stay so we can love ye more."

I slide off the side of the bed and kneel on the floor beside her, still holding her hand. I press my lips upon her cold skin, and I pray.

The hours pass in a blur that turns into days. I haven't left her side and can feel myself getting weak from lack of food and rest. I thought she might be getting better when she began moving and mumbling words I couldn't decipher. But yesterday, a fever set in, and my hope is turning into a hard knot in the pit of my stomach.

"Lord Galloway," Beatrice calls from behind me. She will ask me to leave again to get food and rest, and again I will tell her no.

"Do'na bother askin' me to leave, Beatrice. Ye know I can't." I can hear the dehydration in my voice as I rest my forehead on Ella's hand.

"I know, sir. I brought the babe for you to see. And I thought maybe it would do Ella some good."

My head jerks to the right, where I see Beatrice standing, cradling my sleeping son. I feel my throat close with emotion as I look upon the reason my beloved wife is unconscious, holding on to her life by a thread. I love him so much, I know it in my heart, but I am so angry that his mother might die because he was born. It isn't his fault, I know that, but he is the evidence of this terrible nightmare, and I feel as if a blade has severed my chest open, searching for my heart as I wonder if I will ever get past the anger and regret.

"Is he well?" I ask.

"Yes, m'lord. He has taken to the wet nurse very well. He may be the healthiest babe I've ever seen, not to mention the most adorable," she says with pride as she tickles his plump cheek with her finger.

Time stands still as I realize that I'm smiling for the first time in a week.

"Bring him here," I say.

Her smile beams as she walks toward me. I have rejected seeing him, only having the energy to focus on Ella and not wanting to face my clouded emotions. Beatrice never quit trying though, and is clearly pleased that her efforts have finally paid off.

"He is very special, m'lord," she boasts as she hands him to me.

"Aye, well, he gets that from his mother."

I take my son from her and am surprised at how heavy he is. I hold him close, welcoming the comfort of having him in my arms. My finger glides across his rosy cheek, and I'm startled by the contrast of my scarred and calloused hand next to his soft and supple skin. Just then, his mouth opens to release a yawn that stretches wide and ends with his lips puckered out as if he were offering a kiss. I hear Beatrice laugh from behind me and can't help but join in.

"He is quite adorable," I agree, noticing the dark lashes resting against his cheeks.

I move closer to Ella so I can lay her hand on his head.

"He's so healthy, Ella. Ye did...ye did good." My voice breaks before I can say more as I fight to hold back the tears. It's no use, though. Seeing her frail hand rest upon his vibrant cheek brings the fear and anger back to the surface, and I am unable to stop them from crashing together in my gut.

"Here now. Let me take the babe back to his nursery," Beatrice says with sympathy. "Today was a good first step. He needs to know you're here, sir, that you care. And now he does."

I give him back to her and move to lie down next to Ella. I feel sick now. I'm weak and tired, I smell like a street wretch, and I can't even bring myself to be strong for my newborn son. My hands are tied, and the only thing I can do for my dying wife is pray. And I have. I've prayed so much it hurts, and she's only gotten worse.

"Ye should have been better by now, Ella," I say, resting my head next to her hip. I can feel the heat of her fever through the blankets. "Yer so hot, my love. Do ye want me to remove some of these?" I ask, sitting up to pull the blankets further down over her legs. I turn to the window, noticing that it is shut, so I get up to open it and let in some fresh, cool air. After fidgeting with the latch, I pull the window open and let the breeze rush in as if it were waiting to gain entrance. It smells so good in contrast to the illness in this room that I stand there with my eyes closed and take several long deep breaths, relishing the noticeable boost of energy.

When I open my eyes, I see the green grass and greener forest beyond. The sun is bright today and accentuates all the details of this complex landscape. I think about how much Ella loves the outdoors and how her faerie blood comes to life when she's exposed to nature.

I quickly turn to Ella. "My God! Could that help her?" I ask myself through a strained whisper.

I turn to look back at the forest, recalling the story of her taking my father there to die. It was a generous thing to do for an aged man desperate to be reunited with his beloved wife in heaven. But could it bring life back to Ella?

"Ella!" I call as I turn and run back to her bed. "Ella, I'm taking ye to the forest! Do ye hear me? I'm taking ye to yer favorite place, faerie maiden," I finish with a kiss on her damp forehead before scooping her and the blanket up in my arms and turning toward the door.

Her head is rested against my chest for the long walk to the entrance of the wood. I must force myself to walk gently so that she isn't jostled, feeling a strong sense of hope replace the suffocating fear I've lived with for days. As soon as we enter the line of tall trees and thick undergrowth, I feel a shift within me. That sense of renewal and oneness that comes from a strong connection with nature.

"Can ye smell the trees, Ella? The plants? The air is especially fresh today," I tell her as we make our way down the trail that leads to the ancient oak. "When yer all better, we can come here every day if ye want. You, me, and our son, just as we talked about so many times."

I turn off the main trail and make my way to the massive oak that has fascinated me since I was a child. Once we reach its majestic canopy, I sit down on the grass and get Ella comfortable in my lap, pulling the blanket off so she can be touched by the cool fresh air.

"There we are, my love. Does that feel good on yer skin?" I ask, pushing the hairs away that are stuck to the dampness on her face. Her pallor is so different out here, so much whiter than it is indoors. She seems almost transparent, the faint blue of her veins crisscrossing under the surface of her skin.

I untie the ribbon of her shift to let more air in as I lean forward to press my lips to her brow. "I love you, Ella. I love you so much." I begin to gently rock her, wanting her to wake up, so she will realize where she is and take a deep, fortifying breath of this healing air. This is where she gains her strength, I've seen it. I've seen her fully blossom in the cradling arms of nature.

My mind relaxes, and the tension releases from my body as the spirit of this land consumes me. Without thought, I start to hum, a gentle rhythm that began more than a thousand years ago. Before long, I am crooning her with the old Gaelic songs my grandmother taught me. The ones that sing to the beauty and magical powers of the forests and the glens, the rivers and streams, the songs that feel as if they are connected to my soul. I close my eyes, my forehead gently touching hers, and let the beautiful sound of the Gaelic melody vibrate around us.

We are surrounded by a peace I haven't felt in many years. *This feels so good*, I think to myself as my hand rests on Ella's chest, where I can feel the gentle beating of her heart and pray that it will only grow stronger.

The tickle of something landing on my wrist distracts me, so I lift my head and open my eyes to find there is a small flower resting upon my skin. Before long, there is another and then another. I still the rocking motion and watch as tiny leaves and flowers begin to rain down upon Ella from above. I'm frozen as my heart begins to pound inside my chest. *Could it be?* I wonder as my shaking hand picks up a tiny leaf. It is small and dense and clearly bruised to release its scent. I bring it to my nose and confirm the earthy musk of heather, the hearty plant whose resilience can withstand the harshest conditions and whose medicinal properties have been valued for thousands of years. But what is more, the delicate flowers that are now sprinkled all over her body and continue to fall from the sky are white and not the common purple of most Scottish heather. I pick up a tiny bloom and smile, recalling the legend that says when you happen upon the rare white heather, you are in the presence of faeries, a symbol of good fortune.

I keep my focus on the continuous flow of tiny leaves and bell-shaped blossoms. I will not disrespect them by trying to catch a glimpse as they put forth such effort to help my beloved wife. I am astounded by what is happening, and my gratitude gets lodged in my throat as it overwhelms me. I know they chose this plant for a reason, and I recall my mother's remedy books that speak of the power of white heather, not only when steeped into teas or worked into poultices, but to smell it, to touch it, to be in its presence is said to bring forth its wisdom and the energies of healing and protection.

"Thank you," I say with a thickened voice as the tears well up in my eyes.

I pick up a tiny sprig and roll it between my fingers to release the healing aroma. The herbal scent reaches my nose as I bring it closer to Ella's. My stomach flutters. Did she just take a deeper breath? Perhaps it is my imagination, but I could swear she did. I quickly begin picking up more leaves, squeezing them, and breaking them before placing them on the slightly raised bone in the center of her chest, where she can easily smell them.

She did it again! I know this time it was real, and a tingle of excitement races through my body.

"Ella!" My hand caresses her face as I try to encourage her eyes to open.

Before I can say more, I am startled by the loud, shrieking cry of a hawk. I look up to find him perched upon a low branch of the oak tree. He is quite striking as his white feathers stand out in sharp contrast to the dark background of leaves and branches. But his piercing yellow eyes give me pause as they glare at me with unexpected intent. He calls again, seeming louder this time as I watch his mouth open wide, eyes still focusing solely on me. I can sense that he has a purpose but cannot fathom what that might be. It raises chills on my skin as he cries out again, the high-pitched scream echoing around us.

The stare down continues until the sound of rustling leaves distracts my attention. My head jerks to the right. "Christ!"

I instinctively pull Ella closer for protection as my mind registers that an enormous white stag is walking toward us. *My God!* It must be the same one she talked about seeing on the far ridge of the estate. It is an impressive beast. Looking up at its tall stature and full rack of antlers is an awesome sight, but its snow-white coat makes it seem otherworldly.

"Have ye come to see Ella?" I ask as it stops a few feet away. Its calm, assertive demeanor seems to answer my question without words. "She is'na well," I say, fully aware of the oddity of speaking to a wild animal. But my instincts seem to understand that at this moment, it is of no concern. That he is here to help her, and that is all that matters. "She struggled with the delivery of our son." I must stop as the significance of his presence and the stress and fear of the past week overwhelm me. Again, I rest my forehead upon hers as my eyes squeeze shut, and my jaw clenches hard to rein in my emotions as my arms wrap tighter around her.

The warm, humid air of the stag's breath rushes across the side of my face and down my neck, forcing me to pull back from Ella. His wide snout is barely a foot away, and we are surrounded by the heat of his proximity. His scent reminds me of Magni when I brush his shiny coat—pungent, earthy, and masculine, yet the stag has the added distinction of green plants and crisp air. His knowing eyes stare at me for a moment before he grunts and lifts his head, then does it again. My hands are truly shaking now because I believe the beast wants me to move out of the way.

"I...I can'na leave her," I say with clear skepticism.

He grunts again, then bends his head forward, almost impatiently, and nearly spears my face with a point of his massive antler.

"Oh, I see. Forgive me. I fear I am a bit ignorant when it comes to this sort of...communication," I reply, letting a bubble of anxious laughter escape as I turn to gently lay Ella upon the grass. The mass of heather flowers and leaves shift and fall about her body as I get her comfortable. Her color is better; I can already see the difference, a slight hint of pink on her cheeks and lips. When I move back, sitting several feet away, I know I can see her chest move as her breaths become deeper and stronger. I feel my own chest expand with the release of pent-up tension.

The stag moves closer to Ella and bends his head low, bringing his nose close to her side. I can see his nostrils moving as he sniffs her, taking his time to slowly move around her body. He stops when he reaches her lower abdomen and begins moving in small circles before pressing his snout gently on her womb. A dull ache forms once again in my throat as I witness what I believe to be an answer to my prayer—perhaps even a miracle.

A few minutes later, he moves up toward her chest and hovers there, pressing only a few times between her breasts, then moves to the center of her forehead and rests there for several long minutes. Another tear follows the wet trail streaking down my face. Is this a dream? Am I in heaven, having already died from a broken heart? What I am seeing cannot be real, yet I can feel the energy of whatever it is that is happening right now. Still, my logic fights a mighty battle against the truth before me, screaming defiantly in my head.

The stag finally lifts his immense head, crowned with those magnificent antlers, and stands tall and proud before us. He turns and looks up toward the massive branches of the oak and lets out a loud bellow that vibrates in my chest and echoes through the forest. It sounds like a war cry, that haunting call to action that rallies forces to charge into battle and defeat the enemy with fearless ambition. Perhaps he is calling on the forces of nature to defeat the illness that is trying to take Ella's life, or it could be a call to her spirit, demanding she fight and win the battle. When the silence returns, it is strange and heavy in my ears. Then suddenly, it's broken by the high pitch call of the hawk I had forgotten was there. My heart is pounding in my chest when the white stag bellows again, the opposing sounds blending into a melody that reverberates around us, then drops his head to nudge Ella's side, jostling her as if to wake her up.

The hawk cries out again and again, the pauses between each cry long enough to allow the silence to deafen the forest. The rhythm becomes hypnotic as the fierce sound becomes more and more powerful as if this magnificent bird of prey is chanting an ancient prayer that only the forest remembers. Gooseflesh spreads across my entire body as I continue to witness something surreal yet, more beautiful than I could ever imagine. Then, without warning, Ella's eyes open, and she looks directly at the regal stag standing over her. She blinks several times to adjust to the light, then lifts the corners of her mouth into a small, knowing smile that nearly blinds me.

Thank you, thank you, thank you, I repeat in my head as I watch her small hand reach up and gently rest on the stag's face. His eyes close in a slow blink before lifting his head to stand tall once again. He looks toward me, lets out a muffled grunt, and turns back to the forest, slowly disappearing into its dense camouflage while the swooshing sound of a bird in flight echoes above.

I rush to Ella's side, pulling her frail body into my arms.

"Ella! My love. Yer awake, yer alive." I pull away, my trembling hands holding her head so that I can stare at the eyes I have begged to open, I have dreamed of looking into again. "My God! I can'na believe what I've seen. 'Tis a miracle, a true gift." She looks at me, the weakness still evident in her eyes. But she's awake, and she's smiling at me once again. "I love ye so much, Ella. I've never been more scared in all m'life. I thought ye would'na make it through. I begged, and I prayed, but nothing helped until I brought ye here. Ye can'na believe what has happened, what they did fer ye."

Her hand comes up to push my hair behind my ear. "You did the right thing, Alasdair. Everything is alright now."

My lips press hard against her forehead as I weep from hearing the sound of her voice. "Christ, Ella," I say through the strangled grip on my throat.

"It's alright, Alasdair. Look at me." My eyes meet hers. "Tell me, how is my boy?"

THIRTY-ONE

Ella

"You're staring at me again," I say, sitting comfortably in my bed while Callen sleeps soundly next to me.

"Aye. I can'na take my bloody eyes off o' ye," Alasdair replies with a serious face. "And I do'na sleep at night fer wanting to stare at ye to make sure yer still breathing."

"That makes me so sad, Alasdair. You're going to exhaust yourself with worry. Come here," I say, wanting to do anything I can to ease his mind. Taking his hand, I continue, "I am fine now. You must have faith that I will remain that way. Fate would not have brought us together to simply tear us apart so soon. It may want to challenge us, ensuring we understand the depth of our love, but not take us away from one another. Look at me," I say, encouraging him to bring his eyes to mine and away from our locked hands. "I fully believe that with all my heart. Don't you?"

His eyes are fierce as they roam the features of my face, and mine cannot help but notice the lines of worry that now accent his.

"Aye. I do. But when ye've been scared that badly, it leaves a wound, and this one is'na small. It will need time to heal."

It hurts my heart to know how terribly he suffered, and in many ways, I completely understand, having lived with the fear he may never return home. But Alasdair saw his nightmare day in and day out. The potential for the worst outcome was high —he could see that, and it terrified him.

"I understand. Truly, I do."

"I know ye do. So, when ye find me staring at ye, just smile and know that alone is the best medicine I could have."

"I think I can do that."

"I do have to admit," he says, coming over to sit next to me on the bed, "it makes me feel a wee bit better knowing that ye were dreaming through most of it and not in pain."

"Yes, me too," I say with a laugh. "Though I call it a dream because I don't know what else it could have been. I can assure you, though, I have never had a dream like that before. It was like an ongoing tale that I was living and witnessing all at once. And it was as vivid as this moment sitting here with you."

"Ye did'na tell me that. What were ye doing? And do ye know where ye were?" he asks with genuine curiosity.

"Well, I don't know where I was specifically, but it must have been here in Scotland. The people were dressed in traditional Scottish wardrobe, like that of the Highlands, but much older. There was a village...it seemed old as well, or perhaps it was a very remote location. Either way, it was nothing like the cities I'm familiar with," I explain, wondering if he thinks it strange. "Though mostly I was in the forests or exploring nearby streams collecting herbs and roots, then taking them back to a cottage where I worked them into what I believe were medicinal remedies." It does seem strange to have such a vivid recollection of a dream. "I must have dreamt that I was a healer of some sort. I have to say, I find the idea of it all rather appealing."

"Fascinating, it must have some significance to who ye are, to yer ancestry perhaps." He pauses then as Callen moves in his sleep, clearly having a vivid dream of his own. "If yer interested in learning about healing herbs, especially in this area of Scotland, the library is full of books that will teach ye anything ye want to know. It was a hobby of my mother's, and she collected extensive samples. I still have them all stored in one of the pantries off the kitchen."

"Oh! That's wonderful, Alasdair. I think I would like to learn more about the healing arts. In the dream, I felt...very content. I would say it was as if I was doing what I was meant to do. And I can assure you, I would much rather do that than sit around the parlor working tiny stitches into a piece of fabric until my eyes hurt." We both laugh at that notion. "Do you know that is what I was taught a proper lady does with her free time? Can you even imagine such a life?"

"Not so much fer you. But perhaps it is fitting fer some other ladies I have known," he replies.

"Ladies, you have known?" I question with a raised brow.

"Not like that, my little vixen. Other women in general. Most ladies do'na like traipsing through the woods and racing horses over hurdles like you do." He explains, showing off his dimple with a knowing grin. "Tellin' ye true, it seems like a good fit fer ye, learning about the herbs and whatnot. It may not be what's expected of ye, but that is of no mind. You will decide how ye spend yer time and what ye care to learn. It's always been my belief that it's a woman's right to do so."

"Well, that is very admirable of you, dear husband," I say, taking his hand in mine and pulling him forward so that I can kiss his beautiful mouth. "Our daughters will be very pleased to know they can be educated and free to think for themselves. I know I was always grateful my father allowed it for me."

Alasdair's face turns sullen, like a mask of despair has replaced his joyful glow.

"What is wrong?" I ask with concern.

He doesn't answer right away. Then finally admits, "I do'na want ye to have more children, Ella."

"What?!" I exclaim. "You can't be serious. You literally just said it is my choice how I want to live my life! And I want more than one child, Alasdair," I vehemently state.

He stands abruptly and walks to the window across the room. I can see his jaw clenching hard, then notice his hands balling into fists with the same rhythm. I don't say another word, giving him time to think about what I have declared.

I look down and notice my hand is wrapped around Callen's, my thumb fitting perfectly in his tiny palm. My heart swells again with love for my beautiful, healthy boy. It's as if every time I look at him, it expands inside me.

"It's because I love you so much, Alasdair. I look at Callen and see that love in his creation. I can't put into words how happy it makes me to see how he looks like you. What if we have a daughter that looks like me or, better yet, your mother? Then I can see her with my own eyes, and you will get to see her again."

He drops his head, jaw still ticking as he tries to control his emotions. "Ella, ye almost died right before my eyes. 'Twas a miracle that brought ye back, and I can'na expect that to happen twice." My stomach sinks when he turns to face me. The anguish I see there speaks of the fear and pain he went through, and I suddenly feel selfish, and thoughtless.

"I'm sorry, my love. I shouldn't push so hard after what you've been through. You're right, the wound will need time to heal, and when it has, we can discuss it again," I offer, wanting to ease the worry that mars his handsome face.

"The last thing I want to do is argue wi' ye. Time is too precious fer that. Not to mention, yer a fierce little fighter, and I'm afraid I do'na have the strength to keep up." He agrees with a half grin that is weak and laced with sadness.

"Do you have the strength to come give this fierce little fighter a fierce little kiss?" I ask playfully.

One eyebrow instinctively raises, full of implications. "Aye, I can. And if ye keep smilin' at me like that, I'll be inclined to give ye more than merely a kiss."

"That is a very intriguing threat, Lord Galloway. But I'm afraid the doctor has given me strict orders when it comes to that kind of activity," I reply as he sits back on the bed and leans in to touch his lips to mine.

"I can work around those orders, ye know that don't ye, faerie maiden?" His rich voice turns velvety smooth as his mood shifts back to that with which I am accustomed. Then he takes my mouth in a deep and sensual kiss, pushing me back into the pillows.

I hear myself moan as he awakens my desire. The sound encourages him to kiss me harder as a flush of pleasure settles between my legs. I moan again just before he pulls away.

"Call fer the nursemaid. I will'na do this in front of our son." His breaths are heavy on the command.

"Are you sure we should..." I stammer.

"Ella. Do ye trust me?"

"Of course I do."

"Then ring the bell." The rolling R and slow command tighten my breasts to hard points as I reach over and pull the toggle. "Verra good. Once she leaves, the only thing ye need to do is lie back and relax. I'll do the rest."

Over the next few days, I began to feel more myself. I've had a voracious appetite, and the kitchen staff has made sure I have an ample variety of food choices at any given moment. Alasdair wanted me to stay in bed, but after the first day, I was already tired of staring at my bedroom walls and didn't care if I slept another wink for days. Eventually, I moved over to the window seat. Callen and I would get comfortable there, surrounded by pillows and bathed in sunshine, and I would continue getting him used to nursing on my breasts and pray my milk would come in stronger. There was very little when I first woke up from the strange coma I was in, but the midwife has me drinking a special tea that nourishes lactation. It seems to have worked well as Callen now nurses contently and falls fast asleep afterward with a full belly.

Today I plan to venture out of my room, not only for the change of scenery and a bit more exercise, but also to go to the library to research Alasdair's mother's collection of herbal remedy books. I can't stop thinking about the dreams I had. Whether that was merely a dream or a vision from a past life, as Alasdair has suggested, is of no matter, I'm intrigued, and I want to know more.

In the hallway, I take my time walking to the stairs as my head is undeniably light, and I still have some pain leftover from Callen's difficult delivery. Once there, I grab onto the railing and take one step at a time. I barely make it three steps before Beatrice squeals from below, startling me.

"Dear God, child! What in heaven's name are you doing out here? Climbing the stairs, no less!"

Before I can answer, she hurries up to me, wrapping her arm around my waist to help guide me back to my room.

"Beatrice," I say. "First of all, you seem to have forgotten I just gave birth to a very healthy baby boy, which means I am no longer a child. Secondly, I am not going back to my room. I am going to the library. If you would like to assist me in doing so, I welcome the help. But I am not going back to the confines of my bedchamber." We both stare at each other with defiance, but I will win this battle. "If you'll excuse me."

"Fine," she replies tersely. "I will help you to the library, but Lord Galloway will not be pleased when he finds out."

"I'll deal with Lord Galloway."

When we enter the library, I realize how much I've missed this room. This has always been my favorite place to relax and read while Alasdair sits at his desk to work. The smell of old books and a low-burning fire brings me a sense of instant comfort.

"Thank you, Beatrice. That wasn't so hard, was it?" I ask with sugary sweetness.

"You may be as sarcastic as you like, but I still say you should be resting. You don't want to make yourself weak by overdoing it."

She really is adorable when she's flustered with me. "I am not overdoing it. I will be sitting here reading books, not running to the stables to take Willow for a run. Although that is what I would love to do more than anything." That last part came out as somewhat of a mumble.

Beatrice doesn't respond even though I know she heard what I said. She just gives me a firm brow and tight lips before saying, "I'll be back shortly to check on you."

Shrugging off Beatrice's short-lived ire, I walk over to the wall of windows that line the far side of the room. It is truly a stunning view that overlooks the manicured hedges and flowers that hug the stone walls of the manor, across the unblemished lawn to the tall trees of the forest beyond. How I miss it there, my enchanted forest. Chills spread down my arms and legs as I think about opening my eyes and finding that magnificent white stag so close, I could touch him. I can still hear the hawk's ear-piercing call and feel the warmth of the stag's breath as he waited patiently for me to come to. I close my eyes to relive the moment again. I can feel him nudging my body, pressing on my belly while the pleasant smell of heather surrounds me. Before opening my eyes, I tell them all another silent thank you.

Thinking of the white heather my little flying friends chose to encourage my strength and consciousness, I turn to the shelves that Alasdair said hold the volumes his mother collected over many years. There is a pique of excitement as I walk slowly along the shelves filled with books that give me a noticeable boost in energy. At the far end, close to Alasdair's desk, are two wide shelves that hold what must be at least forty books. "My heavens!" I exclaim and run my fingers along the spines of one reference after another: *The Healing Herbs of Scotland; Plant Remedies; Teas, Poultices, and Tinctures; Healing Herbs of the Highlands; The Healer's Handbook.* I'm so enthralled with all my options, I don't even know which one to choose. I want to read them all right now, then I laugh in giddy excitement. I pick up *The Healing Herbs of Scotland,* figuring that it would certainly have plenty of good information.

I read through the various applications of white heather. A tea made from the flowers is used for stomach pain, the stems and leaves for urinary issues, hot poultices for rheumatic pain; it can even be used for emotional problems. I continue reading the extensive list of potential uses and think to myself that it must be one of the most universally beneficial plants in existence.

At the bottom of the page, it elaborates on the spiritual powers of heather, that it protects against violent attacks, and that it brings about healing and good luck and empowers sensuality.

The last paragraph, though, makes the hair stand on my neck. *Heather is commonly associated with faeries, especially white heather. Some say that faeries are near when you happen upon the uncommon white blooms.* I stare at the words, acknowledging the nervous tick of my heart beating in my chest.

"I'm beginning to believe there are no longer coincidences in my life," I say to myself through a hushed laugh, then close the book and put it back on the shelf.

I glance down at the second shelf. It is immediately obvious that these books are much older than the ones above. I kneel and find that some don't even have a typical spine with a title exposed; they are simply yellowed, tattered pages between two thick covers and held together with brittle leather ties. As I reach for what appears to be the most worn of the collection, a strange feeling comes over me, and my heartbeat begins whooshing loudly in my ears. Maybe I am overdoing it. I am a touch lightheaded and maybe a little chilled. Trying to ignore it, I admire the cover that is nothing more than a thick piece of hide with a rudimentary embossed vine pressed into it, adding a simple design. I run my hand across the worn surface, wondering at its history and the strong sense of nostalgia. But when I open the cover and see the scrolled handwriting of the author, I cannot contain the gasp that escapes as my fingers come up to cover my mouth.

The dream. I saw this there...wherever that was, in the cottage where I would take the herbs I had collected and store them or mix them into various concoctions. It was lying open on a nearby table, its unique handwriting easy to distinguish, flowing, and precise. *Isla Sutherland – Healer's Journal.*

I smile at her beautiful script. She clearly put effort into making this special and took pride in her work. How strange it is that I have a sense of my own pride. The next few pages are filled with what she considered basic tonics and remedies for the most common ailments. She drew detailed illustrations of leaves and flowers to help identify them, noting if certain ones had close similarities and how to distinguish one from another. Her descriptions are neatly presented and easy to read and understand.

About five pages in, she started journaling the various patients she saw—the first one is dated September 7th, 1571. I feel a tickle of excitement as if I have found some hidden treasure. Isla continues, describing a festering wound on an elderly man's foot. She believes his healing time will be long as his age is working against him to help it close with fresh skin. In another entry, a young family has been stricken with food poisoning, likely from tainted meat. She feels certain they will recover but has concerns about the youngest, a boy of only two years. There are several instances of teeth that need to be pulled. Most did not seem serious, but one woman needed to be treated for a festering rot in the gum and possibly the bone. Isla packed the wound with a paste of wild garlic and added clove for pain.

"Dear Lord, that sounds dreadful, poor woman," Again, I voice my thoughts aloud. I can't imagine how terrible it must have been. Although, I'm sure she was relieved when Isla changed the dressing and had her rinse with a tincture of honey and whisky. She probably asked for a little extra of that sweet concoction to take home.

Thumbing through the pages of her journal takes me back to the time and place I visited in my mind after Callen was born. How strange it is that I have such a connection to that dream and now to Isla's journal. Seeing her beautiful script and reading her detailed recollections is like visiting an old friend

I've longed to see for ages. It's as if she's talking to me, teaching me about the medicinal remedies she used to heal the sick and wounded.

Through her writing, I can sense her emotions. She cares deeply for her patients and their well-being. I can feel her satisfaction in successfully treating an ailment, be it minor or serious. Yet, when I happen upon her first loss, a young man with a severe battle wound in his abdomen, I have to blink away the tears that blur my vision. She was deeply distraught and sought out the guidance of her mentor to help her through.

"I'm so sorry," I whisper as my fingers glide along her words of sorrow and defeat. I have a deep yearning to comfort her and let her know that she is a gifted, compassionate healer, but sometimes life and death are given up to a higher power. Perhaps with time, it was something that became easier for her to accept.

I turn the page. "My God!" I gasp, my hand quickly going to my chest. Staring at me from the yellowed page is a man so striking and so familiar I feel my stomach sink as if the floor dropped out from under me. He is handsome yet intimidating, and through this sketch, Isla managed to capture the intensity of his glare. Why does my heart seem like it will pound right out of my chest? Why did she draw his portrait? And why does he remind me of Alasdair?

On the facing page, she answers my question but leaves more that I am desperate to ask.

The MacLeod chief's eldest son came back today. Lachlan MacLeod is his name. I didn't know why he was here—I figured it had to do with his brother's death, that perhaps he had more questions. But what could he ask? It was obvious that Duncan had lost too much blood and that the wound could not be repaired. Lachlan waited a long time before speaking, staring at me with a severity that made my chest hurt. I could sense a deep longing within him that awakened my feminine spirit. He finally spoke, offering his gratitude for helping his brother pass from this life to the next. He said it was a gift that I gave his brother and their family, letting Duncan know that he was safe and he could let go and begin his next journey. I could sense that Lachlan wanted to say more, and I desperately wished that he would. Instead, he came close, forcing me to look up at him. I felt my knees go weak, then he gently caressed my face, and I could have sworn his hand was trembling. How could this powerful man be so tender, and what could ever make him afraid? Certainly not me. Yet the look in his eyes said otherwise. He offered me compliments, even jested a bit, surprising me with his laughter. Then he asked my name. Something about my answer displeased him, and he turned and left without another word, leaving me with a terrible urge to weep.

I quickly turn the page, hoping to find more, wanting to know if he came back to her. Did Isla ever see him again? Why did he act as if he cared for her, then turn and leave when she told him her name? A thousand other questions are racing through my mind, but there was nothing more about him. I skim through the rest of the journal, my eyes searching for the name Lachlan or MacLeod, but find nothing. I pull more journals off the shelf, five of which were Isla's, and hurry through the pages, desperate to find something that would tell me if they ever met again, but to my dismay...I fear I will never know.

THIRTY-TWO

Alasdair

The past few months have not only been healing for Ella but for me as well. I needed to see her as vibrant as I remember, that glow on her cheeks and the sparkle in her eyes. The smile that makes me want to conquer the world, simply so that I can give it to her. I can feel the wound closing, the one that flayed me open emotionally after watching her light fade and living day in and day out with the fear it would never shine bright again. It is a relief to finally be free of the heavy burden that fear left behind. Nonetheless, I am still not ready to broach the topic of having more children. The wound hasn't healed entirely, it is still tender, and beyond that, I'd like to enjoy our firstborn a while longer before thinking about having another.

Callen grows bigger by the day, and I do not recall ever seeing a bairn as healthy as him. Ewan, as expected, has assured me that my son is the healthiest, most handsome lad in all of Scotland, that never has he seen a babe such as him and professes to have seen many in his twenty-six years. As a proud father, I will happily take the compliment. My only concern at this point is how spoiled the little lad will be. Between Ewan, Beatrice, and more than half the staff here at Galloway, Ella and I will have our work cut out for us to ensure he is solidly grounded and grows into a man of dignity and self-discipline.

Sitting at my desk, I look over at the shelves that hold my mother's collection of books that have become Ella's obsession —after doting on her son, of course. It pleases me that she has found such great interest in the healing arts. But I still get gooseflesh every time I see the time-worn journals of Isla Sutherland. It is strange that they have been on that shelf, right next to my desk for so many years, yet I never took the time to read them, having never really had an interest in plants and herbs the way my mother did. But when Ella showed it to me, my breath stopped short in my chest. It was familiar, as was her name, but when she showed me the drawing of Lachlan MacLeod, I felt a flush go through my body that triggered a sharp headache around my eyes. Thinking about it now causes me to close them and rub my temples. I wish Nanna were here to help us understand so many of the inexplicable events that Ella and I have encountered. Our connection, from the moment we met in London, was quite remarkable, but here in Scotland, it is something else entirely.

Without Nanna's wisdom and her gift of sight to help me confirm otherwise, I can only surmise that Ella's detailed dream, where she saw Isla's journal sitting on a table, had to be a vision from a past life. If that is true, I wonder if it is connected to her ancestry, the line that I believe is that of the Fey. Humans without faerie blood have had past-life visions for hundreds of years or more, but Ella has a connection with nature that is uncommon and a sensual passion that distinguishes her from most. How many times have our souls found each other and loved one another as deeply as Ella and I do now? How far back in time does it go? Where did it begin? I feel certain that Isla Sutherland and Lachlan MacLeod are part of the puzzle. Did our souls belong to them? Considering our reactions to the journal and his portrait, it seems likely, and that was over two hundred years ago. Does it go back further than that?

"Truly fascinating," I quietly say to myself as I write my thoughts down in my own journal. Putting them to paper seems to help my mind sort through the strange events of my life. Faerie blood, past lives, souls reunited, the magical events of the forest and its creatures—any rational person would think me insane should I even suggest it to be true. With that, I close my eyes and say another silent thank you to Nanna for teaching me to appreciate those things in life that cannot be explained. To respect the power of fate.

The rough sketch of Lachlan enters my thoughts again followed by the longing to see an image of Isla. Was she the ethereal blonde woman with blue eyes in the vision I had? Was Lachlan consumed by her beauty and charm and spirit the way I am with Ella's? Isla's brief description of his reaction to her says he was, and I'm certain it did not take Lachlan long to know that her outer beauty, as exquisite as it was, could not compare to the inner. There is something special about the spirit of these women, this soul that travels through time and ensnares the men that it loves.

My blood heats at the thought of pleasuring my wife, my passionate little faerie maiden who drives me mad with her natural desire for carnal play. I think about how she has teased me over the past several weeks, pushing my limits of self-control. Her doctor and the midwife gave strict orders of abstinence, though we have not abstained from the pleasures of oral sex, something my lady wife is exceptionally talented at administering.

"Christ," I say through gritted teeth. My cock is so stiff it's painful. As I wonder what Ella is doing right now and where I can find her, a knock at the door startles me.

"Come in," I curtly announce.

A maid enters. "Pardon me, m'lord. Lady Galloway asked me to deliver this." She hands me a folded piece of paper.

"Thank you," I say, focusing on the wax embossed with Ella's personal seal.

There is a sense of anticipation as I break it open, knowing that today is the first day our abstinence will no longer be required. But when I read the elegant script of my wife's hand, I feel my bollocks tighten, and my shaft begins to throb.

> *Alasdair,*
>> *Please come to my bedchamber. I have something special*
> *for you.*
>> *Ella*

My chair slides back with a sound that echoes loudly through the silence while I tuck the note into my pocket and make haste to the staircase, not bothering to wait for my erection to subside. In the hallway that leads to Ella's room, my steps are loud as I widen my stride to get there faster.

I stop outside her door, wondering what I will find on the other side, hoping I have not read into the meaning of her note incorrectly. The click of the latch is loud against the hollow silence of the hall, its harsh contrast extraordinarily erotic. Once inside, I face the door, not yet turning around. The hairs stand up on my neck as I sense her presence without seeing her. She's naked, I can feel it reaching out to crackle along my skin like a strike of lightening. My fingers twitch as I wait a little longer, relishing the desire that has engulfed the room. When I turn to find her lying on the bed, her beautiful creamy skin bright against the ornate bed cover, her hand gently massaging the delicate folds between her legs, my hands ball into fists as I try to maintain control.

My steps are slow and heavy as I make my way to the bed. She watches me, her pale skin flushing pink, then red, while her fingers move faster. Lying next to her, she has neatly placed the blindfold, binding ties, and tasseled crop that we haven't enjoyed since I left for battle almost a year ago. It's strange to think that much time has passed, even stranger to think of all that has transpired. I push away the thoughts of fear and desperation that constantly try to dominate my mind. They certainly have no place here tonight.

Bringing my eyes back to Ella, I see hers turn black as they drift down to where my swollen cock is trapped inside my breeches. With measured control, I reach down and pick up the crop, rolling it in my hand a few times before taking a steady grip. I let the fringed leather strips tease her skin lightly as they drift across her belly, then down to where her fingers continue to rub intently against her clit.

"That belongs to me," I say, using the tip of the crop to move her hand away from her beautifully wet cunny. She smiles at me, so I tease the inside of her thigh, then circle the plush fur of her mons with light touches that coerce the panting breaths that drive me mad. "Sit up," I command, taking a step back to watch her get comfortable. I love it when she doesn't know what to expect. Her desire to let me control her pleasure is easy to see, and I wonder if she understands how much she has control over me.

"So, ye want to play this way, do ye?" I ask, stinging one nipple with a quick snap of the crop.

She inhales sharply. "Yes."

"I'm pleased to hear it," I reply.

I lean over to grab the blindfold, placing the cool silk over her eyes, relishing that familiar twinge of excitement in my gut.

Once it is comfortably in place, I take a moment to admire how beautiful she is, then take her voluptuous mouth in a devouring kiss I know she was not prepared for. Her head is held steady in my hands as my tongue takes her deeper and deeper until her moans vibrate through my chest. In one quick move, I've got her on her feet and turn her around so that her back presses hard against me. Her head falls onto my shoulder, exposing the tender flesh of her throat, so perfect and unmarred, waiting to be marked by our passion. I cannot resist taking her delicate skin, sucking hard while I squeeze firmly on the erect points of her breasts, feeling the wet release leak out onto my fingertips.

Abruptly, I turn her around, taking her mouth again as I continue to tease her bosom, spreading her maternal essence across the fullness of her mounds. My fingers bear down, and our mouths separate as she pulls away to gasp for air. I kiss a trail down her throat and across her chest, making my way to her tight bud. My tongue plays with it before I pull it into my mouth, letting her sweet milk seep out to wet my tongue.

Without warning, I pull away and grab her hands, placing them on the bedpost. "Keep them here. Do'na move," I say next to her ear, then move around to kiss her open mouth. "Yer milk is so sweet. Can ye taste it on my tongue?"

"Yes," she replies against my lips.

"Good. Now, tell me if this is too tight." I take my time, both to enhance her anticipation and perhaps a touch of fear, savoring the eroticism as I bind her delicate hands.

When I am finished, I step back to admire how beautiful she is. Pale, flawless skin, and a body that is still lush with the feminine curves of motherhood. Another silent prayer is spoken in my mind. *My God, how I love this woman!* My hand hovers above her skin, her heat and mine, mingling in the small space in between. She flushes again on a sigh as her back arches slightly, lifting her beautifully round arse in silent invitation. She will have to wait for that.

Her long hair is swept up in braids and curls, exposing her full back and slender neck. I step closer, bringing my nose to her hairline, where her scent is rich with her elegant aroma.

"Ye smell so bloody good. My mouth waters wi' need to taste yer sweetness," I say, lips gently brushing the outer edge of her ear, "to slide my tongue along the folds of yer wet cunny." Her breath hitches. "Would ye like that, faerie maiden?"

"Yes, Alasdair, please."

Before she can beg for more, I take the tender skin of her shoulder in my mouth, sucking hard as my hand comes around to slide between her wet folds and tease her swollen nub. She rests her head back onto my shoulder, those supple lips opening seductively to let her cries escape.

"Ye have the lips of a temptress," I growl, biting down on her soft lobe while my fingers continue to play. "They make me mad with need." My explanation is accentuated by my stiff erection pressing into the softness of her bum. Her breath catches again, opening her mouth wider, so I bring my wet fingers up to coat her lips, then dip them in to tease the tip of her tongue. "Wrap yer lips around it, let me watch ye taste yer sweet essence." And so, she does, with a sensual mastery that shatters my resolve to take this slowly. "Stop!" I command and quickly pull my fingers out of her mouth.

Taking the tasseled crop in hand, I tease her shoulders with light touches. "Are yer arms getting tired?"

"No."

"Good. I want ye to stay like this fer a bit longer." Again, my accent has thickened, even to my own ears.

I continue to caress down her side, coming close to the edge of her breast, then further to her waist, where I graze the front of her hip. Her spine arches, her head falls back, and somehow, I am once again stunned by her raw sensuality and ethereal beauty. Blindfolded, hands bound, exposing her trust in me as easily as she does her desire. There it is, the shift within me, like the awakening of something primal, something older than history as we know it. It drives my need to have her, to take her, to ensure she knows that she is mine, that I am hers.

My hand reaches up and firmly grabs onto her jaw, turning her head toward me so I can devour her mouth and she can taste the intensity of my desire. She matches my hunger with her lips and tongue, the sound of her moans vibrating through my soul like a beloved song from our ancient past.

"My God, woman," I say against her lips. "The need I have fer ye...the love..." I kiss her again. "There are no words fer it."

"Show me. I want to feel it." Her mouth pushes against mine. "I *need* to feel it."

My hand lets go, and I step back, taking a moment to stare at the reason I exist. "Ye are everything to me, Ella." I move to stand behind her while I untie my cravat and unbutton my vest.

I remove my boots a bit slower and drop them on the floor louder than I normally would. Anticipation is a powerful tool in this moment. I intend to utilize it to its fullest potential. The shifting air that passes her skin as I exaggerate my movements, the sound of me intentionally taking my time—it will all enhance the pinnacle and make the journey there that much sweeter.

Smack!

The leather tassels sting her bum, her blood rushing in to brighten the mark.

Smack!

Again. Her sharp inhale stiffens my cock.

Smack!

Again.

Again.

Again.

I pause to let more blood surge under the surface. Her arse is bright with it, and I cannot stop myself from kneeling down and letting my mouth feel its warmth. A moan escapes as my lips glide along the tender, heated skin before sucking it hard into my mouth. Her cries dictate my next move as I push her firm cheeks apart and slide my tongue through her wetness, wondering if she's already climaxed.

"Oh God, Alasdair!" She tries to bend forward but can't. Instead, she lifts herself on her toes, pushing toward the pressure, desperately needing more.

I know if I continue, she will release within seconds. I lick my way back to her tender cheek and kiss the reddened skin just like I do her mouth—open and aggressive, lips and tongue swirling against its warmth. My teeth scrape the surface, but I want more. I want to have her flesh between them—the top of her hip, along her side, up, up, just enough pressure to heighten her need. When I reach her shoulder and neck, I suck hard again as my hand rubs slow circles, preparing her arse for another round of pleasure-pain.

She loves it, possibly more than I do, the euphoria that only this kind of lovemaking can induce. The soft strips of leather caress her brightened skin, barely teasing the surface until I pull back and snap the tips with a perfectly measured flick of the wrist. She bites her lip, and I wonder if it is too much until she pants, "More," on a heavy exhale.

My spine tingles with another surge of everything that makes me a man, enthralled by everything that makes her a woman. My woman. *Smack!* She is strong. *Smack!* And powerful. *Smack!* Clever and bold. *Smack!*

I drop the knout to the floor and release a feral growl through gnashed teeth, while I spread her apart and drive my rigid shaft home, thrusting hard as she screams out my name. Her erotic cries push my ferocity as my hips slam against her. My hands clamp tightly, one on her hip, the other on her shoulder, holding her steady through the impact of my fury.

"Ella!" I strain through the taught muscles gripping my core.

"Yes!" The instant response breaks free on a heavy exhale. "Yes!" Her wet channel pulsates around me as her orgasm breaks free. She pushes herself toward me—I can't hold back; the pleasure is too intense. "Christ!" I try to articulate, but the word becomes a strained hiss through the force of my release. Calling out, my head falls back as the sound of my pleasure echoes around the room, mingling with hers in an age-old harmony that can only be heard when a man and woman come together and reach the peak of carnal passion.

My God! What was that? I wonder as I try to keep some momentum. It still feels so good I don't want to stop, but my head is light, my body tingling. Her knees start to weaken as her climax ebbs, so I wrap my arm around her waist as the other reaches up to untie her hands from the bedpost. Once they are free, she rests against me while my hips continue rolling toward her, my shaft holding on to the last of her contractions.

Both arms wrap around her now, forming her sated body around mine, wanting as much contact with hers as possible.

"Ye feel so fucking good in my arms, Ella," I say against her ear. "Ye smell so good...taste so good." I kiss her temple, then lick the salty perspiration from my lips. "I love ye so much, faerie maiden. So bloody much."

She turns to face me, her slender hands coming up to caress my face, fingers gently running through my hair. She doesn't speak right away, just gazes into my eyes, and in hers, I can see the whole world and its elaborate history. I see time travel backward, then forward, then I see it stand still. I see the Holy Creator and all the heathen gods and goddesses of ancient times, then further still to the Fey ancestor with whom her blood is shared. *Thank you.* Again, a silent prayer. *I will cherish your soul through eternity.* Again, a silent promise.

My breath catches on a sharp inhale. Her eyes flashed brightly, I know they did, that luminous blue green of a rare gemstone. But why? The reason is of no mind. Because when she speaks, I feel as if I've been strangled with emotion. For her voice is not that of Ella but of an angel—its sound so beautiful and rare that it is only sung in the cathedrals of heaven, yet familiar in a way that makes me want to weep.

"Thank you, Alasdair. I have always cherished you, and I always will."

Epilogue

"Nanna! Nanna! Look what Miss Penny gave me!" young William exclaims. He is the youngest of our three great-grandchildren.

"What do you have there, lovey?" I ask, knowing full well what they are.

"Miss Penny made special little sweet cakes fer me to give to the faeries!" he says with the adorable, accented voice of a child. "Can we go to the forest? Please, Nanna, please!"

Every time I hear them call me Nanna, it reminds me of Alasdair. He is the one that insisted our grandchildren call me that name. It was an endearing tribute to his own grandmother, one that I felt honored to accept.

"Of course. I could use some fresh air."

"Grand-da always said that the forest is yer favorite place to be. He told us that ye are friends wi' the animals *and* the faeries. But we already knew that because Mamma told us that when she was little, she would only see them if she went wi' you to leave them gifts." His round rosy cheeks lift with his smile, enhancing the boyish sparkle in his eyes.

"Yes, well, that may be true. But your mother forgot to mention how rambunctious she was and that she would scare everything within earshot if I didn't keep my hand over her mouth and repeatedly tell her 'Shhhh!'" I explain with exaggeration and my finger to my lips. Of course, William thinks that is hilarious and throws his head back in laughter.

His mother, Anne, is our second grandchild and likely the strongest willed of all eleven. I remember teaching her that demanding what she wants rarely guarantees that she will get it, especially when it comes to faeries. Thankfully, by the time she made it to her teenage years, she had mellowed into a charming young lady that stole the heart of an equally charming young man. She is now the Duchess of Hamilton, and this darling lad in front of me is the next in line for the dukedom.

"Let's go, let's go, Nanna!" he says excitedly, pulling me with him to the door.

"Alright. Let me grab my shawl. There's a bit of a chill in the air."

Before long, William and I are entering the forest, and I am immediately overwhelmed with the sense of comfort and nostalgia I felt the first time I walked through this magical place. It is home to me—the rich, moist scent of green like a simmering pot of freshly made stew waiting by the kitchen hearth. It brings specific memories to the forefront of my mind, taking me back to those special moments in time with the people I love most. I pause, then take another full inhale and try to hold back the tears welling up in my eyes.

"Come, Nanna, come! Over here!" He runs ahead of me, too excited to consider patience.

"I'm coming, love. I'm not as fast as I used to be. There was a time I could have raced you through these trails...and won!" I yell to his retreating figure.

When I finally catch up, he has neatly placed the sweet

treats on the flat stone my eldest son, Callen, named the faerie table when he was just a boy. There are several places in the forest where we leave goodies and treasures for our little flying friends, but this one is the closest to the trail, and considering William's attention span, this is always his first choice.

"See what I did? I made a circle with them. Do ye think they will like that?" he asks with a sudden seriousness.

"Oh yes! They will be very pleased with your effort. They love designs and pretty things about as much as they love sweets. You did very well."

"Thank you, Nanna. I'm excited to see what they leave in return."

"I am, too. I've spent over sixty years coming to this forest, leaving my little friends presents, and my excitement to see what they left the next day has never waned."

"What is the best present they ever left ye, Nanna?"

"Oh, well, they've left me so many, and I love them all, of course. Most of the time, they will leave herbs that I use for healing, but they did leave me a gold ring once. It's the one your great-grandfather always wore. I remember giving it to him. He studied it, inspecting it from every angle...he was so serious," I say with laughter. "Then he slid it onto his finger, looked up at me, smiled, and said, 'I love it, Ella. 'Tis perfect. Tell them I said thank you.'"

William's eyes are wide as he asks, "Where did they get a ring that would fit Grand-da? His fingers were huge."

"I can't say for sure, but it's a question I pondered many times. I imagine it was very old. You could see markings on the inside that were worn. It must have been lost in the forest, perhaps even by a relative of your great-grandfather's. It would have been nice to know its history, but nonetheless, it's still a meaningful gift with an equally meaningful story."

I stop for a minute and look at this handsome little boy. He has Alasdair's long, dark lashes framing those striking turquoise eyes. My chest tightens before I say, "William, I want you to do me a favor. I want you to collect the prettiest stones and pebbles you can find. They have to be special; you see— they cannot be ordinary or plain. Look for ones that have colors and lines or patches, something you think the faeries would love. Can you do that for me?"

"Yes, I can do that. I'm very good at looking for things," he states confidently, proud to have been given an important task.

"Good. I want you to collect twelve spectacular stones while I go to the clearing just over there. I'll see if there are any I can find as well. Is that alright?"

"Yes, ma'am. I will start right now!"

I give him a wink and a smile, then turn to head for the clearing that overlooks the sea.

The wind pushes hard as I leave the protection of the trees, wrapping my skirts around my legs. It's cool as it seeps through the layers of fabric. I close my eyes, remembering the day Alasdair made me dance—in this very place—completely naked. It was his thirty-eighth, birthday and that was his only request for a gift. I hesitated for obvious reasons, but it was also a chilly day like today, a hard wind blowing in from the west. A smile lifts the corners of my mouth as I see myself undressing slowly, teasing him with coy flirtations. He had to help me with the stays, but beyond that, I could handle the rest. He kept telling me how magnificent I was, that never has there lived a woman as beautiful as me. And then, in the brisk air blowing hard across the sea, I danced for my beloved husband. I showed him how much I loved him with my body, through movements that spoke to me from my heart, that felt right in my soul. My arms reached up to the sky, my back arched forward and backward, side to side. It felt so good, so freeing, and Alasdair loved it. When I eventually danced my way to him, stopping to take his hands in mine so that we could dance together, I found his face wet with tears. He made love to me there. He was tender that time, holding me close in his arms, crooning me with words of love in his native tongue.

"I miss you so much, Alasdair," I say through my tears as I walk toward the edge of the clearing and look out to the horizon. "So much, my love." I close my eyes and see his beautiful face, those eyes, that smile. I picture myself caressing his cheek, my thumb dipping into that dimple that always gave me butterflies when it appeared. "Thank you for visiting me in my dreams." My eyes open and squint at the sun's bright reflection shimmering across the rough surface of the water. Every night, he is there. Sometimes laughing, sometimes serious. Together with the children when they were young, riding horses and fishing in the stream. Sitting quietly together in his study, me reading about herbs while he worked at his desk. Making love. I stop as a sob breaks free, but I swallow down the rest. "Please don't stop. Please don't stop visiting me. Please come see me every night and let us relive our beautiful life together." I wipe my face. "Remember when you said in the note you left me, *I thank God every day that our souls found each other again. Let us grow old joyously, knowing they will do so from now through eternity.* I was young when you wrote that, and I loved it for its sweetness, charm, and romance. But now, they are the words that comfort me. They give me strength and profound happiness, knowing we will be together again, that I get to love you again and be loved by you." The words come out as barely a whisper through the thickness of emotions strangling my throat. "I will know my time is soon when you no longer visit me in my dreams. I will come searching for you then, and I will find you. I will find you, my love."

I turn back to the forest, the wind pushing me toward the entrance. I slow my pace, wanting the tears to dry and my sadness to hide away once again. I don't want to burden sweet William with the heaviness of my grief. Alasdair has been gone barely two months. I promised him I would be strong, and I have been, considering. Our children and their families make it easier as Galloway Castle is always filled with the love that Alasdair and I created. We had three sons and one daughter, and my beloved husband's legacy will live on through the dignity, honor, and integrity he instilled in them.

Once I am back in the company of tall trees and pillowing ferns, I regain my composure, and I can hear William talking to himself just up the way.

"Did you find the prettiest ones?" I ask, smiling at him diligently working the stones into his display.

"Yes. And now I'm adding them to my design with the cakes from Miss Penny. Look at this one!" He reaches up to hand me a particularly beautiful stone that is mostly white with dark veins through it and one patch of burgundy. "I think that it is the best one."

"Oh! I must agree! That is quite lovely. Your arrangement will be extra special now," I say, handing him the last piece to set in place.

"All done," he announces and stands up, hands on his hips, looking down at the faerie table so perfectly set in graduating circles.

"All done and *well* done. Now, can you help me with one more thing?" I ask, taking his hand in mine.

"Yes, Nanna, what else can I help ye with?" He loves having responsibilities, and I can't help but smile as he puts on his best grown-up facade.

"I need you to help me pick some flowers like these," I say, leaning down to pick a few stems with white blooms from along the edge of the path.

"I can do that!" And off he goes, skipping down the path, filling his hands with as many flowers as they can hold.

Just before the trail ends that leads back out onto the moor, I call to him, "William! Come back over here!"

He runs back to me and asks, slightly winded, "What is it? Are these fer the dining table?"

"No. This way. Follow me."

And so, he does. A short way off the main trail to a small clearing with a beautiful ash tree on the north side. Not far away, two burial stones lie side by side. We approach slowly, and I kneel to place my flowers on one, then direct William to put his on the other.

"What do they say, Nanna?"

I swallow a few times before answering, "This says Willow, and that one says Magni."

"Wasn't that Grand-da's horse?"

"Yes. And Willow was mine, but more than that, she was my dearest friend."

William doesn't say anything more. He just reaches up to hold my hand, knowing that is what I need right now. I give a gentle squeeze to show my gratitude. He waits patiently while I say a prayer, then lets go while I kneel and rest my hand on her grave.

"You keep them company...I'll see you soon, my girl."

Deep inside you, in the realm of past lives, intuition,
    perhaps a sixth sense,
there exists knowledge of which you are unaware.
It controls you without your say then plays tricks on your
    mind.
History says it is magic and you know that magic is an
    illusion.
So you fight against it with your pride,
With your ego,
Your will.
Fight as you might, it has insight beyond your conscious
    thought.
Beyond your will.
Beyond any choice you could make.
Beyond logic.
Yet...
When you let go, when you are finally set free of your
    self-imposed restraint,
And you embrace your soul's desire, you can accept that
    your soul has a mate.
Don't be afraid.
Don't be afraid of its power over you.
Accept that it is all consuming,
It is pleasure,
It is pain.
It can destroy you, then recreate you.
Indulge in its unimaginable passion,
in the taste,
the touch,
the kiss...the release,
the sound of my name escaping your lips.
Know that your tears on my tongue mean I will protect
    you.

Know that in the warmth of your arms I am grounded.
Know that when we are together, no matter where we
    are, we are home.
Know that without question, without doubt,
You are mine,
I am yours,
Again,
and again,
and again.
For eternity.
-Alasdair Stewart

Acknowledgments

I cannot thank my family enough for their love and support. To my awesome husband, Nick, who listened while I read each chapter aloud and didn't laugh at my rendition of Alasdair, Scottish accent and all. To my amazing daughter, whose wisdom and honesty I rely on. She is always the first person to read my finished manuscript before it goes to the editor. To my sweet son, who still won't read my books, but is so genuinely excited when I get good reviews and ratings. He even bought me books for Christmas to use for research while writing the next two books in this series. The three of you mean everything to me, I love you so much.

Thank you to Linda Russel (Foreword PR & Marketing – forewordpr.com) for helping me get my books published and setting up all the promotional "stuff" that is more daunting than writing a book. She makes it a smooth process with her many years of experience and her professionalism. You're the best!

Thank you to Marisa Wesley (Cover Me Darling – covermedarling.com) for another amazing cover. Marisa is so sweet and professional and very patient.

Thank you, Shari at Madhat Studios, (madhatstudios.com) for doing another great job formatting my manuscript for ebook and print, as well as editing and proofreading. Shari is an amazing writer with many wonderful books available on Amazon and her website www.sharijryan.com

Thank you to Sarah Pesce (Lopt & Cropt editing - loptandcropt.com) for editing my book. The editing process is challenging, but I truly love it because I gain so much as a writer.

Another big thank you to Michele Fitch for proofreading and for being so supportive.

Thank you, to Lori, Heidi, Missy, and George for all your support and for taking the time to read my book before its release. Your input is *so* appreciated! Love you guys!

And thank you to all the readers of my first book The Essence of Fate. So many of you reached out with kindness and support through emails, messages, and reviews. I am forever grateful for your encouragement, and I look forward to hearing from you again.

CPSIA information can be obtained
at www.ICGtesting.com
Printed in the USA
JSHW030817190622
27150JS00002B/16

Contents